THE BEGINNING OF CIVILIZATION
Mythologies Told True

Book 2

KIYA AND HER CHILDREN

Rise and Fall of the Titans

Second Edition

Dennis Wammack

Kiya and Her Children: Rise and Fall of the Titans, Second Edition
© 2021, 2024 Dennis Wammack. All rights reserved.

Hardback ISBN: 979-8-9860246-9-1
Paperback ISBN 979-8-9903998-0-8
eBook ISBN 979-8-9903998-1-5

Characters, places, and events in this work are fictitious unless otherwise identified in the appendix. Any names, characters, companies, organizations, places, events, locales, and incidents are either used in a fictitious manner or are fictional. Unless identified in the appendix, any resemblance to actual persons, living or dead, actual organizations, or actual events is purely coincidental.

This is the Second Edition. Changes of consequence made to the First Edition of Kiya and Her Children, ISBN 979-8-9860246-1-5, are detailed in the appendix.

Disclaimer: Within the six-book series, historical names are drawn from Greek, Egyptian, and Biblical references to protohistoric figures. Other names are derived from Sanskrit and Proto-Indo-European languages. Many characters, places, and events are inspired by well-known mythologies, but the narrative is not necessarily consistent with the myth. No effort has been made to provide historical accuracy of time or place or a scholarly development of technologies and themes. Histories spanning thousands of years have been compressed into hundreds to provide a single narrative across the series. Connections are made between characters who would realistically have lived in different epochs.

For rights and permissions,
contact Dennis Wammack,
denniswammack@gmail.com.
denniswammack.com

Cover design by the author using artificial intelligence resources.
Books are printed and distributed by IngramSpark, Nashville TN.
Published by DCW Press, Birmingham AL, dcwpress.com.

B2seHC-240618

DCW PRESS
A Boutique Publishing Company

TABLE OF CONTENTS
PART I. CLAN OF THE SERPENT

1. Vanam
2. The First Family Campfires
3. Kiya
4. Rivermaster and Sagacity
5. Winter Solstice Festival 17
6. The Banished

PART II. TITANS

7. A New World
8. The Founding of Tartarus
9. The Emissary
10. The Oceanid Trade Mission
11. The Seduction of Pumi
12. The Sundering of Vanam
13. Winter Solstice Festival 18
14. Birth of an Empire
15. Consolidation
16. The First Marriage

PART III. OLYMPIANS

17. Cronos
18. Hestia, Zeus, and Athena
19. Decline
20. Titanomachy
21. Dionysus
22. Gigantomachy
23. Fall of the Titans
24. Triumph of the Olympians

APPENDIX

Author's Notes
Greek Mythology Primer
Glossary of Names and Places

KIYA AND HER CHILDREN

Rise and Fall of the Titans

Second Edition

###

PART I. CLAN OF THE SERPENT
1. Vanam
In the 42nd year from the birth of Vanam

Vanam dismissed the hunters from the hunter's fire and signaled Kiya.

Kiya dismissed the women from the gatherer's fire and obediently followed Vanam into the nearby grove. She turned, raised her tunic, fell to her knees and elbows, and waited.

Aggressively, he entered her and thrust until he was sated. He savored the moment, withdrew, rose, straightened his tunic, grunted, and left.

Kiya waited until he was gone and then rose. *I should be grateful. He seldom comes to me anymore. I've borne him five healthy sons and am the most respected woman in any tribe. What more does he want from me?*

She straightened her tunic and returned to her family.

Vanam was sitting on his resting stone, ignoring their daughters playing nearby. He did not acknowledge her approach.

"Did I please you?" she asked.

Vanam glanced at her, shrugged his shoulders, and replied, "You were fine."

"Is there more I could do? You don't seem pleased if I move or reach to touch you. I would do more if I knew how." *I want more than 'fine.' I want to provide you with joy. To please you. To excite you.*

"You're fine," Vanam replied. "You're available when I call you. That's all I want."

Her effort to engage in meaningful conversation ended as it always ended, without meaningful conversation. She tried a different tack. "Your children adore you. They are proud their father is chief of a great tribe."

Vanam glanced up. "The females are not mine. You accumulated them from other tribes." He paused. "And the males? Are they mine? They seem to be sons of a different man. They are more like girls than men. Their thoughts are always elsewhere. They cannot hunt or track or dress game. They do not think of the things men think about. They think of

---

PRINCIPALS: Kiya, Vanam, Pumi, Valki | ELDER TITANIDES: Themis, Mnemosyne, Phoebe, Tethys, Theia, Rhea | ELDER TITANES: Rivermaster/Oceanus, Sagacity/Coeus, Starmaster/Crius, Watchman/Hyperion, Piercer/Iapetus, Cronus

women's things, just like my little brother. Maybe Pumi fathered them instead of me."

Kiya offered a gentle laugh as she, at last, replied, "No, Vanam. I have mated with no man but you. If your sons are not to your liking, blame me; not them. You have never guided them or told me that you wish them to be hunters. They don't know your expectations. And they *do* wish to be like Pumi. He is their father's little brother and the most respected man in the land. For one who isn't a chief, of course. Pumi respects and loves you. He has never asked me to mate. He is certainly *not* the father of any of your children."

Vanam rose, stared at her, sneered, and spat out, "Address me as *Chief* Vanam. Mate with whomever you wish. Your sons are an abomination."

He stormed off to nowhere.

Kiya glanced at her daughters who studiously kept their heads down and continued their play.

Vanam's words festered in Kiya's mind. *I knew our relationship had weakened, but I did not realize it had sunk to this. Becoming chief has changed you, Vanam. You were so attentive before becoming chief. Is the pressure too great? Does the great success of Pumi lessen your self-worth? I would help you, Vanam, if I knew how. But you verbally abuse my children and now cast me into the company of other men.*

She looked at her younger daughters, playing nearby. *Our relationship is wonderful and warm. You giggle and laugh as I tell you stories of my childhood and about boys and their nature. But my sons are a different matter. I expected Vanam to provide their training and education. I have never counseled them in any matter. They keep to themselves, away from both of us.*

Kiya suddenly saw her sons in a new and chilling light.

A light brightly illuminating that upon which it fell.

ELDER OCEANIDS: Metis, Tyche, Clymene, Eurybia, Amphitrite
ELDER OLYMPIANS: Hestia, Demeter, Hera, Hades, Poseidon, Zeus
OTHER: Philyra, Dionysus, Heracles, Outis, Enceladus, Littlerock, Porphyrion

2. The First Family Campfires

Several days passed.

The hunters left for the hunt. That day, Kiya did not lead the gatherers into the countryside as was normal but instead asked Panti to lead them. She then asked her five sons if she could travel with them. "I would like to see what my sons teach themselves and how you spend your days." She now realized that they had no guidance during their daytime activities. It was well past time that she, since Vanam would not, took an interest in their development. All five boys were excited that a parent—an adult—was interested in them. The older two were old enough to hunt but, as far as she knew, neither had ever been allowed.

"Yes, Mother, please," said Secondson. "Can you prepare food for us? I will plan our day to show you all the places we go and the things we do. We can start as soon as you have prepared."

Kiya was surprised by Secondson's precocious response. She looked at the other boys for signs of disagreement, but they seemed to accept his pronouncement. *I know less about my sons than I know about my mate. What kind of woman am I?*

"You are my wise child," she replied. From this day forward I shall call you 'Sagacity.'"

Sagacity replied, "That would please me, Mother. Thank you."

Kiya retired to prepare provisions. When she returned, the boys, too, were prepared with their hunting pouches containing who knew what.

Sagacity declared, "Well, let's be off. This way, Mother. Let me know if you tire. Follow me."

The band obediently fell into line behind Sagacity and Kiya. They walked, not trotted, westward toward a band of trees. Entering the sparse forest, Kiya heard running water in the distance. Her oldest son suddenly became animated, ran toward the sound of water, and called back, "This way! Follow me."

Without objection, the other boys fell into a single file and followed Firstson. Kiya made her way to the stream where the boys hunched over

PRINCIPALS: Kiya, Vanam, Pumi, Valki | ELDER TITANIDES: Themis, Mnemosyne, Phoebe, Tethys, Theia, Rhea | ELDER TITANES: Rivermaster/Oceanus, Sagacity/Coeus, Starmaster/Crius, Watchman/Hyperion, Piercer/Iapetus, Cronus

watching Firstson poke at rocks and move them around. He altered the water flow to create new eddies and expose small fish and things that swam rapidly away. The boys were intrigued. Firstson held up his hand to silence their chatter, "Wait, there should be a frog somewhere over here." Firstson crossed to the other side of the stream and pushed back a pile of leaves. A large frog jumped high into the air at the unexpected intrusion.

The three younger boys gave chase and the oldest of the three, Thirdson, caught the frog before it could hop again. All laughed with delight. Thirdson asked, "What will I do with it? Eat it?"

The five boys looked at Kiya who was apparently to be judge and jury. Kiya studied the frog for a moment and then gravely asked the group, "How does my council advise me in this matter? Does the frog live or is it to be our lunch?"

Firstson: "Lunch!
Sagacity: "Throw lots!"
Thirdson: "Let it go!"
Fourthson: "Kill it!"
Fifthson: "Keep it as a pet!"

"Oh, dear," Kiya said. "There is no consensus here. Return the prisoner to from where he came. He will not be so fortunate the next time he is captured."

This appeared to be a popular decision. The prisoner was returned to his abode, unscathed. The boys continued their exploration of the stream and its inhabitants. Kiya watched with interest.

Finally, Sagacity announced, "It's time to eat and regain our strength. Do you have nourishment for us, Mother?"

"Why, yes, I do. Both food and drink" replied Kiya. "Shall I prepare a place for us?"

"Yes, please," said Sagacity. "On the knoll over there will be suitable."

Kiya withdrew a large blanket from her gathering bag and placed it neatly on the ground. She took various breads, meats, and sweets from the bag and placed them on the blanket. She withdrew a stoppered urn and told her sons "I also have an urn of water sweetened with different herbs and

ELDER OCEANIDS: Metis, Tyche, Clymene, Eurybia, Amphitrite
ELDER OLYMPIANS: Hestia, Demeter, Hera, Hades, Poseidon, Zeus
OTHER: Philyra, Dionysus, Heracles, Outis, Enceladus, Littlerock, Porphyrion

spices which may be to your liking. But know that many hunters will not drink this mixture for fear of being likened to a woman."

The five boys exchanged glances as they considered this information. "We see no dishonor here," Sagacity replied. "Let us taste this water and decide for ourselves that which is appropriate."

"What a wise and manly decision," she replied to the group. *They're communicating only with their eyes. There is more to my sons than their father sees. Or perhaps he does!*

As they ate and drank, Kiya turned the conversation to Firstson as she said, "There is one here who knows more about streams and water than even the scholars at Tallstone."

Firstson's face brightened with the recognition of his knowledge. Sagacity opened his mouth to respond but Firstson gave him no chance. Firstson cut him off with, "I remember attending a winter festival and trying to find someone interested in water. Everyone listened but the talk always went to sky or stone or building or planting or animals. There wasn't any interest in water, which must surely be the most important thing in nature after the sun."

"I have never thought about that," Kiya replied. "But, yes, we can live a long time without those other things but only a short time without water. Perhaps water is the most important thing there is."

Firstson sat happily basking in his mother's interest. The other four boys were impressed. Perhaps they would hold their oldest brother in even higher esteem.

"From this day forward," Kiya told Firstson, "I shall call you 'Rivermaster.'"

"'Waterboy' would be better," Sagacity quietly interjected.

The boys stared at one another in silence. Kiya had thought that 'Rivermaster' would be accepted with celebration.

Finally, Firstson spoke, "Yes, 'Waterboy' would be better."

"I see," replied Kiya; not seeing at all. "And why is this?"

PRINCIPALS: Kiya, Vanam, Pumi, Valki | ELDER TITANIDES: Themis, Mnemosyne, Phoebe, Tethys, Theia, Rhea | ELDER TITANES: Rivermaster/Oceanus, Sagacity/Coeus, Starmaster/Crius, Watchman/Hyperion, Piercer/Iapetus, Cronus

"Because," Firstson began without emotion, "our father has told us that we will never be men. That we will remain boys all our lives or, worse yet, become girls. He has told us that we will never become hunters and that we are useless to the tribe. He pities us and is embarrassed because you present us as his children. That is why 'Waterboy' is better, Mother. It is a name that will not make my father mad at me."

Kiya wondered, *Can this be true?*

The five boys stared at her expectantly and apparently in complete agreement with Firstson. She knew then that his words were true.

Kiya replied, "I see no dishonor here. Let us taste this water and decide for ourselves what is true." She stared at Firstson and demanded, "*Are* you 'Rivermaster,' Son?"

Her oldest child silently held her gaze. The other four boys looked back and forth between their brother and their mother—waiting.

The boy rose, straightened his back, and looked at each brother. "I am 'Rivermaster.' Now, let's find some colored rocks for Brother Fifthson."

"What a delightful idea," Kiya said as she stood. "You all go on ahead and I will catch up after I pack the remains of our lunch." She wanted to give the boys time to themselves to come to terms with this development. Strangely, Kiya was not upset. She now understood her sons and her mate. Why this was Vanam's attitude, she did not know, but he had drawn a clear line between himself, her, and their—her—children. She would now journey across that line without consideration for *Chief* Vanam's desires. *Vanam is a man of great strength and temper, but I am not afraid. I will raise my children to be not afraid. A mother cannot bestow manhood onto her son but perhaps a boy's brothers can. Colored rocks? Well then, let us look for colored rocks!*

The afternoon was spent as Kiya and her sons scoured the creek bed for stones streaked with color. None were found. Fifthson was disappointed. There was nothing to add to his collection.

They arrived back at camp late. The women's fire was already burning. The older women and children, including Kiya's three youngest daughters, were gathered around it anticipating the evening's activities. The gatherers, including Kiya's three oldest daughters, were not yet

ELDER OCEANIDS: Metis, Tyche, Clymene, Eurybia, Amphitrite
ELDER OLYMPIANS: Hestia, Demeter, Hera, Hades, Poseidon, Zeus
OTHER: Philyra, Dionysus, Heracles, Outis, Enceladus, Littlerock, Porphyrion

around the fire. Their daily collection of plants was bountiful. Sorting and storing the plants by their use would take a while longer. They were meticulous with their craft and would not be hurried.

The male children ran and rough-housed. She told her three youngest sons to join the other boys. Rivermaster and Sagacity would be out of place with the younger boys since both were old enough to be on the hunt. Yet here they were with Kiya and not on the hunt or around the fire. She had never noticed before where the two boys were at this time of day, so she asked, "Where do you two go in the evening?"

"Oh, we find a spot away from the noise and review our day," Sagacity said. "If we found some good rocks, we build a fire and study them. The colors and patterns can be quite interesting."

"How nice," Kiya said. "It's too bad we didn't find any. A fire just for us would be nice." Kiya stood silently and considered her family. Her immediate family, not her tribal family. *I know little about my sons other than none are interested in the hunt. But one knows everything about water, one is more articulate than me, one loves colored rocks, and my adopted daughters are delightful and smart. But soon enough, Vanam will have me trade my daughters to other tribes. I won't be able to laugh with them, to teach them how to handle males, how to gather plants, and how to experiment to achieve different results. At best, my sons will be traded to other tribes because Vanam dislikes them. They aren't like him. They embarrass him.*

She looked toward the heavens with sadness. *Sister Valki, you are wise. What should I do? Would you remember I once said, "Rather than finding what the plant will do, decide what you want to be done, and find the plant to do it?" We both laughed. I see now that we laughed with fear because no one has ever tried because this is not the way things are done. To leave the path of 'the way things have always been' is terrifying. To do something different is uncharted, dangerous territory. You could be left behind by the tribe. Perhaps banished.*

Kiya saw that which she wanted. *I will NOT do things the way they have always been done! I shall make my own path!*

Strangely, she was not afraid.

PRINCIPALS: Kiya, Vanam, Pumi, Valki | ELDER TITANIDES: Themis, Mnemosyne, Phoebe, Tethys, Theia, Rhea | ELDER TITANES: Rivermaster/Oceanus, Sagacity/Coeus, Starmaster/Crius, Watchman/Hyperion, Piercer/Iapetus, Cronus

The First Family Campfire

She said, "Rivermaster, build us a fire. Sagacity, gather your brothers and sisters. Tell them I want us to gather around Rivermaster's fire. Tell Fifthson to bring his rocks. His family wishes to learn about rocks."

A surprised Rivermaster gathered the necessary materials and built a circle large enough to hold a fire for his family. He found a rock suitable for his mother to sit on. By the time Sagacity had gathered his brothers and sisters, the fire was burning, Kiya sat on her rock; hands folded in her lap. Fifthson arrived and arranged his collection of precious, colored rocks in front of his mother.

The children approached the fire tentatively, unsure of what protocols were in place. Was this fire only for females? Would there be a different fire for the males? In any case, where would the children sit in relation to adults? They arrived and stood around the fire in confusion.

Kiya said, "We are one family. Sit in a circle around Rivermaster's fire. My two oldest daughters, sit on either side of me, and then a son and then a daughter. Rank is for members of our tribe, not for members of our family. I am told that my oldest son is an expert in the knowledge of water. I bestowed him the name 'Rivermaster.' You have a brother wiser than your mother. I named him 'Sagacity.' And Fifthson is a collector of colored rocks. I did not know these things before today. It is my wish that each of us knows the other. I have asked Fifthson to begin by showing his family his collection of rocks."

She paused, waiting for reactions.

The concept of "family" was foreign. They were members of a tribe, each member having specific expectations, always aware of rank, and always observing established protocols. For a female to show interest in the dealings of a male was not wise. Certainly, a male would never show interest in the dealings of a female. And children? Do not be the child that crosses an adult, not even a young adult. Retribution is swift and without mercy. Her children cast unsure glances at one another; not wanting to be the first to commit.

Sagacity took control from his mother. He said, "Themis, you are the oldest, sit on Mother's right. Mnemosyne, you sit on her left. Thirdson,

ELDER OCEANIDS: Metis, Tyche, Clymene, Eurybia, Amphitrite
ELDER OLYMPIANS: Hestia, Demeter, Hera, Hades, Poseidon, Zeus
OTHER: Philyra, Dionysus, Heracles, Outis, Enceladus, Littlerock, Porphyrion

sit next to Mnemosyne, and then Phoebe, Fourthson, Rhea, me, Tethys, Rivermaster, and then Theia and Themis. If I left anyone out, make yourself a place."

Her children took their assigned places. The females were nervous sitting next to a male around a campfire. The children were excited to be sitting around *any* campfire. There was no laughter, no giggles, no bantering. All was serious. Deadly serious.

Kiya said, "Fifthson, show us your rocks, tell us about them."

Hesitantly, Fifthson began. He picked up a rock the size of his fist and held it high for all to see in the firelight. The stone reflected deep blue stripes alternating with thin gray striations. He began. "You have to look carefully to find these colored rocks. In creek beds and near foothills where the earth has been washed away. When you clean them and crack them open, beautiful colors might appear. Some stones can be separated many times to create smaller stones of pure color. Deep blue, bright green, pretty red."

He talked into the night about his collection of rocks. Fifthson came upon a necklace he had made by piercing a hole in five thin, colorful stones and placing a cord through them. He had never thought that his mother might care about his obsession and care enough to let him show off to all his brothers and sisters. Fifthson was still young and not accustomed to recognition from anybody in any form. Tonight, sharing his treasures with his brothers and sisters by their campfire, he burst with pride and a feeling of belonging. Belonging to his mother, to his brothers, to his sisters. With joy and a little fear, he presented the colorful stone necklace to his mother. "Mother, would you wear this necklace I made?"

Kiya was taken aback and shocked to receive a gift, a beautiful gift from her child, her youngest son. It was so unexpected. "Why, Fifthson, it is beautiful. I will be proud to wear it every day. I shall show it to all the other women. What you have made and given to me is wonderful, I shall treasure it forever. Look, you have pierced holes in the stones. From this moment forward, I shall call you 'Piercer.' Would that please you?"

For a boy to be given an adult name, especially one as young as he, was a high honor. His two oldest brothers had been given proper names only

---

PRINCIPALS: Kiya, Vanam, Pumi, Valki | ELDER TITANIDES: Themis, Mnemosyne, Phoebe, Tethys, Theia, Rhea | ELDER TITANES: Rivermaster/Oceanus, Sagacity/Coeus, Starmaster/Crius, Watchman/Hyperion, Piercer/Iapetus, Cronus

today. His eyes widened. After staring at his mother for a few moments, he replied, "Y-yes, Mother."

The girls were overcome with excitement; gifts, names, sitting around a fire, seeing and learning about beautiful things. They clapped their hands and shrieked together with delight, "Pier-cer ... Pier-cer ... Pier-cer ... P..."

Piercer turned red. He looked for a retreat but there was none. He could only stand there, staring at the ground, with no more words to say.

Kiya said, "Piercer, think of the wonderful things you could do with your rocks if you were an apprentice stone cutter. But now, it is late. Rivermaster, escort your sisters and brothers back to our sleeping area. I will extinguish the fire and be along shortly."

Phoebe rose, walked to Piercer, stooped down, and embraced her brother. "'Piercer'—that is a lovely name, a manly name. Carry it with pride. I love your collection of rocks. I had no idea that a rock could be so beautiful. I am proud that you are my brother and that we are in the same family."

As the others left, Rivermaster said, "I will take care of the fire, Mother."

"Thank you, Son, but I will stay a few moments to collect my thoughts. Make sure everyone gets back safely."

He nodded and joined the others, walking and talking back to their beds.

Kiya continued to sit and stare at the dying fire. She looked into the distance where the women's fire had burned and was now extinguished. *The women will have talked about me. How the chief's mate, his elder woman, had abandoned her post to build a separate campfire. A campfire mixing men, such as they are, and women, and children together without regard to rank. Vanam would certainly want to know of this! What will Vanam think? What should I do?*

She considered her question. *The answer is clear. 'Decide what I want done and find the plant to do it.'*

The night had exceeded her expectations. *My three oldest daughters were upset that they had been called from the women's fire. But they excitedly joined discussions of rocks and new names. My daughters addressed their brothers without notice of rank or position. My sons responded in kind. The fire had brought everyone closer together. Phoebe made a strange comment to Piercer, 'I'm so glad we are in the same family.'*

ELDER OCEANIDS: Metis, Tyche, Clymene, Eurybia, Amphitrite
ELDER OLYMPIANS: Hestia, Demeter, Hera, Hades, Poseidon, Zeus
OTHER: Philyra, Dionysus, Heracles, Outis, Enceladus, Littlerock, Porphyrion

But she was talking about those gathered around this campfire, not of their tribe. This is a new way of looking at 'family.' Why does this statement feel so strange? So right?

She sat quietly for a moment. *I have left the path of the way things have always been. Where do I wish this path to lead?*

She laughed and said out loud, "I must find the right plant!" Kiya rose, extinguished the campfire, and went to her bed.

Kiya and Panti

Sunrise.

The camp bustled with activity as the women prepared for their day. Kiya found Panti.

Panti would have replaced Palai as the tribe's elder woman except Vanam had become Chief at the same time Pala had left the tribe. As the new chief, Vanam appointed Kiya to be the tribe's new elder woman. Panti was older than Kiya and had far more experience in matchmaking and dealing with issues that arose among the women. Kiya's appointment was not met with universal approval because Panti would have been Palai's natural successor. But it was grudgingly admitted-that Kiya was a superior master of their art, both in identifying and usage of that which they gathered. What Kiya lacked in experience was offset by her knowledge and intelligence. Panti never objected, but still, the slight was with her. Kiya remained solicitous of Panti's advice; even when not needed. Panti took over the duties of the chief gatherer when Kiya remained in the camp, such as yesterday.

"Panti, I need your help," Kiya said.

"You need to remain in the camp again, today?" Panti asked.

"No. I need someone wise to talk with. You are the wisest person in the tribe. Can we work side-by-side today so that we can talk about things?"

Panti brightened with the warm words. Her mood shifted from "put-upon" to "needed." She said, "This sounds serious. Are you with child, yet again?"

Kiya laughed. "No, no. That, I could handle easily enough. No. I wish to talk of things not so easily handled. Will you join me in the fields?"

PRINCIPALS: Kiya, Vanam, Pumi, Valki | ELDER TITANIDES: Themis, Mnemosyne, Phoebe, Tethys, Theia, Rhea | ELDER TITANES: Rivermaster/Oceanus, Sagacity/Coeus, Starmaster/Crius, Watchman/Hyperion, Piercer/Iapetus, Cronus

Book 2. The Beginning of Civilization: Mythologies Told True

"Yes. I look forward to it I shall find you and we can talk as we gather."

Kiya thanked Panti and donned the broad-rimmed headpiece she wore in the fields. Each continued their preparations for the day.

The gatherers finished their morning routines and walked to the fertile fields far from the camp.

Panti found Kiya advising three younger women on their art. "Do they learn anything?" Panti asked.

"Yes," Kiya replied. "They learn well and will be excellent additions to whichever tribe accepts them."

The three young women giggled. Compliments, becoming women, finding a mate, going to a new tribe. What was not to giggle about?

Kiya and Panti strolled off, monitoring the women in the field.

"So, what do you think?" Kiya asked.

Panti replied, "I think what I'm told to think, Elder Woman."

Kiya laughed. "Well said, Panti. Now, what do you think?"

Panti replied with caution, "About what, Kiya?"

Kiya was silent for a while. "About Chief Vanam. About how he leads the tribe. About how he cares for me. About how he cares for his children. Yes, start with Chief Vanam, and let's see how it goes from there."

This time, Panti was silent for a while, then said, "Oh," and was silent a while longer. "I would never question my chief in any matter or find fault with anyone in my tribe. You know that."

Neither woman spoke for a long time.

Then Panti released her long-repressed diatribe. "Vanam is a much better chief than Talaimai. Our tribe prospers under Chief Vanam. This is what matters. That he mates with other women and pays little attention to you or his children is of no consequence to our tribe's well-being. Your two oldest sons handicap our tribe. They are old enough to be contributing to our welfare. Has Vanam not decided on what to do with them? I assumed he directed you to trade them to another tribe, even without compensation. Maybe the strange people at Tallstone would want them.

ELDER OCEANIDS: Metis, Tyche, Clymene, Eurybia, Amphitrite
ELDER OLYMPIANS: Hestia, Demeter, Hera, Hades, Poseidon, Zeus
OTHER: Philyra, Dionysus, Heracles, Outis, Enceladus, Littlerock, Porphyrion

There is nothing for you to do. Everything will come to pass as it always comes to pass." She calmed herself, then offered, "Your necklace is beautiful. Where did you get it?"

"Piercer, my youngest son, made it from rocks he had collected. No mother has ever received a better present."

The two women worked on in silence. Kiya said, "The day grows hot. Let's find shade and rest." As they walked toward a shade tree, they inspected younger women's harvests; complimenting or cajoling as needed. After resting and eating, they continued their day, gossiping and sharing knowledge.

As the day was ending, they led their gatherers back to the camp, Kiya said to Panti, "It is you who should have been our tribe's elder woman; not me. Vanam did our tribe no favor by appointing me. I wish to spend the next few days with my children. Will you take care of the gathering duties?"

It was not a question.

The Second Family Campfire

Upon returning to camp, Kiya found her older sons and said, "I enjoyed our family gathering around your campfire last night. Shall we do it again tonight? Will the others approve?"

"Yes, let's," Rivermaster said. "Piercer found some stones in the creek bed today. They're small but interesting. Especially where they were found in the water. They were in a place I would not have expected."

Kiya replied, "How exciting! We will have to hear from both of you. And maybe your sisters can tell us about what they found in the fields today."

"That would be interesting," said Sagacity. "Who knows what goes on in the minds of women when they are out gathering?"

Kiya laughed. "Yes, who knows?"

That night, her family gathered around their second family campfire. Food was shared, and all was good. Piercer showed off three small stones. Their surfaces were streaked with dull red. He was considering breaking them open to see how deeply the colors ran, but he had not yet decided.

Rivermaster explained how he was surprised to find them on the edge of the bank, out of the water. Colored stones were usually found by picking up all the pebbles from the bottom of the stream and sifting through them. He was unsure how these had gotten out of the water so he would have to pay closer attention in the future.

Sagacity stood. "All that's interesting, but let's find out what our sisters search for and how they know when they have found it. Plants may not be as interesting as water and rocks, but they are still useful. Themis—did you have a successful day? Tell us about it." Sagacity sat down.

Themis, Tethys, and Phoebe looked at one another. A female did not talk about gathering with males. *Of what interest does a male have in this?*

Mnemosyne spoke up. "Yes, tell us. I have had some training, but I have never been on a real, honest-to-goodness gathering. Was it exciting? Are you pleased with your harvest? Was Panti pleased? I saw her receiving and sorting everything from all the gathering sacks."

Themis's eyes brightened and she excitedly began to speak.

Sagacity glanced at his mother as she listened to Themis with rapt attention. *How strange. What they do excites them. There are a lot of different plants and they each probably do different things and taste different. Maybe there is more to gathering than one would imagine. It's better than killing animals, I suppose.*

The night and conversations went on. The fire drew each closer together. At last, Kiya asked her youngest son, "Piercer, why don't you ask Chief Vanam to make you an apprentice stonecutter? Wouldn't this help you master knowing what's inside your colored rocks?"

Rivermaster and Sagacity tensed. Piercer was too young to comprehend the implications of what was being proposed. Piercer said, "That would be fun. I could cut my rocks open and give them pretty shapes. Do you think he would let me do that?"

Kiya said, "I don't know. Why don't you ask Rivermaster and Sagacity?"

Rivermaster was horrified.

Sagacity stared at his mother. *You know what you do, don't you, Mother?*

ELDER OCEANIDS: Metis, Tyche, Clymene, Eurybia, Amphitrite
ELDER OLYMPIANS: Hestia, Demeter, Hera, Hades, Poseidon, Zeus
OTHER: Philyra, Dionysus, Heracles, Outis, Enceladus, Littlerock, Porphyrion

Sagacity quickly replied, "Yes, Piercer. We will advise you tomorrow on what to say and how to say it."

Kiya continued, "And my two oldest sons are young men. You should be contributing to our tribe's well-being. Your father has not told me how you should do this. Has he told you?"

Rivermaster and Sagacity exchanged glances.

It was Sagacity who spoke. "You know full well, Mother, what we will *not* be, and he gave us no alternatives. We will talk with Piercer tomorrow, and we have two more brothers. The five of us will have a full day of discussions. After that, we will all know what to say and how to say it."

Kiya nodded. *Tell him what you wish to become, my sons. And how to make it so.*

The Third Family Campfire

The next day, Kiya asked Panti if her three oldest daughters might be excused from the day's gathering so she might better instruct them in the ways of men.

Panti, with an air of resentment, acquiesced to Kiya's request as she led the women into the gathering field. An older male child, oversized spear in hand, maintained watch over the playing children. Although both Rivermaster and Sagacity were older, neither son had ever been given this responsibility. For the first time, Kiya took notice of the slight.

She and her three oldest daughters walked through the children, gathering her three youngest daughters around them. They walked toward the south, away from both the gatherers in the east and her sons presumably in the creek toward the west.

Kiya said "I spent one entire day with my sons and now wish to spend an entire day with my daughters. Let us talk about boys and babies and the things we can do with plants."

"Let's talk about what we can do with boys," Phoebe interjected. "Especially what I can do with Sagacity."

The girls giggled.

"Are you attracted to Sagacity?" Kiya asked.

PRINCIPALS: Kiya, Vanam, Pumi, Valki | ELDER TITANIDES: Themis, Mnemosyne, Phoebe, Tethys, Theia, Rhea | ELDER TITANES: Rivermaster/Oceanus, Sagacity/Coeus, Starmaster/Crius, Watchman/Hyperion, Piercer/Iapetus, Cronus

"Oh, yes!" Phoebe replied. "He is so smart. He knows things that nobody else knows. I could listen to him talk for hours. And he is so handsome."

"All of my sons are handsome. And Sagacity is not your blood brother. I adopted you from a northern tribe. He might be a good mate for you."

Everyone giggled.

"And Rivermaster is so manly, so interesting," Tethys offered.

"Well, girls, let's divide up your brothers. Thirdson is close to manhood. Who claims him?"

Giggles turned to laughter.

Phoebe turned serious. "Will we be allowed to remain with our tribe, Mother? Or are we to be traded away?"

Kiya replied, "I will do what is best for my family."

The girls remained silent. These were not the words of an elder woman.

For the remainder of the day, her girls found interesting plants. Kiya identified each plant with the proper name and explained its various uses. "And, sometimes, you just must experiment with what different combinations of plants might do. And, sometimes, you might need something new done and you will need to find the plant to do it."

That night, Kiya and her family gathered around their third personal campfire. Kiya noticed that Phoebe had taken a place beside Sagacity and that Tethys sat beside Rivermaster. Flames danced.

Kiya said, "This will be our last gathering for a while. It is disrespectful enough to build a separate fire from the women. The hunters return tomorrow. I certainly cannot build a separate fire from them."

"Mother, I built the fires, not you," Rivermaster said. "I bear responsibility for their judgment."

Kiya smiled. "Yes, I understand. Nevertheless ..."

Sagacity changed the subject, "We discussed our situations today. We each have a proposal for our father and intend to request an audience at tomorrow's campfire. We are uneasy, but our proposals are well thought

ELDER OCEANIDS: Metis, Tyche, Clymene, Eurybia, Amphitrite
ELDER OLYMPIANS: Hestia, Demeter, Hera, Hades, Poseidon, Zeus
OTHER: Philyra, Dionysus, Heracles, Outis, Enceladus, Littlerock, Porphyrion

out and advantageous to the tribe. We have high hopes that he will be pleased with our proposals and will decide favorably for us."

Phoebe listened to Sagacity with rapt attention and wide eyes.

The campfire brought them closer together.

PRINCIPALS: Kiya, Vanam, Pumi, Valki | ELDER TITANIDES: Themis, Mnemosyne, Phoebe, Tethys, Theia, Rhea | ELDER TITANES: Rivermaster/Oceanus, Sagacity/Coeus, Starmaster/Crius, Watchman/Hyperion, Piercer/Iapetus, Cronus

3. Kiya

The hunt had been good. Six antelope were killed. A light-hearted Vanam led his hunters triumphantly into the camp of adoring women and cheering children. The game was laid out to be butchered. Life was good.

Kiya stayed back while Chief Vanam performed his routine rituals of return. Finally, he retired to his tent and sat down to rest. Kiya brought him a drink and sweet bread. Vanam perfunctorily thanked her and noticed her necklace of colored stones.

"Where did you get that necklace?" he asked.

"From a young admirer," she replied, fingering the necklace. "Your youngest son. He made it himself and gave it to me. I was thrilled. I bestowed him the name 'Piercer.' I hope you don't mind."

"Mind?" Vanam grunted. "No. It's good that one of them is good for something. Maybe I should make him an apprentice stonecutter. What do you think about that?"

Kiya replied, "That sounds wise, but I know nothing of such things. I know the strengths and weaknesses of our women, but the affairs of the males are beyond my understanding. Whatever you decide will certainly be best for the tribe. More sweetbread?"

The next evening Chief Vanam sat in front of the brightly burning campfire. On his right sat Kiya, the tribe's elder woman. On his left was his skywatcher, Voutch, and next to him was Valvuna, Vanam's second-in-command. Littlerock, the tribe's stonecutter, sat nearby. The hunters sat around the campfire discussing concerns from the recent hunt. The women sat behind the hunters, gossiping. The children quietly played in the background.

Vanam spoke, quieting the noise. "How many spears and spearheads did we lose?"

Valuvana went into detail identifying what was lost during the season, what remained, and what was needed. Littlerock explained the recent unavailability of proper rocks for forming spearheads but the next time they passed near Rockplace he could create an oversupply of the critical equipment. Voutch announced that the tribe would journey to the next

ELDER OCEANIDS: Metis, Tyche, Clymene, Eurybia, Amphitrite
ELDER OLYMPIANS: Hestia, Demeter, Hera, Hades, Poseidon, Zeus
OTHER: Philyra, Dionysus, Heracles, Outis, Enceladus, Littlerock, Porphyrion

camp on the third sunrise and that the tribe would pass near Rockplace after the next camp. Kiya identified young women who would be available to trade to other tribes if they attended the upcoming Winer Solstice Festival. She praised several gatherers for their outstanding contributions to the tribe and praised Panti profusely as an outstanding inspiration and leadership of the women.

Vanam listened intently and said, "It is doubtful we will attend the Winter Solstice festival. We might do well to devote our energy to hunting rather than play."

No one spoke.

"Valvuna, what do you think about that?" Vanam asked.

"Well, mighty chief. Whatever you decide. But the games are exciting, young women are plentiful, the various foods are different and delicious, and there is usually a great deal to be learned of hunting techniques and I do enjoy winning the games of strength. We have not attended the festival in many years but whatever you decide will be best for the tribe."

Vanam sat thinking. *Yes. My tribe enjoys renewal at my little brother's creation each year. His little festival grows larger and larger. He adds more and more monoliths to his little observatory. More tribal chief sitting stones. More apprentices to his little guilds of learned people. More builders and farmers for Valki's little farming communities. She feeds all the tribes gathered at the little festival from her einkorn fields. I provide the tribe with food and warmth all the other seasons but what excites them is my little brother's winter solstice festival. Something is wrong with this.*

He said, "I will think upon your words and decide before we break camp." He paused. "Are there any problems that I need to resolve?"

From the children's area beyond the circle of women, a voice asked loudly, "Chief Vanam, may I and my brothers approach you with requests for your consideration?"

The voice belonged to Rivermaster. His words had been chosen carefully. Sagacity had suggested most of their words. Each of the brothers had memorized and rehearsed what they were to say to their father. Rivermaster and Sagacity agreed that Rivermaster, as the oldest, should be their spokesperson, even though Sagacity was much better with words.

PRINCIPALS: Kiya, Vanam, Pumi, Valki | ELDER TITANIDES: Themis, Mnemosyne, Phoebe, Tethys, Theia, Rhea | ELDER TITANES: Rivermaster/Oceanus, Sagacity/Coeus, Starmaster/Crius, Watchman/Hyperion, Piercer/Iapetus, Cronus

Vanam looked at the speaker and recognized him as his oldest son. He said, "You may approach." His eyes tightened. His five sons walked to the chief and faced him. "All right, Firstson, what is your problem?"

Rivermaster replied, "I have been given the name 'Rivermaster' because I am not worthy to be a hunter and that is my problem. I am no longer a child, and I must contribute to my tribe. Since I am not skilled enough to be a hunter, I request that you consider adding a Scout to your tribe. Large tribes have a scout and you have made us a large and wealthy tribe. Consider commanding that I teach myself how to be a Scout. I would report back to you at the times you require, Chief Vanam!"

Rivermaster had learned his words well and had spit them out not allowing Vanam time to become angry or regale him for the name Rivermaster. He had glossed over Vanam's humiliation that his oldest son was not skilled enough to be a hunter while giving Vanam an out for removing him from the tribe and stroked Vanam's ego with the reference to a 'large and wealthy tribe.'

Vanam replied, "Said well enough, Firstson. You may go."

"My name is Rivermaster."

Sagacity stepped between the locked stares of Rivermaster and Vanam. "Ah, my Chief. If I may make a similar request. My problem is the same as Firstson's. I will never make the first-rate Scout that Firstson will become; the envy of all that hear his reports to you. But I would like to accompany Firstson as his apprentice. It may take both of us to capture enough food to live on since neither of us is an accomplished hunter. But between the two of us, we can capture enough food to survive. I hope you will look favorably upon my request."

Vanam said, "If not enough game, you can live on berries and grass."

Sagacity laughed. "Berries, yes. Grass? Better to starve, Great Chief."

Vanam grunted and said, "There are three more of you."

Sagacity pushed Thirdson to the front. Tentatively, Thirdson began, "I am not yet a man, but I am interested in the moon and the lights in the sky. If Master Voutch needs an apprentice, my interest and dedication to

ELDER OCEANIDS: Metis, Tyche, Clymene, Eurybia, Amphitrite
ELDER OLYMPIANS: Hestia, Demeter, Hera, Hades, Poseidon, Zeus
OTHER: Philyra, Dionysus, Heracles, Outis, Enceladus, Littlerock, Porphyrion

his skills would be unfailing. If you think me worthy, I would like to be considered as Master Voutch's apprentice skywatcher."

Sagacity thought, *A bit stilted but good enough.*

"Next," commanded Vanam.

Fourthson said, "Father, I am still a child, but I would like to be taken on some training hunts to see if I am worthy."

Sagacity pushed Piercer to the front as he thought, *Good, Fourthson. You spoke well.*

Piercer said "I like rocks. They are interesting. If you believe that Master Littlerock should take an apprentice stonecutter, I would like for you to consider me."

Sagacity stepped aside so that Rivermaster could address Vanam. "You are kind to listen to our trivial problems, Chief Vanam. Thank you for doing so. Are we dismissed to return to the children?"

Vanam sat staring at them, coldly. *You and the next little bastard are certainly not mine. Kiya should have at least told me that I was raising children that my little brother planted inside her. But, at least, you are both smart enough to leave the tribe before I banish you. And Firstson had the testicles to stand up for himself. Maybe Fourthson will turn out to be a hunter. At least he is willing to try. And Fifthson, another of Pumi's little bastards? Anyone who asks to become a stonecutter will never be worthy of being anything other than a stonecutter. Piercer, was that his new name?*

Vanam glanced at Kiya, who sat watching the fire, a frown on her face.

She was thinking, *My sons, I am so proud of all of you. You spoke so well. You stood up for yourselves and your choice of words was so skillful. Even Pumi could not have manipulated thoughts and desires toward his own goals so skillfully.*

She frowned slightly as she remembered Pumi. *When you looked at me, you were always so intense. So demanding. So desiring. But you never asked me to mate. I bore Vanam five fine sons. He despises them. You would be so proud of them. Pumi.*

Chief Vanam said, "My decisions are made. Firstson and Secondson will part the tribe at this camp breaking. They will try to become 'scouts' and if they survive, they will report to me at the Winter Solstice Festival, which we will attend this year. Littlerock, take Fifthson as an apprentice

---

PRINCIPALS: Kiya, Vanam, Pumi, Valki | ELDER TITANIDES: Themis, Mnemosyne, Phoebe, Tethys, Theia, Rhea | ELDER TITANES: Rivermaster/Oceanus, Sagacity/Coeus, Starmaster/Crius, Watchman/Hyperion, Piercer/Iapetus, Cronus

stonecutter. Voutch, talk with Thirdson. If you think he is capable and so wish, you may take him as an apprentice. Valvuna, is Fourthson capable of being a hunter? I doubt it! But take him and find out. Let me know his worth." He paused. "We have had an excellent season. We break camp in three sunrises. You are dismissed."

"'Rivermaster,'" Rivermaster muttered to himself.

The Understanding

Kiya retired to her sleeping area. Her daughters soon joined her. Kiya asked them to find their brothers and sleep elsewhere tonight; she would like time alone with Vanam. The girls looked at one another, giggled, and left. Kiya put out flavored water and bread for her mate and waited.

Eventually, Vanam came. He seemed relaxed and took the proffered water. "The problem of your sons has taken care of itself," he said as he sat down. "And much to my liking. I may even get one hunter out of the lot. Valvuna will forge Fourthson into a hunter. I know he will. Fifthson is slight and weak, so making him a stonecutter was brilliant. Stonecutting is a lowly craft but necessary and not in the least an embarrassment. A skywatcher son might be a source of a bit of pride. A skywatcher is below only chief. The two girl-boys will be gone, probably forever. Yes, much to my liking."

Standing behind him, Kiya bristled at the characterizations of her sons. *They are fine young men. They just didn't turn out to be hunters. Rivermaster and Sagacity may surprise you. I know you are disappointed that you don't see a chief among them. Chief Talaimai was fortunate that he had you as a son. You are a wonderful chief. Talaimai retired in peace knowing you lead his tribe.*

Vanam said, "I plan to get rid of your daughters at Winter Solstice. Two or three are old enough to take mates, anyway, aren't they? The others could be bartered away with them. Maybe with all of them gone, I can start over trying to sire a leader. You say that they are all my sons but we both know that none of them are like me. They are weak and inept. No one believes that I am their father. Do you think that you bear me an adequate son if you put your mind to it? You have not done well, so far."

Kiya thought, *Well, Vanam, exactly what effort did you put into raising your sons? I seem to remember that you spoke harshly to them before they could walk.*

ELDER OCEANIDS: Metis, Tyche, Clymene, Eurybia, Amphitrite
ELDER OLYMPIANS: Hestia, Demeter, Hera, Hades, Poseidon, Zeus
OTHER: Philyra, Dionysus, Heracles, Outis, Enceladus, Littlerock, Porphyrion

She asked, "Get rid of our daughters? But it was you who took them from other tribes to curry favor with their chiefs. They are not of this tribe and can take mates from within your tribe. You need not 'get rid of them.'"

"I have decided! Get rid of them all at Winter Solstice. I will keep the three youngest boys. I will start fresh and have Panti watch you at all times to make sure you don't mate with anyone but me. You will bear me manly sons. Hunters. Sons I can be proud of. Not girl-boys like Pumi."

Angry, Kiya responded, "I will *not* get rid of my daughters. You will *not* get rid of your boys. I have given you five fine male babies. You are their father. They are all gifted. You are the only one who believes them inferior. I shall bear you as many children as you can sire but you will *not* get rid of any of them. And none of them are girl-boys and if they were, what difference?"

Vanam stood and faced Kiya. "You will get rid of the females at the Winter Solstice Festival and if the two older ones happen to survive and show up, I will banish them! Do you understand?"

"None of what you said shall come to pass! Do *you* understand?!"

Vanam slapped her hard enough to knock her to the ground and stood glaring over her.

Slowly, she rose and, inches from his face, smiled sweetly as she hissed, "None of what you have said will come to pass. Strike me again or try to 'get rid' of my children, then as you sleep in the night, I will cut off your penis and testicles. I will fashion a necklace and wear these things around my neck. I will go to each female with whom you have mated and say to her, 'Look what I have around my neck. I took these things from the great *Chief* Vanam. He is like a woman now, perhaps we can invite him to go gathering with us.' Do you doubt my words, *Chief* Vanam? Do you think me too weak or too timid to do that which I say? As you lay sleeping, *Chief* Vanam. You may kill me and face the shame from your tribe, or you shall do as I command, *Chief* Vanam. You will never touch me again and you will never threaten my children again. You are dismissed!"

He could have easily killed her but instead glared, spat, "Bitch," turned, and stormed away.

PRINCIPALS: Kiya, Vanam, Pumi, Valki | ELDER TITANIDES: Themis, Mnemosyne, Phoebe, Tethys, Theia, Rhea | ELDER TITANES: Rivermaster/Oceanus, Sagacity/Coeus, Starmaster/Crius, Watchman/Hyperion, Piercer/Iapetus, Cronus

She stood silently and watched him leave; empty of emotion; strangely not caring; relieved. *You were so kind when you accepted me. So considerate until you became chief. You think Pumi is the father of your sons. I gave you no reason. But you are correct. Your sons are not like you. They are not like other boys. They think rather than act. They are content to stay within their own thoughts. They don't seek the praise of others. But neither are they like Pumi. Pumi could move among hunters and women and skywatchers and children without regard to their station. And all respected him, even as a child. All thought of him as helpful even as he bent their will to his. Pumi loves you, Vanam. His success is not your failure. You are great by every measure. To every man, to every woman. Still even to me. I am now your burden. You will never be free of jealousy until you are free of me. Vanam. Oh, Vanam.*

The Fourth Family Campfire

The next day Kiya found Panti and told her it would take a while to become official, but Panti should take it upon herself to take over the duties of the elder woman for the tribe. "Make whatever excuses you think necessary."

Kiya found Themis and told her to gather her sisters and brothers at nightfall. "Have Rivermaster build a family campfire far away from the hunters."

She then found Chief Vanam with the hunters, approached him without permission, and said, "Chief Vanam, I can no longer handle the stress of being an elder woman. I am not worthy of the position. Panti is wiser than I, and handles the gatherings better than I. I request that you dismiss me from this heavy burden and tell Panti that she is now the tribe's elder woman."

She returned his unblinking glare.

Vanam replied, "As you wish. You may go."

Vanam returned to his conversations, daring anyone to question the exchange.

Rivermaster had built the fourth family campfire. The family gathered around it. The heat and the flames were comforting, inviting closeness and intimacy. Phoebe sat close to Sagacity; Tethys to Rivermaster.

"My sons spoke well at the meeting. You spoke plainly and confidently. I am proud of you," Kiya said.

Sagacity replied, "Rivermaster and I are extremely fortunate. Our requests could have infuriated our father. We crafted them as best we could. We

ELDER OCEANIDS: Metis, Tyche, Clymene, Eurybia, Amphitrite
ELDER OLYMPIANS: Hestia, Demeter, Hera, Hades, Poseidon, Zeus
OTHER: Philyra, Dionysus, Heracles, Outis, Enceladus, Littlerock, Porphyrion

are thrilled that we are set free to explore whatever lands we wish. Our three brothers received the positions they requested. It could not have worked out better for us, but our mother appears to have paid a painful price for our triumph. Will you tell us what has happened?"

Kiya was taken aback. That she had asked to be removed from her position would be common knowledge by now. That her sons connected her resignation with their requests from their father surprised her. "Why, Sagacity, there is no reason my removal need be tied with your speaking to your chief."

"I see," said Sagacity. "You had rather keep us uninformed and imagining the worst rather than trusting us with the truth."

"You are too forward with your mother! You will show respect!"

"Yes, Mother," Sagacity replied. "Of what, then, shall we talk?"

Kiya was quiet. No one spoke.

Finally, she said, "Chief Vanam has lost respect for me. I will not have it. But he is chief, and his orders must be obeyed. I will not obey his orders, so it is only honorable that he be free of me. My family is here, around this fire. I will protect my family even against the orders of a chief. I may be an unworthy member of this tribe and unworthy to be the elder woman, but I intend to be a worthy mother to my children. There, you have it."

The children reflected on her words.

Phoebe asked, "Were you told to trade us to the next tribe we encounter?"

Kiya replied, "Yes. I refused!"

"This is wonderful!" exclaimed Sagacity. "What do you think, Rivermaster?"

"It's interesting. We sit around our campfire in defiance of custom. We can all be banished if our father decides to punish us, a fate worse than being left to be eaten by wolves. I don't fear it. Neither do you, Sagacity, although my sisters might be fearful of such a thing."

"Oh, no, no, no," Phoebe exclaimed. "That would be exciting. We could start our own tribe. We can learn to farm from Sister Valki. Brother Pumi can teach our brothers whatever they want to know. Fourthson might learn how to bring us game. We would have a family campfire every night. We would make do quite nicely."

"My goodness," laughed Kiya. "My children are smarter than their mother. It will never come to banishment, but you have a wonderful plan if it did. I could not be more delighted."

"But," said Sagacity, "let's make a plan in case the worst doesn't happen. Let's decide what we want."

Themis intoned, "And find the plant to make it happen."

Sunrise

The tribe began breaking camp. Kiya gathered her sons and daughters at the site of the family campfire to say goodbye to Rivermaster and Sagacity. Little speeches were made about how they would gather at the upcoming Winter Solstice Festival, which was only three seasons away, how the two newly designated scouts would easily survive on their own for three seasons, how no one should worry, and how everyone was going to be all right. Kiya provided each of her sons with a bag containing food and drink. Unexpectantly, each of their sisters also provided food that had been saved from their own rations. Piercer gave each a colorful shard to be used for cutting and skinning.

As the two scouts turned to leave, Tethys ran to Rivermaster, embraced him, said, "Stay well," turned, and hurried away in tears. Phoebe, seeing this, broke down, ran to Sagacity, hugged him, turned, and quickly joined Tethys. The two young men, never exposed to such a thing, were at a loss.

Kiya looked at them, and said, "It is the way of women. Be safe, my sons."

The two looked at their mother, then toward the two retreating young women, and then at each other. Sagacity replied, "Keep everyone together, Mother. We will see you in three seasons." They turned and trotted away to explore unknown lands.

Later, before the tribe's departure, Panti found Kiya and told her, "It is done! Chief Vanam has made me elder woman. You will come to me only with problems; do not approach Chief Vanam again for any reason. To prevent confusion among the women, I will not allow you to accompany the women into the gathering fields. You are to stay in the camp with the

ELDER OCEANIDS: Metis, Tyche, Clymene, Eurybia, Amphitrite
ELDER OLYMPIANS: Hestia, Demeter, Hera, Hades, Poseidon, Zeus
OTHER: Philyra, Dionysus, Heracles, Outis, Enceladus, Littlerock, Porphyrion

children. When we reach Tallstone, I will trade you, your daughters, and, if they survive, your two oldest sons to other tribes. Your three oldest daughters may accompany the women when gathering until that time. Your three apprenticed sons may stay with our tribe. Chief Vanam is merciful; he wishes you no humiliation; only riddance of you, your daughters, and your two oldest sons. The less said about this, the better."

"I understand," replied Kiya. "You are kind and merciful."

< >

Kiya, her daughters, and her two youngest sons followed behind the women as the clan began its run to the next camp. Chief Vanam and Moonman led the tribe. Thirdson ran with Voutch as his newly appointed skywatcher apprentice. Fourthson stayed close to Valvuna.

The morning wore on. As they ran, Kiya said, "We and your two oldest brothers will be traded to another tribe at the festival. I intend to ask Panti to trade us all to Valki at Urfa. I believe Valki will look with favor upon us. What do my daughters think of this plan?"

Themis answered, "That would be wonderful, Mother! Surely, Aunt Valki will trade for us. We are accomplished at gathering and would not be a burden. I'm sure she could make good use of our brothers. How exciting!"

Little Theia said, "Maybe I could be useful by making things for Aunt Valki to trade."

Themis asked, "And what would that be, Little Sister?"

She answered, "Well, I have been thinking about a stupid thing, but the thought won't go away."

"Well, let's hear it," Kiya said. "If it's stupid, we will be entertained. If it's not stupid, it will be interesting. Either way, it will be pleasant to hear."

"I don't know how to explain," Theia began. "But when women leave to gather, they carry empty baskets and sacks. When they return after a good day, their sacks and baskets are filled and are heavy to carry. Mother has let me help sew bags together before, so I have a little bit of experience. I think I could sew tunics with large bags sewn directly into them so the plants would be easier to carry. I could sew in many pockets so the plants

---

PRINCIPALS: Kiya, Vanam, Pumi, Valki | ELDER TITANIDES: Themis, Mnemosyne, Phoebe, Tethys, Theia, Rhea | ELDER TITANES: Rivermaster/Oceanus, Sagacity/Coeus, Starmaster/Crius, Watchman/Hyperion, Piercer/Iapetus, Cronus

could be divided in the field and the plants would be mostly sorted at the end of the day. And nobody's tunic fits well. I could make a tunic to fit the exact shape of each woman. Surely this would be more comfortable."

"Yes," Kiya said. "These could be traded at the Winter Solstice Festival. Once seen, any woman *could* make them, but won't because they never have before. They will think that the only way to get one is at the festival."

"And, Theia," Themis exclaimed, "you forget about the hunters. The skins they wear look and smell like they were pulled directly from a carcass. Think how excited someone like Valvuna would be if he had a tunic cut to fit only him and emphasize his muscles. He is vain, you know, always parading and preening in front of the women. You could sew a tunic to fit him alone, but, oh dear, it would take much more time so it would cost twice, no, ten times the price of a premade tunic."

"Make one for him at this festival, Theia," Phoebe said. "When the tribes return for the next festival, everyone will have heard about how good Valvuna looks in his form-fitting tunic. Tell him how much it would normally cost but *give* it to Valvuna. The festival after this one, the hunters will be lining up to be measured for one of their own. And by that time, you will be ten times as fast, but you would, of course, charge the higher price. And, if a chief wants the special model with sewn-in lion's mane or serpent skin trim, only available to tribal chiefs', the price would be ... oh, my goodness, I don't know what."

"You don't think it's stupid?" Theia asked.

As they continued their fast trot, Kiya listened to her daughters laugh, banter, and make suggestions. *Upon this path, we may perish. Upon this path, we may prosper.*

ELDER OCEANIDS: Metis, Tyche, Clymene, Eurybia, Amphitrite
ELDER OLYMPIANS: Hestia, Demeter, Hera, Hades, Poseidon, Zeus
OTHER: Philyra, Dionysus, Heracles, Outis, Enceladus, Littlerock, Porphyrion

4. Rivermaster and Sagacity

At parting, Kiya had looked at them, and said, "It is the way of women. Be safe, my sons." The two looked at their mother, then toward the two retreating young women, and then at each other. Sagacity had said, "Keep everyone together, Mother. We will see you again in three seasons." They had then turned and trotted away to explore unknown western lands.

And Now

Sagacity said, "All right, we need a plan if we are to become great scouts."

Rivermaster laughed a bitter laugh. "Our father will judge us the same no matter how well we do. Let's survive three seasons, if for no other reason than to present ourselves at the festival. He doesn't really expect to see us again."

"That's a good plan. Short on details but certainly a good plan! More specifically, I propose traveling for one season toward the southwest. I don't think our tribe has been any farther west than we are now, and south, as I understand it, will take us in the general direction of Tallstone. Any better suggestions?"

"No. To the southwest it is and, oh, the wonders we shall find!"

"Food and water will be wonder enough. And no starving bears."

"Let us begin, Brother. To the southwest!"

< >

The two traveled on through barren, uninviting land. After a day's travel, the vegetation began to thicken and rolling hills appeared. Another day found them at the beginning of a forest. A half-day farther, they stopped. Before them lay a swift river of immense width. Rivermaster was transfixed. *I never imagined a stream could be this size.*

Sagacity said, "All right, great scout, do we turn and follow the river, or will you figure out a way to get to the other side of this thing?"

They lay down their equipment and sat, staring at the river. After a while, Rivermaster stood and said, "We can swim across." He ran to the water, jumped in, and began to swim toward the far bank."

PRINCIPALS: Kiya, Vanam, Pumi, Valki | ELDER TITANIDES: Themis, Mnemosyne, Phoebe, Tethys, Theia, Rhea | ELDER TITANES: Rivermaster/Oceanus, Sagacity/Coeus, Starmaster/Crius, Watchman/Hyperion, Piercer/Iapetus, Cronus

Sagacity thought, *You are insane, big brother. No one can swim this thing!*

Nonetheless, Sagacity rose and followed his brother into the swift waters.

The river wrapped itself around them. Over them. Around them. Pulling them down. Locked in liquid embrace. "Come to me," the river sang. "Stay with me."

A violent undertow caught Sagacity. He went under. He flailed. He could not breathe. He could not rise.

"You shall be my lover," the river sang. "Stay with me forever."

Sagacity had no air left. A strong hand grabbed his hair and pulled him up until his head was above water. He gulped air. The two swam as best they could. Through overpowering currents. Across a river with no bottom. Across a seemingly infinite distance.

"Stay with me," the river sang. "We shall be together forever. I will embrace and protect you. Stay with me. We will be as one."

The brothers swam, sank, floated, pulled each other, sank, gasped, and eventually found footing on the far side. They collapsed on their backs, exhausted, on the muddy riverbank.

"We are great scouts," Rivermaster gasped with pride.

"We left our supplies on the other side," Sagacity replied.

"Oh, yes. We did." Rivermaster sat up and dejectedly stared at the river. *You are a river. I am your master. You will do my bidding. You will tell me your secrets.*

Sagacity eventually sat up and observed his brother deep in thought. He silently rose and wandered into the nearby thicket to find something—anything—to eat.

As Rivermaster stared, movement upstream captured his attention. The trunk of a fallen tree was floating in the strong current, riding the river, floating on top of the water. He studied the movement of the tree. Where it floated, how it turned, and when it turned back. *We could use the tree to keep our heads above water and to rest on. One of us could swim pulling the tree while the other rested. We can use it to ride on the river.*

ELDER OCEANIDS: Metis, Tyche, Clymene, Eurybia, Amphitrite
ELDER OLYMPIANS: Hestia, Demeter, Hera, Hades, Poseidon, Zeus
OTHER: Philyra, Dionysus, Heracles, Outis, Enceladus, Littlerock, Porphyrion

Rivermaster rose and went into the thicket searching for a perfect section of a tree. The brothers met in the late afternoon; one with food, the other with a plan. They ate the nuts and fruits Sagacity had gathered, then returned to the thicket and to a tree trunk Rivermaster had found. The tree had broken into several pieces after being blown down by a strong wind. Each man still had their cutting stone tied around their waist. They were able to cut away undesirable limbs and fashion a log Rivermaster thought might be suitable. It was small enough that the two could drag, carry, push, and roll their creation to the muddy riverbank.

"Now," said Rivermaster, "we must fashion a rope the length of five men. We passed some vines growing in trees and dead vines easy to get to. Come on, let's see if we can do this before nightfall." The vines were found, and the rope was easier to construct than they dared hope. "Let's make a couple of extra," Sagacity suggested. "They may prove useful."

Night had almost fallen when they returned with ropes for their *river-rider*.

"Tonight, or in the morning?" Sagacity asked.

"Now. We still have the strength and there is light enough to see by."

They looped the center of the long rope around their river-rider and securely fashioned the ends around their waists. They began pushing the river-rider into the water. Rivermaster stopped, looked at it, and then at the water. "Wait," he commanded. He stood thinking, untied the rope from around his waist, and plunged into the darkening thicket. He returned after several minutes carrying two long tree limbs. "These may be useful in pushing our log in shallow water and maybe even guide us in deep water."

Rivermaster refastened the rope around himself and grasped Sagacity's shoulder. "We will die becoming great scouts or else live and become great scouts." They both laughed as they pulled their river-rider into dark waters. The trip back was difficult, but they once more crossed the river.

Upon reaching the other side, they beached their river-rider, walked upstream, and found their abandoned equipment. Rivermaster told Sagacity to set camp. They sat around their small campfire reviewing the day's events. Late in the night, they finally lay down upon their bedding.

PRINCIPALS: Kiya, Vanam, Pumi, Valki | ELDER TITANIDES: Themis, Mnemosyne, Phoebe, Tethys, Theia, Rhea | ELDER TITANES: Rivermaster/Oceanus, Sagacity/Coeus, Starmaster/Crius, Watchman/Hyperion, Piercer/Iapetus, Cronus

Before falling into a deep, exhausted sleep, Rivermaster said, "We are great scouts!"

They slept well past sunrise. Sagacity awoke and sat up to find Rivermaster sitting by the river, staring at it. Sagacity went into the brush to find something edible to supplement the rations in their traveling pouches. Upon returning with an abundance of edible plants, he broke camp and prepared their breakfast. Rivermaster had not moved.

"Shall we eat and then cross the river, yet again?" Sagacity asked.

"Our first crossing was almost fatal. Our second was strenuous, but not especially difficult. Let's make our third crossing pleasurable and so easy that even Piercer could cross with his colored rocks."

Sagacity said, "'Rivermaster,' 'Great Scout,' 'Oldest son,' 'Son of the chief.' You let these names go to your head. Let's just get back across the river and continue exploring."

"Did you learn nothing from our second crossing? Come with me." Rivermaster led Sagacity into the thicket. They searched for a fallen tree.

After a long search, Rivermaster found all the pieces he required. The two brothers fashioned, as best they could with their cutting stones, a log like the one waiting for them on the bank. They muscled the log to the waiting river-rider and laid it parallel to it, the width of a man apart. They returned to the thicket and gathered a dozen saplings and branches Rivermaster had selected. These were returned to the river-rider where Rivermaster fashioned them into the shapes he desired. He tied five strong saplings across the two logs. They wove vines, twigs, and leaves between the cross-saplings making a pad on which they could lash their supplies and equipment. They fashioned six poles from the remaining branches and saplings. Two were made into smooth long poles that they could use to push off the bank. Branches and leaves were left on the bottom of the remaining four. They tied their equipment and supplies to the woven pad. And last, they tied their original long rope to the forward, strongest cross-sapling. With this rope, they could alternate swimming and pulling their craft across the river.

In the early afternoon, they sat back and admired what they had made: a new, improved "river-rider."

ELDER OCEANIDS: Metis, Tyche, Clymene, Eurybia, Amphitrite
ELDER OLYMPIANS: Hestia, Demeter, Hera, Hades, Poseidon, Zeus
OTHER: Philyra, Dionysus, Heracles, Outis, Enceladus, Littlerock, Porphyrion

Sagacity said, "I believe that you have fashioned a new creation, Brother. Nothing like this has ever existed before. This should bring you respect from our father. Whether it's useful is beside the point. If it can carry us across the river, you will truly be 'Rivermaster.'"

They sat in silence staring at their craft and the river.

Rivermaster noticed the last, unused sapling lying nearby. He retrieved it and tied it to rise vertically at the rear of the river-rider. "The sapling is tall and will help us find our craft after we cross the river and beach it."

"Yes," Sagacity replied. "And it will blow in the wind as we cross, cheering us on, telling the world, 'Here be great scouts.'"

They laughed, embraced, and then pulled their craft into the river. They each mounted a log, took a long pole, and pushed themselves into the river's current. They experimented with paddling with the four remaining leafed branches. By the time they reached the other side, they could control their creation at will.

They beached and safed their river-rider. The tall mast was visible far up and down the riverbank.

"To the southwest," proclaimed Sagacity. They continued the exploration which had been so rudely interrupted by the river. The river seemed to sing, "Farewell, my master."

Rivermaster mused as they walked. "This river will keep Eastern tribes away from this side. Few from the east will have found this land. Someday, I must learn where the river begins and where it ends, and if it is this daunting its entire length. I assume it has a beginning and an end. I doubt if any tribe on this side of the river has ever encountered tribes from our side of the river. Will they be like us? Will there even be tribes on this side? We must learn these things. Being a scout gives us great knowledge and great power. Perhaps we *will* become worthy in our father's eyes."

Oursea

They trotted southwestward for four days. The land sloped continually downward. They took note of the terrain, animals, and vegetation. Then, toward nightfall at the end of the fourth day, they came to the end of the world. Before them lay endless water. They saw no land on the other side. Rivermaster fell to his knees in awe. Water without end!

Sagacity stood staring at the water with amazement. *Enough water for you, big brother? What shall you do with all this water?*

Sagacity said, "Let's make camp. We can spend the evening considering our course of action."

"Yes," Rivermaster replied, still on his knees. "Let's make camp."

Sunrise

They followed the shoreline northward. Later, Rivermaster saw land rising above the water toward the northwest, a mountaintop, perhaps? They quickened their pace. Eventually, a shoreline appeared jutting into the sea. In the late afternoon, they were able to turn due west onto the landmass.

They found a landmass surrounded by water on all sides save the narrow land bridge which was the only connection to the mainland. They found mountains, a great plain with all manner of animals, vegetation, and colored stone. Coves contained sea creatures beyond imagination. They found a fertile land; a rich land; a wondrous land. They had adventures. They killed a bear. The land was devoid of human life.

They both said, many times, "We are great scouts. Father will be pleased!"

After five quarter-moons, they set out northeastward to return to their river-rider and then for their rendezvous at Tallstone and the judgment of their father.

Urfa

After five days, they came to the great river and eventually found their river-rider. They crossed and set out directly east to find Tallstone.

After a morning's run, they came upon men working in a grove harvesting wood. The men identified themselves as *builders* and invited the two scouts to visit. The builders were from the settlement of Urfa and said, "Yes, we know the location of Tallstone. We will all go to the Winter Solstice Festival which begins in a quarter moon.

ELDER OCEANIDS: Metis, Tyche, Clymene, Eurybia, Amphitrite
ELDER OLYMPIANS: Hestia, Demeter, Hera, Hades, Poseidon, Zeus
OTHER: Philyra, Dionysus, Heracles, Outis, Enceladus, Littlerock, Porphyrion

The builders were interested in the lands that lay to the west, especially the frequency, height, and girth of any trees. The scouts shared their knowledge of the land up to the great river but not about the land that lay on the other side. The builders were interested when Rivermaster mentioned the river rider he had built. A construction that a man could ride to cross the great river. They wanted to know the details of its construction; why Rivermaster constructed it as he did; what tools he used, and how it performed in the river. They insisted that the two scouts go with them to their settlement. Their chief, or master as they called him, would be interested in this river-rider. No Builder had ever built such a thing before. Their questions were endless. "What size are these *fins*? What do they do? This thing carried your weight and your gear across the top of the water?" And on and on.

The builders suggested returning to Urfa for the evening meal and, at sunrise, being taken and shown this strange new creation. They returned to Urfa, a strange place with all manner of buildings and constructions; some were made of mud and stone, but most were built of wood. The scouts were introduced to the builder's master, Putt, who questioned them even more intensely about the river-rider.

Rivermaster used sticks and bark to show, as best he could, what he had done.

Putt questioned, "You say that you crossed the great western river on this thing?" He motioned his apprentices to take the visitors into the nearby 'house,' while Putt remained squatting, staring at the sticks and bark.

The apprentices and scouts approached a great house and then climbed *stairs* onto a *porch*. They entered the house where a woman stood over a *counter* kneading bread. An apprentice announced, "Mother Valki, these are strangers we met while harvesting wood from the western grove. They are Scouts from the north."

"Welcome," Valki said. "We gather for our evening meal at sunset. Join us and tell your stories. For what tribe do you scout?"

"We are from Chief Vanam's Clan of the Serpent," Rivermaster said.

She stopped her work, turned, and stared at him. "Chief Vanam and Kiya, you must know them."

PRINCIPALS: Kiya, Vanam, Pumi, Valki | ELDER TITANIDES: Themis, Mnemosyne, Phoebe, Tethys, Theia, Rhea | ELDER TITANES: Rivermaster/Oceanus, Sagacity/Coeus, Starmaster/Crius, Watchman/Hyperion, Piercer/Iapetus, Cronus

Rivermaster said, "They are our parents."

She went to them and embraced them. "You are Kiya's sons! How wonderful! I met you many years ago at Tallstone when you were still small children. And now you are scouts! How wonderful! Come sit on the front porch and let me hear of my old tribe."

She called a young woman to take over her task and led Rivermaster and Sagacity to the porch where they all sat in 'chairs.' Another young woman brought a drink for them.

Rivermaster asked Sagacity to tell their story. As usual, Sagacity said more than he should; things Phoebe had told him about words between their parents. Valki listened intently, shaking her head in understanding, and asking delicate questions, which led to even more explanations. When he had finished, Valki knew even more than they about their family's situation.

Valki said, "Well, Kiya is a wise and determined woman. Good things shall come to pass from all of this, and I know she is proud of her two Scouts."

Rivermaster asked her not to repeat any of these words to anyone for any reason until all had come to pass; one way or the other. They all agreed that it would be bad if any word of this conversation made it back to anyone in the Serpent clan.

Valki agreed to total secrecy until decisions had been made. She then said, "It is time to gather for evening meal." A young girl took them to a room in another building and told them to wash their bodies, especially their hands, and then to gather in the main room of the building for the evening meal. They did as they were told and, upon entering the great room, found tables of food and people sitting in chairs around the tables.

Valki saw the two scouts enter and called them to the head of the table where she had set aside chairs for them on either side of her. She attracted everyone's attention and introduced the two scouts by name and tribe. The diners welcomed them in unison. Valki gave everyone leave to take whatever food pleased them and to enjoy it.

The builders spoke enthusiastically about their upcoming adventure to learn of new construction that could cross the wide river that they knew to lay to the west. Everyone was interested in hearing of what land lay on

ELDER OCEANIDS: Metis, Tyche, Clymene, Eurybia, Amphitrite
ELDER OLYMPIANS: Hestia, Demeter, Hera, Hades, Poseidon, Zeus
OTHER: Philyra, Dionysus, Heracles, Outis, Enceladus, Littlerock, Porphyrion

the other side of the river, which none had ever ventured to cross. And, of course, the upcoming festival was also on everyone's mind. The conversation was animated and loud.

After evening meal was over, Valki called Putt. "I have a request, Putt. My dear friend, Kiya, will attend the festival for the first time in years. Construct a chair befitting her rank. Design it so that it may be transported between camps, as needed. When you are finished, deliver it to her sons to place as they think appropriate. Can this be done before the festival?"

"Yes, Mother Valki," Putt replied. "My apprentice, Enceladus, excels at building these constructions. He is strong and talented but sometimes belligerent. I will direct him to use our best wood and twine in its construction and to design it with a high back and space so that different figures may be engraved as you think appropriate."

"Excellent. Enceladus came to us as a battered older boy, as I remember; trampled on a training hunt. Their Chief assumed he would soon die or at least be useless as a hunter."

"Yes, Mother Valki. The tribe was from the Far East and was aggressive. They put great significance on strength and endurance. Their loss has been my gain."

"Excellent," Valki said, again. "Now, I will discharge our two guests to you so you may continue your plans for tomorrow's excursion."

Evening pleasantries were exchanged. The two scouts left with Putt to select the apprentices to accompany them on the next day's journey to inspect the river-rider.

Putt and the River-rider

The troupe arrived at the river-rider in the late afternoon. The apprentices derided the rough cuts and poor selection of building materials, but Putt held up his hand to silence them.

He walked to the vessel and ran his hands over it, examining each cut, each binding, each part; including the tall limb, topped by leaves, rising high in the rear of the vessel. He would periodically look to the river; imagining how each piece worked with every other piece to negotiate the river. "You say that you place these poles with leaves on the bottom into

PRINCIPALS: Kiya, Vanam, Pumi, Valki | ELDER TITANIDES: Themis, Mnemosyne, Phoebe, Tethys, Theia, Rhea | ELDER TITANES: Rivermaster/Oceanus, Sagacity/Coeus, Starmaster/Crius, Watchman/Hyperion, Piercer/Iapetus, Cronus

the water to help you control the direction of the vessel? The leaves on the pole on the back of the vessel flutter in the wind when you cross? You can orient the vessel in the water and use the poles to push the vessel? More than one rider may cross?"

Finally, Putt stood, looked at Rivermaster, and proclaimed, "It is magnificent. Can we cross the river before nightfall?"

"Yes. Sagacity and I will carry you across and back again while the others make camp. You can take the place of Sagacity on our return so you can learn to control it."

The three men crossed the river; each noting how far downriver they traveled during the crossing. They discussed their return as they rested on the far shore for a few minutes. They then set out on the return crossing. Putt was neither accomplished nor particularly skilled with his tasks. Still, eventually, they made it back to their original side although much farther downstream. Rivermaster and Putt walked the shore back to the launch site while Sagacity doggedly pulled the river-rider in the shallow water using the rope tied to its bow.

"An interesting experience," Putt told his troupe when he arrived back at the launch site. "I have several ideas to improve efficiency. We will discuss them tomorrow. Now, let's retire for the night. Tomorrow will be strenuous."

The day's activities and experiences had left the two scouts exhausted; they slept a deep, peaceful sleep. The builders were full of questions and ideas; they slept fitfully; visions running through their heads.

When the two scouts awoke, well after daybreak, the builders were already busy performing their assigned tasks. Putt suggested that his apprentices be given training crossings, two trainees at a time, to familiarize them with the operation. Putt could see no immediate benefit in building these things, but as creation follows need; need follows creation. That, plus proper creation was mentally stimulating, and proper creation could certainly benefit from skilled craftsmen.

The day was spent crossing the river to train the builders; Putt crossed twice more; experimenting with different poles and wooden shapes. Several other builders requested a second crossing. As everyone gathered around the evening campfire, Putt announced that he was pleased with

ELDER OCEANIDS: Metis, Tyche, Clymene, Eurybia, Amphitrite
ELDER OLYMPIANS: Hestia, Demeter, Hera, Hades, Poseidon, Zeus
OTHER: Philyra, Dionysus, Heracles, Outis, Enceladus, Littlerock, Porphyrion

the day's activities and that Rivermaster and Sagacity could now leave for the festival. "Our work should be completed by the time you return. And, oh yes, Tallstone is a half-day due north of Urfa."

The next morning, the two scouts departed and set off to return to Urfa and then on to Tallstone.

And to their fate.

5. Winter Solstice Festival 17
In the 43rd year from the birth of Vanam

Once more, the Clan of the Serpent set up camp, hunted, gathered, and again broke camp. This time their destination was the yearly festival at Tallstone.

Theia had spent the previous season taking her new craft seriously. She experimented with cutting tools to develop the finest, most exact cuts. She experimented with her needles of bone and wood to make the smallest, most precise stitches. She experimented with strands of gut and fibers to make the thinnest, strongest thread. She practiced making a form-fitting dress for Phoebe, who had more curves than her older sister and most of the tribe's women. In the evenings, Phoebe would collaborate with her on designing a generic dress to facilitate gathering. Theia took to her craft as much as her Uncle Pumi had taken to his stonecutting. Once tentative and withdrawn, she was now driven and relentless. She was only a child, but a child entering an adult world on her terms with an art and craft that she alone had conceived, with which she had been given the adult responsibility to make happen. She. Theia!

Phoebe had spent her time in the gathering fields but without incentive to perform. She was, after all, to be evicted after this season. She gathered at the rocky edge of the field, staying out of sight of Panti, gathering plants plus stones streaked with color.

Kiya and her children brought up the rear of the tribe as they traveled to Tallstone. Mnemosyne invented a traveling song and began to sing. Her sisters joined in.

In mid-afternoon, Vanam and his Clan of the Serpent arrived at Tallstone.

Members of the various guilds were in the fields around the vast festival site to greet arriving tribes. Their duty was to guide incoming tribes to an appropriate campsite based on tradition and the tribes' size. The guild masters had delineated two dozen campsites of various sizes by placing tall wooden posts into the ground. The posts were seared with various icons. Twelve tribes had already made camp.

An acolyte from the Agriculture Guild saw the Clan of the Serpent approaching. He went to greet them and lead them to their designated campsite. Vanam's tribe was one of the two founding clans of the festival

ELDER OCEANIDS: Metis, Tyche, Clymene, Eurybia, Amphitrite
ELDER OLYMPIANS: Hestia, Demeter, Hera, Hades, Poseidon, Zeus
OTHER: Philyra, Dionysus, Heracles, Outis, Enceladus, Littlerock, Porphyrion

and, as such, their traditional camp toward the south was always reserved for them, whether they attended or not. Their wooden posts were seared with the icon of the serpent. The tribe proudly marched to their premier site; past other clans, past the large athletic area laid out for foot races, feats of strength, endurance, wrestling, spear-throwing accuracy and distance, wrestling, and other manly competitions.

The acolyte was especially proud of Urfa's great serving areas which were seen in the southern distance. One area, designated by the tall wooden posts seared with an icon of bread, contained tables with loaves of cooked bread; free for the taking for poor tribes, although contributions of skins, threads, or rare plants were accepted from the wealthier tribes. Another area contained ovens where attendants busily baked even more loaves of bread. Nearby were large urns containing raw einkorn; also free for the taking; contributions accepted. Far behind the serving areas were empty fields. Many shallow, long trenches had been cut by agriculture guild docents. Portable private stalls were located over the trenches. Stalls allowed men and women to relieve themselves in privacy. As the trench was filled, a docent would move the stall down the trench and cover the waste with dirt. This kept the entire campsite clean and encouraged crop growth during the next growing season.

The tribe passed near the great receiving house lined with benches facing the large front porch. Those seeking a *Last Camp* and resettlement in Urfa would soon gather on these benches. They would counsel with Valki or one of Urfa's elder women to discuss their needs and desires.

And then, Chief Vanam saw the four corner posts marked with the sign of the serpent. His tribe had returned to the site where they had first made camp seventeen years ago before there was a Winter Solstice Festival, before there was Tallstone, and before there was Urfa. The site where Vanam had been passed the mantle of chiefdom during the first Winter Solstice Festival.

Vanam directed Valuvana to oversee setting up the camp. No one should leave the site until the festival was proclaimed to begin. Vanam then set out to find Chief Nanatan, chief of the great Clan of the Lion.

PRINCIPALS: Kiya, Vanam, Pumi, Valki | ELDER TITANIDES: Themis, Mnemosyne, Phoebe, Tethys, Theia, Rhea | ELDER TITANES: Rivermaster/Oceanus, Sagacity/Coeus, Starmaster/Crius, Watchman/Hyperion, Piercer/Iapetus, Cronus

Kiya had been directed to claim space at the far southwest corner of the site; a space too small for her and all her children. *Our tribe has grown larger in the past years. Everything is cramped. A much bigger site will surely be allocated next year. Vanam will have a large space. Space for himself and a random woman. Women.*

Her children did not complain about the cramped quarters. Thirdson observed that their site was in a corner away from the other sites. It would be easy for him and his brothers to find a suitable sleeping place in the nearby woods and let their mother and sisters have the entire area to themselves.

Phoebe protested, but Thirdson pointed out that maybe the males could find a suitable place for a campfire. His sisters were delighted, his mother proud.

Kiya was surprisingly at peace, but her children's excitement was palpable.

Rhea said, "This is where we belong. Campsites are so constricting and boring. Mother, how did you live so long, running from camp to camp, tending women? This place is alive and exciting."

"Yes, it is exciting," Themis said, "because it's different. I remember coming years ago. It has grown much larger, and I don't want to face that. You all go on without me. I want to walk in the woods and think."

Phoebe would have none of that. "I want to get into the thick of things!"

The Opening Ceremony had evolved. Valki of Urfa now met with Skywatcher Littlestar, Master of Tallstone, Chief Nanatan, and all other attending chiefs beneath the tall stone obelisk on the morning of the new season. At noon, it was Valki who would stride upon the stage erected yearly for this occasion, excite the crowd, and introduce the dignitaries in attendance. After getting the crowd excited, and to the sound of beating drums, she screamed over the excitement, "Let's go have a festival!" and signaled the great horn to blow.

The great horn sounded. The festival began. Each person began the festival in their own way.

Kiya's sons immediately ran toward the playing fields.

Pumi found his older brother, Chief Vanam, and extended his arms to embrace him.

ELDER OCEANIDS: Metis, Tyche, Clymene, Eurybia, Amphitrite
ELDER OLYMPIANS: Hestia, Demeter, Hera, Hades, Poseidon, Zeus
OTHER: Philyra, Dionysus, Heracles, Outis, Enceladus, Littlerock, Porphyrion

Vanam ignored Pumi and retired arm-in-arm with Chief Nanatan to inspect the festivities and mingle with the other chiefs.

And so ... The Festival Begins

The great trumpet was heard. The festival had begun.

Pumi

Pumi, ignored by his brother, set off to join Littlerock at the tall stone.

The masters of the various guilds joined Littlestar and Pumi at the tall stone to receive the mass waiting to see, touch, or speak to Pumi. Pumi was acknowledged by all to be the greatest stonemason who had ever lived. In his youth, he was the most celebrated stonecutter in the land. His spearheads and cutting blades were still the finest available. Some said that he had single-handedly conceived and built Tallstone. Pumi, with Littlestar, received each person in turn. They introduced those who wished to be apprenticed to one of the five guilds to the appropriate Guild Master, who then assigned those who might prove worthy to an apprentice within the guild for further, deeper discussions.

Eventually, a familiar stonecutter stood before Pumi. Neither spoke for a long time. The stonecutter fell to his knees and touched Pumi's feet with his forehead. Pumi drew the man to his feet and said, "Littlerock, my friend. I rejoice to see you. We will meet over a campfire as soon as all is calm."

"Yes, Master, "But allow me to introduce my apprentice." He pushed Piercer to face Pumi. "Piercer, this is my great master, Pumi. Pumi, this is my apprentice, Piercer."

"You have an excellent master, Piercer. Littlerock is quite accomplished and a wonderful teacher. Your name is interesting. Is there a story there?"

"Yes, Master, I pierced holes into colored rocks and made a pretty necklace that I gave to Mother. She gave me my name."

"Colored rocks? I have noticed rocks that contain color but never paid attention to them. Do they make better spear points than regular rocks?"

"I don't know, Master. I only began a season ago. I have much to learn. But I like colored rocks."

PRINCIPALS: Kiya, Vanam, Pumi, Valki | ELDER TITANIDES: Themis, Mnemosyne, Phoebe, Tethys, Theia, Rhea | ELDER TITANES: Rivermaster/Oceanus, Sagacity/Coeus, Starmaster/Crius, Watchman/Hyperion, Piercer/Iapetus, Cronus

Pumi laughed. "Well, keep me apprised of your progress. I need to know how colored rocks may be different than regular rocks. I look forward to finding a woman wearing a pretty necklace of rocks."

"You already know her, Master," Littlerock said. He paused, "Piercer is Kiya's youngest son."

Pumi's expression did not change. He stared at Littlerock. "Kiya?"

"Yes, Master. We need to talk. Before you leave, find me. We must talk."

Littlerock left, taking Piercer with him.

Pumi thought, *Kiya? Vanam? Talk? Yes, Littlerock. I shall find you!*

The next in line addressed Pumi. Pumi was delighted to talk with him.

< >

An hour into the evening meetings, the Clan of the Serpent skywatcher, Voutch, stood before Pumi with his apprentice. After introducing himself, Voutch introduced his apprentice, Thirdson.

Voutch said, "It is right that Thirdson follows in your footsteps. You are the only person who was both an acclaimed stonecutter and an acclaimed apprentice skywatcher. I saw you meet Piercer. He is the fifth son of Chief Vanam. Well, Thirdson is his third."

"Excellent," Pumi said. "Is Kiya your mother?"

"Yes, Master," Thirdson replied. "But she and all my sisters and my two older brothers will be traded to another tribe during the festival, and I will never see them again and I love my mother and brothers and sisters."

"I see," Pumi said. He looked to Voutch for an explanation.

"Thirdson, don't bother Pumi with gossip!" To Pumi, he said, "I apologize, Master. Thirdson has not been taught proper respect."

Pumi replied, "Affairs of my old tribe are always of interest. We will talk more tomorrow night at the council of skywatchers."

Voutch beamed and put his hand on Thirdson's shoulder. Then both ambled off to join the festivities.

Pumi thought, *Yes, Littlerock, my friend. I shall most certainly find you.*

ELDER OCEANIDS: Metis, Tyche, Clymene, Eurybia, Amphitrite
ELDER OLYMPIANS: Hestia, Demeter, Hera, Hades, Poseidon, Zeus
OTHER: Philyra, Dionysus, Heracles, Outis, Enceladus, Littlerock, Porphyrion

The day wore on. Everyone in line was addressed and attended to. Sunset came. Pumi found Littlerock.

Littlerock told Pumi all he knew of the problem with Kiya and her children. He did know the 'why' but the 'what' was self-evident plus Piercers' comments unknowingly shed some light on the 'why.' It might be that Vanam was jealous of Pumi or maybe Vanam thought Pumi was the father of some of his sons. The details were not clear but animosity toward Pumi appeared to play a part in the problem. On the positive side, Piercer had made amazing progress as Littlerock's apprentice, exceeding all expectations. The boy loved working with rock. Littlerock assumed that Piercer would not be expelled from the tribe, but it was not a subject Littlerock brought up with Vanam. Pumi and Littlerock talked into the night. It was decided Pumi should not seek an audience with Chief Vanam and this was not an issue Valki should be brought into, at least for now.

Pumi would instead seek counsel from Chief Nanatan.

And so ... The Festival Begins

The great trumpet was heard. The festival had begun. Kiya dismissed her children into the excitement.

Kiya

Kiya walked toward the great house with benches in front. In front was a tall post engraved with a house, the symbol of Urfa.

She and Valki had been thrown together by their respective mates; the brothers Vanam and Pumi. But the relationship evolved far deeper than a simple tribal association. The minds of the two women, in their own ways, ran deeper and more complex than other women of their time. As the years progressed, they fed off each other's intellect and questioning of the nature of things. Valki had founded Urfa near an unexplained patch rich with wild einkorn and as a Last Camp for her tribe's elder woman, Palai, and their elderly skywatcher, Moonman.

The two women had not seen one another in five years. Vanam had inexplicably ceased leading his tribe to the yearly festival, preferring instead to lead his tribe to the hunting fields toward the east. Valki had devoted her years to domesticating and creating fields of einkorn. Kiya,

PRINCIPALS: Kiya, Vanam, Pumi, Valki | ELDER TITANIDES: Themis, Mnemosyne, Phoebe, Tethys, Theia, Rhea | ELDER TITANES: Rivermaster/Oceanus, Sagacity/Coeus, Starmaster/Crius, Watchman/Hyperion, Piercer/Iapetus, Cronus

the devoted mate, raised her children. She had, however, experimented with creating various elixirs, salves, and medicines. What mixtures of plants would promote healing, increase endurance, and decrease the effects of aging? She experimented with herself, her children, and her fellow clansmen. All were acclimated to Kiya's unending inquiries into their health and how they felt that day. She desperately needed the mental stimulation and practical advice available from her only peer—Valki.

Kiya also needed empathy and guidance for her familial situation.

The day would be a full day for everyone. Pumi worked with the Astronomer and Stonemason guilds to support Tallstone activities. Valki worked with the Builder, Agriculture, and Shepherd's guilds to support Urfa activities. While Pumi received accolades for the festival; Valki provided the infrastructure; food, campfire wood, facilities, water, a refuge for the old, trash management, and things of that nature.

Kiya did not intend to see Valki on this day; perhaps tomorrow she could re-introduce herself and Valki might have time to visit. In the meantime, Kiya would tour the Urfa area. She walked past the great house; assuming that is where Valki would be. The benches were already filled with older people and people with infirmities. They would all be met by Valki herself.

Kiya walked to inspect the tables filled with bread. The tables had been assembled and stocked for several days. The poorer tribes tended to arrive early, sometimes they were in the midst of starvation. The availability of bread saved lives. The poor tribes had little to exchange in return; nothing was expected. These tribes would remember the kindness and would be generous in future years as their fortunes improved.

Tables had been designated for various contributions in exchange for the goods taken. Skins of all types, animal bones suitable for repurposing, exotic plants, dried meats, surplus spearheads, string and rope made from intestines and fibrous plants, linens fashioned from hemp, baskets, and any other item of possible value were gladly accepted. Elder women stood near the tables to advise on the purpose and how to use the private stalls in the fields toward the south, to encourage the poorer tribes, to thank those who contributed, to discuss any unusual properties the item might have, and to gossip. These women were the clearinghouse for all information. The contributions the women received made it possible for

ELDER OCEANIDS: Metis, Tyche, Clymene, Eurybia, Amphitrite
ELDER OLYMPIANS: Hestia, Demeter, Hera, Hades, Poseidon, Zeus
OTHER: Philyra, Dionysus, Heracles, Outis, Enceladus, Littlerock, Porphyrion

the citizens of Urfa to maintain their village during the year and then host the great Winter Solstice Festival.

Kiya talked with several women to admire all they were doing and how efficiently they did it. "To feed this many people is impressive." She did not mention that she was once the mate of the Chief of the Clan of the Serpent. She would be an embarrassment to her tribe soon enough.

She visited the tables containing the bread. She took no bread but wondered if she had, would a colored stone be an appropriate exchange? As far as she knew, the stones had no unusual purpose; they were simply pleasing to the eye. She turned to leave but reconsidered. She stopped and waited until the women at the table were not busy. She then approached, showed them her necklace of stones, and inquired about the desirability of colored stones. The women gathered around to excitedly admire the necklace. Not only were the stones 'pretty' but they might be functional. A young woman explained that with each loaf of bread given, the recipient was asked the name of their tribe. A small river pebble would be placed into a box containing many slots; the slot into which the pebble was placed indicated the tribe that received the loaf. "Not only can we count how many loaves were given, but Pumi can also tell which tribes took how many loaves. This information seems to be of interest to the guild masters. "A handful of small stones is certainly worth a loaf of bread, but I might take a few of them for myself to make a necklace. I would replace them with river rock, of course."

Kiya laughed, "Of course." She filed the woman's words away for future consideration.

Their elder woman, silent so far, now asked, "Which is your tribe?"

This was the subject Kiya had been avoiding but there was no way to not answer truthfully. She answered, "Clan of the Serpent."

The elder woman's face brightened. "Oh, then you know Elder Woman Kiya and Chief Vanam!"

Kiya stared back, blankly. *Here we have it. There is no way past this. I was foolish to think that I could avoid this and the* dishonor it brings.

She answered, "I am Kiya."

PRINCIPALS: Kiya, Vanam, Pumi, Valki | ELDER TITANIDES: Themis, Mnemosyne, Phoebe, Tethys, Theia, Rhea | ELDER TITANES: Rivermaster/Oceanus, Sagacity/Coeus, Starmaster/Crius, Watchman/Hyperion, Piercer/Iapetus, Cronus

Book 2. *The Beginning of Civilization: Mythologies Told True*

The elder woman became alert and presented herself. "I am Paravi, once Elder Woman of the Clan of the Auroch. I am now on Urfa's Council of Elders. I am honored to meet you. Valki has spoken highly of you many times. Have you not yet presented yourself to Mother Valki? She will be insulted if you ignore her. Come, I will escort you to her."

Kiya could remain silent, but protocol demanded she clear all misconceptions of rank. "You are kind, but I am no longer the elder woman of my tribe. I requested Chief Vanam relieve me of the burden of leadership. The tribe's new elder woman is Panti who is more accomplished than I in everything but the knowledge of plants. To transfer leadership to Panti was a joy to me, to Panti, and to our women. I cannot present myself to Valki as an elder woman. I feel that I should wait until she has finished her duties, and I can approach her as a common woman."

Paravi was unsure how to proceed with this information. She said, "Wait. I will consult with Mother Valki." Paravi scurried off to the large house.

Within moments, Valki burst from the house followed by Paravi. Valki hurried to Kiya with extended arms. "Sister, how can you neglect me so? It is a joy to see you after all these years. Come into the house. We have much to discuss!" She took Kiya's hand and began pulling her toward the house.

Following, Kiya said, "Valki, so much has changed. Nothing is as it was."

"That is wonderful news," Valki replied. "Change is so interesting, don't you think?"

They entered the house. It was alive with newcomers. Urfa's elder women busied themselves acclimating the newcomers to their new environment.

Valki took Kiya through the main room to a smaller room in the back which could be closed off for privacy. They then sat in chairs facing one another.

Valki said, "Putt insisted that he make me a place where I could be away from the people. Unnecessary, perhaps, but nice for private gossip. Now, let us gossip." She leaned forward and looked expectantly at Kiya, smiling.

Kiya was silent for a while; then the words burst forth.

Valki listened intently, shaking her head when appropriate. Kiya finished her story with eyes closed and silent tears.

ELDER OCEANIDS: Metis, Tyche, Clymene, Eurybia, Amphitrite
ELDER OLYMPIANS: Hestia, Demeter, Hera, Hades, Poseidon, Zeus
OTHER: Philyra, Dionysus, Heracles, Outis, Enceladus, Littlerock, Porphyrion

Valki stood, walked to Kiya, leaned over, and embraced her. "Sister," she said, "much of this I already knew. If Vanam will trade you to Urfa, everything will be easy enough. You and your children can settle here. Ask or beg Panti to trade you but don't let Vanam banish you. Panti will have a great influence on Vanam. Banishment would be a big problem because Urfa is home to many elder women. My council would not accept a banished woman and her children into Urfa. That would go against everything they believe in. I would need time for them to work out among themselves how such a thing would be handled. I can have the builders help you until that time. Now that we have a plan, let's take a long walk and have a good cry."

They laughed a little laugh and left through the back door for a long walk.

Kiya returned to her sleeping area late that night.

None of her children were there.

And so ... The Festival Begins

The great trumpet was heard. The festival had begun. Each daughter set off on their own grand adventure.

Mnemosyne

Mnemosyne walked toward the great house with facing benches. She had never seen such things. Not a house; certainly not benches. *What strange and wonderful devices. What a strange and wonderful place. Is this to be my family's destiny?*

When she arrived, she found an ancient woman sitting in a chair that would rock back and forth with only a little effort. *How interesting. She is the oldest person I have ever seen. What stories does she have to tell?*

She approached the woman and said, "Great Mother, I am Mnemosyne of the Clan of the Serpent. Will you speak with me?"

The woman quickly leaned forward in her rocking chair, held out both hands, took Mnemosyne's hands, pulled her near, and with squinting eyes, looked at her. "My child, Clan of the Serpent was my tribe long ago. I was the elder woman for Great Chief Talaimai before Chief Vanam took the robe of power. I am Palai."

"Great Mother, I know of you. My mother, Kiya, has spoken of you often."

PRINCIPALS: Kiya, Vanam, Pumi, Valki | ELDER TITANIDES: Themis, Mnemosyne, Phoebe, Tethys, Theia, Rhea | ELDER TITANES: Rivermaster/Oceanus, Sagacity/Coeus, Starmaster/Crius, Watchman/Hyperion, Piercer/Iapetus, Cronus

The gossip between the two women began. After a long discussion, Mnemosyne said, "You were here at Urfa's beginning; before the beginning; as Mother Valki tamed the wild einkorn, as the buildings were built. Tell me their stories, every detail. Leave nothing out."

Palai laughed and said, "What joy you bring me, child. To relive the days of my youth with someone who cares."

Palai raised her hand. A young docent ran to her. Palai said, "Bring us food and drink. We will need sustenance for all my stories to be told." The docent hurried off to fulfill her command.

Palai began "In the beginning the land was empty and nothing stood. Then Pumi came and created Tallstone. Then Valki came and created Urfa."

Mnemosyne took in every word, imprinting them into her mind. It was late when Palai said, "Such is the story of Urfa. Did it entertain you?"

"Yes, Great Mother. Every word. If I come back tomorrow, can you tell me the story of the tall stone?"

Palai laughed. "Yes, child. But you must promise to hold my stories close to you. I will pass soon enough. I have need for a teller of my stories."

"I promise, Great Mother Palai. I will tell your stories forever."

And so ... The Festival Begins

The great trumpet was heard. The festival had begun. Each daughter set off on their own grand adventure.

Themis

Themis watched her sisters disappear into the crowd. She then turned and walked back toward the woods. She stopped at her family's sleeping area. *After we are traded at tomorrow's campfire meeting, Panti may not allow us to return to get our belongings; especially if we are banished. Mother is sure that Father would not do such a thing, but I'm not. Mother has a lot on her mind. She may not be thinking about these things. To be safe, I will move our belongings into the woods until after all is decided. I may appear foolish after it's over, but I have appeared foolish before.*

She continued into the nearby wooded area. She needed to think plus find a suitable place to temporarily hide her family's belongings.

ELDER OCEANIDS: Metis, Tyche, Clymene, Eurybia, Amphitrite
ELDER OLYMPIANS: Hestia, Demeter, Hera, Hades, Poseidon, Zeus
OTHER: Philyra, Dionysus, Heracles, Outis, Enceladus, Littlerock, Porphyrion

A hundred paces in, she heard, "Sister, is our family well?"

She froze. "Sagacity? Is that you?"

"Yes, Sister, it is me. Rivermaster and I have come to Tallstone as ordered by our father. We will present ourselves tomorrow. Will he receive us with joy or with venom? We are prepared for either."

"Sagacity, how did you fare? Was it difficult? Did you almost die? Where is Rivermaster? We have been worried about your well-being since you left. I am overjoyed to see you. You look so good. More manly, even." She walked to him and gave him a big hug. She had seen Phoebe embrace him and it seemed appropriate.

"We had many adventures and have much to tell. Many wonderful discoveries were made. Rivermaster is out scouting the festival. But are my sisters and Mother well? Do things go better for our family or worse?"

Themis and Sagacity told their stories to one another. They both hoped for the best but prepared for the worst.

PRINCIPALS: Kiya, Vanam, Pumi, Valki | ELDER TITANIDES: Themis, Mnemosyne, Phoebe, Tethys, Theia, Rhea | ELDER TITANES: Rivermaster/Oceanus, Sagacity/Coeus, Starmaster/Crius, Watchman/Hyperion, Piercer/Iapetus, Cronus

6. The Banished

Sunrise.

Day two began.

Pumi rose to seek an audience with Great Chief Nanatan.

Valki rose to meet with her Council of Elder Women and masters of the guilds providing support for Urfa's contributions to the festival.

Kiya rose to seek an audience with her Elder Woman Panti.

Mnemosyne rose to meet with Great Mother Palai.

Themis rose to enter the nearby woods.

The boys rose, after sunrise, and ran to the athletic fields.

So began the second day.

< >

That evening, Chief Vanam held his tribal council meeting. Valvuna organized the campfire area and gathered the hunters and gatherers. He lit the fire as the sun set and nursed it to a suitable council fire. Chief Vanam soon appeared and took his place at the head of the fire between Voutch and Panti. Vanam went through routine tribal matters and then recognized Voutch to present his concerns with the weather, tracking, and the sky. Voutch noted that his new apprentice, Thirdson, was a competent student. Vanam then recognized Panti to present women's concerns. Panti went through the routine reports and ended with, "Chief Vanam, you must now address the problem with Kiya and her children."

The tribe grew silent; they waited.

Chief Vanam commanded, "Woman Kiya, come face your elders, bring your daughters; old and young."

Kiya and her daughters came forward and faced Vanam.

"Woman, you have been negligent with your duties in the gathering fields, you have been disrespectful to your elders; you have disobeyed the commands of your chief. These shortcomings will not be tolerated. You are a danger to your tribe. You and your daughters will not be allowed to remain in the Clan of the Serpent. Panti, what say you in this matter?"

Panti answered, "Great Chief, today Kiya requested that she and her children be traded to the city of Urfa. Yesterday, Valki of Urfa came and offered great riches for Kiya and whichever of her children came with her. This trade would add wealth to your tribe and would rid you of their presence."

Vanam snorted. *Trade you to Urfa, Kiya? You would love that, wouldn't you? You could visit my little brother any time. You could be his little plaything! Trade you, Kiya? I think not!*

He replied, "Trade? That is for the honorable. There will be no trade. This woman has strained my tribe past its limits. My clan will be avenged. I hereby banish Kiya and her daughters. I expel them all! They will be titans, corrupted and without hope, forever. Anyone who finds one in our camp—kill them. No one in this tribe or any other honorable tribe is ever to look upon them again. Her three young sons may stay. They are acceptable. Panti, escort these females out of my camp."

Before Panti could rise, a voice from the back of the hunter's circle asked, "And we, Father, what is to be our fate?" The speaker, Rivermaster, and his brother, Sagacity, approached the elders without invitation. They stood facing them.

Vanam was not pleased. "Ahh, the two girl-boys who would be scouts. You both live. I am surprised that you found enough carrion to sustain you. Do you have a report manly enough to be allowed to stay in this tribe? Give it to me. Now!"

Sagacity began, "Great Chief Vanam ..."

Rivermaster cut him off mid-sentence. "Yes, Father. We found much. Big fluffy, beautiful clouds hung above our heads, fields of beautiful flowers with which we could make garlands for our heads as we skipped across the fields. We found ..."

"Silence!' Vanam roared. Valvuna rose and stepped forward, spear in throwing position. Vanam held up his hand. "You will not receive a man's death, girl-boy. Both of you are banished with the females. Anyone else?" Vanam demanded. He waited; daring anyone to speak.

PRINCIPALS: Kiya, Vanam, Pumi, Valki | ELDER TITANIDES: Themis, Mnemosyne, Phoebe, Tethys, Theia, Rhea | ELDER TITANES: Rivermaster/Oceanus, Sagacity/Coeus, Starmaster/Crius, Watchman/Hyperion, Piercer/Iapetus, Cronus

Book 2. The Beginning of Civilization: Mythologies Told True

Piercer had been quietly listening as his mother was banished. as his sisters were banished, as his two beloved older brothers were banished. He could stand it no more. Unsteadily, Piercer rose to his feet. "May I go with them, Great Chief?"

Thirdson rose to his feet and quietly asked, "And me?"

Vanam sneered at the two boys. "Yes, I banish you along with the rest of your pathetic family." He paused for a moment. "If I remember correctly there is one more of you." He glared at Fourthson daring him to move.

Fourthson stared back at his father. Fourthson's mentor, Valvuna, had been complimentary of Fourthson's hunting skills. Valvuna had told him, "You received all the manly skills in your family. You will be a great hunter. When the time comes, it will be you who Vanam appoints chief. By then we will be the largest and greatest tribe in all the land. I have great expectations for you." Heady words for a boy not yet a man, spoken by the second in command of his tribe. *Father is daring me to stand. I have said nothing against my tribe. Yet, he is daring me to stand. I can remain silent and become a great hunter, maybe the chief of the tribe. I need only to sit in silence.*

Chief Vanam sanctimoniously broke his stare toward Fourthson.

Fourthson rose to his feet.

Vanam asked, "And now you, talented hunter Fourthson. For what reason do *you* wish to leave your tribe?"

Fourthson replied, "I wish to live with honor and dignity. There is none in this tribe."

Valvuna sprang to his feet, spear poised, waiting for the command to release it.

A voice spoke from outside the council area. "Do not soil your camp with the blood of disrespect. Banish them all to oblivion."

Vanam was livid before the voice spoke and to speak to him at this moment was a danger to every living creature nearby. Vanam glared toward the voice that had offered the unsolicited suggestion. It was Chief Nanatan; the only human Vanam considered to be his equal. Recognizing the speaker, Vanam calmed.

ELDER OCEANIDS: Metis, Tyche, Clymene, Eurybia, Amphitrite
ELDER OLYMPIANS: Hestia, Demeter, Hera, Hades, Poseidon, Zeus
OTHER: Philyra, Dionysus, Heracles, Outis, Enceladus, Littlerock, Porphyrion

"You are hereby banished, Fourthson. Panti, escort these vermin from our ground. Kill any who enter our camp again."

Panti and Valvuna came and began pushing Kiya and the older daughters toward the edge of the camp, motioning her other children to follow.

"May we gather our belongings?" Kiya asked Panti.

"NO!" Panti snapped. Arriving at the edge of the camp, Panti stopped the troupe, turned to face them, held out her arm, and pointed toward the dark woods. "You are banished from this tribe. May no worthy person ever look upon you again. GO!"

Rivermaster and Themis quietly led the family toward the woods.

Kiya was the last to go. She said, "Thank you, Elder Woman Panti. You are kind and merciful."

Kiya then stepped onto the path which lay before her and her children.

PRINCIPALS: Kiya, Vanam, Pumi, Valki | ELDER TITANIDES: Themis, Mnemosyne, Phoebe, Tethys, Theia, Rhea | ELDER TITANES: Rivermaster/Oceanus, Sagacity/Coeus, Starmaster/Crius, Watchman/Hyperion, Piercer/Iapetus, Cronus

PART II. TITANS
7. A New World

"That did not go well," Sagacity said after they were out of earshot of the camp.

"I am proud of all of you," Kiya said. "Each of you remained calm and maintained your dignity. But Rivermaster, your response was so ... flowery."

"It's what he wanted to hear, Mother. I regret my choice of words. It was not dignified."

Tethys said, "You sliced him open and exposed his emptiness, Rivermaster. I will stand beside you in battle with any creature that may exist."

Themis broke in. "That's all well and good but we must find our campsite. It's around here someplace."

"You made camp?!" Kiya asked.

"Yes," Themis replied. "Sagacity and I moved our belongings before we were banished ... just in case. We certainly didn't want Piercer's rock collection left behind if he were thrown out with us."

"You saved my rock collection?" Piercer asked. "I was ready to die to steal it back!"

"Stick with me, little brother. We're going to do all right. Now, go find the clearing. It's someplace in that direction," Themis said, pointing toward the south. The children set off to find the clearing.

The adults followed, exchanging observations of their predicament.

"Here it is!" Fourthson shouted. "Over here!"

They entered the clearing. Sleeping beds had been laid out in one corner with their provisions nearby. In the center, a fire pit waited for a flame. At the head of the pit was a sitting chair, legs on rockers, carved with intricate designs.

Kiya stared at the camp in amazement. "My children ..." was all she could say.

"Good work, Fourthson," Themis said. "All right, everyone. Let's build a family campfire!"

ELDER OCEANIDS: Metis, Tyche, Clymene, Eurybia, Amphitrite
ELDER OLYMPIANS: Hestia, Demeter, Hera, Hades, Poseidon, Zeus
OTHER: Philyra, Dionysus, Heracles, Outis, Enceladus, Littlerock, Porphyrion

Rivermaster began flaming the fire. Sagacity led his mother to the chair. "Sit down and rest. You have had a long day. Themis will bring you food and drink."

Kiya sat in the rocking chair. She could only shake her head in amazement at what her children had done *Their foresight. Their planning. Their cleverness. And this chair? My elixirs and potions and salves ... all saved? My children have done all of this. From where did this chair come?*

Kiya felt an all-encompassing sense of affection and overwhelming love for everyone around her. For her family.

She said, "We are Titans; outcasts, despised, unworthy of being looked upon. Let us raise ourselves to the pinnacle of success, a family overflowing with riches to share with all who ask. Let us build a place even grander than Urfa. A place that challenges the knowledge of Tallstone. Let us love those who despise us. Let us work toward the day that they rejoice that they ever knew us."

She raised her drinking cup into the air and proclaimed, "Long live the Titans!"

Her children responded in kind, "Long live the Titans!"

< >

The campfire burned. They grew closer. They talked of wonderful things.

Rivermaster said, "I have a story of our crossing a great river." He told their story. All listened with rapt attention, reliving every word.

Sagacity said, "Now is my turn to tell a story. The story of a great land full of wonder and wonderful things. It is surrounded on three sides by an immense sea, edged on two sides by mountains, a cliff of solid white rock, animals of many and wondrous kinds, many fruit trees, wild grains, fertile fields, a small river, and a great flat plain beneath the entrance; and did I mention colored rocks in the river and at the base of the mountains. It is a glorious land; five days westward run from the river. We spent most of the season exploring the area. The land does not appear to be frequented by hunters or any other people. It is a wonderful land that we wish to take our family to see. This is the end of my story."

Piercer listened with excitement.

PRINCIPALS: Kiya, Vanam, Pumi, Valki | ELDER TITANIDES: Themis, Mnemosyne, Phoebe, Tethys, Theia, Rhea | ELDER TITANES: Rivermaster/Oceanus, Sagacity/Coeus, Starmaster/Crius, Watchman/Hyperion, Piercer/Iapetus, Cronus

"What wonderful stories you tell," Kiya said as she clapped her hands together. "Now tell me the story of the chair in which I sit."

Rivermaster told their story, including their conversations with Valki and the builders they had left engrossed with building a better river-rider.

"Ahh," said Kiya. "So Valki did hear gossip about us. First-hand and detailed gossip."

Tomorrow, they would go to the river-rider on the banks of the great river, but, for this night, there were stories to be told.

Mnemosyne imprinted every word into her memory.

First Followers

There was no urgency in rising early or in hurrying to the river. They rose late and walked leisurely, enjoying their adventure. The two older boys carried their belongings on two poles stretched over their shoulders.

"Builder Putt was impatient to start improving our river-rider," Rivermaster said. "It will be interesting to see if he can improve upon perfection. Regardless, we can all make it across the river in due course. It will simply take us many crossings to transport us and our belongings. But I think you all will find it exhilarating to ride across a river on top of the water. It's an interesting experience."

As they walked, Tethys locked her arm with Rivermaster's and placed her head against it. "I look forward to our crossing the river but promise to keep me safe, Rivermaster. I will be *so* frightened."

Silently, Phoebe rolled her eyes, but she *did* take Sagacity's arm in hers.

< >

They reached the river-rider in the late afternoon. The builders were working feverishly. Perfection had been improved upon.

Before them lay strange sights. "You arrive too early! We still have much to do," exclaimed Putt as he ran toward the Titans. "We have only begun to construct a suitable place where our 'boat' can rest when it is not crossing the river. Look! Our first boat is not yet even complete. We must learn from this boat and then it will take us many seasons to form the

ELDER OCEANIDS: Metis, Tyche, Clymene, Eurybia, Amphitrite
ELDER OLYMPIANS: Hestia, Demeter, Hera, Hades, Poseidon, Zeus
OTHER: Philyra, Dionysus, Heracles, Outis, Enceladus, Littlerock, Porphyrion

material and to construct a boat that will safely and easily carry all of you and your equipment across with one crossing. Tomorrow afternoon, at least. Give us another full day to ensure this boat is water-worthy and will carry the weight we hope it will carry."

Kiya told Putt of their banishment from their tribe and that "You probably should not associate with Titans."

Putt responded with a quizzical look and said, "That is stuff for elder women and tribes. We are builders. Come and see what we have built."

The Titans stared at the scene in silence. Rivermaster and Sagacity knew the nature of a river-rider, but the concept of a 'boat' was overwhelming, even to them. "Yes, yes," Rivermaster stammered. "We will certainly camp out of your way while you complete your—'boat.'"

Putt replied, "Yes, and the 'dock.' Thank you for your patience, Rivermaster. This has been a greater project than I had first imagined. There is more here than we yet know. When all is complete, I shall invite all at Tallstone to come, and, together, we will all understand what you have brought to pass!"

Rivermaster thought, *I? What 'I' have brought to pass?*

But he remained silent as he stared at the next generation of river-riders—a boat.

Sagacity said, "We will set our camp downstream from your dock and not interfere with your work." He motioned the Titans to follow him.

Five older children, four girls, and a boy with only one eye followed them. Out of range of the builders, the oldest girl ran to Rivermaster and asked, "May we come with you? The builders will not let us help. They say we get in their way, but maybe we can help *you*."

Tethys, now a woman, but not that many years older than the child, looked upon her with disdain. *What an impertinent child. She shows no respect to her elders and addresses a male without permission.*

The irony of her thoughts did not occur to her.

Rivermaster replied, "Yes, you may. But how will you help us?"

PRINCIPALS: Kiya, Vanam, Pumi, Valki | ELDER TITANIDES: Themis, Mnemosyne, Phoebe, Tethys, Theia, Rhea | ELDER TITANES: Rivermaster/Oceanus, Sagacity/Coeus, Starmaster/Crius, Watchman/Hyperion, Piercer/Iapetus, Cronus

"We will gather firewood and find berries and whatever else you want."

Mnemosyne asked, "Will you and your sisters sing campfire songs to us?"

"Yes, yes, yes, we will sing you campfire songs. What is a 'campfire song?' What is a 'sing?'"

Mnemosyne laughed. "My sisters and I will teach you campfire songs."

Rivermaster said to the leader, "You and your friends will be a great help. What is your name?"

The girl looked upon Rivermaster with big eyes, awe, and worship. Tethys was not amused. "My name, Great Rivermaster, is Metis. These are my sisters; Tyche, Clymene, and Eurybia. And the boy? Who knows or cares who *he* is?"

The boy spoke. "I am Outis. I am a friend of Breathson, and I know about frogs and birds and turtles and bees and snakes and a little about fish."

Metis rolled her eyes and said, "He's just a boy."

Rivermaster laughed.

Sagacity tried to build the campfire, but the four young girls scurried to perform all the necessary tasks before he could begin. Metis, already aware of feminine protocols, competition, and rivals, sweetly asked Tethys, "May we help you set up your sleeping places?"

Tethys sniffed the air and replied, "If it pleases you."

The camp set, the fire started, and the family circle complete, Kiya motioned the newly acquired children to sit behind her on either side. They were thrilled to be so honored.

"Not so fast, Mother," Mnemosyne said. "We were promised campfire songs. Let them stand before us and sing."

The four girls ran to surround Mnemosyne and stood waiting to learn how to sing.

Mnemosyne had never taught girls how to sing nor did she know any campfire songs. *But ... how hard can it be?*

ELDER OCEANIDS: Metis, Tyche, Clymene, Eurybia, Amphitrite
ELDER OLYMPIANS: Hestia, Demeter, Hera, Hades, Poseidon, Zeus
OTHER: Philyra, Dionysus, Heracles, Outis, Enceladus, Littlerock, Porphyrion

With trial, error, and laughter, Metis, Tyche, Clymene, and Eurybia learned campfire songs and how to sing them.

Sunrise

The Titans rose the next morning to the sounds of scurrying girls bringing berries and fruits to the eating area. Metis immediately came to Rivermaster and asked if he wanted a good morning song sung to him.

Tethys was not amused; Phoebe was.

Rivermaster smiled, but said, "We will hike downstream after we eat. I will show you a cove with many fish and water creatures. If you like, I will teach you how to harvest these things for food. You can sing walking songs as we hike."

The four girls looked at one another and ran off to make up walking songs. The four were creative and enthusiastic in their inventions of words, melodies, and harmonies. They were just getting their first song polished when the troupe came upon the cove.

"We crossed this place while pulling our river-rider from where we landed on our re-crossing. Over in that corner by the tall grass will be frogs, and look, over on that rock, a turtle is sunning. There will be several large fish out in the center and many smaller fish; but beware of serpents, their bite is painful and sometimes fatal. The simplest way to capture a large fish is with a gathering bag. Remain still and let the fish swim inside looking for food and then raise the bag out of the water; you will have caught our evening meal. The trick is to move slowly and not call attention to yourself. Keep the quietness of the place and you will be rewarded with its bounty."

The girls looked at one another, removed their gathering sacks from their waists, and cautiously waded into the water. They moved slowly, with sharp eyes looking for any sign of movement in the water, especially serpents.

Toward the center, Tyche became exceedingly still and gently lowered her bag into the water with its opening wide. Slowly, she moved the bag through the water, then suddenly withdrew it. Tyche's eyes widened as the bag squirmed and thrashed in her hands.

The girls quietly but quickly returned to the bank and peered inside her bag.

PRINCIPALS: Kiya, Vanam, Pumi, Valki | ELDER TITANIDES: Themis, Mnemosyne, Phoebe, Tethys, Theia, Rhea | ELDER TITANES: Rivermaster/Oceanus, Sagacity/Coeus, Starmaster/Crius, Watchman/Hyperion, Piercer/Iapetus, Cronus

Rivermaster reached in and removed a large fish. He quickly and expertly took his cutting knife and removed the head. "Now," he announced, "we will learn how to prepare fish for our mid-day meal."

Everyone looked at Tyche with admiration.

"More, we need enough fish for everyone," Metis said as she directed the other three girls back into the water. "And the turtle. We need to know how to prepare turtle."

"We could make it our pet," Outis offered.

"It would prefer being our lunch to being your pet," Metis retorted.

So, the day was spent. The Titans and the four girls and one boy had never suspected that there was so much to know about water. Still water, running water, deep water, shallow water, controlling the flow of water, the forces water could bring to bear on objects in its way. Water. Endless water. Rivermaster taught the five children how to swim and immersed them in his knowledge and his passion. They were enthralled and apt students. The day went quickly. The fish was cooked over an open fire. The turtle in boiling water with onion. They decided to camp another night at this excellent location. Campfire and fishing songs were sung.

Outis mourned the turtle. *I would have named him 'Hardshell.'*

The Naming of Riverport

The group returned to the river port location late the next morning. The builders had completed the boat and were adding niceties to the surrounding area. The boat itself was in the water tied to the 'dock.' An artificial wooden walkway was raised out of the water parallel to the river. This allowed people to board the boat without getting their feet wet. There was another artificial walkway perpendicular and even with the dock raised above the muddy bank. This allowed people to walk from the grassy area, over the muddy area, and directly to the boat dock without getting their feet muddy. The river would certainly rise above its current level so this nicety would allow a permanent docking location for the boat, and it would not have to be pulled in and out of the water for each use. The boat was the length of four men and the width of one. It could easily fit eight people with room for equipment and supplies. There were

ELDER OCEANIDS: Metis, Tyche, Clymene, Eurybia, Amphitrite
ELDER OLYMPIANS: Hestia, Demeter, Hera, Hades, Poseidon, Zeus
OTHER: Philyra, Dionysus, Heracles, Outis, Enceladus, Littlerock, Porphyrion

brackets upon which 'oars' could be placed for rowing across the water. There was a movable plate in the back that could be shifted according to the need to control the direction the boat would attack the water.

And, fixed to the back of the boat, was a tall pole upon which hung a cloth flag marked with a trident. Putt proclaimed this to be the insignia of Rivermaster and his followers. "This is Rivermaster's boat landing port," Putt proclaimed. "Welcome, Rivermaster."

The Titans stared at these creations with incredulity. The walkways by themselves were impressive. The boat was unbelievable. Rivermaster fought to maintain his self-composure. He, himself, had been credited with conceiving these structures.

Rivermaster asked Putt, "Will your boat carry us across safely? It appears to be too large to stay above the water without sinking."

"Of course," Putt replied. "As long as water does not enter the boat by seeping through or by coming over the edge. It sinks deeper in the water the more weight it carries so be aware of your weight, but otherwise, the boat has carried me across many times during its final construction. It is easy to guide and force the boat through the water. We took what you taught us about the poles and the limbs with leaves in the water. With that knowledge, it was simple enough for a builder to make a more perfect shape. This boat is flat and straight. It will take us several seasons to cut and form the wood into curved shapes. But we can then create a boat with a more perfect form which should carry even more people and weight. What do you think? Are you pleased, Rivermaster?"

"Why, yes. But should you not name it 'Putt's Place'?"

"It is yours to name," Putt replied. "But I would like to construct a small house nearby to allow at least one person to stay here as a river-crossing guide and to watch over the place throughout the year. They could trade a river crossing for whatever goods they might negotiate."

Metis exclaimed, "Name it 'Riverport,' Great Rivermaster. And can girls be taught how to steer this boat? Can I and my sisters have your river-rider thing for ourselves? Can we stay here and live in this wonderful place? We will be careful to do as you command! Don't say 'no' yet, Great Chief Putt. At least think about these things before saying no."

PRINCIPALS: Kiya, Vanam, Pumi, Valki | ELDER TITANIDES: Themis, Mnemosyne, Phoebe, Tethys, Theia, Rhea | ELDER TITANES: Rivermaster/Oceanus, Sagacity/Coeus, Starmaster/Crius, Watchman/Hyperion, Piercer/Iapetus, Cronus

Metis stared at Rivermaster with large, pleading eyes. Rivermaster looked at Putt and said, "We will discuss these matters." Metis knew when to be quiet. Not yet a full woman, she knew the manipulation of men.

Rivermaster crossed the swift river several times with Putt and his builders. They identified problems with the boat and identified what worked well. Metis, Tyche, Clymene, and Eurybia were allowed to learn how to control the boat. Everyone became adept at guiding the boat back to the dock. Tyche was adept at throwing the rope from the boat around the strong post on the dock to pull the boat to the dock. She suggested putting another rope in the back so the boat could be moored parallel to the dock. Putt looked at Tyche with pride. The girls could remain at Riverport if they wished but reports on its condition would have to be made periodically to Urfa. The Titans' last night at Riverport was spent around the campfire with the builders and children singing river songs.

Outis, Enceladus, and Metis asked if the Titans would allow them into their tribe. They promised to do as told, work hard, and not eat much.

< >

Midmorning, the next day, Rivermaster and Metis carried the Titan's equipment and supplies across the river. Tethys was not pleased. She waited impatiently upon the dock. Upon their return, several more crossings were required to ferry all the Titans and their new charges across the river. Once all were across, the Titans waved goodbye to their new friends and began their five-day trot westward.

With sadness, Tyche, Clymene, and Eurybia watched them go. Then ferried the boat back to Riverport; there to care for it and guard it with their lives.

Journey

The troupe began their run southwestward talking among themselves. Enceladus, ten times stronger than the others, carried his own equipment plus Kiya's plus miscellaneous common equipment.

Fourthson was much farther back walking with Outis. Fourthson kept encouraging Outis to keep up, but Outis stayed far in the rear. At last, in exasperation, Fourthson demanded, "You are huge, twice as large as any of us, Outis. Why can't you keep up?"

ELDER OCEANIDS: Metis, Tyche, Clymene, Eurybia, Amphitrite
ELDER OLYMPIANS: Hestia, Demeter, Hera, Hades, Poseidon, Zeus
OTHER: Philyra, Dionysus, Heracles, Outis, Enceladus, Littlerock, Porphyrion

Outis replied, "You are all pretty." He trotted on, saying nothing more.

Fourthson said, "Oh, that explains it."

The troupe trotted on, now in silence. Waiting for more exchange between the two lagging behind.

After a while, Fourthson said, "Are *you* pretty, Outis?"

"No, I am ugly. That is why I cannot be with any of you."

"Well, you *are* different, Outis. Having only one eye and being so big and all. How did you wind up with only one eye, anyway?"

Outis replied, "I was born with one eye smaller than the other one. The elder woman cut on it to try to make it larger, but the cuts inflamed the side of my face. The Chief wanted to leave me under a tree to die but the elder woman let my mother keep me and nurse me until the festival. The women at Urfa accepted me and saved me but my face grew back ugly making me look like this. The other boys shunned me except for my friend Breathson. Breathson let me follow him around and let me learn how to make friends with animals. Breathson didn't like people, but he loved animals and made friends with them. He liked me a little because no one else liked me. He did not teach me, but he would answer my questions because I wanted to know how to make friends with animals. Because they didn't know I was ugly."

Fourthson offered, "Being different isn't the same as being ugly, Outis. I won't say you are pretty, but, on the other hand, you are not particularly ugly, either. Sisters, what do you think? Is my friend ugly or simply different?"

Kiya held up her hand and said, "This is a good time to rest. Daughters, help your brother."

The troupe stopped, laid down their equipment, and then circled Outis and Fourthson. Outis cowered from the attention.

Sagacity said, "You *do* have only one eye. I had not noticed."

Themis said, "Let us study you. What do you think sisters? Is he ugly?"

Phoebe said, "He is different, but he is not ugly."

PRINCIPALS: Kiya, Vanam, Pumi, Valki | ELDER TITANIDES: Themis, Mnemosyne, Phoebe, Tethys, Theia, Rhea | ELDER TITANES: Rivermaster/Oceanus, Sagacity/Coeus, Starmaster/Crius, Watchman/Hyperion, Piercer/Iapetus, Cronus

Tethys offered, "He reminds me of a hunter who fought and conquered a ferocious bear."

Rhea said, "I would mate with him when my time comes."

Themis said. "Rhea, you would mate with a fish,"

Metis shouted, "Can you do that? Is that even possible? I mean, what would my children look like? Which half would be fish and which half human? Maybe all my children would be fish! I could be the mother of a thousand minnows."

Kiya admonished, "Children!" She then quietly said to Outis, "You are different, Outis, but you are not ugly. Even if you were, what difference would that make? You should respect us as we respect you. You will run with your family and not hold back. Am I understood?"

Outis did not understand but he would try his best to do what he was told to do. He looked at his new friend, Fourthson, with gratitude and admiration. He said, "You have watched over me and made me whole. Thank you, Fourthson."

"You do watch out over things, all things, Fourthson," Kiya said. "'Watchman.' Is that a fitting name for him, children?"

"Watch-man ... Watch-man ... Watch-man ... W..." the girls chanted.

"Yes, Mother," Sagacity said. "Watchman is a fitting name."

They gathered their equipment and resumed their trot to the southwest.

The addition of Enceladus to their family had been fortuitous. The high-back chair he had built for Kiya was built for easy transport from camp to camp. To address the transportation issue, Enceladus had also built a carrying sled for it. It was supported by long timbers on either side so that four men could easily shoulder the sled during runs, or two men could shoulder the front and drag it behind them. Enceladus was strong enough to pull the sled by himself. The sled had the added advantage of being able to store Kiya's jars, urns, mixing utensils, and her large collection of elixirs, salves, ointments, and exotic plants. These items had always been carried by volunteers which were readily available when she had been the tribe's elder woman, but volunteers were limited to her family members

ELDER OCEANIDS: Metis, Tyche, Clymene, Eurybia, Amphitrite
ELDER OLYMPIANS: Hestia, Demeter, Hera, Hades, Poseidon, Zeus
OTHER: Philyra, Dionysus, Heracles, Outis, Enceladus, Littlerock, Porphyrion

since their banishment. Enceladus' concept of the transportation sled was a wonderful addition to Kiya's family's base of knowledge. As he pulled the sled, Enceladus considered improvements that he might make.

Oursea

Eventually, a little time after high-sun, they came to the sea. Metis fell to her knees in wonder. All stared at it with silent awe and then walked to the water's edge. They waded up to their knees while Metis swam as far as she dared and returned but remained in the water with it up to her neck. The others rested for a while on the banks staring at the distant horizon.

Finally, Rivermaster said, "I named this body of water "Oursea." We will follow the shoreline northward and make camp when we see land on the horizon. From there, it will be less than a half-day run to the land connecting the shore to the island. Sagacity and I agree that we should consider settling on the island. Let's explore it, then decide our course."

Toward dusk, a sliver of land appeared on the horizon separating the sea from the sky. Rivermaster continued their run with a quickened pace. The moon and stars provided sufficient light. They soon reached the land bridge that connected the almost-an-island to the mainland.

Rivermaster declared that here is where they would camp for the night. The camp was made, a campfire built, Mnemosyne told stories, and songs were sung.

Sunrise

Metis and Enceladus were in the water as the sun rose. Metis swam far from shore with bags with which to catch fish. Enceladus scoured the shoreline for crabs and whatever other sea creatures might inhabit the bank. Outis was in the nearby woods seeking small game.

Kiya's daughters rose and began searching for edible plants.

Everyone gathered around the now-extinguished campfire at mid-morning. Metis had captured only two fish, but they were huge. Enceladus had an assortment of small crabs and other such creatures. Outis had not captured an animal, but he had discovered a dense patch of shrubs bearing edible berries plus some random nuts. The daughters had gathered more

PRINCIPALS: Kiya, Vanam, Pumi, Valki | ELDER TITANIDES: Themis, Mnemosyne, Phoebe, Tethys, Theia, Rhea | ELDER TITANES: Rivermaster/Oceanus, Sagacity/Coeus, Starmaster/Crius, Watchman/Hyperion, Piercer/Iapetus, Cronus

plants than could be consumed at one meal. They prepared and ate their morning meal as they stared out over the land bridge.

Rivermaster decided to remain at this camp for another evening. He wanted the Titans to scout the land bridge. They spent some of the morning walking north until they again came to the water. They then knew the breadth of their narrow land bridge. They spent the afternoon exploring and familiarizing themselves with the entrance to their promised land. They returned to the camp just after sunset.

The family fire was built, they ate from their bounty, and Mnemosyne told stories. Songs were sung.

Sunrise

The camp was broken. The troupe gathered and stared toward the west.

Kiya commanded, "This will be our land. This is the path we follow. This is our destiny. 'Long live the Titans!'"

The Titans entered the land within Oursea.

Exploration

The women mentally cataloged the plants as they walked through the land. Enceladus and Outis cataloged the trees and various living creatures that appeared. Rivermaster paid close attention to streams and ponds. Watchman searched for signs of game.

And for Piercer, the land was rich with colored rocks. Kiya had forbidden him to collect any more rocks until a permanent camp had been decided upon. The weight of his growing collection was already onerous to transport even with the new sled pulled by Enceladus. But Piercer committed the colored rock locations to memory. He would someday return to these places and harvest the greatest collection of colored rock the world had ever seen.

And soon, it was Outis' time to become excited. "A bee! Look, it's a bee!" He ran toward one of the few plants that were flowering during this season. He stopped and let the bee fly to another flower. Rivermaster signaled they would rest while Outis did whatever it was that Outis did. Outis watched and watched some more. Eventually, the bee took off with

ELDER OCEANIDS: Metis, Tyche, Clymene, Eurybia, Amphitrite
ELDER OLYMPIANS: Hestia, Demeter, Hera, Hades, Poseidon, Zeus
OTHER: Philyra, Dionysus, Heracles, Outis, Enceladus, Littlerock, Porphyrion

Outis close behind. The bee flew toward a patch of wood, and then into the hollow of a dead tree. Outis noted the location of the tree and how many bees were entering and exiting the tree. Satisfied, he returned to the troupe. "This is wonderful. This will be a source of sweet honey and the wax Mother Valki uses to make ointments and things. I know how to move the bees to whatever location we choose. Sometimes I can make two hives out of one. If we locate them near flowers they like, they will share their honey and wax without getting too mad when we collect it."

After Outis had all the information he needed, the troupe continued their journey. The land rose higher and became more rugged as they traveled. Oursea receded farther below them. Toward their right, mountains loomed, and toward their left, the sea. The more rugged the land, the more colored the rock. Piercer wanted to veer toward the mountains. Tethys wanted to remain close to the sea. Within a short time, they had to choose. The sea to their left suddenly gave way to a vast expanse of land, a great and fertile plain, stretching as far as their eyes could see.

"Here," Sagacity said with an outstretched arm. "This is the land of plenty of which I told you."

The land sloped down dramatically from where they stood. Down and down to the plain where the shore was level with the sea. Tethys and Metis did not wait. They began running wildly down the slope to the shoreline of Oursea.

Piercer looked longingly toward the mountains.

Kiya said, "This view is magnificent. I have never seen more beautiful or impressive landscapes. Make camp here, Rivermaster. We will consider all that lays before us."

Around the campfire that night, it was decided that they would split into two parties, go opposite ways, and meet here on the afternoon of the third day to share their findings.

Rivermaster, surprisingly, would lead to the mountains. It must be the mountains, he reasoned, that was the source of all the freshwater they had seen. Piercer knew from experience that the rugged highlands would find colored stone in abundance. Tethys, of course, joined Rivermaster's party.

PRINCIPALS: Kiya, Vanam, Pumi, Valki | ELDER TITANIDES: Themis, Mnemosyne, Phoebe, Tethys, Theia, Rhea | ELDER TITANES: Rivermaster/Oceanus, Sagacity/Coeus, Starmaster/Crius, Watchman/Hyperion, Piercer/Iapetus, Cronus

Metis had already left to explore the great coastline.

Themis and the remaining daughters chose to explore the great plains. Sagacity would lead the plains party. Kiya, partly with the wisdom of a mother and partly by desire, chose to stay at the camp. She said, "I will remain here. Everything can be seen from here. This view is so magnificent that I could stare at it forever."

Farewells were said. Each party left for their adventure. Kiya, with pride and confidence, watched them go.

And so ... Into the Mountains

Rivermaster retraced his steps to a stream they had crossed. He examined it closely, then turned northward to seek its source in the mountains. The group ran at a fast pace. The terrain turned rocky and then mountainous. Piercer wanted to stop many times, but Rivermaster maintained the pace until they were entering a mountain. The stream grew wilder. Large rocks with color abounded; there, for the picking up. What treasures there must be for the taking? Raw materials for stone cutters and builders were everywhere. Higher they hiked; wilder, grander.

And so ... Into the Plains

Sagacity's party walked down the long, rugged incline toward the plains. Reaching level land, at last, the girls spread out to explore.

Sagacity stopped and turned to look from where they had come. They had accidentally taken the only navigable path to the plain; a gentle slope compared to the westerly straight-down drop-off; a cliff. A cliff from the higher land from which they had come straight down to the plain upon which they stood. But more than that, the cliff was stark white. Void of color. It was the cliff of pure white rock: 'marmaros.' *Where is Piercer when you need him? Even I know that this is a discovery of consequence. I don't know why. But it is too impressive not to be of consequence.*

And so ... At Water's Edge

Metis ran along Oursea; sometimes swimming far out, sometimes rolling in the sand. The sea; Oursea, my sea, and maybe Rivermaster's. Maybe. Metis was overwhelmed with some unknown feeling. Love, perhaps? For the sea? For her sisters? For life itself?

ELDER OCEANIDS: Metis, Tyche, Clymene, Eurybia, Amphitrite
ELDER OLYMPIANS: Hestia, Demeter, Hera, Hades, Poseidon, Zeus
OTHER: Philyra, Dionysus, Heracles, Outis, Enceladus, Littlerock, Porphyrion

And so ... At Overlook Point

Kiya stood looking at the sea, mountains behind her, a fertile plain below, and a gentle wind blowing around her. *I am free. Free of Vanam's disdain. Free of the responsibility of the tribe. Free of the fear that I cannot properly care for my daughters. That my sons will be destroyed by their father. Free. Looking at an unknown sea. Oursea.*

She waited in peace as her children explored their fertile land.

PRINCIPALS: Kiya, Vanam, Pumi, Valki | ELDER TITANIDES: Themis, Mnemosyne, Phoebe, Tethys, Theia, Rhea | ELDER TITANES: Rivermaster/Oceanus, Sagacity/Coeus, Starmaster/Crius, Watchman/Hyperion, Piercer/Iapetus, Cronus

Book 2. The Beginning of Civilization: Mythologies Told True

8. The Founding of Tartarus

They gathered on the third day; except for Metis, who was nowhere to be found. At the family fire that night, discoveries were revealed, and stories were told. It was decided that Rivermaster and Sagacity would discuss and agree upon a plan for settling the family and the plan would be presented at the next family fire.

On the evening of the fourth day, Rivermaster and Sagacity had agreed. "Our land is large and full of all manner of resources. It will take many people and many years to properly develop and inhabit the land. The Titans will build a permanent camp, maybe like Urfa, in the middle of the great plain. It is fertile and bountiful. All parts of the island will be accessible from this location. We will add citizens as we can and develop our settlement while respecting the beauty of where we live."

Kiya requested that a spear be driven into the ground at the exact center of their land.

On the fifth day, Rivermaster and Sagacity led the family to the center of the great plain.

Rivermaster had driven the spear into the ground. "Here," he said. "This is the center of our great plain." The Titans spent the remainder of the day exploring their new surroundings.

That night, the spear was replaced with a large rock, and the family fire was built around the rock. The family gathering was spent exchanging information, worrying about the whereabouts of Metis, Mnemosyne telling stories, and singing.

Kiya stayed behind after the others retired for the evening. She reflected. *What shall we do now? It is too much! What shall I do? Sister Valki taught me to solve unsolvable problems by breaking them into small, solvable problems.*

She sat in her high-back chair sleepily looking out over the dying embers. *This will be a nice place to live but so would that overlook place. I will name it Overlook Point. Maybe Piercer should build a place there to store his colored stones. He wouldn't have to move them so far. Have Rivermaster and Tethys mated? Will they grow together? Honey. Outis said that he could make the bees live close to us. All they want are houses around flowers that they like. The cliff of marmaros rock. Piercer was so*

ELDER OCEANIDS: Metis, Tyche, Clymene, Eurybia, Amphitrite
ELDER OLYMPIANS: Hestia, Demeter, Hera, Hades, Poseidon, Zeus
OTHER: Philyra, Dionysus, Heracles, Outis, Enceladus, Littlerock, Porphyrion

excited. So much white rock. If we can't find the right flowers nearby, perhaps we can move the right flowers from other places. I wonder if Piercer could exchange the rock around our fire with marmaros rock. That would be pretty. Maybe we could build our home with the marmaros rock. Our city. A city of marmaros rock. 'Tartarus.' I shall name our new home 'Tartarus.' Will the children be pleased? Valki learned how to grow endless einkorn from einkorn she found growing wild. Could I do that with flowering plants? An endless field of flowers that bees love. Endless bees. Endless honey. Honey to trade. With Theia's beautiful garments. With Piercer's necklaces of stones. Where? How? Valki cannot let us trade with Urfa. Pumi cannot let us trade with Tallstone. The other tribes would be incensed. Pumi. Did you ever really desire me? Did I only imagine it? Even when I pleased Vanam, he never looked at me with the intensity of Pumi. Riverport. We can trade with Riverport. It is said to belong to Rivermaster. We can get Riverport girls to trade for us. Maybe live there. Tyche, Clymene, and Eurybia already live there. They are all we need. I trick myself into thinking things that were never true. Pumi always got what Pumi wanted. He was patient. Had he desired me, he would have made me come to him. Ask him. Beg him. Where is Metis? Is she safe? Riverport. We could have our own little marketplace. Maybe no one would be offended if we traded at Riverport. My elixirs. We could trade them, too. An elixir to heal. To conceive a male child. A female child. No child. Long, long life. No! That is only for my family. Not even they know of it—yet. Themis has wondered why I do not appear to age. She does not notice how young they all look. Did Pumi notice? The northeast. Visitors would come to our home from the northeast. We need a pathway from the highland to our hearth that is inviting. Lined with flowering trees. Outis and Enceladus could move the trees we desire. The path will be wide and inviting with resting places. Our hearth will be surrounded by fragrant bushes. And running water. And tame fish. And tables like Valki's. And chairs for everyone. Our hearth will be beautiful. Beyond beautiful. But no one comes to our home. But if they did come, our hearth should be inviting and beautiful. Would Pumi come? Valki has a nice house. She greets her guests with warmth and respect. She had so many houses. Urfa. Tallstone. Riverport. Trade. Titan trade. Pumi.

Kiya rose and went to her bed.

Sunrise

The family gathered.

Kiya announced, "This place shall be named 'Tartarus'—Land of the Titans."

PRINCIPALS: Kiya, Vanam, Pumi, Valki | ELDER TITANIDES: Themis, Mnemosyne, Phoebe, Tethys, Theia, Rhea | ELDER TITANES: Rivermaster/Oceanus, Sagacity/Coeus, Starmaster/Crius, Watchman/Hyperion, Piercer/Iapetus, Cronus

To Piercer, she said, "Tomorrow at sunrise, go to Overlook Point, the place that we camped at the top of the entrance, take Enceladus with you. Build a shelter where I can visit and gaze over our great plain. Build it so that we may greet any visitors who might come to our land. Build it so that you can store your colored rock and make a place where you can fashion your rock. Replace our center stone with a rock in the shape of the tall stone at Tallstone. Build a fire pit around it. Make it three paces across. As the days pass, place carved marmaros sitting rocks every three hundred paces in a straight line between our fire pit and Overlook Point so that all can travel between these two places with happiness."

To Rhea, she said, "Tomorrow you and Outis explore the fields to our west. Find pretty and fragrant bushes to plant around our patio. You and your sisters move the bushes here. Also, consider what trees we might someday plant beside our sitting rocks leading to Overlook Point. And flowers—Outis must tell you which flowers the bees will find pleasing. You will either move the flowers or perhaps we can learn to grow a field of these flowers."

To Enceladus, she said, "Let Outis describe a home that bees would move into and then build one ... no ... build many. And all of you choose a suitable spot nearby for a field of flowers and a home for bees."

To everyone, she said, "We must all plan our new home, both for now but especially how it will grow and what we wish it to grow into. Urfa was built without a plan and simply grew as needed. Tartarus shall have a plan for growth. Tartarus will be a place of great beauty and great joy. And Rhea, as you explore tomorrow, do not mate with Outis. It is not your time for such things."

Rhea glanced at Outis and smiled.

Kiya said, "Now go, all of you, make your plans, make these things happen."

Rivermaster and Tethys walked around the immediate area looking outward; talking about what was needed and where it should be placed. Sagacity and Phoebe retired much farther away, looking back and circling the center as they talked. The others broke into their respective groups and made plans for the coming days.

ELDER OCEANIDS: Metis, Tyche, Clymene, Eurybia, Amphitrite
ELDER OLYMPIANS: Hestia, Demeter, Hera, Hades, Poseidon, Zeus
OTHER: Philyra, Dionysus, Heracles, Outis, Enceladus, Littlerock, Porphyrion

As he and Phoebe exchanged ideas and circled the center rock from a great distance away, Sagacity saw a future. He called Rivermaster and Tethys to join them and exchange thoughts.

Sagacity's Vision

Around the family campfire that evening, Sagacity revealed his vision.

"A walking path will encircle the fire pit at a distance of 300 paces. Every building will be built on the path facing the fire pit. Mother's home will be built directly to the south with a home for her sons on one side and a home for her daughters on the other. A straight walkway will connect the circular path at Mother's house to the fire pit.

"A meeting and feasting area for events and gatherings will be built around the fire pit. There will be a great table with many chairs. Perhaps Rivermaster can add waterways for both pleasing sound and utility.

"An area for toilets will be built across the circular path to the northwest. A straight path will connect the fire pit to the toilets. Beds of flowers will be planted on either side of this path.

"Another path will lead from the fire pit to Overlook Point in the northeast and will cross the circular path. Here we will widen the path into a wide road and there place a building for any guests we might receive.

"Mother will plant her trees and shrubs and flowering plants in a manner to maintain the symmetry and simplicity of our design. Each building will be of a similar size and design and be made with marmaros stone. Colored stones can be tastefully incorporated into all areas. Perhaps Thea can create pleasing fabrics for outside decoration and utility.

"As our city grows, a circular road will be added 900 paces around our fire pit. We will plant fields in the west on the other side of the road. Here Outis will build structures to home whatever wild creatures he may bend to his will, including homes for wild bees. Across this circular road to the east, we will create camping areas, athletic fields, and large public fields. We shall remember the gatherings at Tallstone but with a plan rather than haphazardly growing as needed.

"The Titan area to trade colored stones, honey, crafted clothes, and wonderful elixirs will, of course, be prominently placed. That no one ever comes is of no importance but if they *do* come, the glory and organization of Tartarus will overwhelm them. That, plus it will be pleasing to all Titans, regardless. Titans can use the fields to train and practice spear hunting and knife fighting with wild animals in close combat. Women as well as men because wild animals might also include wild men.

"Permission to enter our land must be received at Overlook Point. Once given, the roads will be wide and straight to our fire pit with pleasing sights and smells along the way. Enceladus must recruit other builders to join us and build that which we need. Piercer will require assistant stonecutters. Housing must be placed for each of these guilds.

"Our Mother must approve the design of every building, all that is planted, every stone that is laid. If she is pleased, then we are ALL pleased.

"My vision is only a start which each of us must improve upon but, at least, we have a plan upon which to begin our discourse."

All sat in silence absorbing Sagacity's vision laid out before them and planning what they must do at the coming sunrise.

Sagacity and Phoebe Plan

Sunrise. Each team was ready.

< >

Sagacity and Phoebe walked to the planned location for Kiya's home.

Phoebe said, "We need to outline the area with stone so we can visualize its size and placement. I'll ask Piercer and Enceladus to transport a sled of stone. That would be useful for placing our buildings. And, Sagacity, what do you think about fixing a tall post to our fire pit center stone? Theia could make a large, colorful flag to wave from the top. On a clear day, maybe it could be seen from Overlook Point."

Sagacity replied, "Yes, that's a wonderful idea. Plus, we could raise a flag post at the entrance at Overlook Point that could be seen from here. It would make it easier to build a straight road between the two points."

"And," Phoebe said excitedly, "Theia could make different colored flags for Overlook Point to signal when a visitor was coming, and how many, and their importance."

ELDER OCEANIDS: Metis, Tyche, Clymene, Eurybia, Amphitrite
ELDER OLYMPIANS: Hestia, Demeter, Hera, Hades, Poseidon, Zeus
OTHER: Philyra, Dionysus, Heracles, Outis, Enceladus, Littlerock, Porphyrion

"You are the wisest of us all," Sagacity said. "I am glad that you will walk around with me,"

She thought, *'Walk around with you,' Sagacity?*

"Thank you," she replied, somewhat coolly. "Now, let's lay cornerstones for her home and plan what Mother should see each time she walks from her quarters to our gathering place."

Rivermaster and Tethys Plan

Sunrise. Each team was ready.

< >

Rivermaster and Tethys walked northward 300 paces and turned to face the fire pit. "Water," Rivermaster said. "What need have we of water there? And how would I get it there?"

Tethys replied, "Well, if we are to live here, we need a good source of water; to drink, to cook, to bathe, to irrigate the plants we are charged with planting. Plus, the sound of running water is music from the earth, plus the beauty of it."

"Yes, yes. I understand," Rivermaster snapped. "Water. Much water. A constant supply. The nearest river is far away. We now transport the water here in urns on Enceladus' sled. Yes. We need to make a river flow to this place. I have never built a river. Where do I get water for a river?" He became silent.

She waited a few moments before speaking. "The Overlook is much higher than this place. That, plus the land runs slightly downhill even after the sharp drop from the overlook cliff. There are all the streams you could want at the foot of the mountain above the cliff."

He said, "Yes, yes. You are right. I could dig a trench from the cliff to here and another from there to the mountains. That might work but the loss of water to the earth from here to there would be great."

Tethys replied, "There is much marmaros rock. Could that be used?"

"Yes, yes. Marmaros rock! We could form a manmade river running along the road to the fire pit. And a large lake to accumulate water beneath the

PRINCIPALS: Kiya, Vanam, Pumi, Valki | ELDER TITANIDES: Themis, Mnemosyne, Phoebe, Tethys, Theia, Rhea | ELDER TITANES: Rivermaster/Oceanus, Sagacity/Coeus, Starmaster/Crius, Watchman/Hyperion, Piercer/Iapetus, Cronus

cliff. There would be a large waterfall over the cliff making a pleasant sound for Mother when she is visiting Overlook Point. I can size the waterfall to provide just the right amount of water we need at Tartarus. The overflow could be used to water whatever crops we might plant. Yes! This can be done! We will need builders and rock masons! I have a plan to get the water here, Tethys! A plan on what to do with it when it gets here shall be easy."

Outis and Rhea Plan

Sunrise. Each team was ready.

< >

Outis and Rhea walked due west.

Outis talked of the bees they had seen in the hollow of the tree. "That nest would be hard to move. I would be stung many times, and the bees would be furious with me. Let's find a nest hanging openly under a shelter. We can disconnect it from the overhang and place it in a suitable box Enceladus can make for me. There are groves of trees and fields in this direction. Let's look there ..." He chattered on and on.

Rhea thought, *He is certainly talkative. He has spoken more words since we left this morning than he has the rest of the time he has been with us. I wonder if it's because I smiled at him last night when we joked about mating. We were joking. Themis was mean to me. Of course, I do ask her a lot of questions about mating. She is the oldest. That doesn't mean that I want to do it; just understand it before I have to do it. Mating is important. It will decide who my children are. I can't be too careful. I'm sorry, Outis, but I will probably not mate with you. But you are nice. You might make a good father. It is because I joked with you, isn't it? The mere thought that I might accept you has made you comfortable with me. You have never mated, have you? You have never dared try. I'm glad that you are comfortable with me but I'm not ready, Outis. Sorry.*

"... do you think?" Outis was saying.

"What!???" Rhea asked.

"We must find a place with flowers. Which way do we go, do you think?"

"Oh ... that way," she said absent-mindedly pointing toward the northwest. "There will be flowering plants that way."

ELDER OCEANIDS: Metis, Tyche, Clymene, Eurybia, Amphitrite
ELDER OLYMPIANS: Hestia, Demeter, Hera, Hades, Poseidon, Zeus
OTHER: Philyra, Dionysus, Heracles, Outis, Enceladus, Littlerock, Porphyrion

They walked toward the northwest. Outis was still talking. They soon saw a patch of flowers near a grove of trees in the distance. He ran toward the flowers and stopped at the edge of the patch. He studied it intently. Then he saw the bee. Keeping his focus on the bee, he commanded Rhea, "Dig up this plant with roots and all. Leave plenty of dirt around the roots. We will plant this flower immediately when we get back to Tartarus." He patiently tracked the bee into the grove with Rhea following.

You are passionate about things, Outis. You are smart and kind. Perhaps I WILL mate with you when my time comes. You run deeper than you appear.

Outis saw the hive. He was thrilled. "This colony can be easily moved to our camp. I will hardly get stung at all. I may be able to separate the Queen's comb into pieces so that new Queens will be born, and new nests formed. The Queen is everything to the hive. If the Queen is happy, then all the bees are happy. Except for the ones stinging you, they are angry. You and your sisters move as many of these flowers as you can to wherever you decide that you want the bees to live. Keep the flowers alive and blooming as best you can. Maybe Mother Kiya can guide you."

Have you ever even seen an unclothed woman, Outis? I am not yet grown but I am more a woman than a child. I have seen male parts but never one that's ready to mate. Themis said that they are disgusting to look at. Even more so than when they're just hanging there. That's disgusting enough. I wonder what one looks like. Themis told me ways to satisfy an aroused male without having to actually mate with him. Young ones, anyway. Like you, Outis.

Outis said, "I have to find Enceladus quickly and have him build us many bee boxes. You must get your sisters and have them start moving the flowers to their new home. I can move the nest as soon as the flowers are planted, and I have a box to put the bees in."

Before they became women, Kiya would counsel her daughters on the nature of men and the nature of mating. "The act of mating is natural and is not difficult or painful. You will master the technique before your first mating is complete. A baby may or not result from mating. I will tell you in good time how you can influence the outcome. You may want a baby to happen, or you may want a baby not to happen. Either way, come to me. I have elixirs for these things. Children usually take the characteristics

PRINCIPALS: Kiya, Vanam, Pumi, Valki | ELDER TITANIDES: Themis, Mnemosyne, Phoebe, Tethys, Theia, Rhea | ELDER TITANES: Rivermaster/Oceanus, Sagacity/Coeus, Starmaster/Crius, Watchman/Hyperion, Piercer/Iapetus, Cronus

of their parents. Because of this, choose who fathers your babies well. A male may come to you wishing to mate with you. If so, choose what you wish to do carefully. Your decision is easy if you wish to mate with him. Find a private place, face away from him, raise your tunic, and put your knees and elbows on the ground. He will do the rest. If you don't wish to mate, then choose your best response. Most men will accept 'Thank you for your offer but I had rather not.' They will simply leave and find another female. A few are more aggressive. These you must either accept or be prepared to do him physical harm. The threat of physical harm usually stops them, but you must learn and be prepared to do the things that I will show you. Finding a male who will agree to protect you is a joyful occasion in a woman's life."

Kiya had taught Rhea these things. *Is that all there is? Really? Is that all there is?*

Themis had provided more forward-thinking information. "There are ways to satisfy a hunter's request and you don't actually have to mate with him. Just play with his thing long enough and he will eventually be satisfied. Besides, most of the time they finish before you even realize that he is inside you. If a hunter can continue long enough, you might get some pleasure out of it. One time there was a handsome hunter from another tribe that wasn't in a hurry to finish. He took a long time, and it became pleasurable. But most hunters don't want to take the time. A few wish to enjoy your company but most want to get it over with as quickly as possible with any woman available."

Rhea thought, *Leave it to chance? How can you predict? How do you tell one from the other? Mating just because some random male wants to mate doesn't make sense. It's my body. It should be my decision. But how do I decide? I have no experience in these matters. I need experience.*

The evening was coming. Rhea found a perfect tree to stand beneath. "Outis, it's been a lovely day. You have shown me so many wonderful, exciting things. Now, come stand before me. I want to show *you* something."

Outis obediently walked to face Rhea. She slowly pulled her tunic over her head and tossed it to the ground. She smiled as she leaned back against the tree and intensely stared at his groin.

ELDER OCEANIDS: Metis, Tyche, Clymene, Eurybia, Amphitrite
ELDER OLYMPIANS: Hestia, Demeter, Hera, Hades, Poseidon, Zeus
OTHER: Philyra, Dionysus, Heracles, Outis, Enceladus, Littlerock, Porphyrion

With wide-eyed surprise and a strange stirring, Outis stared at Rhea's naked body. In a far recess of his mind, he heard the words, "Take off your tunic, Outis. I want to see something."

Enceladus and Piercer Plan

Sunrise. Each team was ready.

< >

Enceladus and Piercer strolled toward Overlook Point discussing how many new spears must be made to mark the edge of the pathway so that it could be made straight. They knew the approximate direction between the two points, but Mother Kiya had been adamant that the road must be perfectly straight. The spears would probably be moved many times before the road would be perfectly straight.

When they finally arrived, Enceladus set off to the right toward the grove to scout for trees suitable to be harvested for building material. He had spear shafts to make, chairs, and a suitable shelter to build for when Mother Kiya came. Plus, whatever structures and tables Piercer would need for his rock project. It would require the rest of the morning simply to identify suitable trees.

Piercer set off to the left; there to sit and study the area in detail.

They met again in the early afternoon. Enceladus said, "Now I have an idea of where my building material is. There is much I can harvest that will not reduce the vitality of the grove and will allow the remaining trees to grow even stronger. Tell me what I need to build."

"Let's start with two chairs. One for Mother and the other for a visitor. Let's place the two chairs where we think they would most please Mother. Once we place them, we can design a structure around them. We can then mark the outline with either your wood or with my rock. After we decide that, we can decide exactly where my building will be, and what it will look like, and then outline it. Then we can finally decide the exact spot of the entry into our land, drive two spears into the ground to mark it, and then go get Mother to come and look. If she approves, I will replace the spears with marmaros obelisks like the one at Tallstone.

"Wonderful," Enceladus said. "I will build the chairs immediately. You harvest some marmaros the size you think we should line the path to Tartarus with. Until then, we can use them to outline our buildings."

"Good thinking!" Piercer said. "I will finally get to work with my rocks! I have decided where to cut without destroying the beauty of the cliff."

Toward nightfall, they had a good start on their respective projects and would be able to come to a good stopping point the next day. The two chairs were not yet finished but were serviceable for sitting. The two men positioned the chairs and sat in them as they talked into the evening. The chairs were relocated several times to afford the best view as the night came.

Piercer announced that he had found stones necessary to complete a project he had promised Rivermaster and Sagacity long ago.

Themis and Mnemosyne Plan

Sunrise. Each team was ready.

< >

After everyone else had departed on their projects, Themis and Mnemosyne sat down at the fire pit with their mother.

"Do we need a better layout for our family gatherings?" Kiya asked.

"Oh, I don't know. This works well enough, and it has served the family well since forever," Mnemosyne replied.

Themis said, "Forever is since Mother built our first family campfire not that long ago. The campfires made us a family and kept us close, but things will change. We already have added several new family members. More are sure to come. We need to maintain intimacy but maintain flexibility depending on the number of people. And remember, the day will come when we must entertain visiting tribes and candidates to join our camp. We need a layout to prepare a great deal of food and serve it on a patio large enough that many people can both eat and stand around to talk."

Kiya said, "All right, Daughters. I like it! Design a patio worthy of our new home."

ELDER OCEANIDS: Metis, Tyche, Clymene, Eurybia, Amphitrite
ELDER OLYMPIANS: Hestia, Demeter, Hera, Hades, Poseidon, Zeus
OTHER: Philyra, Dionysus, Heracles, Outis, Enceladus, Littlerock, Porphyrion

Two Gifts

For seven days and nights, ideas were presented, discussions held, and decisions made. Kiya stepped off every step, inspected every location, and approved the placement of every rock and path. On the seventh night, the entire family gathered around their campfire. Sagacity described their plans in detail and requested final approval from his family.

"If it pleases their Queen then all bees are pleased," Rhea announced. "Does this plan please our Queen Bee?"

Kiya laughed. "Why, I believe the plan does please me. You have all worked so hard and so wisely on this; how could it not please me? Besides, if details interfere as we build, we are wise enough to make corrections as we go. But do my children approve?"

"Yes, my Queen!" they replied in unison.

Kiya laughed with delight. She then paused and said, "My sons, my daughters, all my children—this will be our last nightly gathering around our campfire. We have outgrown our need for it and will soon outgrow its space. Henceforth, we will gather around the long eating tables we have discussed, and which Enceladus has already built. Let us celebrate our long, difficult journey to this place with a song. Mnemosyne has composed a song for Titans. She will sing it now."

Mnemosyne, embarrassed for perhaps the first time and feeling the weight of change upon her shoulders, rose. She sang her song. The younger children cried.

Kiya said, "Nicely done, Daughter. And now, do we have any other family business?" She glanced in the direction of her two oldest sons already knowing there was.

"Yes, Mother," Rivermaster said as he rose to his feet. "Sagacity and I each have a gift to give. It is a long time in the giving because the gifts have just recently been completed and the time for giving had not yet come. All needed to be perfect." His voice had begun to tremble.

Sagacity rose and continued. "The color of the stones had to be perfect, and they had to be perfect stones." His voice was weaker than usual. "Time was required so that the craftsmanship was perfect."

PRINCIPALS: Kiya, Vanam, Pumi, Valki | ELDER TITANIDES: Themis, Mnemosyne, Phoebe, Tethys, Theia, Rhea | ELDER TITANES: Rivermaster/Oceanus, Sagacity/Coeus, Starmaster/Crius, Watchman/Hyperion, Piercer/Iapetus, Cronus

Each withdrew a small pouch. Each slid the pouch to the woman sitting beside him and quietly said to her, "This is for you."

Both women picked up their respective pouches and hefted them in their hands, clasping their pouches tightly. They both stared wide-eyed into the eyes of their benefactors.

All attention was on the two sisters. Finally, each opened their pouch, their eyes never leaving the man's gaze. They pulled the contents from the pouch, and both finally looked down at their gift.

They gasped.

Rivermaster said, "Piercer had to find stones to exactly match the color of your eyes."

Sagacity said, "The bear claws were taken from the bear that attacked Rivermaster when we first found this land."

Rivermaster said, "We both would have died had not Sagacity jumped on its back and distracted it. He gave me just enough time to take my knife and pull it deep across the bear's throat."

Sagacity said, "But not in time to keep the bear from slashing his claw across Rivermaster's chest. After we knew that Rivermaster wasn't dead, but the bear was, and we recovered from our surprise, we both agreed that we must make necklaces for each of you from his claws."

Rivermaster offered, "We considered his teeth, but a necklace of bear's teeth is not feminine, and we wanted the necklaces to please you. Do you like yours, Tethys?"

Neither Tethys nor Phoebe changed their expression. They both continued to stare.

"Slashed across your chest?" Tethys finally asked.

Rivermaster replied, "Just a flesh wound. It healed. It doesn't bleed anymore."

Tethys did not change her expression. She handed the necklace back to Rivermaster. "There is a rock on the shoreline that I sometimes sit on alone at night. Come to me there. Then put the necklace around my neck." She rose and silently began walking toward the shoreline.

ELDER OCEANIDS: Metis, Tyche, Clymene, Eurybia, Amphitrite
ELDER OLYMPIANS: Hestia, Demeter, Hera, Hades, Poseidon, Zeus
OTHER: Philyra, Dionysus, Heracles, Outis, Enceladus, Littlerock, Porphyrion

Phoebe smiled at Sagacity and said, "Let us walk toward the mountains. You can show me how to best wear my beautiful necklace." She took him by his hand and led him into the night.

Kiya said, "What a perfectly wonderful family campfire. It is an affirmation that the path we travel is true. We go well into our unknown future my children, thank you all."

Piercer exclaimed, "What's happening? Why are they leaving? Do they like their necklaces?"

Under the table, Rhea kicked him.

Sex Talk

At the next family evening meal, Rivermaster and Sagacity, each, in turn, ceremonially stated that he would protect the young woman who stood beside him and be responsible for her wellbeing. There was much celebrating with singing and some speeches, some longer than others.

Rhea thought about the relationship between Rivermaster and Tethys and between Sagacity and Phoebe. *Tethys and Phoebe appear happier than usual this morning. They probably mated last night. Was it like mother describes it or was it more like Themis and her handsome hunter? Will my sisters tell me if I ask? Rivermaster is handsome but doesn't often laugh. Sagacity is not as handsome, but he laughs often and is inquisitive about everything, not just water.*

After evening meal, Rhea went to Themis and Mnemosyne and said, "We need to talk to Tethys and Phoebe about mating."

Themis said, "You are relentless, Rhea. There are some things a woman wishes to keep to herself."

"This isn't one of them. Let's get them."

Mnemosyne laughed and said, "Let's."

They found the four celebrants standing and laughing together near the great table. Themis said, "All right sisters, you can visit your protectors anytime. Right now, visit us. Let's walk to Oursea."

Neither woman was eager to leave their new mate, but Themis was insistent, and Rhea said 'Please,' which was not a normal word from Rhea.

PRINCIPALS: Kiya, Vanam, Pumi, Valki | ELDER TITANIDES: Themis, Mnemosyne, Phoebe, Tethys, Theia, Rhea | ELDER TITANES: Rivermaster/Oceanus, Sagacity/Coeus, Starmaster/Crius, Watchman/Hyperion, Piercer/Iapetus, Cronus

The two women took their leave, and all headed to the beach, laughing and giggling.

Halfway to the beach, Rhea suddenly asked, "How was it? Did they please you or did they just get it over with? Tell us everything."

Themis laughed. "Hush! Rhea. They will get around to these things as we talk." To the other two, she said, "Forgive Rhea's brashness. She has a fixation on mating. She wants to know everything about it without having to do it. She is just a brash, young, inquisitive, obnoxious child. So, tell us, how was it?"

Tethys and Phoebe looked at one another wide-eyed, shocked in disbelief, blushed, and, in unison said, "It was wonderful!"

They walked and talked about many things.

Rhea absorbed every word.

Metis and Her Sisters

The family sat talking at their master dining table. Visitor's tables, empty for now, were located on either side of the master table. As the family talked, sounds were heard in the far distance from the direction of Oursea.

Rivermaster rose, walked to the edge of the patio, and stared into the distance, listening intently. He turned back toward his family and announced, "It is the sound of singing; the Walking Song, I believe."

The family rose as one and ran to join Rivermaster. As they listened, the singing drew closer, the music clearer. There were smiles and laughter as the four figures came into view. The figures stopped, finished their song, and then jumped up and down squealing with delight.

Their leader, Metis, ran to Rivermaster and stood before him. "Great Rivermaster, please don't be angry with me. This place is so wonderful that I had to bring my sisters here. Your Riverport is still safe. Tyche, Clymene, and Eurybia already had girls that could replace them. There are now many sisters in Urfa who love Riverport and easily learn what is to be done there. Please let my three sisters join us! They can help you because they love the rivers and the sea as much as you."

ELDER OCEANIDS: Metis, Tyche, Clymene, Eurybia, Amphitrite
ELDER OLYMPIANS: Hestia, Demeter, Hera, Hades, Poseidon, Zeus
OTHER: Philyra, Dionysus, Heracles, Outis, Enceladus, Littlerock, Porphyrion

Metis then turned to Tethys, who stood close to Rivermaster, her hand touching his shoulder. Metis instantly realized there had been a change in relations. That this was now a mated pair! *I knew this would happen! Well, that's good! Now I can go ahead and ask!*

Metis said to Tethys, "Great Tethys, you love the water just as Rivermaster loves the water. I and my three sisters love the water as much, maybe even more. We wish to follow you and Rivermaster and do whatever you tell us to do. We have no mother or father. Will you be our mother?"

Kiya quickly coughed. "Metis, we are thrilled that you have returned and brought your sisters. Of course, they are welcome here. We have been so worried about you. Your request of Tethys will be well considered but, for now, come join us and nourish your bodies. While you dine with us, perhaps Mnemosyne can sing us a dining song. We will then discuss these new developments and what is to be done."

The four girls giggled, clapped their hands, ran to a visitor's table, and sat down. No one had said, "No."

Kiya had bought enough time to consider the return of Metis and her sisters plus her request; a request of great significance not to be taken lightly. *Tethys is neither old enough nor experienced enough to be anyone's mother; especially not a precocious, outgoing, probably already mature older girl. It would be more than Tethys could handle even if she agreed. Besides, both Tethys and Rivermaster deserve time to explore their world with each other so their bond will strengthen. Why would the child ask such a thing? Metis is as self-sufficient as Tethys. Perhaps more so. I cannot permit Tethys to accept this request.*

Mnemosyne sang a welcome song. Everyone applauded. The newcomers especially so.

After the applause ended, Tethys said, "Metis, my sister, I am honored that you have made such a request of me. I am so flattered. We can talk about this in the coming days. You may decide that you don't even like me. I was obnoxious to you when we first met. Let us get to know each other better. Is that all right?"

"Of course, Sister Tethys," Metis said brightly. "You appear to already have your hands' full training Rivermaster to be a good protector. New

PRINCIPALS: Kiya, Vanam, Pumi, Valki | ELDER TITANIDES: Themis, Mnemosyne, Phoebe, Tethys, Theia, Rhea | ELDER TITANES: Rivermaster/Oceanus, Sagacity/Coeus, Starmaster/Crius, Watchman/Hyperion, Piercer/Iapetus, Cronus

daughters might be too much to handle. Yes, you are right. But will you at least be my sister?"

Tethys replied, "Let's talk later."

Kiya relaxed. A pleasant meal was enjoyed. After finishing their meal, Metis said, "My sisters and I need to go on a night-time swim. The four girls rose and turned toward the sea as Tethys watched on.

As the girls began to leave, Tethys called out, "Metis, there is much for your sisters to learn of their new home. Make them stay here and learn. Let's you and I go for a swim."

Kiya tensed. *Be careful, my child.*

Tethys took Metis's hand as they walked the long walk to the sea. Tethys told of the necklace given to her by Rivermaster and how they were now a mated pair. Metis listened intently and assured Tethys that she understood, and she was so happy for the both of them because they both loved the water more than they loved the land and that was a powerful bond between them and was not to be broken by any man or woman and she was not jealous of that bond and she wished to have a bond like that with her three sisters and the sea.

They reached Oursea and sat down on the shore.

"Now, Metis. Why did you ask me to be your mother?"

Metis withdrew her hand and sat silently. She finally said, "Because ..." and again sat in silence. "Because I don't know what to do around men or with men or about men or what is expected of me or how to know what is expected of me. I was older when my real mother gave me away. In our camps, I had seen hunters in their little hunting cloth, bouncing around, exposing that thing between their legs. My sisters were given away much younger than I was. Builders and guildsmen are always fully clothed, so my sisters don't even have as much experience as I do. They ask me questions I cannot begin to answer. We had only the elder women at Urfa to ask but they are old and cold and short with us. I know men have that thing there, but I don't begin to understand it." She stopped and choked back a sob. She was again silent for a while and then continued, "Because my insides are rotting out. Every month a little more leaves my body and

ELDER OCEANIDS: Metis, Tyche, Clymene, Eurybia, Amphitrite
ELDER OLYMPIANS: Hestia, Demeter, Hera, Hades, Poseidon, Zeus
OTHER: Philyra, Dionysus, Heracles, Outis, Enceladus, Littlerock, Porphyrion

I don't know how to stop it and now I have given the sickness to Tyche. Last season, her insides started coming out like mine. I am sorry, Sister Tethys. I was wrong to ask that thing of you. I'm so sorry."

With that, Metis rose and ran crying into the water.

Tethys stood and watched the girl run neck-deep into the sea. *She is not so different than me, Rivermaster. Can you understand? We were both given away as children. I was the lucky one. I was not left in a wilderness to die. Another tribe accepted me. I was the luckier one. A loving woman accepted me as her own child. To raise me. To teach me. Metis was not so lucky. Food and shelter were gracious gifts that Urfa gave her. Love and teaching and nurturing? Not so much.*

Tethys rose and entered the water. *Our childhoods could easily have been switched. She could be Kiya's daughter. I, a daughter of no one.*

She reached Metis, standing neck-deep in the sea. Sobbing violently. Tethys reached out and put her hand on the girl's shoulder. *I have received much in life. Not because I am me but because the fortune of my birth was great. Metis's fortune was not as great. Metis is as worthy as I. Maybe more so. But it is I that have so much and she so little.*

Tethys turned Metis to face her, put her left arm around Metis, and pulled her close. *Will you understand, Rivermaster? Will you be a father such as your own? Caring nothing of your daughters and despising your sons? We talked of leaving Tartarus and exploring this great sea. Having four daughters would certainly slow us down. But they love the sea more than either of us. I understand much about water because it interests you. Water interests you because of the challenges. The possibilities. The beauty of it. But it is not your soul as it is theirs.*

She placed her right hand on Metis's head and pressed it firmly to her breasts. She looked up toward the endless, beautiful heaven. *Rivermaster, you never realized that it was inevitable that you would mate with me. You are so naïve. Now you would have not only me but also four daughters with which to contend.*

Tethys brushed Metis's hair with her lips as she brought her lips close to Metis's ear. *Will you understand, Rivermaster? Will you forgive me?*

Surrounded by the all-encompassing sea—under the moon's soft light—as inexorably as then becomes now—these words were said, "I am thrilled

---

PRINCIPALS: Kiya, Vanam, Pumi, Valki | ELDER TITANIDES: Themis, Mnemosyne, Phoebe, Tethys, Theia, Rhea | ELDER TITANES: Rivermaster/Oceanus, Sagacity/Coeus, Starmaster/Crius, Watchman/Hyperion, Piercer/Iapetus, Cronus

that you and your sisters wish to be my daughters, Metis. Of course, I will be your mother. I have so much to tell you all. And there will be laughter."

< >

Tethys and Metis returned to the patio.

Kiya had been watching for their return with trepidation.

Rivermaster was distracted talking to the three wide-eyed young girls about rivers to the north and how he hoped to deliver water from there to here. Tyche excitedly asked if there would be waterfalls anywhere or would the stream be swift running water. Rivermaster was impressed and said, "That is an expert question. What do you think?"

Tyche replied without hesitation. "Waterfalls would be best. Not as much water would be needed for one thing. For another, the sounds would be nice, and they are pleasing to the eye. They couldn't be high because the slope is not great. You could add fish and turtles to the ponds the waterfalls fall into. That strange one-eyed boy that came with you would like that. He could give them all names."

Rivermaster was taken aback. That was his plan plus some. It had taken him two days to formulate it.

Kiya saw Tethys and Metis returning. They were holding hands. *Oh no, daughter! Don't do it. You are not yet ready for such things. Consult with me. You must not do this to yourself and Rivermaster.*

Tethys and Metis approached Rivermaster. Tethys whispered, "My mate ..."

Rivermaster, interrupted from a fascinating conversation, turned and stared at her dumbly. "Yes, Tethys?"

"My mate ..." she repeated and continued to stare at him with a cowed look.

Rivermaster stared at her and then glanced toward Metis, who was staring at him with open fear. With slow comprehension, Rivermaster stared back, "Do you two have something to tell me?" he asked.

Metis replied, in terror, "Y-yes. Mother and I have something to tell you."

Rivermaster, without expression, stared a moment at Tethys, then at Metis, and then at the three young girls staring back at him, motionless

ELDER OCEANIDS: Metis, Tyche, Clymene, Eurybia, Amphitrite
ELDER OLYMPIANS: Hestia, Demeter, Hera, Hades, Poseidon, Zeus
OTHER: Philyra, Dionysus, Heracles, Outis, Enceladus, Littlerock, Porphyrion

with fear. He said, "You all understand, do you not, that my sleeping quarters are cramped with the addition of Tethys. The four of you had better be quite close because our quarters will be extremely cramped tonight. I will arrange for larger quarters tomorrow. But for now, I believe it is customary for daughters to hug their father."

The four girls squealed and ran toward him with outstretched arms. Tethys watched, relieved. And silently cried.

Kiya's other daughters clapped and chanted, "Nie-ces ... Nie-ces ... Nie-ces ... N..."

Only by her iron-clad will did Kiya hold her tongue. *Too young, my children. Too young.*

PRINCIPALS: Kiya, Vanam, Pumi, Valki | ELDER TITANIDES: Themis, Mnemosyne, Phoebe, Tethys, Theia, Rhea | ELDER TITANES: Rivermaster/Oceanus, Sagacity/Coeus, Starmaster/Crius, Watchman/Hyperion, Piercer/Iapetus, Cronus

9. The Emissary

Master Littlerock of Tallstone arrived at Overlook Point and introduced himself to Watchman, who was working there while Piercer was in Tartarus.

Watchman said with excitement, "Yes, you may have an audience with Queen Kiya." *We have a visitor! We have a visitor!*

"Follow those rocks to our greeting place. I will tell her you are coming."

Puzzled by the response, Littlerock said, "Thank you," and began the long descent toward the plains. Watchman ran to a tall pole, raised a green flag, and blew into a horn which made a loud noise.

Littlerock eventually arrived at a circular path with a manmade lake to his right. He was met by Themis, who welcomed him and escorted him the short distance to the entrance of the path leading to the Titan's patio. They stopped at the entrance and Themis exclaimed, "Mother, Master Littlerock of Tallstone has come to visit with you!"

He saw Kiya standing at the end of the path of white stone leading to the patio. He walked the path to face her and began, "Great Queen Kiya …"

Kiya stood and held up her hand for silence. "Queen is a title my younger children call me with affection, not a title for formal greeting. But thank you for the proffered honor. I am simply 'Kiya.'"

"Great Kiya …" Littlerock began again.

She again held up her hand. "I and my children are banished from the company of good people. We are Titans desiring only to live among ourselves and with whatever other outcasts may care to join us. I must insist that you address me as 'Kiya.' Now, come, let us sit and visit!"

She led him to the large dining table and signaled Enceladus to bring refreshments.

"Kiya," Littlerock began again and paused.

She smiled, "I know you, Master Littlerock. You were our tribe's Master Stonecutter and Piercer's master for a while. How could I not know you? But why do you defy the command of your chief? Why do you dare

ELDER OCEANIDS: Metis, Tyche, Clymene, Eurybia, Amphitrite
ELDER OLYMPIANS: Hestia, Demeter, Hera, Hades, Poseidon, Zeus
OTHER: Philyra, Dionysus, Heracles, Outis, Enceladus, Littlerock, Porphyrion

counsel with the banished? And you are now 'of Tallstone;' not 'Clan of the Serpent?'"

It was Littlerock's turn to smile. "Piercer was an apt student. He learned quickly, but he has much more to learn. His fascination with colored stone is intriguing. There is much that I could learn from him. But I counsel with you upon command of my Master, Pumi of Tallstone. During the festival, I asked Chief Vanam if I could make my Last Camp at Urfa. He was more delighted to release me than I expected. Perhaps because of my past association with Pumi or even with Piercer. He granted my release and after the festival had ended and all tribes had gone, I made my way from Urfa to Tallstone to join the Guild of Stonemasons. Pumi greeted me with warmth. I no longer belong to any tribe and am free from the customs of the tribes and the old tribal women of Urfa. Our kind is free to come and go as is our nature. So, I am here, Great Kiya. Pumi commands me to give you his warmest greetings."

"So, Pumi is free to acknowledge my existence?"

"Free or not, he sends the same greetings. But Pumi obtained Chief Vanam's leave to do whatever he wished to do. Maintaining goodwill among all tribes has always been Pumi's goal. And Pumi is clever when obtaining that which he wishes."

Kiya thought, "Yes, I am aware of this." *Almost everything.*

Themis was looking at her mother. *Your mind went away for a moment, Mother. Where did it go?*

Kiya said, "And now, what is it Pumi wishes to do with me?"

Littlerock said, "He would enjoy visiting your land; meeting your children; hearing your stories; establishing communications and trade between your land and Tallstone. Tallstone and Urfa are the most important trading centers in the world. That your land could rise to greatness is not possible; nonetheless, trade would help all concerned; no matter how little."

Kiya silently considered his words. *Trade, you say. Perhaps my children have more to offer than you might think.*

She said, "Yes, Littlerock, I look forward to seeing my dear friend in the warmth of our new home and discussing such things. In three seasons,

PRINCIPALS: Kiya, Vanam, Pumi, Valki | ELDER TITANIDES: Themis, Mnemosyne, Phoebe, Tethys, Theia, Rhea | ELDER TITANES: Rivermaster/Oceanus, Sagacity/Coeus, Starmaster/Crius, Watchman/Hyperion, Piercer/Iapetus, Cronus

perhaps, when the moon is full? I need time to prepare for his visit. Can you make this visit so?"

"Yes, Kiya. I shall make it so. Now, do I have your permission to visit Piercer? I miss his excitement when opening a stone."

Kiya rang a small bell. A young, strong-looking male ran to her and stood waiting. "Enceladus, ask Piercer to join us. He has a visitor from far away who wishes to speak to him."

Enceladus said, "Yes, Queen Mother" and ran to carry out her command.

Kiya laughed. "I will counsel Enceladus that sometimes it is not proper to address me with affection. In the meantime, we gather for evening meal at sundown. You will join us."

"I look forward to the delight of your company and the food. Of course, I gratefully accept your kind invitation."

"Invitation?" Kiya asked with a smile. "It is not an invitation, Master Littlerock. The Queen commands it."

Littlerock laughed. "You are most gracious, Kiya. And now, I see my apprentice running this way. May I greet him?"

Kiya saw Piercer fast approaching and nodded, "Yes, of course."

A Gift for Pumi

Kiya stood alone—thinking. She then walked to Theia's room.

Theia sat at her worktable sewing a garment for Rivermaster. "Sit and join me, Mother. What shall we talk about?"

Kiya sat down at the desk. "Theia, if you were to sew a garment for the Grand Chief of all the Heavens, what would it be made of? How would it look?"

"Something grander than a chief's robe? A robe for the Chief of all Chiefs?"

"No. For someone who does not want to be Chief of all Chiefs. For one who only wishes to embrace the sky; to listen to all that the sky will reveal to him. For one who cares not what esteem a chief would hold for him. For Pumi of Tallstone. For a gift to celebrate his traveling to see our family, here in our land. Yes, a gift for Pumi."

ELDER OCEANIDS: Metis, Tyche, Clymene, Eurybia, Amphitrite
ELDER OLYMPIANS: Hestia, Demeter, Hera, Hades, Poseidon, Zeus
OTHER: Philyra, Dionysus, Heracles, Outis, Enceladus, Littlerock, Porphyrion

"Pumi is coming here, Mother. How exciting! Does he not know that we are banished?"

"Yes, Theia, he knows, but still, he is coming. In three seasons with the coming of the full moon. His acolyte, Littlerock, has come to establish communications and he agrees that this would be a suitable time. I would like to send Littlerock back with a gift for Pumi. I can think of nothing more in the interests of my family than a garment made specifically for him by the best seamstress in all the lands. One who happens to be a Titan. How long will it require you to make such a thing?"

"We must first design it. Let me call my sisters. We will design something worthy of the master of stone and heaven. It will take days to make. How many days do we have?"

"As many as you need, Daughter. I shall make sure your brothers keep our visitor entertained. There are enough colored rocks in this land to entertain men for a long time."

"Oh, what fun! I will gather my sisters now." Theia rose and ran from the room calling for each of her sisters. Kiya rose and left the room with confident certainty.

Later, the women met at the great table.

Theia told them, "I don't have a great deal of material to select from. We have no hunters to bring pelts or furs or skins. What little I have is of poor quality and certainly not fitting for a chief's garments. We could send Watchman into the plains to bring down an antelope, but the skin would not have time to age properly."

Suggestions floated across the table.

Theia: "We can take all our clothes and get enough material to make a cloak of some kind."
Mnemosyne: "You can distract from the lack of material by incorporating colored rock into the design."
Theia: "We can find feathers and maybe harvest a snakeskin."
Phoebe: "Make him a fine headpiece. Less material but distinctive."
Tethys: "He has everything he needs. What more can we add?"
Rhea: "Send him urns of honey. We harvest a great deal. Honey is

always appreciated."

Kiya: "Piercer has some exquisite stones. Make him a belt or a necklace or a bracelet.

Themis: "Pumi likes obelisks. Piercer could make him an obelisk of colored stone."

Clymene: "I can get some turtle shells. They are sometimes pretty."

Metis: "We can use fish scales."

"Well, girls," Kiya said, "For nothing to work with, I think we have some good ideas. Go to your quarters and don't come back naked but otherwise bring back every article that Theia might be able to use. Let us see what material we have to work with."

Within the hour, all had returned and laid their possessions on the great table. They studied their collection closely.

Sagacity and Enceladus walked by on their way to work on the circular path. They stopped and stared in amazement at the collection of items on the table. "What, my dear women, are you doing?" Sagacity asked.

Theia explained their problem. "Oh," he replied, paused, and then asked, "Would a bearskin do you any good?"

"A bearskin!" Theia exclaimed. "Where would I get a bearskin?!"

"Oh, there's one somewhere up in the mountains. Rivermaster could find it better than I. It's the one he killed. We didn't want to kill it. It was a beautiful creature. Its fur was light brown, almost white. We tried to run away but ... At any rate, we killed it, skinned it, and preserved the pelt as best we could. We left the pelt in a cave out of the weather. As a sign of respect, we ate as much of the bear as we could. But that was a lot of bear meat. So, anyway, should we go get the pelt?"

"Yes, that would be lovely," Phoebe said to Sagacity, "Ask Rivermaster to bring it to us as soon as you can. I will reward you handsomely."

"All right!" Sagacity said. "Come on, Enceladus, let's find Rivermaster."

Theia said to Kiya, "Piercer keeps most of his colored rock at Overlook Point. You love to visit there, Mother. Why don't you go and see what he has in the way of blue stones; or anything that might look good on an almost white cloak? Some of those strange men at Tallstone wear big

ELDER OCEANIDS: Metis, Tyche, Clymene, Eurybia, Amphitrite
ELDER OLYMPIANS: Hestia, Demeter, Hera, Hades, Poseidon, Zeus
OTHER: Philyra, Dionysus, Heracles, Outis, Enceladus, Littlerock, Porphyrion

cloaks with big hoods. If the bear were large enough, maybe I make one of those with some kind of 'sky' motif, but I am sure we will have enough for at least a cape or wrap or something like that."

The women were excited. They had gone from nothing to a great deal with which to work.

"Yes!" Kiya said. "I believe we can present Pumi with a fine gift." Her eyes briefly glazed over. *One worthy of Pumi.*

Themis was looking at her mother. *Where do you go when you speak of Pumi, Mother? Where exactly do you go?*

They then prepared for their nightly gathering. There was singing.

Sunrise

Enceladus accompanied Kiya to Overlook Point. There was always work for Enceladus wherever he might be. Today, they carried food for Piercer and Littlerock and anyone else who might be there helping. Outis and Piercer's brothers would sometimes show up. A temporary enclosure had been built for Piercer and his stones.

His stones were organized with great love and care and stored in boxes built by Enceladus. The afternoon of their arrival had been spent with Piercer showing Littlerock his collection. Littlerock was impressed with the craftsmanship, but, mainly, a new world had opened before him. Littlerock's life had been spent making spear points and cutting tools, sitting rocks, and markers. He knew which rocks could be honed to extremely sharp blades and was a master at honing them. The new world Piercer had opened was a world of beauty and potential. Who knew what new capabilities lay in these colored stones? The two examined rocks and talked far into the night.

The line between Master and Apprentice blurred.

Sunrise

They rose early and Piercer introduced Littlerock to marmaros stone. Littlerock had marveled at the white cliff on his walk from Overlook Point to Tartarus but now he could examine the material up close. Piercer usually spent each morning cutting marmaros; Tartarus had an insatiable

PRINCIPALS: Kiya, Vanam, Pumi, Valki | ELDER TITANIDES: Themis, Mnemosyne, Phoebe, Tethys, Theia, Rhea | ELDER TITANES: Rivermaster/Oceanus, Sagacity/Coeus, Starmaster/Crius, Watchman/Hyperion, Piercer/Iapetus, Cronus

appetite for the white rock. Fortunately, it was an easy rock to cut but was extremely hard and durable. It could be used to build almost any structure. Buildings, roads, obelisks, even riverbeds. But not boats. Piercer had not been able to build Metis a boat from marmaros.

Piercer had been alerted that his mother would be visiting by the sound of the great horn and the flying of his mother's flag atop the pole. It was hard to see but by squinting and staring long enough, one could find the flag in the far distance. He estimated the time his mother would arrive and timed their morning projects accordingly. Piercer planned to visit with his mother and then take Littlerock to the mountains where there was an abundance of all manner of different colored rocks.

Piercer took Littlerock to his mother's formal greeting place. Two chairs and a table were there surrounded by an outline of where a permanent structure would someday be built. Chairs were relocated and the outline was rearranged each time Kiya visited. Patience, planning, and persistence were becoming a way of life.

Piercer's timing was perfect. They arrived at the greeting place minutes before Kiya and Enceladus. Upon arrival, Kiya smiled at Littlerock and embraced her son. Enceladus inspected the area for tasks he could begin.

Kiya went to her chair and motioned Littlerock to sit beside her. She prepared and placed their lunch on the table in front of them. Piercer improvised a sitting rock and sat down to inspect his lunch. Enceladus began to walk, pulling his sled, to where he knew Piercer would have stacked marmaros in need of transport to Tartarus.

As they ate, Kiya told Piercer that she wished to send Pumi a gift for his kindness to them. Something with blue stones attached. "Wouldn't blue stones remind him of the sky and the lights in the heavens? Do you have any blue rocks that might be appropriate, Piercer?"

Rocks. Piercer's favorite subject. "Of course, I have blue rocks. What size? Polished and shiny or natural rough ones. With or without holes pre-pierced? Polished ones would be better. They would be shinier—like stars. Rough ones would be more like the sky. Would you mix the two together? What are you attaching them to? I will go get both boxes, shiny ones and rough ones. You can choose better when you hold them."

ELDER OCEANIDS: Metis, Tyche, Clymene, Eurybia, Amphitrite
ELDER OLYMPIANS: Hestia, Demeter, Hera, Hades, Poseidon, Zeus
OTHER: Philyra, Dionysus, Heracles, Outis, Enceladus, Littlerock, Porphyrion

Piercer jumped up, ran toward his enclosure, then stopped and turned around to speak to Kiya. "It might be easier if you came to my house, Mother. There are many boxes, and they are heavy."

Kiya and Littlerock rose and made the trip to Piercer's house.

There was a sitting area outside his modest enclosure, a great flat rock at its center. Here Piercer would study, catalog, and work on his stones. Many unprocessed stones lay on the table. He swept these to one side as he called for Enceladus to come and help him. They went into Piercer's hut where he identified three large, heavy boxes. These boxes, Enceladus brought to the table; one at a time. "Sit here, Mother," Piercer said, pointing to a sitting stone made of marmaros. "These are my boxes of mostly blue stones. I have some other rocks that contain rocks of blue mixed with other colors." He took the top off the first box. "In this box are stones I have polished to be smooth. You can see that they tend to be much shinier than these," he said as he took the top off the second box and showed her the contents. "These rocks are natural and rough, but I am learning how to cut them open to expose more blue. I have become more expert at this since we got here, and now I have a good place to work." He took stones from both boxes and spread them out on the table. "Look through these and see if you see anything you like. Take your favorite ones because this is a gift for Pumi, and we Titans must present our best for him."

Kiya thought, *I have never said such a thing to you, Son. Where did you learn this?*

She said, "Thank you, Piercer. Help me select them. I see pretty ones, but you see not only the pretty but also the quality. Let's select twelve from each box; one from each of us."

"Thirteen," he replied. "One for extra measure; for the future."

Kiya laughed. "Perhaps I should rename you 'Little Sagacity.'"

"No, Mother. I am Piercer."

"Yes, you are," she said as they selected thirteen stones from each box.

Having selected twenty-six stones, Kiya leaned back and considered them. "Theia can create a beautiful garment with these. Thank you, Piercer. I am so proud of the things you can do and that you are my son."

PRINCIPALS: Kiya, Vanam, Pumi, Valki | ELDER TITANIDES: Themis, Mnemosyne, Phoebe, Tethys, Theia, Rhea | ELDER TITANES: Rivermaster/Oceanus, Sagacity/Coeus, Starmaster/Crius, Watchman/Hyperion, Piercer/Iapetus, Cronus

"You're welcome, Mother. I have more if you need more."

She collected the stones and rose to go. "Oh, what is in the third box?"

"Those are rocks that aren't really rocks. I don't know exactly how to classify them or how to work with them. I found these in a cave in the mountains by accident. Look at this," he handed her one. "On one side, it's a plain, gray, rather ugly round rock but turn it over and look."

She rotated the rock, looked inside, and gasped.

"I broke this one open by accident," he said. "I picked up two identical ones and just smashed them together. I must have struck that one at a critical place because it just split into two halves. Look at what's inside. It's pretty, isn't it? I haven't had enough time to properly study them."

The rock was plain on one side but the side that had been split open was a hollow cave, full of rising flat rectangular surfaces, like monoliths in miniature. Each monolith was a different shade of beautiful blue. Catching and emitting light. Reflecting light off myriad surfaces. Kiya sat back down and stared at the hollow cave of blue monoliths. She asked, "Can you make this into a walking stick? Make it a top in some way?"

He studied the rock. "I don't know Mother. It is a beautiful thing, like a clear night full of lights. Let me study it. The walking stick would need to be distinctive. Something worthy of carrying this strange stone. But I don't yet see the walking stick in my mind."

"Very well," she said. "If something worthy can be made, please make it. I would like to present it to Pumi when he visits us." She rose. "I have had a wonderful time, Piercer. You are a gracious host. Now I must take your stones to Theia and see how she can use them."

She then walked to the trailhead and began the long descent home. Enceladus traveled with her, pulling a sled of marmaros.

After they had gone, Littlerock said to Piercer, "I have a thought. Actually, several thoughts. Can you keep a secret?"

< >

At Tartarus, the Titans prepared for their evening meal. Sagacity had named the Titan evening meal, "Dinner."

ELDER OCEANIDS: Metis, Tyche, Clymene, Eurybia, Amphitrite
ELDER OLYMPIANS: Hestia, Demeter, Hera, Hades, Poseidon, Zeus
OTHER: Philyra, Dionysus, Heracles, Outis, Enceladus, Littlerock, Porphyrion

Seating at the three tables was fluid and evolving depending on who was attending and who arrived at what time. The two mated couples usually sat on either side of Kiya, who always sat at the head of the main table.

The remaining males usually sat across from each other on one end of the table on Kiya's left while the younger girls tended to sit at the lower part of the table. Themis and her older unmated sisters usually sat across from each other at the table on her right.

Rhea usually sat far from Outis because Outis was becoming friendlier than she wanted.

Piercer was missing. He was at Overlook Point working on his projects.

Littlerock sat at the foot of the main table.

Themis casually noticed that Littlerock had an unbroken view down the table, down the pathway, to the door of Kiya's house, which was in the process of being built. *We should make this view particularly beautiful. This is the scene a guest will see and remember. Enceladus can plant trees along the path. Maybe put poles with colorful flags on top between the trees. We could make this walkway extremely pretty. Maybe some torches to light the way at night.*

Themis snapped from her reverie.

There was a copious selection of food. A special table had been built at the edge of the gathering patio. The table was made of stone and designed so that a fire could burn beneath the top, keeping the stone top warm. As food was cooked at the nearby fire pits and ovens, it could be placed on this table to keep it warm until served. One fire pit was designed for cooking fish, another for cooking cuts of meat, and another designed to hold skewers of meat intermingled with wild onions, peppers, potatoes, and other savory plants. There was, of course, an oven for bread.

As they ate, Kiya talked to Littlerock about the evolution of their city. "We build what we can when we can. There is no great hurry. Whatever is most needed, we build as time and material are available. But we always consider how to make it the most pleasing to the eye and how it will relate to its surroundings. We accept anyone wishing to join us. More immigrants are always needed, and our land will generously support many more of us. We work throughout the day, poor Enceladus especially. He is so overworked. His great strength is helpful with so many tasks. Tartarus needs many more such as him."

Throughout the dinner, Metis and her sisters constantly checked on their mother and father in case additional food or drink might be needed; if anything needed to be taken away; or, maybe, if they should sing a song.

As sweetbreads were served by the senior daughters, Tethys said, "I have a request. I would like my daughters to sing a Sweetbread Song."

The four girls squealed, jumped up, and ran to stand on either side of Kiya. With a loud and joyous voice, they sang a Sweetbread Song.

Littlerock took note of everything. *They have built all of this in a short time. More impressive is that this is only infrastructure. I expected none of this. Pumi expected none of this. Vanam expected none of this. And fury will come with his knowing.*

< >

After several days, Rivermaster returned to Tartarus with the bearskin. It was huge and had cured perfectly. Everyone gathered around to admire the fur and thrill that their brothers had been able to defend themselves against such a creature. Tethys stared at it with amazement and pride.

Theia was beside herself with excitement. *At last, I have material with which to make a proper garment. I shall be able to make something wonderful with this. Many wonderful garments.*

Theia said, "Come to my room, Sisters. Let's lay it out and place Piercer's blue stones on it and decide what we will make."

The sisters scurried to Theia's room with its sewing workshop. The men milled around Rivermaster to hear of his expedition into the mountains and search for the cave containing the bearskin.

"Did you see any more bears?" Sagacity asked.

"Yes. Several. Two much larger than this one. I avoided making them mad. I kept my distance and changed my path. But entering the mountains is a dangerous place. We must remember to always be vigilant there."

The Titanes looked at Rivermaster with admiration.

ELDER OCEANIDS: Metis, Tyche, Clymene, Eurybia, Amphitrite
ELDER OLYMPIANS: Hestia, Demeter, Hera, Hades, Poseidon, Zeus
OTHER: Philyra, Dionysus, Heracles, Outis, Enceladus, Littlerock, Porphyrion

Founding of the Sisterhood

Metis and her sisters went to Tethys with an idea. "Mother, Theia said that she didn't have material with which to make garments. Does she have enough now?"

"She has enough to make a gift to send to Pumi. That is all she was worried about."

"But what about new dresses for the women and maybe some new tunics for the men? Our clothes are old and worn."

Tethys laughed. "We have clothes enough to cover our bodies. That is all we need. Besides, Theia doesn't have enough material to make us clothes. Maybe we can trade honey or necklaces at Riverport at the festival and get some nice linen. She could make a few new pieces for those most in need."

"Let me and my sisters return with Littlerock. Urfa has the things we need. Surly we have things to trade."

Tethys frowned and knelt to look at Metis at eye level. "We cannot go to Urfa because we are Titans. Outcasts. We are scorned by all decent people."

Metis persisted. "But Master Littlerock doesn't scorn us. And Pumi doesn't scorn us. And am I scorned because I am a Titan? No one ever told me that I was an outcast; just a Titan."

Tethys smiled a sad smile. "Littlerock and Pumi are special people plus they no longer belong to any tribe. But you are right. No one ever expelled you from a tribe. You were not cast out. I don't know if becoming a member of the Titan family makes you an outcast or not. I'll ask Mother."

"If we are not outcasts, then Tyche, Clymene, Eurybia, and I should be able to trade at Urfa or any tribe we encounter. I have never traded before, but I have watched and listened to the elder women trade. It was great fun to listen to. They played a wonderful game. They got to tell lies and it was not dishonorable to lie because everyone knew that everyone was lying so it wasn't really lying. Whoever could tell the biggest lie got the best of the trade. I studied their faces and their bodies and their words. I'm good at knowing who would get what for how much and when. I saw many traders not get the best deal they could if they had countered with a bigger lie. I think we could get fair trades."

PRINCIPALS: Kiya, Vanam, Pumi, Valki | ELDER TITANIDES: Themis, Mnemosyne, Phoebe, Tethys, Theia, Rhea | ELDER TITANES: Rivermaster/Oceanus, Sagacity/Coeus, Starmaster/Crius, Watchman/Hyperion, Piercer/Iapetus, Cronus

Tethys listened in rapt silence. *I'm the mother and you're the daughter? Hmmm.*

Tethys said, "Let's go talk to Mother. This is a lot to consider."

Meanwhile, Piercer arrived in Tartarus in the early afternoon. He went directly to his master. They retreated to the hastily erected guest house in which Littlerock was staying and emerged two hours later. Piercer then sought an audience with his mother.

His mother was meeting with Tethys but allowed both stonecutters to enter her chambers. Kiya said, "Tethys has posed an interesting question; are her daughters outcasts like her?"

Piercer looked puzzled but Littlerock understood immediately. "This circumstance has never before been encountered. There is no precedent for it. It would require a council of all chiefs and elder women in the land to decide the question."

Kiya sat in silence, thinking. She then said, "I believe I'm chief of all this land, and I am sure my children would agree that *my* decision is all that is needed here. Her children and others who join us are Titans but *not* outcasts. Only those of us who were cast out cannot mingle with the tribes outside of our land, *but* the title 'Titan' would confuse and irritate the tribes they might introduce themselves to, especially the elder women at Urfa."

She paused, thought more, and said, "Tethys, your daughters love the sea, the streams, and every gathering of water, wherever it might be. Ask them if the title 'Oceanids' pleases them. If it does, they, and whoever becomes their sisters may introduce their kind as 'Oceanids.' Titans they are and Titans they remain, but they may also have the title 'Oceanid.' Regardless of their title, your daughters are free to go to Urfa and trade. Go and make arrangements."

Tethys smiled broadly, said, "Thank you, Mother," and left to plan with her daughters.

Piercer, still confused, stayed behind with Littlerock.

Littlerock said, "A quick and decisive decision, Kiya. One that can be defended, but all people will not agree with it."

ELDER OCEANIDS: Metis, Tyche, Clymene, Eurybia, Amphitrite
ELDER OLYMPIANS: Hestia, Demeter, Hera, Hades, Poseidon, Zeus
OTHER: Philyra, Dionysus, Heracles, Outis, Enceladus, Littlerock, Porphyrion

Kiya replied, "I suppose not, but there are many who do not agree with any decision. Let us see what happens. And now, what requirement does Piercer have for his mother?"

"Oh. I brought you this to see if you like it." He handed her a long, narrow, cloth-wrapped package.

She laid it on her table and carefully unwrapped it. She looked at the contents with wide eyes. "It's magnificent, Piercer. However, did you design this?"

"Littlerock helped. He suggested the walking stick be made of marmaros stone. I cut it to look like the tall stone at the center of Tallstone. I carved the icon of all the tribes and invented a symbol for Tallstone. I put it above the others. Do you like it?"

"Oh, my son, it is gorgeous. This will be a perfect gift to give him when he arrives. But how did you embed the blue rock into it?"

"That was easy enough. Just carve the hole exactly the right size with a little lip at the bottom. I coated the inside with sticky mortar and slipped the rock into the hole. I added a couple of shims to make sure it could never fall out."

She rose and embraced her son. "What a glorious day to be a Titan!"

Outside her quarters, in the distance, the squeal of Oceanid sisterhood could be heard.

Oceanid Traders

That evening, all gathered for the family dinner. As they ate, they talked about exciting things. Theia left early to return to her project.

Metis talked about their trading project. "Mother Kiya is going to give us healing ointments to trade. Outis said that he could harvest honey from the wild hive. Piercer is going to give some necklaces and bracelets and we think that simple colored rocks might be popular. Theia dyed some strips of cloth and made colorful headbands and gave us some nice reed hats like the one Grandmother once wore in the gathering fields. We have much to trade, I just hope we can be good traders."

"Enceladus is overworked," Kiya said. "Perhaps he could go with you to Urfa. It would be a pleasant break for him, and you are traveling with a great deal of treasure. Think about it, Enceladus. You would be trapped

PRINCIPALS: Kiya, Vanam, Pumi, Valki | ELDER TITANIDES: Themis, Mnemosyne, Phoebe, Tethys, Theia, Rhea | ELDER TITANES: Rivermaster/Oceanus, Sagacity/Coeus, Starmaster/Crius, Watchman/Hyperion, Piercer/Iapetus, Cronus

with four young, outgoing women. On second thought, maybe it would be more restful to stay here and work."

As unaccustomed as he was, Enceladus laughed.

Sunrise

Theia found Kiya already sitting at the family table. "Mother, it's finished. Come and see if you approve." They walked to Theia's chamber. Laid out on her table was a robe of bearskin and above that, a headpiece of bearskin. The fur was the most beautiful color Kiya had ever seen. But, even more, the fur emphasized and highlighted the stones sewn into them.

"I used the polished stones in the headpiece," Theia said. "Don't they sparkle like lights in the sky? And look at the robe. Twelve of the rough stones are positioned so that straps can be used to open and close the robe as much as he might like. I call them 'buttons'. I placed the largest stone on the leather band which ties the robe around the neck as a decorative piece. I love the roughness of the stones and the color of the blue against the fur. What do you think?"

Kiya said, "This exceeds all my hope, Theia. These are gifts worthy of a great person. I am pleased. Wrap them in a manner suitable for presentation to a powerful man we wish to become our ally."

Theia smiled at the recognition. *If the queen is pleased, all are pleased.*

She said, "Thank you, Mother. I will wrap them nicely."

Kiya returned and joined those at the table. Littlerock was busy extolling the hospitality of the Titan tribe. All rose when Kiya joined them. She waved for all to sit.

Littlerock continued. He described the excitement of developing an entirely new attitude toward rocks. Colored rocks. He and Piercer had discovered, in only a few days together, new properties these rocks held. "To be as old as I and discover a new passion makes me young again."

Kiya replied, "Perhaps I can someday help you with staying young."

"I have enjoyed my visit to Tartarus, Mother Kiya. Sadly, I must leave at the next sunrise. The young ones asked to travel with me as far as

ELDER OCEANIDS: Metis, Tyche, Clymene, Eurybia, Amphitrite
ELDER OLYMPIANS: Hestia, Demeter, Hera, Hades, Poseidon, Zeus
OTHER: Philyra, Dionysus, Heracles, Outis, Enceladus, Littlerock, Porphyrion

Riverport. Enceladus has agreed to carry all their trading items. I have hope that the coming seasons will be beneficial to us all."

"Theia will bring the gifts to present to Pumi to encourage him to visit us. I trust you will present them with our kind regards?"

"Your gift will ensure that he comes, and Pumi has a way of making that which he desires come to pass."

Kiya said, "Wonderful!" *And does Pumi still desire what he once desired?*

Themis was looking at her mother. *To where does your mind go, Mother?*

Preparations were made. The day passed.

PRINCIPALS: Kiya, Vanam, Pumi, Valki | ELDER TITANIDES: Themis, Mnemosyne, Phoebe, Tethys, Theia, Rhea | ELDER TITANES: Rivermaster/Oceanus, Sagacity/Coeus, Starmaster/Crius, Watchman/Hyperion, Piercer/Iapetus, Cronus

10. The Oceanid Trade Mission

Sunrise.

A light breakfast was eaten. The troupe gathered. Hugs were given. Excitement overrode tears.

Littlerock had packed his belongings including the Titan's gifts to Pumi. He also carried a large featureless rock that had been split open to reveal myriad strange structures inside plus a collection of smaller red rocks. These rocks did not behave in the manner a rock was expected to behave. These treasures were for Littlerock's personal study.

Enceladus had loaded his sled with the trading items Metis and her sisters had collected from the tribe. A great many items.

The four young Oceanids ran and hugged their parents in a tearful goodbye.

All were prepared. They set off on their grand adventure. The Oceanids broke into a raucous traveling song.

They traveled with haste and reached the great river on the morning of the fifth day. They traveled upstream until they saw Riverport on the other side. Enceladus took a mental note that markers and some way stations would have made the trek easier. They stood on the banks across from Riverport so that the Portmaster, Doris, could ascertain how many people and how much baggage needed to be transported. She selected an appropriate vessel and sent one of her captains, a girl not yet a woman, across to ferry the troupe back across.

The captain reached the other side and spoke respectfully to Littlerock who, she remembered, was a stonecutter of great significance, but, otherwise, just an elder traveler. But she became excited upon learning of her women passengers. She raised the flag to show that she was transporting a great dignitary, perhaps even Metis. "All must be on their best behavior!"

Before they docked, word spread through Riverport that Metis might be onboard. The girls gathered around to hopefully meet her. The story was told that Metis could swim underwater for an hour, catch a fish in her mouth, eat it, and swim for another hour before coming up for air. The older girls thought the story apocryphal, but the younger children believed it might be true. Metis, ever one for a grand entrance, greeted each admirer

ELDER OCEANIDS: Metis, Tyche, Clymene, Eurybia, Amphitrite
ELDER OLYMPIANS: Hestia, Demeter, Hera, Hades, Poseidon, Zeus
OTHER: Philyra, Dionysus, Heracles, Outis, Enceladus, Littlerock, Porphyrion

with a touch on the shoulder and a warm greeting. One could never have too many sisters.

Doris was excited to see her four sisters but was somewhat relieved to hear that they were here on a trade mission and would not be staying. Doris's position as Portmaster was safe.

After the baggage had been unloaded, Littlerock said goodbye and continued on to Tallstone. The traders spent the night singing with their sisters.

Sunrise

The Oceanids set off for Urfa. Arriving, Metis presented herself and her companions to Paravi. "We are Oceanids from the far west come to trade."

The girls seemed familiar, but she could not place them, nor did she recognize the tribe, 'Oceanids.'

"You are all so young, children. Why did your elders not come with you?" Paravi asked.

Metis explained, "We gathered our items to trade by ourselves. Our elders said that we would gain experience and that anything we could trade for would be acceptable. Our elders did not wish to travel this far just to trade what we have to offer."

"I think I see," Paravi laughed. "There are two smaller tribes camped to the east of Tallstone. Gain your experience with them. If you are not successful, return to Urfa, and our traders will give you a little something for what you have."

"Smaller tribes?" Metis said. "I would prefer to trade with those who have much to trade."

"Yes, I'm sure you would, Sweet. But the traders at Urfa are quite skilled and deal only in large transactions. You understand, I'm sure."

"Very well," Metis said. "May we tell the tribes that Great Elder Woman Paravi directed us to them?"

"You certainly may, and on your return home I would be delighted to see what items you may have received in trade."

PRINCIPALS: Kiya, Vanam, Pumi, Valki | ELDER TITANIDES: Themis, Mnemosyne, Phoebe, Tethys, Theia, Rhea | ELDER TITANES: Rivermaster/Oceanus, Sagacity/Coeus, Starmaster/Crius, Watchman/Hyperion, Piercer/Iapetus, Cronus

"You are kind and merciful, Great Elder Woman Paravi," Metis said. The four young women smiled and then left to return to Enceladus who had remained behind tending their treasures.

On the path to Tallstone, Tyche said, "That was not exceedingly fruitful."

Metis laughed. "It was exceedingly fruitful. Honey and seashells are the only items we have for trade their traders would not recognize as being made by Titans. That would complicate things and put us at a disadvantage. These smaller tribes will not associate us with Titans. The name will not even come up. No, Sister. The first round of talks goes to the Oceanids. When we get to Tallstone, let's split up and get all the information the Scholars have about these two tribes, and I hear they are a nosy bunch."

The Oceanids hurried along, making plans and singing.

< >

It was late evening when they reached Tallstone. Metis presented the Oceanids to second-in-command Master Skywatcher Littlestar.

"Oceanid Metis," Littlestar exclaimed. "Littlerock returned late last evening. I will tell him that you are here. He told me that you came to trade with Urfa. What brings you to Tallstone?"

"Great Master Littlestar, Master Littlerock spoke so highly of you and the Scholars of Tallstone, we wanted to come and see the wonder of Tallstone for ourselves. That, plus two tribes are camping to the west who might trade with us. We are young and inexperienced and might do well to gain experience by trading with smaller tribes rather than starting with the skilled traders of Urfa."

Littlestar laughed. "That may be true, but Littlerock suggested that you might be well matched to trade with even Paravi, herself."

Metis was demure. "Both masters are most kind. May we camp here tonight? We would love to visit and see the wonders of this place."

"Of course, you may. Join our guild for dinner. Afterward, I will ask acolytes to give you a tour and explain what we do here. Exposure to young women will be wonderful training for our young men."

ELDER OCEANIDS: Metis, Tyche, Clymene, Eurybia, Amphitrite
ELDER OLYMPIANS: Hestia, Demeter, Hera, Hades, Poseidon, Zeus
OTHER: Philyra, Dionysus, Heracles, Outis, Enceladus, Littlerock, Porphyrion

Demure Metis replied, "You are sooo kind. We would be thrilled to accept your invitation. And we could also talk about the tribes to the west. Could each of us be guided by our own acolyte? We could learn so much more that way."

Littlestar said, "That would be excellent. We gather near the tall stone at sunset." He left the women to make their camp. *You are correct, Littlerock. With Paravi herself.*

That evening, after her tour, Metis sought Littlestar. "Kind Master, these are poor gifts, but my sisters and I would like to at least give you tokens of our appreciation for your kindness to us so that you will remember us with affection." With that, she handed him seven highly polished stones.

Littlestar inspected the stones. "'These are exquisite, Metis. Thank you. We Skywatchers can use them in our measurements. You will do well with your trading tomorrow."

They exchanged more pleasantries and retired to their beds.

He thought, *With Paravi herself!*

Sunrise

The girls set off to the west toward the two campsites. They chattered among themselves.

Eurybia: "The hunters will all be on the hunt. The women will be out gathering. We may not find an elder to trade with."
Metis: "Someone will be there."
Tyche: "The first camp is the poorer of the two, but they have wildebeest pelts and a few linens."
Clymene: "Starling told me that the first tribe is extremely well off. They only pretend to be poor so they don't have to share with other tribes, and they can make better trades."
Tyche: "Starling?"
Clymene: "Yes, my escort last night. Quite handsome and well-spoken."
Tyche: "Eww."
Clymene: "I didn't let him eww me. We just talked a lot"
Eurybia: "Did we bring any arrowheads?"
Metis: "Yes, Piercer gave me a double handful of good ones."

PRINCIPALS: Kiya, Vanam, Pumi, Valki | ELDER TITANIDES: Themis, Mnemosyne, Phoebe, Tethys, Theia, Rhea | ELDER TITANES: Rivermaster/Oceanus, Sagacity/Coeus, Starmaster/Crius, Watchman/Hyperion, Piercer/Iapetus, Cronus

Metis then said, "Eurybia, you carry the ointments and arrowheads. Offer those first. A poor tribe can always use arrowheads and honey and maybe some healing ointments. Rich tribes have less use for arrowheads and their elder women make their own ointments."

Eurybia asked, "Who told you that?"

"I listen, thank you. Clymene, you carry the honey and seashells. You can offer them depending on what happens with the arrowheads. Tyche, you offer the colored stones for trade only if they are wealthy. I'll offer the necklaces if they are wealthy."

Tyche said, "There's a camp in the distance."

They stopped and Enceladus distributed the items each girl requested and then made himself a spot in which to wait.

Metis presented the Oceanids to the camp elder woman who was dressed in rags and hobbled around. She rasped, "I will be delighted to trade with you. We need so much and have so little, but I do have some linens and a little rope that might interest you."

"Wonderful!" Eurybia said as she placed arrowheads and a jar of ointment on the table. "This ointment heals a hunter's wounds. It works well."

The elder woman inspected the arrowheads and sniffed, "These are of inferior quality, but you appear to be a nice young girl. I believe that I can offer you a fine piece of linen for all of this." She pulled a piece of linen from a pile nearby and placed it on the table.

Eurybia feigned delight with the offer.

Metis broke in, "That linen was made by a child in training. Do you have any of good quality? Something worthy of our trade?"

The elder woman turned to face Metis. They engaged.

Three intense hours later, Metis motioned for Enceladus to come to them.

He arrived. Metis loudly complained. "This elder woman has taken advantage of children. All she was willing to trade were some linens for every valuable thing we had. I am so ashamed."

Tyche whispered to Enceladus, "Pack these carefully. They are exquisite."

ELDER OCEANIDS: Metis, Tyche, Clymene, Eurybia, Amphitrite
ELDER OLYMPIANS: Hestia, Demeter, Hera, Hades, Poseidon, Zeus
OTHER: Philyra, Dionysus, Heracles, Outis, Enceladus, Littlerock, Porphyrion

The elder woman said, "You are quite accomplished Metis. There is another tribe farther on. Go there and offer one of my exquisite linens. Perhaps, you can trade it for their chief's son or at least a hundred pelts."

Demure Metis said, "You are most kind, Elder Woman. Here, I keep this polished stone in my pocket. It means too much to me to trade. Please take it as a gift for your kindness."

The elder woman smiled and bid them good trading.

The Oceanids traveled to the next camp. All went well.

After trading was finished, a third tribe arrived unexpectedly. It was quite wealthy.

Return Triumphant

More Oceanids returned to Overlook Point than had left. Sisters from Riverport had joined them. Upon their arrival, the horn was blown. Flags went up.

After a triumphant entry, all gathered around the family table to meet the newcomers and see what the Traders had brought back in trade. Enceladus began setting items on the table, the linen first.

Metis asked, "Theia, we got a lot of this linen. Is it all right?"

Theia looked at the linen with awe. "They are exquisite, Metis. I have never seen linen so finely made and so strong. There is enough here to make new garments for everyone. More than enough."

"And these pelts?" she asked, as Enceladus stacked many fine-looking pelts on the table.

Theia was in shock by the material with which she had to work.

"Now this is the good stuff," Metis said as she helped unpack rawhide, strong threads, skins of serpents and lizards, and two great horns. "They liked the seashells. Oceanids can retrieve seashells in massive quantities. Piercer can teach us how to pierce holes in them. We could use some of this thread to make seashell bracelets and necklaces to go with your rock necklaces. They would be such fun to wear."

On and on they talked, admired, and thrilled at what lay before them.

PRINCIPALS: Kiya, Vanam, Pumi, Valki | ELDER TITANIDES: Themis, Mnemosyne, Phoebe, Tethys, Theia, Rhea | ELDER TITANES: Rivermaster/Oceanus, Sagacity/Coeus, Starmaster/Crius, Watchman/Hyperion, Piercer/Iapetus, Cronus

After a joyful evening meal, the Titanides and the Oceanids retired to Theia's quarters for planning and gossip. During the gossip, Metis inquired, "Mother, may I ask you a question?"

Tethys replied, "Of course, you can, Metis. What is it?"

"Have you ever mated upside down in a tree?"

Rhea's sweet drink spewed out her nose.

Tethys calmly said, "That's an unusual question, Metis. Why do you ask?"

"We visited Great Mother Valki after our trading was done. She told us all about mating and things. Things I had never heard of before. Different positions and techniques and things like that. I wasn't ready to mate before our trip, but I think maybe I am now. But I have got to find a male that is interested in me and not just any female to mate with, at least that's what Mother Valki told me. She said that we may have to find an interested male and then train him. You never mentioned these things to us. I was wondering why."

"Well, that is interesting, Metis. You may know more about these things than I do. Different positions and techniques, you say? Exactly what else did Mother Valki tell you?"

The women talked into the night with gasps of disbelief mixed with giggles.

ELDER OCEANIDS: Metis, Tyche, Clymene, Eurybia, Amphitrite
ELDER OLYMPIANS: Hestia, Demeter, Hera, Hades, Poseidon, Zeus
OTHER: Philyra, Dionysus, Heracles, Outis, Enceladus, Littlerock, Porphyrion

11. The Seduction of Pumi

The Titans worked feverishly to prepare for Pumi's upcoming visit.

After an evening meal, Themis said, "Mother, we need to talk."

Kiya replied, "Of what shall we talk?"

"Not here, Mother. In your quarters."

"My goodness. Let's retire to my quarters and solve great problems."

Themis, Mnemosyne, Tethys, Phoebe, and Rhea walked with Kiya, in silence, to Kiya's room and made themselves at home.

"You are all quiet and somber," Kiya said. "What problem do we discuss?"

Themis replied, "Mother, you have so much to plan for Pumi's coming. The affairs between Titans and the rest of the world will be decided—our trade and our relations. Not only that, but Pumi is from your old tribe and the brother of Chief Vanam. He is an old friend; a person of much importance to the world; a man deserving of much respect."

Tethys said, "These considerations are best left to your leadership and guidance. It is another subject we wish to discuss."

Kiya asked, "That subject being?"

Phoebe said, "We five already know the answers to our questions, Mother. Our concern is that you don't yet know and your worry over these matters will take your attention away from the other things."

Kiya frowned with the suspicion that this conversation might not be to her liking. Sternly, she asked, "The subject being?"

Themis cleared her throat, paused, and asked, "Mother, do you wish to mate with Pumi?"

Kiya was livid. "THE IMPERTINENCE! THAT IS MY CONCERN! NOT YOURS!"

Themis replied in kind, "MOTHER! CONTROL YOUR VOICE! ANSWER MY QUESTION!"

PRINCIPALS: Kiya, Vanam, Pumi, Valki | ELDER TITANIDES: Themis, Mnemosyne, Phoebe, Tethys, Theia, Rhea | ELDER TITANES: Rivermaster/Oceanus, Sagacity/Coeus, Starmaster/Crius, Watchman/Hyperion, Piercer/Iapetus, Cronus

Flustered, Kiya responded, more calmly, "I shall decide in good time. My daughters need not concern themselves with this."

Phoebe responded, "Dear Mother, we are not here to pry. We are here to counsel. Do you think us witless? Even unmated Rhea has insights for our coming discussion."

Kiya responded, "Coming discussion? This discussion is ended!"

Themis stood. "No, Mother. This discussion has not yet begun. Explain to us why you reacted so violently to such a simple question."

Before Kiya could answer, Mnemosyne quietly said, "The answer is obvious, Mother. This has been weighing heavily on your mind and you have not yet reached a decision." She paused, "Have you?"

Kiya, no longer in control of the conversation, contritely answered, "No."

Themis knelt before her mother, took both of her hands, gazed into her eyes, and said, "You know what you wish to do, but you have yet to accept it. Accepting it opens a world of unknowns and uncertainties. That is why we are here, to counsel you on these things. You may be our all-wise mother, but we have the collected wisdom of two mated daughters, two worldly daughters, and an innocent one with a vivid imagination."

She paused. "Do you want to mate with Pumi?"

Kiya lowered her head, removed her hands from Themis's, and put her hands over her eyes. Meekly, the reply came, "Yes."

All but Themis jumped up with cheers and gathered around her.

Themis: "Now, that wasn't hard, was it?"
Tethys: "This is going to be wonderful."
Theia: "Will you have a child?"
Rhea: "What if he doesn't want *you*?"
Phoebe: "You think he may refuse you, don't you?"
Themis: "He may want you, but he has Vanam to contend with."
Tethys: "And Valki."
Rhea: "And, what if you mate and you don't please him?"
Tethys: "You didn't always please Father, did you Mother?"
Rhea: "What makes you think you would please Pumi?"

ELDER OCEANIDS: Metis, Tyche, Clymene, Eurybia, Amphitrite
ELDER OLYMPIANS: Hestia, Demeter, Hera, Hades, Poseidon, Zeus
OTHER: Philyra, Dionysus, Heracles, Outis, Enceladus, Littlerock, Porphyrion

Themis held up her hand for silence. "Mother, between us, we have all the answers. What Pumi thinks is of no importance. You will give him no choice in this important matter. My Oceanid daughters told us many things concerning mating techniques that they learned on their visit with Great Mother Valki. Phoebe and I have practiced these techniques to the great delight of ourselves and our mates. We will tell you how to please Pumi beyond your greatest desires."

Through quiet tears, Kiya looked at her daughters. The women talked into the night with gasps of disbelief mixed with giggles.

The First Gala

The day of Pumi's expected arrival came. Exactly at the expected time, the horn of Overlook Point sounded. Flags went up. Pumi plus two honored guests plus a party of twelve were on their way to Tartarus.

Torches were lit. The greeting party gathered on the patio. Every girl and woman wore a fine linen dress made especially for and only to be worn when a party of important guests was visiting. Their dresses were all tightly form-fitting sewn specifically for the wearer. Themis had laughed that she would not be able to eat for fear she would rip a seam in her dress. The dresses were knee-length with a finished slit up the left leg to facilitate walking and sitting. The deeply plunging neckline could be adjusted by varying the tension on the fine cord connecting stone buttons on either side of the Vee. The color of the buttons was selected by each female from Piercer's collection of polished stones. Piercer then made each a necklace to match the buttons. The length of each necklace was personalized for the wearer. Each wore a bracelet of seashells. The older ones had applied red berries to their lips. They laughingly referred to this as their 'party dress.' Sagacity quipped that the women were dressed as if they wished to 'attract a decorative male' to their side. He proclaimed each one to be extremely 'attractive.'

Enceladus met Pumi and his party at the circular path and directed them into the adjacent guest house where they could rest and freshen up. He provided all with cups of fresh water and told of the location of the toilets.

He explained to Pumi, "When you are ready, walk down the path toward the fire pit. Titans will be standing in line to introduce themselves to you

PRINCIPALS: Kiya, Vanam, Pumi, Valki | ELDER TITANIDES: Themis, Mnemosyne, Phoebe, Tethys, Theia, Rhea | ELDER TITANES: Rivermaster/Oceanus, Sagacity/Coeus, Starmaster/Crius, Watchman/Hyperion, Piercer/Iapetus, Cronus

and your guests. Sweet or bitter drinks will be provided as will be pleasant conversation on the other side of the fire pit. You will sit at the end of the long table facing Kiya. Kiya sends her deep regrets that she is indisposed and cannot join your distinguished party until mealtime. Will there be anything else, Master Pumi?"

"Yes," Pumi said quietly. "I have a problem requiring some discretion. The elder woman from Urfa, Paravi, does not wish to sit at the same table as Kiya nor look at her unless unavoidable or speak to her or be spoken to by her. Paravi is here as an observer. Only!"

Enceladus replied, "I understand, Master Pumi. I will make the necessary adjustments. It will be as you desire."

Pumi said, "We will be a while. Apparently, we need to dress for dinner."

Enceladus found Themis. They discussed the Paravi problem. Outis busied himself in the cooking area preparing food. The Oceanids stood ready to provide each guest with a sweet or bitter drink, as requested.

Enceladus took a position at the guest house. The door opened. Pumi appeared. "Are you ready, Master Pumi?"

"Yes."

Enceladus led them to the head of the path leading to the gathering patio and loudly announced, 'Titans, I present Master Pumi of Tallstone and his company."

The hosts formed lines on either side of the pathway. At its head was Rivermaster facing Tethys; next was Sagacity facing Phoebe. The Titans, by age, completed the line. Themis, standing in for Kiya, stood at the foot of the line.

Pumi walked to the head of the line, considered what he saw, and stepped aside leaving his entourage to face the Titans.

Pumi loudly announced, "I present Master Stonecutter Littlerock of Tallstone with a guest." Pumi nudged Littlerock to enter the receiving line and speak to each host. Paravi followed close behind, nose in the air, neither speaking nor acknowledging anyone in the receiving line. After each guest finally spoke to Themis, Metis and her sisters asked each if they

ELDER OCEANIDS: Metis, Tyche, Clymene, Eurybia, Amphitrite
ELDER OLYMPIANS: Hestia, Demeter, Hera, Hades, Poseidon, Zeus
OTHER: Philyra, Dionysus, Heracles, Outis, Enceladus, Littlerock, Porphyrion

would prefer a sweet or bitter drink. Paravi realized to her horror, that these were the young trader women.

As Littlerock was speaking to Themis, Pumi pushed three young stonemasons forward and announced, "These three young men were apprenticed to Master Littlerock and are now accomplished stonemasons. They hope you will consider accepting them into your city. They promise to work hard and not eat too much."

The three young men, nervous and confused, made their way down the receiving line.

He waited a few moments and announced, "These three young builders were apprenticed to Master Builder Putt of Urfa and are now expert builders. They hope you will consider accepting them into your city. They promise to work hard and eat less than the stonemasons."

He pushed them into the receiving line.

Waiting again, Pumi then said, "These three young women have studied and worked with the premier farmer in the world—Valki of Urfa. They are learned in the way of einkorn and of moving, planting, and growing all manner of plants. They hope you will accept them into your city."

The girls gaily entered the receiving line without prompting. "And finally, three young men who wish to join your city whom I had to scour the land for. They come from only one tribe from the far, far east. They can do almost anything, and each has the strength of ten men. They are called Gigantes; giants in their ability to perform acts of great strength. They will eat much more than the others."

The Gigantes moved down the line, serious and intense."

Each reached Metis and said, "Yes, I will accept your drink. Thank you."

Metis demurely told their leader, Porphyrion, "I will make yours *very* bitter."

And then, Pumi stepped to the head of the path and stood for a moment. The torches illuminated him. He wore a robe of almost white bearskin. Six blue buttons of stone ran down either side of the front, the buttons were connected with fine rawhide. The color and texture of the bearskin heightened and intensified the rich, dark blue of the buttons. On his head,

PRINCIPALS: Kiya, Vanam, Pumi, Valki | ELDER TITANIDES: Themis, Mnemosyne, Phoebe, Tethys, Theia, Rhea | ELDER TITANES: Rivermaster/Oceanus, Sagacity/Coeus, Starmaster/Crius, Watchman/Hyperion, Piercer/Iapetus, Cronus

Book 2. The Beginning of Civilization: Mythologies Told True

he wore a headband made of the same bearskin. Attached to the headband were twelve highly polished blue stones, catching and reflecting firelight like brilliant stars in the firmament. He then looked at and smiled slightly to Rivermaster and Sagacity; then looked at and smiled more broadly to Tethys and Phoebe; then removed all smile, straightened his back, and stared directly down the line into the eyes of Themis 'standing in for Kiya,' and grandly announced to all present, "I am Pumi of Tallstone."

He then walked the line, graciously speaking to each person. Reaching Themis, he said, "I am sorry Kiya missed this pageantry. Is she well?"

Themis smiled and said, "Sister Mnemosyne did not miss it, she will tell of it in excruciating detail many, many times. And, yes, Mother is well. She feared she could not survive this much fun. She is freshening up and will join you at dinner. And now ..." she motioned toward Metis, patiently waiting for his order.

"Bitter, please."

After allowing everyone to mingle, Themis escorted her guests to their assigned seating at the various tables. She began with the youngest. She instructed them to take their plate to the serving table and take whatever food they might like. She asked Pumi to seat Paravi at the table with the three new farm girls and facing toward the sea.

After all were seated except the senior attendees, Themis excused herself to check on her mother.

She hurried to Kiya's quarters and briefed her on who was there, including Paravi, an extremely snooty elder woman who was probably a spy of some kind. They selected a suitable gift for Littlerock, and Kiya insisted that Paravi also be given a gift. They discussed the presentation. Preparations finalized, with gifts in hand, Themis turned to leave but then turned to again face Kiya. "Remove all concern from your face, woman. You are the most attractive and desirable queen who has ever lived. Act it!"

She turned and returned to the feast. She nodded to Rivermaster to seat the remaining guests. He instructed them to select their food and where they should sit. Rivermaster was the last to re-seat himself. Themis rang a bell. All talking stopped. All instinctively looked down the torch-lit path.

ELDER OCEANIDS: Metis, Tyche, Clymene, Eurybia, Amphitrite
ELDER OLYMPIANS: Hestia, Demeter, Hera, Hades, Poseidon, Zeus
OTHER: Philyra, Dionysus, Heracles, Outis, Enceladus, Littlerock, Porphyrion

The door opened. Kiya stood framed in the door for a moment as she surveyed her domain. She then began her slow walk toward her party. Torchlight illuminated her.

Her children were impressed.

Themis: *MOTHER!!!!*
Sagacity: *My goodness, Mother, you look better than anybody.*
Rivermaster: *She walks like a river flows.*
Piercer: *Mother Kiya, you look different tonight.*
Tethys: *She looks like a nursing mother. Her breasts are so big.*
Metis: *Fluid. Like Oursea waiting to embrace you.*
Watchman: *Her hair shines like a star-filled night.*
Outis: *Is that the smell of jasmine?*

Theia watched her mother closely. *I put too much support in the top and the dress is too tight. I should have made it looser. The slit is too wide. It exposes more leg than I would like. And the vee for the neck may expose too much. Is the color too red? Your makeup is exquisite. Oh, Mother, I hope you like it. You look incredible.*

Pumi stared at her. *You are younger now than when we were not much more than children. How is this possible, Kiya? What potions do you hide? What secrets do you have? Have you mastered time itself?*

Then Pumi of Tallstone, in full regalia, stood to greet the Queen.

All stood.

She slowly passed her chair and held out both hands to Pumi. He left his chair, met her halfway down the table, and took her hands.

"You are as lovely as ever," he said.

"You are as persuasive as ever."

Pumi said, "Your tribe gives a fine festival."

"Well, yes, and let's enjoy the festival while we may. You and I must follow this with serious, awkward negotiations concerning the future of me and my children. But until then, let us laugh and enjoy the evening."

Pumi looked into her eyes. "Serious? Awkward? I will do the best I can."

PRINCIPALS: Kiya, Vanam, Pumi, Valki | ELDER TITANIDES: Themis, Mnemosyne, Phoebe, Tethys, Theia, Rhea | ELDER TITANES: Rivermaster/Oceanus, Sagacity/Coeus, Starmaster/Crius, Watchman/Hyperion, Piercer/Iapetus, Cronus

"Let us enjoy this, Pumi." She smiled broadly and released their hands. Both returned to their seats.

Dinner was loud and festive. As the sweetbreads were being served, Kiya rose and rang her bell.

Kiya began. "We are delighted to have such distinguished guests this evening. I would like to thank Master Littlerock for his interest in our little settlement. My children have selected two gifts for you. One for you to keep for yourself and one to give to any friend you might wish to honor. We Titans express our gratitude that you will counsel with us."

She paused, "Themis, present these gifts to our guests."

Themis took two necklaces to Littlerock. He stood. Themis held up a polished stone necklace of red and gold stone, flanked on both sides by seashells. In the center hung a large rock, split in half, exposing countless small perfectly smooth purple obelisks. Littlerock stared at it with astonishment. "May I place it around your neck?" Themis asked.

He simply shook his head, "Yes."

Paravi had turned her head slightly so that she could cut her eyes to see what was happening.

Themis placed the necklace over his head and said, "I give you a second necklace that you might wish to present to your guest. The necklace would be from you, of course, not from my family. With that, she handed him a similar necklace, missing the large centerpiece but containing many more seashells. Themis nodded slightly toward Paravi in case Littlerock did not understand what he was being asked to do.

Littlerock stood. Confused.

Pumi offered, "Do you think Elder Woman Paravi would enjoy such a necklace, Master Littlerock?"

Paravi stiffened and tore her gaze away from the scene.

Littlerock now understood. "Oh, yes, Master Pumi. Let me ask." With that, he walked to Paravi, now staring straight ahead, sitting as if she were made of stone. He said, "Elder Woman Paravi, I have a beautiful necklace, almost as beautiful as you. Would you accept this as a gift from me?" In

ELDER OCEANIDS: Metis, Tyche, Clymene, Eurybia, Amphitrite
ELDER OLYMPIANS: Hestia, Demeter, Hera, Hades, Poseidon, Zeus
OTHER: Philyra, Dionysus, Heracles, Outis, Enceladus, Littlerock, Porphyrion

his innocence, Littlerock was sometimes slow comprehending a thing, but once comprehending, was quite accomplished in handling it. He held the bracelet to the side of her face.

She cut her eyes toward it. It was magnificent beyond belief. She jerked her head toward the table and said, "Lay it there. I will consider your gift."

Littlerock laid the necklace on the table and returned to his seat admiring the necklace around his own neck.

"Wonderful!" Kiya exclaimed. "I am so excited that we shall have new members for our tribe. Brave new members. Brave enough to leave a world they know and settle in a completely new, unknown land. And with talents that will make our settlement an even more lovely and bountiful place to live. I welcome each of you and look forward to meeting each of you and hearing your story. Welcome, all!"

She paused. "And now, our final gift for a most honored guest. Themis, present our gift to Master Pumi of Tallstone."

Pumi stood and faced Themis. "The citizens of Tartarus are too kind," he said as Themis reached him and held out a long narrow gift covered by linen. "What have we here?" he asked, looking at Kiya, as he took the proffered gift into his hands. He removed the linen from the top and looked down, in disbelief, at a walking stick carved from the finest marmaros rock, covered with the symbols of his civilization; intricate and beautiful. Inset at the top was the large geode of blue crystals complementing the polished blue stones in his headband and sparkling like stars on a cool night. Pumi was speechless. He said nothing but stared without expression at Kiya. His back straightened, he stood, held the walking stick high above his head, and slowly turned so that all could see.

A quarter of the way around, the Titanides could no longer stand it. They began, "Pu-mi ... Pu-mi ... Pu-mi ... P..."

Completing the turn, he held up his hand for silence. He looked toward Littlerock with consternation. "Can we match this, Master Littlerock? I think not. I am embarrassed, Kiya, but at least I have a gift for you. Littlerock told me that he would take care of this matter. I was not allowed to be involved or offer my advice. Master Littlerock, present Kiya of Tartarus with our gift, no matter how inadequate it may be."

PRINCIPALS: Kiya, Vanam, Pumi, Valki | ELDER TITANIDES: Themis, Mnemosyne, Phoebe, Tethys, Theia, Rhea | ELDER TITANES: Rivermaster/Oceanus, Sagacity/Coeus, Starmaster/Crius, Watchman/Hyperion, Piercer/Iapetus, Cronus

Littlerock walked toward Kiya with the wrapped gift held low. When he reached her, he said "Titan Piercer will you join me?" Piercer jumped up and ran to stand beside his Master. Littlerock said to Kiya, "Only this afternoon was I able to inspect this gift which Apprentice Piercer and I discussed on my recent visit. I think you will be pleased. Apprentice Piercer, present Kiya with her gift from Pumi."

Kiya stood. Piercer took the gift from Littlerock and proudly presented it to his mother. Pumi looked on with intense interest. Kiya smiled as she took the gift from Piercer. Seeing the shape of the package and feeling the weight, she froze. She knew what it was without looking. She looked first at Piercer, then at Littlerock, then at Pumi as she removed the wrapping. She stared at it for a moment. Instead of a geode of blue, it contained a geode of green. An infinitely beautiful green encompassing every green of the earth; brilliant, sparkling green. With both hands, she raised the engraved marmaros walking cane high into the air and slowly turned it for all to see.

"Ki-ya ... Ki-ya ... Ki-ya ... K..."

She laughed and waved her cane in the air with one hand. "Isn't this all so wonderful?" she shouted above the revelry. "Everyone mingle and meet your new family. I must now enter difficult trade negotiations with our guest. Go mingle, everyone. Mnemosyne, Oceanids—sing a party song! Goodnight, all!"

With that, she stepped to the side of the path holding her walking stick in her left hand. She looked at Pumi, placed her right hand on her stomach, and held out her elbow as an obvious invitation that Pumi should enjoin his arm in hers and escort her to her quarters.

To negotiate.

Negotiating

They entered her main room. She lit two more torches and laid her walking stick on her table. She stared at it. "It is magnificent, Pumi."

He laid his walking stick beside hers, "They are identical except for the color of the stones."

ELDER OCEANIDS: Metis, Tyche, Clymene, Eurybia, Amphitrite
ELDER OLYMPIANS: Hestia, Demeter, Hera, Hades, Poseidon, Zeus
OTHER: Philyra, Dionysus, Heracles, Outis, Enceladus, Littlerock, Porphyrion

She said, "Piercer calls them geodes. They are a new kind of rock more beautiful than others. He still studies them and has much to learn."

She paused. "Here, let me take your cloak. It looks uncomfortable. Leave on your headband. It looks quite handsome." She removed his bearskin cloak and placed it on a chair on the far wall.

Two chairs faced one another with a small fire pit to provide light between them. She said, "Sit. I will bring us drinks. Bitter, I believe is your preference."

The chairs were oversized. Pillows had been placed in them to make them soft and comfortable. She handed Pumi his drink. Standing, she lifted her drinking cup and said, "May our negotiations be fruitful."

He raised his cup and said, "And may the fruit be sweet." They drank.

She sat but did not sit upright in her chair like Pumi. Rather, she leaned back a little more than one might expect, arms not at her side but spread open laying on the wide arms of the chair.

She remembered her instructions. *Not too formal, not too relaxed. Supreme confidence without looking lazy. Show deference, but without fear. Remember, you are a woman, he is just a man. The right to trade Titan goods at Riverport during the Winter Solstice Festival is all we want. The Oceanids can be our traders. No original Titan needs to cross the river. Is that too much to ask? Once he agrees, then you can move on to other things—to seal the agreement, so to speak. Remember to control your skirt. Shift your leg to show as much or as little leg as appropriate. And the Vee of your dress. If you drop your shoulder exactly right, you can make the strap slide off your shoulder. Don't lean too far back or show too much until after you have our agreement."*

She remembered the consensus of her daughters, *Oh, Mother. You are going to have so much fun.*

Kiya said, "And so, Pumi, what issues must I and my children overcome?"

Pumi replied, "I have a major problem, Kiya. You have another. Mine is Vanam. He has word that you still live. I used my words of persuasion to no avail. He remains angry. Extremely angry. He expected you and your children to wander desolate plains and painfully die one by one. You last, after you watched each of your children die. It was not your banishment he wanted. it was your death in misery. I don't know what you did to create this hatred. I saw it grow within him slowly. After he became Chief, after the birth of his first son. I only saw him at the Winters Solstice Festivals. Each year, he was a little more powerful, a little angrier; with me, with the world, apparently with you. I sought him in the north before I sent Littlerock here as my emissary. He had banished you. I wanted to hear the facts, the truth, from him. Not words distorted by the retelling by many people. He did not welcome me. He did not give his permission for me to contact you as much as he would not forbid it. I cannot soften his heart in this matter, Kiya. If you trade at Riverport, he will bring his hunters and destroy Riverport. He will be enraged when he hears of how you prosper. As horrible as the words, I believe him capable of taking your life."

Kiya responded, "YOU DON'T KNOW WHAT I DID TO HIM! Pumi, is that what you just said? I REJECT the statement, the inference, and the attitude!" Then more gently, "You understand, I'm sure."

"I apologize for my choice of words. But you understand my position."

Kiya asked, "What do the other chiefs think of Vanam?" *You are still a little afraid of me, Pumi!*

"All acknowledge the Clan of the Serpent is the most powerful tribe in our part of the world. They have more hunters, spears, gatherers, and more wealth. Simply more of everything. And Vanam acts the part. He shows deference to no chief. He disrespects the scholars and the work of the people of Urfa. He strides the land as if he owns it. His hunters follow his lead as do his gatherers. He disrupts the peace and tranquility of our land. A Titan presence at Riverport would infuriate him."

"Whether Titans trade at Riverport or not, your problem remains. Our trade adds only a little drama to this landscape.

"My concern is for the safety of your traders, Kiya."

"I see. Your problem is Vanam. What is *my* problem?"

"The elder women of Urfa, of course. Valki would welcome you with open arms, but you know, full well, the elder women will have nothing of it. Paravi came so that she could spy and witness first-hand the despair and desolation the Titans live in. The immigrants from Urfa she allowed to come were all ones she wished to see gone; too lazy, too slow, too

ELDER OCEANIDS: Metis, Tyche, Clymene, Eurybia, Amphitrite
ELDER OLYMPIANS: Hestia, Demeter, Hera, Hades, Poseidon, Zeus
OTHER: Philyra, Dionysus, Heracles, Outis, Enceladus, Littlerock, Porphyrion

different. 'Let them go to those despicable Titan people.' What she sees here will not change things. The elder women of Urfa are rigid, and they simply will not accept Titans."

He hesitated, "You appear amused."

She laughed softly and said, "No, Pumi. I am not amused." She leaned a little farther back in her chair, spread her hands a little farther apart, and stared past Pumi over his right shoulder, deep in thought."

"I can solve your problem, Pumi. Can you solve mine?"

"Oh?" he asked as he clasped his hands and leaned closer.

Kiya shifted her gaze to Pumi, leaned forward, and said, "I see the future clearly. I know myself and I now know Vanam. Vanam was the average son of an average chief; sometimes rich in food, sometimes starving. Vanam had one resource no one else had, a talented little brother who was 'different.' The little brother who could carve things into rocks and inspire hunters. You can fill in the rest of that part of the story. You went on to change the nature of our kind. Tallstone, Urfa. You may not have done that much yourself. But you were always around when new things were getting done. Einkorn, scholars, Tallstone, monoliths, observatories, domesticated animals, towns. And against all this, Vanam worked extremely hard. He was the best hunter in the land. But every great thing he did was lost in the shadow of the latest thing his little brother had done. His wonderful little brother. Then his first son was born, then his second, then more. They grew. He was concerned they would not grow to be great hunters like he was. I see now that he was constantly belittling them. Taking away their confidence. They grew into fine young men, but they were 'different.' Different like his little brother was different. Did you know Vanam constantly accused me of having your children?"

She paused. "Well, did you?!"

"No."

"Well, he did, Pumi. He did!" She closed her eyes for a moment, then said, "He made them different and then blamed me and you for their difference. Truth be told, they are finer sons than he deserved. Isn't that funny? I find it funny. But you see your problem, my dear Pumi? He

PRINCIPALS: Kiya, Vanam, Pumi, Valki | ELDER TITANIDES: Themis, Mnemosyne, Phoebe, Tethys, Theia, Rhea | ELDER TITANES: Rivermaster/Oceanus, Sagacity/Coeus, Starmaster/Crius, Watchman/Hyperion, Piercer/Iapetus, Cronus

thinks you are the father of my sons. It is himself he hates the most, then me, then you. He will never be as good as Pumi of Tallstone. But he will not challenge you; he is not man enough. But for me and my children? If we live and do not suffer, Vanam will not rest."

She stared at her drink for a long time. "Pumi, grant me the right to trade at Riverport during Winter Solstice. The Oceanids can be our traders. No original Titan will cross the river. Is that too much to ask?"

Pumi said, "It's too dangerous, Kiya. You must not do it."

"That is a good answer, but not to the question I asked. Do you forbid it?"

"No, of course not, but ..."

She held up her hand for silence. "Do you respect me, Pumi? Do you respect my judgment? My ability to handle the things which need handling?"

"Of course, Kiya, but ..."

Again, she held up her hand for silence. "I have my plan Pumi, I am confident. You need to do nothing but remain out of my way and let the stars whisper things stars whisper to you. Don't be afraid for me or my people. I see the future. You will like it."

She leaned a little farther back in her chair, uncrossed her legs, and accidentally displayed a little more skin. "Now, that we have our understanding that the Oceanids will trade at Riverport, our negotiations have concluded. Let us now remember our youth."

She sipped her drink. "The first time I saw you, you were a child. A child disappointed that I would not be joining his family. You were so precocious. So very precious." She smiled in remembrance. *But you never even asked me to mate when you grew up and had your chances! I'm getting excited!*

She shifted slightly in her chair; a sleeve accidentally slipped exposing her shoulder.

He said, "We went on our expedition to find new gathering lands. You were so much older and more sophisticated than me. I may have been a little frightened of you."

"Yes, you were."

ELDER OCEANIDS: Metis, Tyche, Clymene, Eurybia, Amphitrite
ELDER OLYMPIANS: Hestia, Demeter, Hera, Hades, Poseidon, Zeus
OTHER: Philyra, Dionysus, Heracles, Outis, Enceladus, Littlerock, Porphyrion

"We found wonderful places, but I got dressed down by my father and you got to sit and snuggle with Vanam."

"We were close, then."

"I never said anything improper, but you never let yourself be alone with me."

"I didn't want you to ask me to mate because I wasn't sure what I would do." She made no pretense of sitting up straight. Just leaned back on the couch and said, "Did you want to couple with me, Pumi? I was a full-grown woman. I knew things. I am alone with you now and you aren't even noticing."

He sat in silence staring at her.

"You look so nice in your headband. I want to see you standing in front of our fire holding your scepter and wearing your bear-skin headband. Nothing else. I will name our son Cronus. I hope you approve."

He sat in silence for a long while, then rose, picked up his scepter, walked to the wall, and let his tunic fall to the floor.

A simple tug at the seam holding her dress together allowed her to remove her dress before he turned back around. He turned, saw her lying there naked, walked back, and stopped at the fire. Her gaze never went to his face. She allowed her eyes to widen and her lips to part as she stared intently at his groin. He began to rise. She stared more intently until he had a full erection. She slowly lowered her left hand, palm up, still staring at the erection.

He walked to her waiting hand.

How do my daughters know these things?

Sunrise

Pumi planned to depart after the morning's meal. All Titans and guests were already gathered before the two leaders appeared. The Titanides discreetly glanced at their mother's face as she approached.

Sagacity asked with excited innocence, "Did the negotiations go well?"

Pumi replied, "Queen Kiya is an excellent negotiator. She received everything she desired."

PRINCIPALS: Kiya, Vanam, Pumi, Valki | ELDER TITANIDES: Themis, Mnemosyne, Phoebe, Tethys, Theia, Rhea | ELDER TITANES: Rivermaster/Oceanus, Sagacity/Coeus, Starmaster/Crius, Watchman/Hyperion, Piercer/Iapetus, Cronus

Kiya smiled a smug smile. The Titanides sat back in relief.

The conversation was animated and happy. Pumi and his entourage finished the meal, gathered their baggage, paid warm farewells, and began their journey back to the east.

Kiya told her children that she would enjoy some time to herself. They would plan their future actions that afternoon.

More tired than she would admit, Kiya returned to her quarters. On the table, she found parchment upon which was written, "My first attempt. Not good but I kept it. I give it to you."

Under the parchment was a small, flat, circular engraved rock. On one side was a figure of a man hunting. On the other, five points of light identifying the constellation Stillhunter.

ELDER OCEANIDS: Metis, Tyche, Clymene, Eurybia, Amphitrite
ELDER OLYMPIANS: Hestia, Demeter, Hera, Hades, Poseidon, Zeus
OTHER: Philyra, Dionysus, Heracles, Outis, Enceladus, Littlerock, Porphyrion

12. The Sundering of Vanam

The visit between the Heads of State had been a tremendous success. Quarter-moons came and went.

Then, the horn sounded at Overlook Point. The flags went up.

Enceladus read the flags and sought Kiya. "Vanam comes. He is accompanied by ten others but none of rank. The warning flag also flies."

"He is earlier than I anticipated," Kiya said. "I thought he would wait until after the festival. He must be angry. We must prepare."

Enceladus trumpeted a horn and then stood behind Kiya's chair, where she now sat. The Gigante Porphyrion hurried to her side and stood at alert attention as everyone within the horn's sound gathered.

When Porphyrion saw all had gathered, he commanded, "Position to Defend!" Instantaneously, all those gathered circled and faced away from Kiya in a crouched, defensive position with daggers drawn. Waiting.

Kiya stood, surveyed the situation, and said in a loud voice, "I am well defended!"

Porphyrion commanded, "Return to Alert!" All immediately replaced their daggers to their hidden places and relaxed. The talents of Porphyrion had been immediately noted by Sagacity and Kiya. He had been tasked with training everyone in Tartarus in his art of self-defense. He was an excellent teacher. They were excellent and conscientious students.

The queen addressed her people. "Vanam is coming with ten hunters. He possibly comes in peace to bring me flowers but, then again, he may come in anger to bring me death. The truth probably lies between. You have been instructed on your response in all cases. In the latter, Porphyrion will command you. Metis, you and your Oceanids will entertain. All Gigantes will remain near my table. All others take your position and be gracious to our guests. Fear nothing. We know ourselves. We know our adversary. We cannot fail."

With that, her daughters joined her at the table; daggers hidden but readily accessible. Her sons went to their quarters to be out of sight unless 'War' was proclaimed.

PRINCIPALS: Kiya, Vanam, Pumi, Valki | ELDER TITANIDES: Themis, Mnemosyne, Phoebe, Tethys, Theia, Rhea | ELDER TITANES: Rivermaster/Oceanus, Sagacity/Coeus, Starmaster/Crius, Watchman/Hyperion, Piercer/Iapetus, Cronus

Enceladus met Vanam and his hunters at the guest house on the inner circular pathway, "Greetings, Great Chief. Which Great Chief may I announce has arrived?"

"Take me to Kiya! Never mind, I see her sitting there." Vanam pushed Enceladus out of the way and stormed toward Kiya and her daughters.

Enceladus reached for his dagger but remembered his rigid training and relaxed. Whether he approved or not, he understood his orders.

Ten hunters followed close behind.

Kiya addressed him as he arrived at the foot of her table, "Ah, Vanam. I did not hear you announced. Please, sit and join us for drinks."

Metis ran up and asked, "Sweet or bitter drink, Great Chief?" The other Oceanids stood nearby looking at the hunters with wide-eyed admiration and giggles.

Vanam was taken aback by the confident reception he and his hunters were receiving. Somewhat less in anger, he replied, "I want no drink from the likes of you. You are to leave this land. You are to remove yourself and all your fellow scum to lands far beyond my reach."

"Oh, Vanam," Kiya replied. "It will sadden me so much to leave this land. How long do I have? Why do you command this? I have broken no terms of our banishment. At least sit and tell me exactly what I have done that you disapprove of. Please. Sit. Dismiss your hunters to be entertained by the Oceanids. They are local girls and were not banished as were I and my children. Please. Sit!"

She waved toward a chair that Enceladus immediately pulled out for him to sit on.

Vanam looked around, waved a hand to dismiss the hunters, and sat down.

Kiya looked at Metis and said, "I believe he prefers Sweet," then looked at Vanam and smiled. "So, tell me, Vanam. What exactly have I done to raise your anger against me?"

"You exist!" he snapped.

"Yes, but Vanam, what is it I have done? Other than 'exist,' of course. Tell me what it is I should have done so that I would not have raised your anger."

ELDER OCEANIDS: Metis, Tyche, Clymene, Eurybia, Amphitrite
ELDER OLYMPIANS: Hestia, Demeter, Hera, Hades, Poseidon, Zeus
OTHER: Philyra, Dionysus, Heracles, Outis, Enceladus, Littlerock, Porphyrion

"You exist! That is the only reason you need! I will not have you near my lands or any land I can travel to or any land I hear of. If I hear of you, then you are too close."

"You aren't giving me much to work with, Vanam. It appears the only thing I can do is pack up my children and move to the ends of the earth. Is that my choice?"

"That is your only choice!"

"And if I cannot or will not do this thing then what will happen?"

"Then I will kill your children while you watch and then I will kill you!"

"Oh, dear. That sounds so distressing." Kiya called to Metis as she tarried making Vanam's drink, "Metis, dear, make Vanam's drink *very* sweet. Make sure each of his hunters partakes in your specialty drinks. And ask Enceladus to prepare a special evening meal for our guests. Understand?"

"Perfectly, Queen Kiya," Metis called back.

"I need to keep you and your hunters properly entertained while I consider my choices. Maybe this sweet drink will sweeten your disposition," she said as Metis delivered the drink.

Vanam merely snorted and stared at her.

"That's the nicest thing you have said to me in ages," she laughed. "But until evening meal is served, at least tell me of your tribe. I am told that you are the greatest chief in the land. Rich and powerful beyond my imagination. Is this true?" Kiya knew her enemy.

He said, "Yes, I will tell you of the greatness of the Clan of the Serpent." He did not remember that Kiya had helped him make it so.

Kiya leaned against the table with her chin on her clasped hands listening with rapt attention. Although, she did once interrupt with "more drink for our guests." Her left strap accidentally slipped exposing her shoulder.

Enceladus announced that food could be obtained at the warming table. Vanam and his hunters had been smelling the wonderful smells of the cooking meats. Kiya had them all sit at her tables. Vanam looked around and saw that he and his hunters were the only ones eating. He observed, "No one but us is eating."

Kiya replied, "Everyone realizes they are not worthy to sit at this table with you. We are getting used to our new station in life."

"Oh," Vanam said, pleased.

As each finished eating, the Oceanids forced more drinks on their guests.

"The little dears are trying to get your hunters to like them," Kiya observed. "Is there any chance of that?"

They are associated with you, but I will at least consider their fate."

"Thank you, Vanam, you are merciful and kind." The right strap of her dress had accidentally slipped down. "And now, the Oceanids want to show your hunters Oursea. Unless you are afraid of me, of course. But they will be close enough to hear if you call them loudly. May your hunters go? I would like to retire with you to our guest quarters so that I can finish our discussion on what it is you wish me to do. I have learned much since we last met. I would like to show you some of it."

Vanam was feeling relaxed and grunted acquiescence. The hunters went to the sea with the Oceanids. Vanam went with Kiya to the guest quarters.

Upon entering, Kiya said, "Your tunic is dirty from your travels. I will have it cleaned for you." She pulled the tunic over his head leaving him standing in only his loincloth. "The loincloth, too!" She placed the loin cloth with his tunic and lit a small fire for illumination. "Sit there." She pushed him aggressively into the chair beside the fire. "I will sit here."

She stepped toward the chair across from him as her tunic slipped from her body leaving her unclothed. She sat down. "Nothing you haven't seen before, Vanam." She leaned back in her cushion-filled chair, arms wide apart, legs uncrossed, knees slightly apart. "Now, dearest Vanam, let me make sure that I understand. I have violated no term of my banishment and now you demand more from me. If I do not meet these new terms, then you will kill my children and then me. Do I understand correctly?"

He mumbled, "Yea. Tha's right." His tongue was thick.

ELDER OCEANIDS: Metis, Tyche, Clymene, Eurybia, Amphitrite
ELDER OLYMPIANS: Hestia, Demeter, Hera, Hades, Poseidon, Zeus
OTHER: Philyra, Dionysus, Heracles, Outis, Enceladus, Littlerock, Porphyrion

"Dear Vanam," she exclaimed with delight as she pulled her legs into a lotus position. He was staring at her as he had when they were young. "Do you remember the other understanding we have? The one about what I would do to you if you threatened my children?"

Vanam thought, *She is threatening me!*

He stood. His arms were heavy; his mind was confused. Anger? Desire? Fear? Confusion.

She held out both hands to him. He reached out to her. She took his hands and pulled him onto her. She whispered into his ear, "Remember the tricks I told you about? Shall I demonstrate a few as we mate one more time, Vanam? Oh, you aren't up for it? Too tired? A long day? Well, tomorrow will be an even longer day."

She whispered, "I know that you can still hear me, my protector. My answer to your demand is 'No!' We will discuss this in the morning but just so you know tonight, my answer is 'No!'" She held his naked body close to her naked body until she was sure he was unconscious.

She rose and dragged him to the large table nearby. She waited a while, sitting in her chair, looking at him lying there. *This night was inevitable, Sweet. You do not know yourself. You do not know me. What chance did you ever have?*

She rose and took her cutting knife from the belt of her discarded tunic. *I could stand here and get teary-eyed and sentimental over this, Vanam. But I think not.*

She placed his limp hand against her bare belly. *I could have been cruel and hurt you. I could have described Pumi's baby growing inside me and the details of how I moaned with pleasure as he put it there. His name will be Cronus. But let's not dwell on these things.*

She held the handle of the knife to her abdomen. *Let Cronus feel the blade, Vanam. He and I will do this thing together.*

She moved the blade with quick and accurate motion. *Easier than gutting a fish. Not as much blood as one would think.*

She staunched the flow of blood and took ointments from inside a drawer in the table. *This one is for healing, Vanam. And this one is for pain. Some of it, anyway. I am not cruel. I do not want to hurt you. I do not have to apply these things,*

PRINCIPALS: Kiya, Vanam, Pumi, Valki | ELDER TITANIDES: Themis, Mnemosyne, Phoebe, Tethys, Theia, Rhea | ELDER TITANES: Rivermaster/Oceanus, Sagacity/Coeus, Starmaster/Crius, Watchman/Hyperion, Piercer/Iapetus, Cronus

but I will. Also, I will give you a supply to carry with you. With good fortune, you will heal well enough. But your mating days are over. If you are wise, you will disappear from the land. You were wise once. Have I made you wise again? We will talk tomorrow. I will take all your spears for safekeeping. Goodnight, Vanam. Sleep well.

She dressed and called for Enceladus. He collected all the weapons which had been left in the area. Kiya thanked him and asked him to check with the Oceanids and make sure all went well with them.

She then took the package to her room where she treated the flesh with oils and ointments to preserve it for a long time. She then went to Theia's room, knocked, entered, and handed the package to her, saying, "I would like to wear this at tomorrow morning's meal, if possible."

"It will be finished by then, Mother. Was it difficult?" Theia asked.

"Not at all, Theia," Kiya said as she was leaving. "One does what one must do. It is only difficult if one is unsure of what one must do. Goodnight."

Sunrise

Kiya sat at the table watching the sun rise as Theia arrived with the necklace. "A long night?" Kiya asked.

"Not at all, Mother. It is only long when one is not doing something one is interested in. This was interesting. Look what I have made." She held a bib to her chest. "It's not a proper necklace. I took a piece of Rivermaster's bearskin and made a bib you can hang around your neck. You can attach anything you want to the bib. I thought about decorating it with seashells or stones or red berries, but I finally decided plain, unadorned testicles and penis would make the most dramatic presentation. What do you think?"

"It's grand, Theia. You made it from the same bearskin that Pumi wears. I like that! You have outdone yourself. Tie it around my neck."

Theia rose and tied the bib around her mother's neck. "It goes well with what you have on, Mother. I think you can wear it with almost anything."

Her other daughters began arriving. Each admired her bib as they laughed and joked. Enceladus brought fruits and nuts for breakfast.

ELDER OCEANIDS: Metis, Tyche, Clymene, Eurybia, Amphitrite
ELDER OLYMPIANS: Hestia, Demeter, Hera, Hades, Poseidon, Zeus
OTHER: Philyra, Dionysus, Heracles, Outis, Enceladus, Littlerock, Porphyrion

Oceanids began coming up from the sea. They joined the women, eating fruits and staring wide-eyed at Kiya's bib.

Metis arrived at the table. "Very impressive, Grandmother! Ouch!"

The Oceanids sat eating, making random comments:
"Mine passed out before he could be any fun."
"Mine didn't even have a self-protection dagger."
"They aren't scary at all."
"Do we get to watch Chief Vanam eat lunch with Queen Kiya?"
"Can we eat lunch with the hunters? That would be a lot of fun!"
"Are we sure they are going to wake up?"
"Are they going to be mad?"

Kiya said, "All are welcome to do as they wish. Everyone did such a wonderful job last night. But remember, we are still in negotiations. Every word we say, every inflection in our voice, every glance must be to accomplish our purpose. There is no room for gloating or smart remarks or angry retorts or snide observations no matter what is said or done. I am sure you all have your daggers hidden on you. Our goal is to simply state, 'We are here. We are staying. Oceanids will trade at Riverport during winter's solstice. We mean no harm. We will do no harm. We will not allow ourselves to be harmed. Go in peace.' And don't add 'or die!' That is for me alone to say. Am I understood?"

Variations of 'yes' were heard; along with one, "Ouch!"

Understanding

Late in the morning, the hunters began straggling up from the beach. They were greeted by enthusiastic Oceanids bringing them nuts and drinks to clear the fogginess in their head. Strangely, none of the hunters noticed Kiya sitting at the head of the main table. They were talking happily with the Oceanids when a roar was heard from the guest building.

"Oh, dear," Kiya said. "I think Chief Vanam just woke up. He may be angry, everyone."

Several hunters looked at Kiya and then noticed her bib. It took long seconds for them to realize what they were looking at.

Vanam came roaring out of the guest house rushing toward the table.

PRINCIPALS: Kiya, Vanam, Pumi, Valki | ELDER TITANIDES: Themis, Mnemosyne, Phoebe, Tethys, Theia, Rhea | ELDER TITANES: Rivermaster/Oceanus, Sagacity/Coeus, Starmaster/Crius, Watchman/Hyperion, Piercer/Iapetus, Cronus

Kiya smiled at him. The Gigantes removed their defensive daggers, letting them be seen. The hunters tensed. Their weapons, they now noticed, were not where they had left them.

As Vanam reached the table, Kiya commanded, "Stop! Don't be the fool, or this disagreement ends here in a pool of your blood!"

The Gigantes took a step forward, their blades in attack position.

Vanam grabbed the end of the table with both hands and clamped down hard. "What have you done, woman?" I will wash this land with your blood and the blood of everyone who has ever looked upon you."

"Oh?" she replied. "I hope you will have a change of heart. We wish you and your people no harm. We wish only to live in peace, without threat. Free to trade at Riverport once each year. This is not too much to ask. This is all you need to agree to. Now, sit down. We will feed you."

"I will stand!"

"Oh, yes. Of course."

To Themis, she said, "Sweet, bring Vanam a jar of the healing ointment and a jar of the ointment to relieve his coming pain."

To Enceladus, she said, "Enceladus, bring these men meat to eat on their way out of our land."

To Vanam, she said, "Vanam, understand that you now live under my sentence of death. Come again across the great river and you will be killed. Whatever men you bring with you will be killed. Attack Oceanids at their trade and you will be killed. Raise your knife against me or my children at any time or for any reason and you will be killed. This is not a threat. This is the agreement you entered last night. It would not have been honorable to kill you when you were helpless, and my terms had not been explained clearly. They have now been explained. I hope you will leave us in peace."

Vanam replied, "A lovely speech, Kiya. You understand that I will return with a hundred hunters and kill you all."

"I shall measure you by your deeds, Vanam. Leave us in peace."

"There will be no peace," he spat.

ELDER OCEANIDS: Metis, Tyche, Clymene, Eurybia, Amphitrite
ELDER OLYMPIANS: Hestia, Demeter, Hera, Hades, Poseidon, Zeus
OTHER: Philyra, Dionysus, Heracles, Outis, Enceladus, Littlerock, Porphyrion

Think hard on this, Vanam. Leave us in peace. Now, leave our land. Do not return. The Gigantes will track you until you cross the river. You will have no weapons. Goodbye, Vanam. May we never meet again. One of us would surely die."

She rose, turned, and left for her quarters.

Vanam glared after her, turned, gathered his men, and stormed up the path toward Overlook Point.

Themis handed a sack of food and ointments to one of the hunters, saying, "He will need this for later. Enjoy!"

After they had gone, Theia observed, "I'm disappointed! No one commented on Mother's beautiful bib."

The Oceanids, too, had observations:
"A hundred hunters against us doesn't seem like a fair fight."
"We would kill them before they crossed the river."
"If they get past Overlook Point, I will be surprised."
"I play fought one. He wasn't good."
"If he brings a thousand, we might have a problem."

No one was afraid.

The Battle of Riverport
In the 44th year from the birth of Vanam

The Titans arrived across the river from Riverport the day after the start of the Winter Solstice festival and made camp in full view of all. Kiya's Riverport spies saw them and crossed the river to make their reports.

The first Oceanid reported, "The Clan of the Serpent arrived and made camp early. They were the first tribe to arrive. Three hunters from the clan have been watching the river. One of them left when he saw your camp being made. Another left when he saw me sail across the river."

Kiya asked, "Have they talked of requiring boats to take them across the river to meet us?"

"No," she replied, "But one girl heard them talking of burning any tables holding trade goods. They seemed to be looking forward to it."

PRINCIPALS: Kiya, Vanam, Pumi, Valki | ELDER TITANIDES: Themis, Mnemosyne, Phoebe, Tethys, Theia, Rhea | ELDER TITANES: Rivermaster/Oceanus, Sagacity/Coeus, Starmaster/Crius, Watchman/Hyperion, Piercer/Iapetus, Cronus

Kiya had her great chair set on the far-side dock; a command post where she could observe the activities of Riverport. Enceladus stood behind her. Her generals, Porphyrion and Themis sat beside her. They discussed strategy. The hope was that Vanam would see them, become enraged, and cross the river with his hunters to attack them. The hunters would make it halfway across the river and then be abandoned to float helplessly downstream to the mercy of whatever found them downstream. Vanam would, of course, be easily dispatched. A minimum loss of life. If the Titans tried to cross the river and enter Riverport, they would be defenseless against a rain of hunter's spears. If there was no change in conditions by the next morning, then the 'Metis Plan' would be initiated.

They sat and enjoyed the sunset and watched the activities of Riverport. That night, Metis swam unobserved to join her sisters at the port. She told them of the excitement to expect and what they should do. She returned with a boat upon which the Titans loaded low-value trading goods. They crossed the river late in the night and set up several trading tables well before sunrise.

Sunrise

The hunters from the Clan of the Serpent finally awoke, looked around, and saw trading tables that had not been there the night before. They walked over and demanded to know what this was. An Oceanid sweetly explained that the Oceanids would be trading here; would they like to trade some goods? A hunter snarled and knocked much of the merchandise to the ground. He was swamped with Oceanids boiling out of the woodwork biting, scratching, and ripping at his tunic. The hunter, with his friends, retreated in disbelief having no idea how to respond to an attack by girls. The Oceanids stood their ground in defiance; daring the hunters to do that again.

Kiya watched in great delight from the other side of the river. Porphyrion and Themis also watched; eyes riveted to the action.

They waited.

Vanam came with five hunters. Kiya saw them and waved at Vanam with an air of glee. Vanam saw her and stormed to the tables and pushed them into the water. Metis restrained her Oceanids but directed them to begin recovering the goods.

ELDER OCEANIDS: Metis, Tyche, Clymene, Eurybia, Amphitrite
ELDER OLYMPIANS: Hestia, Demeter, Hera, Hades, Poseidon, Zeus
OTHER: Philyra, Dionysus, Heracles, Outis, Enceladus, Littlerock, Porphyrion

Kiya stood, put her hands on her hips, and wagged a finger toward Vanam as a mother would scold a child. Vanam stared but otherwise ignored her and walked away from the scene.

Kiya spoke to her counsel, "He ignores my taunts. He will not cross the river to kill me. If I am to fulfill my oath, then I must cross the river and kill Vanam."

"My Queen," Enceladus exclaimed, "let me go and do this thing, or let Gigantes cross the river and kill Vanam and his hunters."

She replied, "Only one of us need die and it is I who must face him. His hunters do only as they are told and do not deserve death. This stain will be on my hands; no other."

Kiya spoke to Sagacity, "If I and Themis die, you will be the leader of the Titans. Return with Porphyrion to Tartarus in defeat. Build an army capable of defeating a hundred hunters. Then enter the hunting grounds you once knew, hunt Vanam down, and kill him. Spare as many hunters as you can but kill Vanam. Do as you will with the Clan of the Serpents. Titans shall trade at Riverport during the festival. If not this year, then next."

To the waiting Oceanid, she said, "Prepare a crossing boat for me and Themis. Prepare another vessel for the Gigantes. I will cross directly to the Riverport dock. Take the Gigantes across downriver as unobtrusively as possible. It must be over before the Gigantes appear lest someone say it was they, and not the Titan Kiya, who did this thing."

"Mother!" Sagacity protested.

She turned, held up her hand for silence, and commanded, "You are Titans! You shall conduct yourself as Titans. Now and forever!"

With that, she embraced each of her children.

Mnemosyne said, "I shall tell the story of this day for all time to come, Mother."

Kiya replied, "I shall try to make the story worth the telling."

Carrying her marmaros walking stick, she boarded the waiting boat. Themis boarded behind her. They crossed the river standing up hoping that Vanam would appear. Vanam appeared. *At last. Something happens as planned.*

PRINCIPALS: Kiya, Vanam, Pumi, Valki | ELDER TITANIDES: Themis, Mnemosyne, Phoebe, Tethys, Theia, Rhea | ELDER TITANES: Rivermaster/Oceanus, Sagacity/Coeus, Starmaster/Crius, Watchman/Hyperion, Piercer/Iapetus, Cronus

Vanam greeted her with cold silence, a wide stance, and crossed arms as she disembarked.

Kiya straightened her tunic as Themis stepped to the dock behind her. Kiya leaned against her walking stick, looked at Vanam, and sweetly said, "Vanam, I believe that you pushed my merchandise into the water. You were commanded not to do that and yet you did. Did I not tell you clearly that this will not end well for you?"

Vanam snorted, "Do as you will, Outcast Bitch!"

Kiya replied sweetly, "Vanam, you stated that you would kill me if I crossed the river. Your hunters heard you say this. Yet, I crossed the river, stand before you, and you have not killed me. Are you not man enough to do so? Are you afraid of a woman? Are you a coward in front of your hunters?"

His nostrils flared.

"A coward, a girl-man just like you accused your sons of being. Oh, I forgot—you are a girl-man, aren't you? I wear your manhood around my neck as a pretty necklace for all to see. Look at this, hunters of the serpent clan. This is why your Chief Vanam is a coward. Look at him and laugh at him."

She nodded to Metis, standing with her Oceanids at the edge of the dock.

The Oceanids began their chant, "Cow-ward ... Cow-ward ... Cow-ward ... C..."

Vanam scanned the crowd in fury.

"Cow-ward ... Cow-ward ... Cow-ward ... C..."

Kiya released her walking stick, raised her left hand, motioned for Vanam to come to her, and screamed, "Come and kill me, you weak, worthless, no-account, girl-boy coward!!!"

Vanam charged Kiya, his spear positioned to kill.

Kiya did as Porphyrion had trained her and which she practiced every morning. She closed her eyes, readied herself, and visualized each step he would take, her muscles relaxed, and she knew the choreography to which her body would now be commanded. She opened her eyes. *Poor Vanam.*

ELDER OCEANIDS: Metis, Tyche, Clymene, Eurybia, Amphitrite
ELDER OLYMPIANS: Hestia, Demeter, Hera, Hades, Poseidon, Zeus
OTHER: Philyra, Dionysus, Heracles, Outis, Enceladus, Littlerock, Porphyrion

She easily sidestepped his rush and slipped her dagger into his abdomen. He stopped. She grabbed his body, held him upright by his neck, and gently pulled the dagger upward toward his rib cage. His intestines spilled onto the dock. She held him tightly and whispered into his ear, "You are the greatest chief who has ever lived, Vanam. You are a better man than Pumi. Everyone says so. You are as great as the stars in the heavens, better than Tallstone. Better than all those pitiful things your little brother did. Can you hear me Great *Chief* Vanam?"

He gurgled a response.

She removed the dagger from his stomach and plunged it into his heart. She held the now lifeless body for a silent moment and then shoved it to the ground.

"Remove this travesty!" she barked at Metis. "Have Oceanids escort him to the most dismal part of the river they can find. And here, have one of them take this as they escort him to eternity." She tossed her necklace of flesh to Themis to give to an Oceanid. "Let her drag this in the water behind him to impregnate the earth with whatever furies he can father.

Enceladus emerged from the background and waited on orders.

She commanded, "Stand back, Gigantes. This is woman's work."

She then looked at Vanam's hunters wide-eyed in disbelief with no idea of what to do. It had been great fun up until just now. She strode toward them with a stern face. "You!" she commanded, "What is your name?"

"Armstrong," he replied. "You knew me when…"

She interrupted without pause. "You are now chief of the Clan of the Serpent. Tell your elder woman and other tribal elders. You are free to continue to roam whatever land you care to roam, or you may join me and settle near my land as you wish; I do not care. Tell your elders that the chief who declared me and my family outcasts is now dead and that I, Kiya, Queen of the Titans, declare our banishment ended. Anyone who disputes this may come and find me. I shall convince them of the truth of my words. You tarry! Why do you tarry? Go immediately and tell these things to your tribe and all others! GO!"

PRINCIPALS: Kiya, Vanam, Pumi, Valki | ELDER TITANIDES: Themis, Mnemosyne, Phoebe, Tethys, Theia, Rhea | ELDER TITANES: Rivermaster/Oceanus, Sagacity/Coeus, Starmaster/Crius, Watchman/Hyperion, Piercer/Iapetus, Cronus

Armstrong, confused but with orders, led his men back toward the camp of the Clan of the Serpent.

Kiya waved to summon the Gigantes to her. "Porphyrion, have all Titans cross the river with all our trade. Display everything; that for the poorer tribes first, for the richest, last, and fill in the middle. Keep all Titans on alert to defend to their death our right to be here. Enceladus, Themis, come with me as we visit this great festival. We will invite those who will listen to visit our traders at Riverport."

Kiya looked around and surveyed the situation. "Am I overlooking anything, Themis?" she asked.

"Only this and your change of clothes, Mother," Themis said as she handed her mother her walking stick.

Kiya walked and faced the Oceanids and the stunned random visitors on the dock. She raised her walking stick and proclaimed, "I salute Metis, the great leader of the Oceanids. I salute the Oceanids. May you always care for the waters of the earth and may the waters always care for you! I salute your greatness! Long live the Oceanids!"

Cheers greeted her proclamation.

She then said to Themis, "Let's go to Tallstone. I will change on the way."

Kiya led them down the road toward Urfa and Tallstone. Passing a grove of trees and out of sight of Riverport, she said to Themis, "Come with me. I will change here."

Out of sight of Enceladus, Kiya fell to her knees, leaned over, and vomited. And again. And again. Her body convulsed. She sat for a moment. "I am not cruel. I did not hurt him. I didn't!" She then stood.

Themis removed Kiya's bloody tunic, cleaned her face, placed a fresh tunic on her, and brushed her hair. Themis stood Kiya at arm's length, inspected her, and proclaimed, "You look fabulous, Mother."

Kiya laughed a strange laugh.

They rejoined Enceladus, and the three resumed their walk to the Tallstone Eighteenth Winter Solstice Festival.

ELDER OCEANIDS: Metis, Tyche, Clymene, Eurybia, Amphitrite
ELDER OLYMPIANS: Hestia, Demeter, Hera, Hades, Poseidon, Zeus
OTHER: Philyra, Dionysus, Heracles, Outis, Enceladus, Littlerock, Porphyrion

13. Winter Solstice Festival 18

The trio walked past the Clan of the Serpents without acknowledging the elders who gathered to stare at her passing.

Then, before them, stood the tall stone, the epicenter of all scholars. And beyond that, the mass of humanity of over twenty-four tribes meeting together in one place, once a year; to trade, to find a protector for young women ready to leave their tribe, for young men to compete in games of strength and games of skill, for women to gather and trade information about the plants and herbs they gathered and new things a woman could do with them, for chiefs to meet and discuss hunting and hunting grounds, and, as always, a place where skywatchers, stone cutters, and scouts could come together to increase their knowledge of their crafts.

And supporting the entire endeavor were the farmers of Urfa, supplying grain and countless loaves of bread.

The trio was a commanding presence.

Boys ran up to openly gape at Kiya saying:
"That's Kiya, Queen of the Titans."
"She has just killed the greatest chief in the land."
"Don't let her stare at you. You will fall dead."
"The Titans are at Riverport. They have more trade than any tribe here."
"Don't let Metis see you misbehaving. They say she can fly up to the heavens and then sweep down upon you like a hawk on a hare."
"That's her protector. His name is Enceladus. He has the strength of a hundred men."
"She killed Chief Vanam without even touching him."
"She spilled his insides on the docks and then sent his body down the river of death."

"Mother, your reputation precedes you," Themis whispered to her mother.

Kiya laughed as she called to an older boy who had been walking with them at a respectful distance. "Young man, come here!"

He hurried over to face her as she leaned on her walking stick. "I seek the richest tribe at the festival. Would you know where they might be?"

PRINCIPALS: Kiya, Vanam, Pumi, Valki | ELDER TITANIDES: Themis, Mnemosyne, Phoebe, Tethys, Theia, Rhea | ELDER TITANES: Rivermaster/Oceanus, Sagacity/Coeus, Starmaster/Crius, Watchman/Hyperion, Piercer/Iapetus, Cronus

"Y-yes, Great Queen Kiya. The richest tribes are the farthest away from the tall stone. Some say the Gigantes are the richest but there are many rich tribes there."

"Good. Take us there. And straighten your back. Stand tall."

The boy threw back his shoulders and marched the trio toward the encampment of the now richest tribe in the land; the Gigantes.

Alcyoneous of the Gigantes

They arrived at the campsite. Kiya asked to meet the chief.

The attendant replied that their chief, Alcyoneous, was not to be bothered. "He is meeting with two other powerful chiefs in his tent. He will not meet with you."

"Return and tell him that he will speak with me! I am Kiya of Tartarus."

The Gigante attendant had never known fear nor did he now, but concern did enter his mind. He did not take orders from a female, especially orders countermanding those from his great chief. Nonetheless, the woman stood there fully expecting her order to be carried out. He stood there a moment too long.

"NOW!" the woman barked.

In unfamiliar territory, the attendant hurried to his chief. "My chief, she says her name is Kiya. She will speak with you now. If you will, of course."

"Kiya? Kiya? KIYA! Of course! Pumi's Kiya. Well, why are you standing there? Bring her to me." He turned to two guests and explained, "She is the chief of a great tribe across the river in the far west. The Titan tribe. Her story is unbelievable. She is from the same tribe as Vanam, Pumi, and the Great Valki of Urfa. All were childhood friends. Unbelievable story."

Kiya entered without her companions. She bowed to the Chief and placed her clenched hand over her heart as a sign of respect. The Chief rushed and gave her a bear hug, a sign of respect and friendship.

"Well, Chief Kiya," Alcyoneous said, "you dare come to the festival? As I understand it, the lesser tribes must shun you; and the powerful Chief Vanam, himself, will kill you on sight. At least I am told such things."

ELDER OCEANIDS: Metis, Tyche, Clymene, Eurybia, Amphitrite
ELDER OLYMPIANS: Hestia, Demeter, Hera, Hades, Poseidon, Zeus
OTHER: Philyra, Dionysus, Heracles, Outis, Enceladus, Littlerock, Porphyrion

The other two chiefs nodded in agreement.

"Great Chief Alcyoneous of the Gigantes, it is my sad duty to inform you that the Great Chief Vanam is dead."

"Dead? How can this be? I met with him only yesterday. He is young and strong; at least strong for one of his kind."

She replied, "He was killed in battle this morning. He attacked someone with the intent to kill."

The chiefs murmured in disbelief:
"Impossible."
"Who would be powerful enough to kill Vanam?"
"An accident, perhaps. Maybe he tripped."
"Maybe ten men jumped upon him."
"Chief Vanam. Dead?"

Alcyoneous asked, "How did he die? Who could kill Chief Vanam?"

"He died with *my* dagger in his heart."

Stunned silence. "*You* killed him, Kiya?"

"Yes, the story is long and sad, and I do not wish to eliminate the joy that is in this meeting. Perhaps I can tell the story around an evening campfire. For now, may I extend the offer of friendship from my tribe to yours? Four members of your tribe have joined the Titans. They are extraordinary men in every way; extremely valuable and courageous. It was Porphyrion who taught me, and all Titans, the art of in-fighting. None of us, even the youngest fears an attack from any man, other than a Gigante, of course."

"Yes, Porphyrion is a master fighter and understands hand-to-hand combat, warfare, and how to build an army as well as any man I have ever known. He had one weakness—a terrible weakness—he could not deliver the killing blow. When Master Pumi came looking for some volunteers to give to this great woman in the West, I had three such men to offer Pumi. I don't remember what I got in return, but I am sure it was a just trade."

He paused and called his attendant. "More figs! Our best figs for my guests." He then remembered that he had not made proper introductions.

PRINCIPALS: Kiya, Vanam, Pumi, Valki | ELDER TITANIDES: Themis, Mnemosyne, Phoebe, Tethys, Theia, Rhea | ELDER TITANES: Rivermaster/Oceanus, Sagacity/Coeus, Starmaster/Crius, Watchman/Hyperion, Piercer/Iapetus, Cronus

He introduced Kiya to the other two chiefs, extolling the virtues and greatness of their tribes.

"With Vanam gone, we may find common ground between our tribes for trade and more planned encounters," one chief offered.

"Well, first, let us wait to make sure he remains dead." The other chief asked, "How dead is he, Chief Kiya?"

"Very," she replied, "and in several pieces."

The chiefs chuckled in admiration of the woman who had supposedly killed the great but not universally admired Chief Vanam.

The attendant arrived with a bowl of sweet-smelling, oddly shaped fruits. "Try this," the Gigante chief said to her, "You will find them to be delicious."

She tasted one and closed her eyes, "Hmmm. They *are* delicious. How long do they keep?"

"Best eaten within the week of harvest but dried and properly stored, up to a year."

"You bring them to trade?" she asked.

"Oh, yes. Figs are one of our most popular trading items."

She asked, "Do you have any specimens we might be able to plant? My land is fertile. Figs might grow well there. Meanwhile, I will take all the figs that you have."

"All that I have?" The chief laughed. "My dear Great Chief Kiya that would be quite a lot."

Kiya laughed, "I would hope so. I have many Titan mouths to feed, and none can be deprived of the sweetness of your wonderful figs. Perhaps you could have them delivered to Riverport tomorrow morning when your traders arrive to select their trade. Your figs would provide a delicious reward for my people there. And there are many mouths."

The chief was now serious, "You have sufficient merchandise to offer such a trade?"

Kiya laughed. "That is up for your traders to decide. But to relieve your mind trade only half what you have and see if I have anything remaining."

ELDER OCEANIDS: Metis, Tyche, Clymene, Eurybia, Amphitrite
ELDER OLYMPIANS: Hestia, Demeter, Hera, Hades, Poseidon, Zeus
OTHER: Philyra, Dionysus, Heracles, Outis, Enceladus, Littlerock, Porphyrion

"Who will decide what you give in trade?"

"Your chief trader or yourself if you deem the trip worthy of your time. I will have my oldest daughter, Themis, show you the grandness of my son's port and then escort you through our trading areas. She would then take you to the restricted area open only to the wealthiest tribes. You will take whatever you wish until our trade for half your figs is fulfilled. But know that for the second half, I shall be far less generous."

Alcyoneous laughed a great laugh. "It will be done!" he exclaimed. "And at tonight's campfire, you will tell the story of Kiya and Vanam!"

Campfire Stories

That night, Kiya told her story at the campfire. Alcyoneous and the visiting chiefs listened with great interest and admiration.

It was then Alcyoneous's turn to tell a story. He chose the story of his son who had died a man's death before he was even a man. "As the ranking boy in the tribe, it was his responsibility to protect the children and older women when the men were hunting. The old women of the tribe saw it all. A herd of antelope came stampeding from the south pursued by lions. The stampede was headed directly toward the children. My son hurried the children and women out of their path, but one child could not escape to safety. My son intercepted the lead antelope, grabbed its neck, and twisted its head to the side, changing its course. The herd turned just enough that the boy made it to safety, but my son could not escape his captive. The old woman saw the lions bring down the weakest antelope and they watched the herd disappear carrying my son with it. She called to her gatherers to search the fields for my son. They found him unconscious; battered, bloodied, barely alive. They made a stretcher, returned him to camp, and ministered to him as best they could. I and my hunters returned to camp the next day. I embraced my son goodbye and had my swiftest runners carry his stretcher to Urfa, where the greatest women of healing in all the lands lived. They ran through the night and well into the next day. They rested there for a day while my son was tended to. The women did their best but declared my son would not live. My hunters then left Urfa to let my beloved son, Enceladus, die in peace."

All clucked at the sadness of the story.

PRINCIPALS: Kiya, Vanam, Pumi, Valki | ELDER TITANIDES: Themis, Mnemosyne, Phoebe, Tethys, Theia, Rhea | ELDER TITANES: Rivermaster/Oceanus, Sagacity/Coeus, Starmaster/Crius, Watchman/Hyperion, Piercer/Iapetus, Cronus

Kiya said, "A story of heroism and greatness. Such stories sometimes live on after their telling. Now, excuse me. I must retire for a short time to attend to women's things."

She left their company and walked toward the tall stone. Midway through his telling, she anticipated the ending. She found Enceladus on one of the sitting rocks which surrounded the monolith. He rose when he saw her approach, but she waved him to sit back down and sat on the ground beside him. "You asked me not to mention your name in the presence of a Gigante. I have honored your request. Now I ask why?"

He sat silent for a while. "I once dishonored my tribesmen. I dishonored my father. I failed to protect my camp. I am ashamed. I have begun a new life. I hope to earn the respect of the Titans and prove myself worthy to be called a man."

"A man must face his dishonor lest it someday destroys him. I ask that you face yours. Here. Tonight."

"What you command, Queen Kiya, I shall do."

"I do not command it, Enceladus. This is *your* decision to make."

He thought and then said, "There is no better place than here. No better time than now. I will face my shame. What shall I do?"

Kiya replied, "I will tell your father that you stand under the tall stone waiting for the stars to whisper your fate. Your Father will decide."

She rose and returned to the campfire. *His loss would be a great loss to the Titans. I fear he will leave. I fear he won't.*

She sat down again at the campfire and said, "Chief Alcyoneous, I request an indulgence. I have another story to tell. One of far greater interest than my first little story."

All consented.

"This is a story as told to me by Master Putt of Urfa when he offered one of his best builders into my service. The story he told me is this: 'The builder who wishes to join the Titans came to Urfa as a boy many years ago. He was brought to us, battered and almost dead, on a stretcher carried by two strong men who had run two full days and a night …'"

ELDER OCEANIDS: Metis, Tyche, Clymene, Eurybia, Amphitrite
ELDER OLYMPIANS: Hestia, Demeter, Hera, Hades, Poseidon, Zeus
OTHER: Philyra, Dionysus, Heracles, Outis, Enceladus, Littlerock, Porphyrion

The stars whispered.

Alcyoneous gasped.

Titan Traders

Even though it was a half days journey from Tallstone, virtually all traders eventually wound up at Riverport. They came to see the blood of Vanam soaked into the dock and toured the lessor trading tables managed by demure Metis. They were provided refreshments by Portmaster Doris and her port Oceanids. Most traders were allowed to at least look upon the Titan riches in the restricted trading area.

The Titans did what they had set out to do! They had established their right to trade, and they were good at it. They had traded all their goods halfway through the festival. They spent the next two weeks trading up from what they had acquired in trade. The figs, those that had not yet been eaten, brought in far more than they had cost. Kiya networked with the chiefs and was accepted by the elder women of Urfa; not happily but fearfully. The Titans, if not embraced, were at least being accepted.

Not until a defeated Paravi extended an invitation for Kiya to visit the Urfa encampment, did Kiya present herself to Valki. Their public official greeting was observed by many people. Kiya had become a celebrity; a position she neither sought nor dispelled. After the formal public meeting, the two women retired to Valki's private quarters, embraced, and cried in each other's arms.

< >

The Titan's departure from Riverport was a spectacle. Metis was in her element of water, high drama, and excitement. Songs were sung as the Titanides crossed the great river.

The return to Tartarus was uneventful. Those returning were met with excitement by those who had remained. There were many stories to tell; and much to catch up on. Metis's first action was to run to the shore of her precious sea. Her second was to shed her clothes and dive in.

Piercer was thrilled to return to his mountains and his rocks. His supply of colored stone had been depleted in trade, but he had learned what products excited the traders. He was anxious to harvest his rocks and

PRINCIPALS: Kiya, Vanam, Pumi, Valki | ELDER TITANIDES: Themis, Mnemosyne, Phoebe, Tethys, Theia, Rhea | ELDER TITANES: Rivermaster/Oceanus, Sagacity/Coeus, Starmaster/Crius, Watchman/Hyperion, Piercer/Iapetus, Cronus

improve his proficiency in turning them into useful and desirable trading items. He was excited that his master, Littlerock, might migrate to Tartarus to study with him.

"There is so much to learn there," Littlerock had told Pumi. "Such opportunities must be carefully considered."

The evening meal was attended by every Titan. Themis and Mnemosyne told their stories; the death of Vanam; the meeting between Kiya and the Gigantes; Enceladus' reunion with his Father; Kiya's reunion with Valki, the discovery of figs, the great wealth their trade had brought the tribe, and on and on.

Kiya commented that she was thrilled that Enceladus would remain a Titan and many at the festival inquired into the possibility of joining the Titan tribe. She had met every chief at the festival. Some had initially spurned her but as her fame and notoriety grew, so did their interest in meeting Great Queen Kiya. An interest she cultivated.

The talk turned to the happenings at Tartarus. The four farmer girls excitedly reported that their projects had proceeded nicely. The einkorn they had planted in the vast field beyond the 600-pace circular path was beginning to show signs of growth. The flowering plants they had found that the bees favored had been successfully transplanted. They were well on their way to learning how to harvest and replant the seeds to increase the density of the plants. They were studying how to transplant and propagate the various shrubs and trees which had been identified to add fragrance to the great meeting-place patio, and the possible trees to line the path from Overlook Point. They were excited about the promise of twelve fig trees soon to be delivered as a gift from the Gigantes tribe. At Urfa, the farmer girls had been restricted to only growing einkorn. At Tartarus, they had been encouraged to expand their art to encompass all living plants. They accepted the challenge. They thrived. The farmer girls had already taken control of their fertile land.

Titans were no longer outcasts. The name 'Titan' was being viewed in a new and different light. They were on their way to becoming a respected tribe in the known and rapidly changing world.

A world that one day might, perhaps, change too much.

ELDER OCEANIDS: Metis, Tyche, Clymene, Eurybia, Amphitrite
ELDER OLYMPIANS: Hestia, Demeter, Hera, Hades, Poseidon, Zeus
OTHER: Philyra, Dionysus, Heracles, Outis, Enceladus, Littlerock, Porphyrion

14. Birth of an Empire
In the 45th year from the birth of Vanam

Seasons passed. Rocks were harvested. Building progressed. Songs were sung. Plants and Kiya's belly grew.

The Birth of Cronos

In the sixth season after the Winter Solstice, Themis commanded that her mother be taken to lay upon the great dining table. The women gathered linen, healing ointments, and heated water. All Titans were invited to attend the impending birth of Cronus. All Titanides were in attendance as were Enceladus, Porphyrion, and Outis. Unfortunately, the Titanes had pressing duties demanding their attention elsewhere.

The child, Cronus, was born perfect in every respect.

In their known world, there were only two female heads of state—Valki of Urfa and Kiya of Tartarus. Without discussion, Themis would become Queen if Kiya became unable to rule. Kiya had many fine sons, but none had the talent nor desire to lead a large clan or manage a great city. Of her daughters, Themis was unquestionably the most capable of doing these things. The birth of Cronus introduced a possible new contender for leadership. Neither Kiya nor Themis were concerned that Cronus might grow to become a more capable leader than Themis. If he did, so be it. This was of no concern to any Titan. No Titan would lift a finger to solicit leadership. No Titan would lift a finger to avoid leadership.

Kiya and her children had consciously left the path of their ancestors. They no longer blindly obeyed the commands of a chief but instead their decisions were based on what benefited the most people regardless of their tribe. Whatever decision was best for the majority of people would be the decision made. They understood that any personal short-term loss would result in future long-term gains, and, if not, what difference?

To do otherwise was outside their comprehension.

Two Women

In the seventh season, the horn blew at Overlook Point. Pumi's flag was raised. He had two respected guests and a company of others.

PRINCIPALS: Kiya, Vanam, Pumi, Valki | ELDER TITANIDES: Themis, Mnemosyne, Phoebe, Tethys, Theia, Rhea | ELDER TITANES: Rivermaster/Oceanus, Sagacity/Coeus, Starmaster/Crius, Watchman/Hyperion, Piercer/Iapetus, Cronus

Kiya was genuinely surprised, but Themis had expected it.

Preparations began immediately. Party clothes were donned. Kiya selected a simple white tunic. Food was prepared. Metis had been experimenting with different herbs and fruits for her sweet and bitter drinks. She was in her element.

The guests were met by Enceladus and escorted to the guest house to freshen up. After a while, Enceladus left the guest house to position himself to announce their guests.

The receiving line formed with Kiya holding Cronus at the end of the line. The guests were seen milling behind the shrubbery ready to make their entrance. Kiya waited excitedly for Pumi to be introduced.

Her blood turned cold as Enceladus announced, "Titans! I present Great Mother Valki of Urfa."

Kiya had not expected this. And yet, how could she *not* have expected this? She had never considered that Valki would know that Pumi fathered her child. How stupid of her. She watched as Valki graciously acknowledged and spoke to each member in the line, which was now quite long. Valki wore a red dress eerily similar to the one Kiya had worn to seduce Pumi.

After forever, Valki stood before Kiya. "Is this your son? May I see his face?" She looked down at the child. "He is beautiful! I am so proud of you and Pumi. I have never been able to bear Pumi a child. I am thrilled that it is you, Kiya, who has given him this gift. I hope to hold him after this pageantry is over. Please, let me hold him, later."

"Titans! I present Master Pumi of Tallstone."

Kiya quickly said to Valki, "Stand by me, Sister. Hold Cronus to meet his guests and his father." She delivered Cronus into Valki's arms. "Let us greet his guests together."

All unspoken issues were acknowledged and resolved.

Pumi stood for a long moment, letting his hosts see him in full glory with headpiece, robe, and walking stick. Before stepping forward, he looked down the long line into the smiling face of Valki holding his son.

ELDER OCEANIDS: Metis, Tyche, Clymene, Eurybia, Amphitrite
ELDER OLYMPIANS: Hestia, Demeter, Hera, Hades, Poseidon, Zeus
OTHER: Philyra, Dionysus, Heracles, Outis, Enceladus, Littlerock, Porphyrion

After speaking to everyone in the line, after kissing Valki on her nose, after taking Cronus's hand into his, after staring for a long time deep into the eyes of Kiya, he turned to the waiting Metis and said, "Sweet, please."

"Dung!" Metis turned and hurried away to replace the Bitter she had waiting for him.

The next guest was Master Stonecutter Littlerock of Tallstone. During the reception, he requested admission into Titan society as an assistant to Piercer so that the two could explore and master the wonders contained in colored rock.

A cheer went up. A chant began, "Lit-til-rock ... Lit-til-rock ...- Lit-til-rock ... L..."

Enceladus announced dinner was ready.

A wonderful visit was had by all.

Pumi and Valki, with their entourage, enjoyed the hospitality of Tartarus for three days. There was much holding and cooing at the babe, Cronus.

After three days, all, except Littlerock, returned to Valki's city of Urfa.

Rivermaster and His Family
In the 46th year from the birth of Vanam

Rivermaster sought counsel with Kiya; with only he and Tethys.

"My, this sounds serious," Kiya said after they had gathered in her private chamber with baby Cronus.

Rivermaster said, "We wish to explore the boundaries of Oursea. I am, after all, a scout. It is time that I scout. Tethys wishes to come with me."

"I see. And your children? What are they to do?" Kiya asked.

Rivermaster hesitated. "I had not considered that."

"You had not considered your children? And you, Tethys?"

"Mother Kiya, would they want to leave you? Leave their home? I don't know. What should we do?"

PRINCIPALS: Kiya, Vanam, Pumi, Valki | ELDER TITANIDES: Themis, Mnemosyne, Phoebe, Tethys, Theia, Rhea | ELDER TITANES: Rivermaster/Oceanus, Sagacity/Coeus, Starmaster/Crius, Watchman/Hyperion, Piercer/Iapetus, Cronus

Kiya, annoyed, replied, "You should do what is right! My children always have my permission to do what is right! Now leave me and come back when you know what is right!"

At the evening meal on the great patio, Rivermaster rose and said, "We have an announcement to make. Metis, would you tell our family what we are going to do?"

Metis rose in extreme excitement. "We are going on an adventure! My sisters and I and Mother and Father are going to travel the coastline of Oursea to see where it takes us. We are going to draw a map and record what we see and talk to all the tribes we meet and maybe set up some ports so we can travel back and forth home by boat. We are going to be Scouts! And swim everywhere in Oursea."

The Titanides all rose and began embracing Tethys and her four Oceanid daughters. There were squeals.

Themis: "We have no song for this. We need a song!"
Mnemosyne: "And a chant. We need a goodbye chant."
Rhea: "How will you live?"
Theia: "How long will you be gone?"
Phoebe: "I'm sad. What will I do without my sister? And my brother, of course."
Themis: "I will be empty without all of you. Metis and her sisters, especially."

Kiya stood, quietened the commotion, and quietly said, "And I shall be all the fuller. My children have chosen a path that will take them to they know not where. Perhaps to destruction. Perhaps to a world of which we have not yet dreamed. I am so proud of you. Bring us back a new world!"

Sagacity rose and embraced his big brother. "Well said, Brother. Well said, Mother. All Titans must now begin to make plans to support Rivermaster's great quest ..." and on and on.

His remarks were punctuated by giggles and random squeals.

The Titanes, along with Metis, discussed whether to take the southerly or the northerly route. Metis observed that she had swum south for great distances but saw little change in the local topology. But no one had any

ELDER OCEANIDS: Metis, Tyche, Clymene, Eurybia, Amphitrite
ELDER OLYMPIANS: Hestia, Demeter, Hera, Hades, Poseidon, Zeus
OTHER: Philyra, Dionysus, Heracles, Outis, Enceladus, Littlerock, Porphyrion

idea of what lay on the northern route. There were mountains to the north, but no one knew what lay beyond the mountains. And, it was imperative that she and her sisters swim every bit of the shoreline.

"Why not?" was the consensus.

Rivermaster decided, "Our ancestral home is toward the north. We will explore the direction from which we came."

It was decided. They would begin their explorations toward the north.

The elder Titanides huddled with Tethys. They were all conversant in reading Mnemosyne's story-telling markings on her parchment, but Tethys would need more detailed training, and new symbols would be beneficial for her notetaking. They would have to travel light. What ointments and potions were mandatory to take? What other supplies would be most helpful? The women recognized that the male and his daughters would begin their journey nearly naked carrying nothing. It would be up to Tethys to have whatever they needed, whenever they needed it, to keep them alive.

Sunrise

Every Titan gathered to eat. All then walked together to Overlook Point and stopped; all but Rivermaster, Tethys, and their four daughters.

"STAY-SAFE-TI-TANS ... STAY-SAFE-TI-TANS ... STAY-SAFE-TI-TANS ... S…"

Almost out of sight, six Titans turned and waved goodbye.

By Order of the Queen

At the subdued evening meal, Kiya said to Enceladus, "Build me a mountain."

Melted Rock

Piercer and Littlerock removed the red stone from the fire and laid it on their worktable. Piercer hit it violently with his heaviest hammer. Again and again. "Look, Littlerock. It does not shatter. It becomes flatter the more I hit it. The red stones are different.

PRINCIPALS: Kiya, Vanam, Pumi, Valki | ELDER TITANIDES: Themis, Mnemosyne, Phoebe, Tethys, Theia, Rhea | ELDER TITANES: Rivermaster/Oceanus, Sagacity/Coeus, Starmaster/Crius, Watchman/Hyperion, Piercer/Iapetus, Cronus

Littlerock said, "I believe the hotter we heat the stone, the easier it becomes to flatten it."

Piercer said, "We can build a larger fire pit and maybe put a top over it to keep the heat inside. It would need to draw air from the bottom to keep the fire burning. Let's see how hot we can make a fire. We need a way to put rocks in and take them out without cooking our hands."

They did these things. They learned.

The family gathered for the evening meal. Mnemosyne sang a forlorn song of family no longer with them.

"That was sad," Kiya offered. "But we should be sad upon occasion. It reminds us to rejoice in those who are at our table tonight. Speaking of which; welcome Piercer, welcome Littlerock. We miss you at our family gatherings. It's good to see you this evening."

"Thank you, Mother. We have been working learning about colored rock."

"Great Queen Kiya," Littlerock said, "Piercer does not do justice to what we are learning. Our knowledge of these things surpasses Tallstone. What Piercer can do with stones is incredible. He has made you a gift in celebration."

"A gift!" Kiya exclaimed with delight.

"Gift! ... Gift! ... Gift! ... G..." her daughters chanted.

Piercer blushed but took a package to his mother. "I made this for you, Mother. I made a smaller one for each of my sisters." To the sound of excited shrieks, he carried a package to each of his sisters and gave an extra to Themis for safekeeping.

"You go first, Mother," Rhea said.

Kiya laid the package on the table and removed the gift. The gift was a necklace; perfectly flat, round, two hands across, with a reddish surface that reflected all the light that fell upon it. She looked at it and said, "It is exquisite Piercer. Of what is it made?"

"That is a rock, Mother. We made it extremely hot and then pounded it flat. You can bend it if you want to. I can fashion it into any shape you like. I suppose we could make drinking and eating vessels with it."

ELDER OCEANIDS: Metis, Tyche, Clymene, Eurybia, Amphitrite
ELDER OLYMPIANS: Hestia, Demeter, Hera, Hades, Poseidon, Zeus
OTHER: Philyra, Dionysus, Heracles, Outis, Enceladus, Littlerock, Porphyrion

The Titanides stared wide-eyed at their mother's gift, then tore into their own. Each held up their necklace, half the size of their mother's but exquisite, nonetheless. "We must put on our party dresses and see how we look wearing our new necklace."

They sped off to their chambers. Mnemosyne stopped, ran back to Piercer, hugged, and kissed him, "It's beautiful Piercer. Thank you so much." She then hurried to join her sisters.

Kiya-considered her gift. "This is a new world of trade, Piercer. You said that you can bend and shape this 'stone.' Will it hold a sharp edge? Can you make cutting devices?"

Littlerock said, "Excellent questions, Queen Kiya. We don't know. We have only last evening mastered the art of making that which you see before you. We don't yet know which color rocks will melt, how hot they must be, what new characteristics they have, or if we can mix different rocks to obtain different characteristics. It appears to be an entirely new art. We have named the colored rock which we can melt 'metal rocks.' Tell us what characteristics you seek from these metals; we will watch carefully for those things."

Kiya said, "You will discover all their secrets, soon enough, Metalworkers. This is as if we just discovered that you could make a house of wood. Keep me educated in this new art. It is extremely interesting. You must train many apprentices. Between polished color stones, stone jewelry, these geodes of yours, and now metals, we have a thriving base of industrious endeavors. We need many trained stone workers just to make goods to trade. How will you find time to unlock the secrets of these metals? You two have so much to do; so many responsibilities."

As Piercer swelled with pride, Littlerock was mentally recruiting possible new staff from Tallstone.

Port Kaptara

Rivermaster and his family explored their seacoast for three full seasons.

One evening, as Tethys prepared fish caught by Metis and roots and herbs gathered by Tyche, Clymene, and Eurybia, Rivermaster went to the shoreline and stared out to sea. Metis did not know where her father's

PRINCIPALS: Kiya, Vanam, Pumi, Valki | ELDER TITANIDES: Themis, Mnemosyne, Phoebe, Tethys, Theia, Rhea | ELDER TITANES: Rivermaster/Oceanus, Sagacity/Coeus, Starmaster/Crius, Watchman/Hyperion, Piercer/Iapetus, Cronus

mind went during these times, but she did understand the sea. It was best to keep the others away from him. She noticed her father looking toward the sky periodically as if he were trying to find something. He was called to dinner which, as always, was delicious.

After dinner, rather than sitting by the campfire, Rivermaster said, "Come with me, Metis. We have a full moon. Let's go explore." It was uncharacteristic and unsafe to explore at night but off they went, into the night.

Away from their camp, Metis asked, "All right, Father, what's the matter?"

"I'm not sure, Metis. I think I have been hearing things all evening. Look north at the sky; that appears to be the reflection of a good-sized campfire. Stay alert, but we need to find out what lives in this land—for your mother's journal."

Metis laughed, "Yes, Father."

They walked toward the light and began to hear sounds. Loud voices argued, angry to the point of violence. Rivermaster and Metis did not understand all the words but enough to know the intent of what was being said. They saw the campfire. It appeared to be two chiefs holding council. Angry council. The two Titans stopped and observed, identifying the principles. They watched until one chief grabbed his spear as he shouted at the other chief. The other chief grabbed his spear and stood. The two chiefs stood glaring at one another.

Rivermaster stepped into the clearing.

All were taken by surprise and turned to face the interloper; the two chiefs included. Rivermaster did not speak. He merely walked to the two chiefs and waved his hand for silence and for all to sit down.

"You!" he said as he pointed to the chief farthest away. With a combination of words they might understand and sign language, he said, "tell me what you want from this meeting."

The chief began to speak and was immediately interrupted by everyone else. Rivermaster only understood half of what they were saying, but he would fill in the other half as best he could."

ELDER OCEANIDS: Metis, Tyche, Clymene, Eurybia, Amphitrite
ELDER OLYMPIANS: Hestia, Demeter, Hera, Hades, Poseidon, Zeus
OTHER: Philyra, Dionysus, Heracles, Outis, Enceladus, Littlerock, Porphyrion

"SILENCE!" Rivermaster roared. "When I wish you to speak, I will tell you. Continue telling me your demands, Chief."

The chief said, "My tribe has been..."

The other chief opened his mouth to speak, Rivermaster shot him an angry glance and with his hand motioned, "SILENCE!"

"... violated, shown disrespect, and humiliated by these no-good outsiders ..."

Rivermaster commanded "Leave out characterizations. Tell me the facts that all can agree upon."

"Well, four of their hunters came into our territory and..."

"It was OUR territory..." the other chief interrupted.

"INTERRUPT THIS CHIEF AGAIN AND YOUR TONGUE WILL FALL OUT AND YOU WILL BE SILENT FOREVER!"

Rivermaster looked toward the first chief and said, "Continue."

"Four of HIS hunters came into OUR territory and mated with two of our women. Both of our women expressly declined to mate but both were taken forcibly, against their will."

Rivermaster held up his hand for silence. He looked at the second chief and asked, "What part of this story do you disagree with?"

The second chief hurriedly began, "It was OUR territory ..."

Rivermaster held up his hand to silence the first chief before he broke in.

"... that the two brazen..."

Rivermaster interrupted, "Leave out the characterizations. Tell me the facts of your dispute."

The second chief continued "Well, they look brazen to me but, anyway, they came into our territory..."

The discussion continued for a long time.

At last, Rivermaster said, "Chiefs, this is what happened. You both agree the boundary between the two tribes is a creek easily recognized by all."

PRINCIPALS: Kiya, Vanam, Pumi, Valki | ELDER TITANIDES: Themis, Mnemosyne, Phoebe, Tethys, Theia, Rhea | ELDER TITANES: Rivermaster/Oceanus, Sagacity/Coeus, Starmaster/Crius, Watchman/Hyperion, Piercer/Iapetus, Cronus

"Yes."

"Yes."

You both agree that these women wandered over the creek in search of plants?"

"Yes."

"Yes, but ..."

Rivermaster held up his hand. "You both agree that the hunters saw the women in their territory and asked them to mate."

"Yes."

"Yes, that is correct."

"When the women declined, the hunters became angry. The women ran back across the creek. The hunters caught them and then all four hunters mated with the two women."

"Yes."

"Yes, that is exactly what happened."

"So, your discussion tonight is to decide who has the grievance and what must be done to correct the grievance."

Both chiefs began simultaneously.

"Yes. I expect ..."

"Yes, they must ..."

"Silence!"

He turned to the second chief and said, "It is your land that was violated. What is it you want?"

"Well, he should not come over here and ..."

"WHAT IS IT YOU WANT?!"

"I want him and his tribesman to stay out of my territory."

Rivermaster turned to the first chief and said, "He doesn't sound neighborly but is that something you and your tribesmen can live with?"

"I can but what about ..."

ELDER OCEANIDS: Metis, Tyche, Clymene, Eurybia, Amphitrite
ELDER OLYMPIANS: Hestia, Demeter, Hera, Hades, Poseidon, Zeus
OTHER: Philyra, Dionysus, Heracles, Outis, Enceladus, Littlerock, Porphyrion

Rivermaster held up his hand and said, "Is that something you can live with? Will you instruct your elder woman to make this clear to your gatherers?"

"Yes. I will do these things."

"Now," Rivermaster said to the first chief, "Your women have been violated. What do you want to satisfy this grievance?"

The first chief hesitated. He was unsure what proper compensation for such an act should be. He stuttered, "Well, I ... Well ..."

Rivermaster finished for him. "It wasn't the women you cared about. It was your neighboring chief and his hunters barging into your land shouting and showing disrespect to you and your tribe. This is what infuriated you. So now, what shall we do to satisfy your grievance? Let me see ..."

The two chiefs muttered among themselves.

Rivermaster said, "This is what you shall do. The two women disrespected the boundary between the two territories. They cannot remain with their tribe. They will come with me. The four hunters disrespected both the women *and* the boundary. They cannot remain. They will come with me. Metis, lead these six people away from here and to your camp."

"Wait! They are our tribesmen," one of the chiefs exclaimed.

"They *were* your tribesmen. We agree that they violated tribal rules. You cannot, or did not, control them. You should be glad to be rid of them but, if not, consider it your punishment. And, too, consider your actions here this day. Neither of you has shown any capability of being worthy to be called chief. You are both petty, argumentative, cannot control your tribesmen, and care little for your clan. You care only for yourselves. I shall leave you to reflect upon your weakness but know this, do not bring your pettiness to the shoreline lest I change my mind. METIS! Take your charges. NOW!"

Everyone looked around in disbelief. Metis came forward and motioned to the two women and four men to follow her. They followed. No one dared stop them.

The second chief snarled, "And who are you that we should obey you?"

PRINCIPALS: Kiya, Vanam, Pumi, Valki | ELDER TITANIDES: Themis, Mnemosyne, Phoebe, Tethys, Theia, Rhea | ELDER TITANES: Rivermaster/Oceanus, Sagacity/Coeus, Starmaster/Crius, Watchman/Hyperion, Piercer/Iapetus, Cronus

Tethys stepped into the clearing and said, "He is Oceanus! He controls the sea, the rivers, and the rain. He controls all water. Obey him. If you do not, remember this, Oceanus controls the waters. *All* the waters!"

Rivermaster, now Oceanus, did not deem to return their stares. He walked in silence back into the grove from where he had first appeared. Tethys and three of her daughters waited until he had passed and then turned to follow Oceanus. Metis waited until they were gone, waved gaily to the two chiefs, and addressed her six new friends with "All right, everybody. Follow me!"

Upon returning to their camp, they divided into two groups. Tethys consoled and comforted the two women; violated and taken from their tribe all in one day. Tyche listened, growing more and more repulsed at what the men had done to the women. She assured them that they were now far better off, and their lives would now be much more enjoyable. The Titanides paid close attention to the two women's responses: piecing together words from their simple language.

The four males did not fare as well. Few hunters had ever received the reprimands and berating delivered to them that night. Oceanus made clear the behavior he expected, and don't ask what happens if his expectations are not met. The six newcomers were fed and bedded down.

The Titans gathered to discuss what was to be done. Metis summed up their problems, "The women can be trained to swim and fish. They would never go hungry. But the hunters? All a hunter is good for is hunting and that doesn't appear to be an option. Maybe we could use them as fish bait."

Oceanus said, "We won't make a port here. The surrounding tribes are not honorable. We will continue traveling for another season. We have a nucleus to build a new port. Let's look for a few more members; some with talents enough to construct a port."

"Oh, maybe I could direct these boys on how to build a port right here. I watched and helped build Riverport. They have the muscle. I have the brains. We just need cutting tools to cut wood. This inlet is rich in fish. The plant life is abundant."

ELDER OCEANIDS: Metis, Tyche, Clymene, Eurybia, Amphitrite
ELDER OLYMPIANS: Hestia, Demeter, Hera, Hades, Poseidon, Zeus
OTHER: Philyra, Dionysus, Heracles, Outis, Enceladus, Littlerock, Porphyrion

Tyche interjected, "Outis has taught me a lot about finding wild bees and harvesting honey without too many stings. We passed several beehives this morning."

Oceanus said, "The problem with this location is the two incompetent chiefs, nearby. We will talk to our new members during our morning meal and then decide how to proceed. In the meantime, sleep well, my family."

Sunrise

Metis roused the two women from their sleep. "Get up, people. You are going to learn the joy of fishing in the morning." Her three sisters joined the on-the-job teaching exercise. "We know how to catch fish," Metis told the two women. "But we aren't going to catch any. So, if you two don't catch our breakfast, we all go hungry!" *A little pressure never hurts.*

Oceanids are natural teachers. They taught the two women the art of swimming and catching fish. They caught enough fish for a modest breakfast for the ten of them.

The women were ecstatic with their newfound skills, even though most of the fish had escaped. The four males begrudgingly admired the prowess of the two brazen women as they ate the fish provided by the two.

Oceanus left them to walk to the shoreline and then stare up the coastline.

Tethys sat silently and listened to the chatter of the newcomers, intuiting meaning to their words. She signaled her daughters to remain silent and listen.

The newcomers appeared to have a sense of relief for their acquisition from their respective tribes. As their chatter continued, the noise of a traveling tribe was heard. Oceanus heard it and walked back to stand in front of the small cooking fire. Metis rose and stood beside him. Twelve hunters appeared in the clearing; then twelve more; eventually more than a hundred men, women, and children were crowded into the clearing.

Oceanus said, "What is it you seek?"

They sought a new leader; one who could command them, lead them with respect, and provide enough food. The two tribes had spontaneously left their old chiefs and wanted Oceanus to become the new chief of all of them.

PRINCIPALS: Kiya, Vanam, Pumi, Valki | ELDER TITANIDES: Themis, Mnemosyne, Phoebe, Tethys, Theia, Rhea | ELDER TITANES: Rivermaster/Oceanus, Sagacity/Coeus, Starmaster/Crius, Watchman/Hyperion, Piercer/Iapetus, Cronus

Oceanus listened and processed their words. He then said, "Go and gather yourselves into groups of ten. Each group select one of your members to speak for the ten. Those selected, return here and I will counsel with you. How long since your bellies have been full?" The general reaction was clear enough: never. "Daughters of the Sea, go gather fish to fill their bellies." Oceanus turned and walked back to the shoreline.

Metis commanded, "All right, everybody. You heard your orders. Divide into groups of ten. Select your captain. Captains come back here after High-sun. It will take a while for The Daughters of the Sea to catch enough fish to feed all of you. You two new women come with us but stay away from the action. I don't want you scaring away our food." She waved impatiently at the gathered throng to start moving.

The Daughters of the Sea plus two caught enough fish to feed everyone in the two tribes.

Tethys directed the preparation of the fish. Tyche and Clymene were directed to go bring back honey. Tyche randomly selected five tribal women to accompany them.

The captains of the eighteen groups gathered.

Oceanus joined the eighteen Captains and said, "Pick your chief from among you." The captains hesitated, unsure how to proceed. They looked to Oceanus for more direction. Oceanus sat in silence, staring back at them. Finally, one of the two women in the group spoke, Aeolus is well respected in our tribe. He acknowledged our suffering when our chief ignored us. He despairs when one of us dies."

Another hunter said, "Achaeous is our best hunter. He fears nothing."

The discussion went on. Oceanus did not speak until the consensus was divided among tribal lines. He then spoke. "Stand before us Aeolus and Achaeous, so that we may hear your words."

The two hunters rose and stood before Oceanus. Oceanus said to them, "It is not I to whom you will speak, it is to your tribesman. Speak to them; any words you will."

The two men were momentarily taken aback but Aeolus regained his composure and said, "I am not worthy to be chief. I do not have the

ELDER OCEANIDS: Metis, Tyche, Clymene, Eurybia, Amphitrite
ELDER OLYMPIANS: Hestia, Demeter, Hera, Hades, Poseidon, Zeus
OTHER: Philyra, Dionysus, Heracles, Outis, Enceladus, Littlerock, Porphyrion

training, skills, or desire. But if chosen, I will always endeavor to be the chief my tribesmen deserve." He was then silent and looked toward his opponent, Achaeous.

Achaeous finally understood that he was to address the captains by saying something. Anything. "I am … the best hunter of anyone. I fear nothing. I am brave and fast and the best hunter of anyone." He was then silent.

Oceanus sat silent as the two speeches sank in. He then said, "I shall now advise you. If I were to follow any man, it would be Aeolus. If I were to stand in battle with any man, it would be Achaeous. Aeolus will delay action to consider all courses. This is a mark of wisdom. Achaeous will be quick to act if any emergency were to arise, such as one of your old chiefs seeking revenge on his old tribe. Whomever you choose as chief will need a trusted general to protect the tribe. I leave at the next sunrise. The Daughters of the Sea will stay with you awhile. The one named Metis provides wise counsel. Your new chief, whomever you choose, will be wise to seek it. Now, choose a chief as you will." Oceanus stood and left the council.

Aeolus turned to Achaeous and said, "I will be chief of this tribe if you will be our tribe's protector." Achaeous nodded in agreement.

Aeolus then looked at Metis and said, "Let my people be fed and a camp made. Achaeous and I will gather the wisest of our tribesmen. You will then meet with us to plan our future in this place."

Metis noticed that she was being ordered around by Chief Aeolus. She smiled approvingly.

Such was the founding of Port Kaptara.

Port Graikoi

The Titans rose before sunrise so that they could embrace and say farewell to Metis before the others continued their westerly exploration. To display emotion in front of the new citizens would not be wise. The young Oceanids instinctively knew they must appear to be in control of all things. Her sisters bid her farewell and then left with their parents.

PRINCIPALS: Kiya, Vanam, Pumi, Valki | ELDER TITANIDES: Themis, Mnemosyne, Phoebe, Tethys, Theia, Rhea | ELDER TITANES: Rivermaster/Oceanus, Sagacity/Coeus, Starmaster/Crius, Watchman/Hyperion, Piercer/Iapetus, Cronus

After the sun rose, Metis rousted Chief Aeolus from his sleep and said, "Chief, wake the women. We will teach them how to catch enough fish to feed your tribe."

Metis was in her element.

< >

Oceanus, Tethys, Tyche, Clymene, and Eurybia made their way west. Tethys recorded mapping information and notes on the land. Tyche would routinely enter the water for her hourly swim and report to her mother; deep or shallow, sandy or rocky, depth at various distances from shore, the abundance of fish, temperature, unusual formation, and any other information of interest. So, they progressed for two more seasons.

< >

"Here," Oceanus said one early afternoon. "We will camp here and explore our surroundings. Tyche, make a careful note of depths and currents. I am going to find any tribes that might be camping nearby."

After Oceanus returned that night, they gathered for the evening meal which had been easily caught by Tyche. Oceanus said, "I found one tribe due north of here. It was a poor tribe, undernourished. I am surprised at how poor the tribes are here in the West. We communicated poorly, but well enough. The land is fertile, the game plentiful, the sea bountiful, yet they suffer. Their hunters are not good, and their women are poor gatherers. I told their chief, Graikoi, to come to the shore at sunrise and I would provide food for his tribesmen. These people lack leadership. Any Titan could make these tribes prosperous in less than two seasons; especially if they set up camp near Oursea."

The five discussed the issues into the night.

Sunrise

Tyche said to her family, "I will catch fish to feed eighty people."

To her mother, she said, "You and Eurybia go gather roots and herbs."

To her father, she said, "Consider sending for Metis. You could leave us here to establish a new outpost. The four of us are smart enough to advise

ELDER OCEANIDS: Metis, Tyche, Clymene, Eurybia, Amphitrite
ELDER OLYMPIANS: Hestia, Demeter, Hera, Hades, Poseidon, Zeus
OTHER: Philyra, Dionysus, Heracles, Outis, Enceladus, Littlerock, Porphyrion

them on how to live properly. Metis is mean enough to teach them what it means to be civilized. Just a suggestion."

She removed her tunic and dove into Oursea.

The tribe arrived at the shore. Tyche had caught and cooked enough fish to feed them all.

After the tribe was fed, the five Titans talked with Chief Graikoi. Oceanus made his offer. "My daughters can teach your women to fish and improve their gathering skills. I can teach hunting skills to your men. Then we will all leave. The tribe will then be in your care."

He paused for the chief to consider his words, then said, "I can call my oldest to come to this place. She has the knowledge to help you bring your tribe to a position of great power. She will stay with you and teach you our ways. But she will not tolerate disrespect, insolence, shortness, or laziness from you or any of your tribesmen. She will disappear into Oursea, and you will never see her again. Now, go and take whatever counsel from your tribe you desire. Return tomorrow after sunrise with your decision. Any of your women who desire to remain will be instructed in whichever art they desire. You may go."

Chief Graikoi rose, bowed toward Oceanus, said, "Thank you, my lord," and returned to his tribesmen. He commanded his elder woman to select five women to remain and learn what they could.

After the chief had gone, Oceanus said, "We need more Titans."

Sunrise

The chief came, his decision made.

Graikoi said, "I want my tribe to become great. I will do whatever I am told to do to make this happen. I will treat your Daughter of the Sea with respect. I accept your offer with gratitude."

"Excellent. You are wise. I shall summon my daughter, Metis, immediately. The Titanide Tethys will remain with you until Metis and her sisters arrive. May your tribe prosper under your leadership." Oceanus waved dismissal to the chief.

PRINCIPALS: Kiya, Vanam, Pumi, Valki | ELDER TITANIDES: Themis, Mnemosyne, Phoebe, Tethys, Theia, Rhea | ELDER TITANES: Rivermaster/Oceanus, Sagacity/Coeus, Starmaster/Crius, Watchman/Hyperion, Piercer/Iapetus, Cronus

After the chief had gone, Oceanus told his three daughters, "Apprise Metis of the situation. Have her make a grand entrance when she arrives. Build two vessels that can be used for trade between the two tribes and a third one capable of sailing to Tartarus."

The Oceanids gathered their traveling equipment and, with hugs, set off to summon Metis and build some sailing vessels.

Toward sunset, Oceanus walked to the shore with Tethys. He put his arm around her as they looked out over Oursea. Looking at the clouds in the sunset sky, he said, "It is time for us to create a child."

Tethys grew closer to him. "So, Rivermaster lives somewhere inside Oceanus. I was afraid my Rivermaster had abandoned me."

He laughed. "Abandon Tethys? Can the rivers abandon the sea? Can clouds abandon the sky? I think not, Tethys. I think these things are united forever. The night is ours alone. A perfect night to create new life. We will name her Amphitrite."

He held Tethys closely.

Thus, Port Graikoi was founded.

Outpost Spearpoint
In the 47th year from the birth of Vanam

Oceanus left before sunrise.

He would travel the coastline for a quarter moon and wait there for Tethys. But as he traveled, the land grew higher. Rather than the sea coming to the land, sheer cliffs arose, with the sea further and further below. He saw no end to the climb in sight. Was this a mountain? He had never seen a landscape such as this. He decided to return to Port Graikoi so he and Tethys could travel this strange new coastline together. He returned slowly, exploring deep inland.

He encountered her on the seventh day. She, one day out of Port Graikoi.

Tethys said, "Our three younger daughters stayed in Kaptara directing boat building. Metis made a grand entrance at Graikoi. Everyone stood and watched with awe as a woman of great beauty and presence rose and walked from the water to their chief. Metis told them, 'I am Metis, a

ELDER OCEANIDS: Metis, Tyche, Clymene, Eurybia, Amphitrite
ELDER OLYMPIANS: Hestia, Demeter, Hera, Hades, Poseidon, Zeus
OTHER: Philyra, Dionysus, Heracles, Outis, Enceladus, Littlerock, Porphyrion

Daughter of the Sea. I am here to serve you so that you may lead your tribe to greatness. Now show me the wonders of your land.' The chief stood up and I think he may have bowed to our daughter. She is in her element. She is excited that Port Graikoi may become a city of greatness. She will spend a quarter moon at Port Graikoi and then alternate between the two ports. She said that too much time with a chief stifles their sense of responsibility. Alternating between the two ports will be a good thing for both chiefs. And Chief Aeolus will be honored to build three sailing vessels if the Oceanids will show him how. He found the concept of trading with Chief Graikoi by water exciting."

Oceanus laughed. "They are all our daughters; natural-born, commanding leaders. Leaders that had rather be swimming naked and giggling."

Tethys laughed, "One must do what one must do. Now show me this strange new land of yours."

< >

They walked for a season.

The land rose to a great height, with sheer cliffs. The land was all rock with no vegetation. The shore turned southward. Tethys took careful notes. After several days of walking south, they turned west to explore the inland. After a little more than a stade, they saw only water. Oceanus shivered. "This is not right. This cannot be. The water we see is level with the land we stand upon. Oursea is more than a stade below us. If this water and Oursea were connected, then both would be at the same level. We must be looking at a shallow inland lake unconnected to Oursea or maybe it discharges water over a high waterfall farther south than we have yet traveled. Wait on me."

Oceanus removed his tunic and dove into the water. He dove as deeply as he dared. He surfaced gasping for air. As he dried his body with his tunic, he said, "It is a sheer cliff. I could not find the bottom. I must have Oceanids come to this place and determine its nature." With that, he tried to drive one of his spears into the ground, but the ground was solid rock. He had Tethys hold the spear as he placed rocks around it to hold it upright. He thought once more and then removed the spear and placed it back with the spear point pointing up.

PRINCIPALS: Kiya, Vanam, Pumi, Valki | ELDER TITANIDES: Themis, Mnemosyne, Phoebe, Tethys, Theia, Rhea | ELDER TITANES: Rivermaster/Oceanus, Sagacity/Coeus, Starmaster/Crius, Watchman/Hyperion, Piercer/Iapetus, Cronus

He stepped back and said, "I shall name this place 'Outpost Spearpoint.'"

They traveled on in silence. And on. They made camp for the evening. He said, "This land is not hospitable. We need to move quickly tomorrow. Our food supply is low, and this land produces nothing. I can see nothing from the cliffs except more of the same."

During the coming days, they found no connecting waterfall. The separation between the two bodies of water grew greater. Oceanus was conflicted. "Which shoreline should we follow? We have discovered a large inland lake. We must find its boundaries. But I feel it my duty to follow the shore of Oursea until we know its nature."

They continued. Finally, the decision could be postponed no longer. The shoreline of Oursea continued due south. The shore of the inland lake went due west. Oceanus decided that he must discover the nature of the inland lake.

They turned due west.

Port Olympus
In the 48th year from the birth of Vanam

Olympus, the home. Olympus, the port. Olympus, the city. Olympus, the mountain.

Port Olympus was built on the coast sixty stades due west of Tartarus. It had taken two long, hard years to simply lay out and build an infrastructure for the port. It was still nothing but a shell. A shell waiting to be completed, waiting to become a great port, waiting to become the grandest structure humanity had ever created.

The shell had sixteen floors. The base was a square, 80 paces on each side. The second floor was a square, 75 paces on each side. The third, a 70-pace square. And so it rose, the next floor was five paces smaller than the one below it until it reached the roof, a 5 pace square. Stairs connected each floor and someday an elevator would rise through the atrium in the center of the structure.

The building would not be even this far along had it not been for the Gigantes tribe. Kiya had sent a message to Alcyoneous that she was in a position to be generous if any of his tribesmen desired to immigrate to her realm; that she had a great building project in mind that far outstripped

ELDER OCEANIDS: Metis, Tyche, Clymene, Eurybia, Amphitrite
ELDER OLYMPIANS: Hestia, Demeter, Hera, Hades, Poseidon, Zeus
OTHER: Philyra, Dionysus, Heracles, Outis, Enceladus, Littlerock, Porphyrion

her capacity to implement in a timely fashion. It would take her people one hundred years to complete on their own but with the assistance of a few Gigantes, she could cut that time in half.

Within a season of sending her emissary, 400 men, women, children, and Alcyoneous himself appeared at Overlook Point. After proper party dresses, receiving lines, pomp, and speeches, Alcyoneous said to Kiya, "The future appears to be in settling in one location rather than moving across the land tracking our prey. Will you accept our tribe into your realm?"

After her delighted acceptance, he asked, "What is this great project of yours?"

The tribe settled to the northwest of Tartarus, near the mountains, in a wonderful land. Their land bordered Great Arc Road being constructed from Port Olympus to Overlook Point.

Return of the Oceanids

On this day, Cronus was with his sister Mnemosyne in Tartarus.

Kiya sat alone on the roof of Port Olympus looking out toward Oursea. This 'mountain'—this 'high place'—this 'Olympus'—which Kiya had commanded Enceladus to build, was complete enough that Kiya could climb the long, unending stairs to the roof of the structure where flooring had been put into place just for her. It was from here that one day flags would fly, and beacons would be lit that could be seen far out at sea. Meetings of great importance could be held in this place. But, for now, it served as a place for her to sit in her special chair from Urfa and fulfill her need to look over her realm; to know all was well; and to look over Oursea, toward where two of her children and four of her grandchildren were.

The speck on the horizon would go unnoticed by most. But Kiya sat high. And the speck appeared to be followed by birds. And the speck appeared to be headed straight toward Olympus. And, if you listened hard enough, if you strained your ears, one could almost believe that the speck was singing a sailing song. Kiya stood and watched the speck grow larger. And louder. Kiya hurried down the stairs.

The Oceanids docked their small raft to one of the posts which had been driven deep into the seabed to one day support the great pier. They jumped into the water, swam, and then waded toward the unfinished

PRINCIPALS: Kiya, Vanam, Pumi, Valki | ELDER TITANIDES: Themis, Mnemosyne, Phoebe, Tethys, Theia, Rhea | ELDER TITANES: Rivermaster/Oceanus, Sagacity/Coeus, Starmaster/Crius, Watchman/Hyperion, Piercer/Iapetus, Cronus

dock. They pulled themselves from the water onto the dock and walked slowly toward the gathering crowd. Their linen tunics clung to their bodies like a second skin. As they walked, they scanned the crowd looking for a familiar face. Seeing none, they continued walking. The crowd parted to let them pass. Kiya had completed her rapid descent down the stairs and arrived at the head of the dock just in time for the crowd to complete its parting, leaving Kiya there to greet the Oceanids. They saw their grandmother, maintained their composure until they reached her, stared at her without expression, then fell to their knees, grabbed Kiya's ankles, and sobbed.

Kiya let the scene play out, then kneeled, took her Granddaughter's hands, pulled them to their feet, and walked with them to construction headquarters. Upon entering, Kiya silently waved her hand. All therein immediately left, leaving the building to the women.

They all embraced and cried.

Family Dinner

All who could be, were there.

Metis had recovered her composure and had reverted to her natural self. Midway through the evening, Metis said, "Uncles, you could help our world if one of you would travel back with me to our outpost ports. The chiefs take advice well, but it would be encouraging if a Titane showed up to see what's been happening and brag on their chiefs a little. Maybe ask if any of their women would like to mate with you; maybe have a child. I don't think the attention would hurt. You could stay a season at each port, and I could bring you back. And I would like a boat worthy of this great port rather than that raft we floated in on. Their shipbuilding techniques are limited."

Phoebe quickly said, "Sagacity is so extremely busy. He could not possibly go. Perhaps one of the younger Titanes. It sounds like a perfect adventure for Watchman or Starmaster."

"Well, whoever," Metis offered. She grew serious and said, "Great Mother Kiya, I have a kind of important story to tell. Aunt Mnemosyne might want to listen."

Mnemosyne thought, *Important to Metis? This is certainly a story to listen to.*

ELDER OCEANIDS: Metis, Tyche, Clymene, Eurybia, Amphitrite
ELDER OLYMPIANS: Hestia, Demeter, Hera, Hades, Poseidon, Zeus
OTHER: Philyra, Dionysus, Heracles, Outis, Enceladus, Littlerock, Porphyrion

Metis leaned toward Kiya. All grew silent. She began. "Father is different, Grandmother. He isn't the same person who left here."

Kiya gathered Cronus into her lap and leaned forward.

"It isn't that he is like a chief or anything. He's kind of more than a chief—more than a king. Mother started calling him a different name. 'Oceanus.' It's kind of like a name, I guess. But it's more like a title like chief or king or maybe all those things. Maybe even more. Not *Chief* Oceanus. Just Oceanus. He wears it well. She first called him Oceanus when he founded the port of Kaptara. That was an exciting adventure. We had just found this beautiful little cove; perfect for sailing a boat into ..."

Union ... Port Kaptara

The shipbuilders built Metis a proper sailing ship; one which displayed the importance, wealth, and technology of Port Olympus.

Starmaster and Metis sailed back to Port Kaptara with an experienced boat builder.

Metis again briefed Starmaster. "They aren't as advanced as the tribes from the east but they're hungry for leadership and direction. Father had a powerful impact on them that I parlayed to maintain control and guide them but now it's time to wean them. You need to instill that they will soon have enough wealth to trade with the other ports; and that they should encourage trade with tribes farther inland so that all surrounding tribes could grow wealthier and more civilized.

Starmaster brought gifts to Chief Aeolus from Queen Kiya.

Their ship was met with awe as they docked at the makeshift port and were greeted by Chief Aeolus, himself. Metis stood and said, "Greetings Chief Aeolus. I have been commanded by the Titans to leave your city. Your tribe has grown in greatness and there is no more for you to learn from a Daughter of the Sea. In my stead, I am commanded to introduce to you the Great Titan, Starmaster."

She stepped aside and Starmaster appeared in full dress including an impressive necklace of polished stones and metal. He nodded toward Metis and stepped from the ship. In his hands, he held one of Piercer's necklaces. Starmaster held it high for all to see. "Chief Aeolus, may I place

PRINCIPALS: Kiya, Vanam, Pumi, Valki | ELDER TITANIDES: Themis, Mnemosyne, Phoebe, Tethys, Theia, Rhea | ELDER TITANES: Rivermaster/Oceanus, Sagacity/Coeus, Starmaster/Crius, Watchman/Hyperion, Piercer/Iapetus, Cronus

this token of friendship about your neck to symbolize our friendship and to promote trade between our lands?"

The chief was overwhelmed. His advisor was leaving him but before him stood a great Titan Lord offering him gifts; a necklace, less impressive than the one worn by the Titan lord, but still more impressive than any necklace the chief had ever dreamed of. He was stunned. Speechless. He glanced toward Metis. She glared back at him and pumped her fist at him. *Now is the time. Be great or not!*

The chief understood. He breathed deeply and said, "I accept your gift. You are gracious to extend such a gift to a poor chief. We shall learn from you and grow our wealth. May the day come that your graciousness is returned tenfold. Please, walk with me, and let me show you our people and our land. I will tell you things we wish to do. Perhaps you could advise me."

They began their tour leaving Metis and the muscular boat builder on the boat.

"Oh, well," Metis said to the young man. "You can be my gift to the women. Just remember to build fishing boats for them and teach them the common language of the eastern lands."

Metis set sail, leaving Starmaster at Port Kaptara for a season.

< >

Metis returned, as planned, to pick him up and carry him to Port Graikoi.

As Starmaster walked to the dock with the chief, he said, "Now remember, select two of your hunters interested in the sky, two interested in building structures with wood, and four women interested in learning how to plant and harvest einkorn. In the season we spoke of, I will send a great ship, far greater than the one you see before you, and the ship will carry you and these tribesmen to the great Winter Solstice Festival. A Festival so great that even the Titans bow to it. Your tribe prospers. You will become known as a great chief to all the surrounding tribes. Remember your teachings and all will be well."

Starmaster boarded the ship.

From the ship, Metis waved to the chief and flashed her best smile.

The chief was weak with excitement he could not show.

ELDER OCEANIDS: Metis, Tyche, Clymene, Eurybia, Amphitrite
ELDER OLYMPIANS: Hestia, Demeter, Hera, Hades, Poseidon, Zeus
OTHER: Philyra, Dionysus, Heracles, Outis, Enceladus, Littlerock, Porphyrion

Union ... Port Graikoi

Metis had brought with her two young men who wished to immigrate to the settlement at Graikoi. They were to be, along with a necklace of stone, his gifts to the chief of Graikoi. One man was an accomplished shipbuilder, the other an accomplished stonecutter. They were both young men highly thought of by the Titans, among their best. The proposition was put forward that those who immigrated to the frontiers would be building new civilizations and would have a high status in their new tribe. They, therefore, must maintain even higher standards. There were many volunteers; only two were accepted. The Titans needed to find more frontiers.

Metis pleaded with Starmaster for him to present the necklace to the chief but let her present the two young men as a gift to the women of the tribe. Starmaster insisted that *he* would present the two men to the tribe's chief.

The ship arrived at Port Graikoi. The scenes were repeated with the same results. Starmaster forgot to present the two young male immigrants to the chief. It fell upon Metis to present them to the tribe's women.

Both tribes had progressed under their chief's tutelage by Metis. The chiefs had been chosen well. They were both the best the surrounding area had to offer. The hope was that both tribes could continue their growth without further supervision.

Metis and Starmaster bid farewell to the people of Graikoi. Metis set sail eastward toward Port Olympus.

Starmaster said, "No. Set sail to the west."

Outpost Kemet

They sailed for the remainder of the day and into the next. The land rose above them. Metis was concerned that there was no beach. The water went to and stopped at sheer cliffs. She dove into the water to test its depths." It's deep but I can touch bottom."

They sailed on. The cliffs grew higher. They followed the coastline as it began to turn toward the south.

Starmaster observed, "Rivermaster and Tethys must have come this way. They would have traveled the high peaks looking down toward Oursea."

PRINCIPALS: Kiya, Vanam, Pumi, Valki | ELDER TITANIDES: Themis, Mnemosyne, Phoebe, Tethys, Theia, Rhea | ELDER TITANES: Rivermaster/Oceanus, Sagacity/Coeus, Starmaster/Crius, Watchman/Hyperion, Piercer/Iapetus, Cronus

Book 2. *The Beginning of Civilization: Mythologies Told True*

"I would love to see Oursea from the land above. Do you think it possible that I could climb the cliff?"

"No," Starmaster replied. "I don't. Don't even try. But Rivermaster and Tethys travel by foot over rough terrain. You and I travel by sea over smooth terrain. As long as you can catch fish for dinner, we can keep sailing our coastline. Catch our dinner. Maybe there is a new frontier to discover."

They sailed on.

The coast eventually turned due south. The sheer, high cliffs remained sheer and high. After a long time, the cliffs became shorter in height. Then, the coast began turning eastward, the land began falling to the level of Oursea, and the beaches returned.

They beached their craft and explored. Inland, it was sand. And more sand.

"The end of the earth?" Metis asked.

"If not, then the end of habitable land."

"What shall we do?" Metis asked.

"I wonder if Rivermaster and Tethys came this way. They would have gone from foodless rocky mountains to foodless unending sand. They are resourceful but this is a brutal landscape. Their goal was to travel the coastline as far as they could. This is the coastline. If they still live, they have had time to be ahead of us. Let's hold course and hope we overtake them."

They sailed on. The shore turned directly east. Still sand. Endless sand. There was no sign that Titans had been this way. On they sailed. Under a brutally hot sun. Then in the distance, they saw green. Could it be vegetation? They sailed on.

They arrived at the green. It was vegetation. The texture of the water was different. Metis jumped in. This water is not as salty. "A river empties into Oursea here. That's where all the vegetation is coming from."

They sailed into a delta filled with sandbars and trees and creatures before unseen. On a bank, Starmaster stared at a lizard as large as a man. "Look there, Metis. That cannot be a friendly creature. Don't enter the water in this place."

ELDER OCEANIDS: Metis, Tyche, Clymene, Eurybia, Amphitrite
ELDER OLYMPIANS: Hestia, Demeter, Hera, Hades, Poseidon, Zeus
OTHER: Philyra, Dionysus, Heracles, Outis, Enceladus, Littlerock, Porphyrion

They sailed among reeds, next to marshes. The landscape became stranger and stranger.

Starmaster said, "Let's find our way out of here and get back to where we came from. We can dock there for the night and enter this land from the desert, not from the water."

"I took good notes on the way we got in here. I hope a giant lizard doesn't try to eat us."

"Well," said the confident Starmaster, "we would at least find out what they taste like."

Sunrise

They stepped out of their anchored boat into the water. They were met at the shore by eight men sitting on strange beasts. They each held a long spear and had a large dagger strapped to their side.

Metis returned to the boat and retrieved some bread, a jar of honey, and some small bead bracelets.

The riders never spoke. They watched.

Starmaster introduced himself in his best Titan tradition. The men simply stared.

Starmaster tried introducing himself again. Still, they stared. Motionless upon their beasts.

Metis was happy that she had worn a cloth dress; one that did not cling to her body after becoming wet. She was not frightened of men but, then again, she was not usually frightened of lizards. These were strange men. Who knew their attitude toward a woman? She took a cleaning cloth from a pocket and placed it over her hair. She then bowed her head and took the bread and pot of honey and placed it midway between Starmaster and the mounted men. She raised her arms heavenward and with a chant, motioned from heaven to the urn. She had no idea what she was doing but it would keep them uncertain of what was happening. She backed away with her head bowed.

She whispered to Starmaster as she backed past him. "I will get daggers and ready the spears in the boat. If they charge, outrun those animals while I throw spears at them."

Starmaster whispered back, "Great plan, but let me try something."

He walked to the jar of honey while staring at their assumed leader, sat down in front of the honey, removed the top, swiped a small piece of bread across the honey, held it up for the leader to see, ate the honeyed bread, and made a hand motion indicating the leader should join him.

The leader dismounted, walked to the jar, stared first at Starmaster, and then at the jar. He sat down, took a piece of bread, swiped it through the honey, and ate it. A tremendously wide smile came over the leader's face. He excitedly pointed to the jar while speaking a language not even close to one Starmaster understood. The other men dismounted and ran to sit down around the jar. They took bread and ate. They were all smiling and laughing.

Starmaster called out, "Demure Daughter of the Sea, bring these men gifts of bracelets. Wear your dagger where they can see it."

Metis returned and gave each man a bracelet of polished stones. They laughed and held up their gifts for each to see. The leader pointed to the dagger on Metis's belt. They all pointed and laughed uproariously; all nodding in agreement in what the Titans hoped was admiration. One of the men suddenly rose and lunged at Metis. Her dagger was waiting at his throat. The man burst into laughter and held his arms wide apart with big eyes. They again pointed at Metis and laughed uproariously nodding in agreement. This time the Titans knew it was admiration.

Demure Metis smiled and retired to her ship.

Looking in hidden places, Metis found that for which she searched. It was a marmaros obelisk Piercer had carved as a decoration for special events. It was half her height and heavy, but she managed to drag it to Starmaster. "I suggest you mark this spot and let them know we will return with more honey. I will go back to the ship and get out of your way."

He nodded his head respectfully toward Metis and said, "Agreed."

Starmaster rose and moved the urn of honey to the feet of the sitting leader. Starmaster then forced the obelisk to stand tall in the sand where

ELDER OCEANIDS: Metis, Tyche, Clymene, Eurybia, Amphitrite
ELDER OLYMPIANS: Hestia, Demeter, Hera, Hades, Poseidon, Zeus
OTHER: Philyra, Dionysus, Heracles, Outis, Enceladus, Littlerock, Porphyrion

the urn had just been. He then looked at the leader, pointed to himself, and said, "Ti-tan."

The leader rose, pointed to Starmaster, and said, "Ti-tan." He then pointed to himself and said "Key-met."

Starmaster pointed to Kemet and said, "Key-met." Kemet smiled. Starmaster then pointed to the honey and said, "Hon-ee."

Kemet repeated the gesture and word.

Starmaster then pointed at the strange beast and raised his eyebrows.

Kemet pointed to the beast and said, "Don-key." He then pointed to Metis and raised his eyebrows.

Starmaster pointed to Metis and said, "Met-is. Ti-tan Met-is."

They both laughed. The beginning of a common language had begun.

With what were elaborate, but logical, hand motions, Starmaster tried to indicate that he would now sail away but would return in one year, to this place, with much honey. He would trade the honey for three don-key.

The men talked among themselves. The leader repeated what had been said, apparently understanding what the hand motion for a circle toward the sky meant. He then pointed to the urn with its remaining honey and said, "Hon-nee" and held out his arms to indicate a BIG urn of honey.

Starmaster laughed, mirrored the arms held out, and said, "MUCH hon-nee." The leader walked to Starmaster, laughed loudly, and gave him a bear hug. The men returned to their donkeys but before the leader mounted, he turned to his new friend, used his arms to make a large circle, laughed, and said "Ti-tan Me-tis. MUCH Hon-ee."

Starmaster repeated the circle and said, "Key-met. MUCH hon-nee."

He returned to the ship. "Set sail, Metis. Get us out of here. If we live long enough, we return in a year with much honey and a ship big enough to carry three of those beasts and maybe a couple of those big lizards. We have a year to find our home and make plans. This is big, Metis. Sail eastward as fast as you can. Let's hope this shoreline takes us home."

PRINCIPALS: Kiya, Vanam, Pumi, Valki | ELDER TITANIDES: Themis, Mnemosyne, Phoebe, Tethys, Theia, Rhea | ELDER TITANES: Rivermaster/Oceanus, Sagacity/Coeus, Starmaster/Crius, Watchman/Hyperion, Piercer/Iapetus, Cronus

Return to Port Olympus

The great trumpet of Overlook Point blew. Flags went up. The site manager of Tartarus sent a messenger to Kiya who happened to be at Port Olympus. Sagacity, himself, escorted the messenger to the top of Olympus where Kiya sat while Cronus played. She watched the sea, she looked over her land, she watched over her children.

"Sagacity, what a pleasant surprise. You and Enceladus build this place yet neither ever join me at the top. The view is breathtaking."

"Yes, Mother. But this messenger from Tartarus has interesting news."

"Oh, what is it?"

The messenger said, "Queen Kiya, these are the flags that were raised: 'Two important guests,' 'In peace,' and 'Port Olympus'; there were no other flags."

"Port Olympus and not Tartarus? Strange, the northern road stops at the camp of the Gigantes. No one can bypass Tartarus to get to the port."

She paused. "Unless they come by sea."

Kiya and Sagacity stared at one another, then directed their gaze southeast toward the coast. A dot soon appeared off the coast, moving swiftly toward Port Olympus.

"Sing me a song, my children," Kiya whispered.

In the distance, if one strained to hear, one could almost believe the dot was singing a sailing song.

Metis and Starmaster had circumvented the entirety of Oursea.

The Mountain Built

Tartarus was complete and fully functional. It served three purposes; as a place for the quarter moon's family dinner, as a reception area for formal receptions for visitors, and as a retreat where family members could escape the chaos of Port Olympus.

When Kiya had commanded Enceladus to build her a mountain, she had merely wanted a high place by the sea so she could look westward out to the sea and eastward over the land of her and her children.

ELDER OCEANIDS: Metis, Tyche, Clymene, Eurybia, Amphitrite
ELDER OLYMPIANS: Hestia, Demeter, Hera, Hades, Poseidon, Zeus
OTHER: Philyra, Dionysus, Heracles, Outis, Enceladus, Littlerock, Porphyrion

Sagacity pointed out the obvious, "We need much larger living quarters, Mother. We have grown so large, and we will continue to grow. Tartarus is simply not large enough for us any longer. If you are to build a mountain, build a mountain in which we can live."

And later, "While we are designing this thing, let's make it a port. If Rivermaster is successful, he may find tribes to trade with us by water."

And still later, "You know, Mother. Even if there are no water trading tribes, I suppose we could establish some outpost ports. Maybe we could send Oceanids to trade from the outposts to our Port Olympus."

And then, "Mother, since we are building this structure, let's make it big and the port large. Perhaps the port will never be used, but still ..."

Then, "You know, Mother, we should have a great circular northern road that connects our port through the highlands to Overlook Point so that traders entering our land can go directly to Port Olympus without coming through our home at Tartarus."

"Quit talking, Sagacity," Enceladus finally said. "You talk too much."

Quarter-Moon Family Gathering

Her family had grown too large and too scattered to join for a family meal every evening on the great patio of Tartarus. Kiya was adamant, however, that every Titan on their island would gather here for their traditional family meal every quarter moon as the sun set. The Quarter-moon gathering would be formal. At each family gathering, there would be feasting and talking, laughter and songs, starting at sundown. Everyone would visit one another through the next day until sundown when each was free to return to their duties. But on this evening and day, they would rest, and all would rejoice in themselves and their family.

And for this gathering; oh, the happiness. Starmaster and Metis were alive. They had sailed north from their port and returned from the south. They had successfully circumvented the border of Oursea. They had stories to tell, and Metis could tell a story well.

Mnemosyne recorded every word.

PRINCIPALS: Kiya, Vanam, Pumi, Valki | ELDER TITANIDES: Themis, Mnemosyne, Phoebe, Tethys, Theia, Rhea | ELDER TITANES: Rivermaster/Oceanus, Sagacity/Coeus, Starmaster/Crius, Watchman/Hyperion, Piercer/Iapetus, Cronus

< >

The next day, Starmaster and Sagacity met.

Starmaster said, "Our plan must include Outis. The creatures there are unbelievable. Do we have anyone accomplished in sign language? I think I and Kemet understand one another well enough. I tried to tell him I would return with much honey in exactly one year, but I can't be sure. Now that we have a vague idea of the extent of Oursea, I believe we could set out on a fast southwest course and arrive at the Kemet outpost in about three days. Right now, the outpost is no more than one of Piercer's obelisks planted on a beach."

Sagacity said, "Where are these people in their development? Greater than our hunters? As great as scholars? As great as the people of Urfa? More like those from Port Kaptara? What kind of people are we working with?"

Starmaster said, "I cannot tell, Sagacity. They are simply different."

The two men discussed possibilities, options, goals, flaws, and dangers. They would formulate a strategy to begin trade with these strange new people and then present the plan at the next Quarter-moon gathering.

Queen Kiya frowned upon mixing family business with family pleasure, but her sons were so excited about all the new ports and the ramifications of expanding trade, and she did enjoy seeing her sons excited. *Who knows what goes on in the minds of men?*

ELDER OCEANIDS: Metis, Tyche, Clymene, Eurybia, Amphitrite
ELDER OLYMPIANS: Hestia, Demeter, Hera, Hades, Poseidon, Zeus
OTHER: Philyra, Dionysus, Heracles, Outis, Enceladus, Littlerock, Porphyrion

15. Consolidation
In the 58th year from the birth of Vanam
Return of the Lost

On the verge of manhood, Cronus rode the elevator to the top of Olympus. He found his mother sitting there, as he knew he would, staring out over Oursea, as he knew he would. He walked over and put his hand on her shoulder.

She looked up at him and placed her hand on his. She said, "It's almost time to light the fire. Even if there is no one at sea to see it, it brings pride to all who see it burning brightly."

"Yes," Cronus replied. "It does." He paused. "Join us in the dining hall this evening. Metis and her sisters will be there. There will be songs."

Kiya laughed. "That would be delightful. They join us so seldom; and never all four at the same time. They always bring me joy."

"Everything always brings you joy, Mother. Come. I will light the fire. We will walk down together."

Cronus lit the great fire atop Port Olympus and held out his elbow for his mother. They walked together down the grand stairway to Kiya's quarters on the floor below. She stopped to change into formal clothes. They then continued to the next floor which contained the Dining Room for the Elder Titans.

Metis saw Kiya enter and ran to embrace her. "Grandmother, you look fabulous!"

Ten of her twelve elder children were in attendance as were the four Oceanid daughters of her missing son and daughter. Enceladus, as always, was nearby. The staff was busy preparing their food and bringing them drink, "Sweet or Bitter?" They talked, they laughed, and they sang.

"Mother, do you remember when you made your grand entrance for Pumi?" Themis asked.

"Yes. I was in my full glory, wasn't I? I remember being so excited, but I tried not to show it. 'Be calm and confident,' I kept telling myself. I am relieved that I no longer must be excited like that. It was all so tiring."

PRINCIPALS: Kiya, Vanam, Pumi, Valki | ELDER TITANIDES: Themis, Mnemosyne, Phoebe, Tethys, Theia, Rhea | ELDER TITANES: Rivermaster/Oceanus, Sagacity/Coeus, Starmaster/Crius, Watchman/Hyperion, Piercer/Iapetus, Cronus

"Excitement is so common, isn't it, Mother?" Themis replied. "Well, I believe your Oceanid granddaughters have a little play they would like to perform for you. Metis?"

The four women jumped up and formed a receiving line at the dining room door. Metis said, "Master Enceladus, would you be so kind?"

Enceladus said, "Of course." He then walked to the door and said, "Metis, would you be so kind?"

Metis said, "Of course."

As Metis opened the dining room door, Enceladus said in a loud voice, "Titans! Allow me to introduce Titane Rivermaster, Titanide Tethys, and their four children."

Kiya fainted.

< >

His hair was full and white as was his beard; her hair was streaked with gray. They were bronze. Their children were swarmed by Titanides as the Titanes worked to revive their mother. There were shrieks of joy.

Rivermaster and Tethys looked down upon their mother with concern. Kiya's eyes fluttered open. She looked up at her lost son and daughter and smiled through her tears.

Rivermaster pulled her into his arms and said, "We are home, Mother. We hardly recognize the place. Let me introduce your grandchildren. This is our daughter, Amphitrite, our oldest son, Achelous, our second son, Alpheus, and our youngest son, Inachus. Tethys lay in a great river as she gave birth to each." He continued, "But our story is long and wending. We will tell it another day. On this day, let us savor being with our family."

The Story of Oceanus and Tethys

They told their story later—at Tartarus—gathered around the patio fire pit. Once more, the family sat together listening to stories, singing songs, and laughing.

The second-generation Titan children played together nearby. Sagacity and Phoebe's young girls, Leto and Asteria, had been raised in the

ELDER OCEANIDS: Metis, Tyche, Clymene, Eurybia, Amphitrite
ELDER OLYMPIANS: Hestia, Demeter, Hera, Hades, Poseidon, Zeus
OTHER: Philyra, Dionysus, Heracles, Outis, Enceladus, Littlerock, Porphyrion

cosmopolitan, sophisticated environment of Tartarus. They were fascinated with Amphitrite, Achelous, Alpheus, and Inachus who had been raised as self-sufficient wilderness explorers.

Starmaster and Eurybia's toddler, Astraeus, ran excitedly between his big cousins.

Piercer and Clymene's baby boy, Atlas, crawled between them all.

At last, Mnemosyne said, "We are ready, Rivermaster. Tell your story."

"'Oceanus!' Tethys announced. Our children and the western world know my husband as 'Oceanus.'"

"Such an impressive name," Kiya said. "I have a son named Oceanus."

Oceanus said, "A son with an impressive story, Mother. A story of seas and lands beyond our imagination. It begins at a place where I tried in vain to drive a spear into the ground; a place I named 'Outpost Spearpoint.' Behind me was Oursea. In front of me was another sea, a sea greater than ours, a sea much higher than ours. Two seas that are not connected at any point but are separated by sheer cliffs less than two stades wide. A cliff that, if removed, would send a flood of water into our lands. The level of Oursea would rise at least one stade; perhaps more. Oursea would cover our fertile plains and rise to make Overlook Point level with the sea, perhaps lower than Oursea."

He paused to let Sagacity and the others consider this information. Sagacity asked, "Can this sheer cliff be breached?"

"We have no power to move it. It is solid rock. Hard solid rock."

Oceanus continued his story. "This was only one of the great seas we discovered. As we walked west along this shoreline, we met many strange tribes. Their language and ways were unfamiliar. Some appeared civilized but most were suspicious of us. They were not much more than brutes. We learned a little of the language used in the region; although most of it is pointing, hand gestures, and facial expressions. But we learned enough words to navigate through their lands. At some point, the land became fertile, and the tribes friendlier. Tethys recorded as much as we could comprehend, yet we were fearful and traveled as fast as we could. Tethys gave birth to Amphitrite in one of the rivers near a group of friendly

PRINCIPALS: Kiya, Vanam, Pumi, Valki | ELDER TITANIDES: Themis, Mnemosyne, Phoebe, Tethys, Theia, Rhea | ELDER TITANES: Rivermaster/Oceanus, Sagacity/Coeus, Starmaster/Crius, Watchman/Hyperion, Piercer/Iapetus, Cronus

people, and the women were trained in the way of childbirth. We stayed for a few days and then continued scouting, along the shoreline, toward the west. Then at last ..." Oceanus's voice trailed off.

Tethys continued, "Then we came to the end of the world. Sea to our left, our right, and in front. Endless water. We turned due north. The land rose to form a tall hill, almost a mountain. We were stopped at the top by a great chasm separating us from a tall hill on the other side. A river far below connected the vast new ocean to the sea we had been scouting. We were confused about what we saw and set up camp. As we rested and considered our options, a gatherer from a nearby camp found us. She was great with child and saw my infant daughter. She was excited and friendly. She and I talked as best we could. Her name was Calpeia. She invited us to their camp, where we were fed and entertained. Their chief was impressed with my husband, who had grown ever more commanding. He and the chief became friends. The seas were important to them and their way of life. This mutual interest was a big reason for their friendship. We stayed for three years learning the language and learning about the seas, their lands, and the people. That is where two of our sons were born. When my time came, Calpeia led us down the path from the top of their land into the water below; between the two great pillars. That is where I gave birth. There was a great celebration with each birth; surrounding tribes were invited. It reminded me of the Tallstone festival, only smaller."

Oceanus continued, "We left their land soon after. We crossed the narrow body of water and continued our journey. After perhaps twelve seasons, we came upon Outpost Spearpoint, untouched. We knew that we had traveled the shoreline of the new, high sea. We had returned to the place where we had left Oursea to follow the shore of the new sea."

"And wiser. Much wiser," Tethys interjected.

"Unbelievably wiser," Oceanus said. "We took up our quest of following the shore of Oursea. We went southward and then eastward to an uninhabitable land of sand. We traveled on and eventually met a tribe that took us inland to a camp in fertile plains beside a great river. In this river, Tethys gave birth to Inachus. The chief of their tribe heard of the birth and came to inspect us. He stared at us a long time and then pointed to me and said, 'Ti-Tan?'"

ELDER OCEANIDS: Metis, Tyche, Clymene, Eurybia, Amphitrite
ELDER OLYMPIANS: Hestia, Demeter, Hera, Hades, Poseidon, Zeus
OTHER: Philyra, Dionysus, Heracles, Outis, Enceladus, Littlerock, Porphyrion

"I replied, 'Ti-tan. Ti-tan Oceanus.' His eyes widened. He ran to embrace me in a bear hug and said, 'Ti-tan Oc-ean-us. Ti-tan Star-mast-er. Little Ti-tan Met-is. Mighty Met-is. Like warrior. You come from the great desert. Not from water like other Ti-tans. How?'"

"I pointed to the heavens, made great circular motions, and said, 'Lost. Many years. Want to go home.' The chief's eyes got big; his face concerned. He said 'Home? Ti-tan home? I take you home.' The Chief took the six of us along their great river and on to Port Kemet where we were greeted by the Oceanid Portmaster. She immediately commandeered a vessel to bring us here where our daughters met us and secreted us to their private quarters. They oohed and aahed over their new sister and brothers. We told them about what had happened to us over the last twelve years. Metis invited us to a party."

Metis exclaimed, "And here they are!"

In Tartarus, there was much love, joy, and laughter.

In the west, there was Outpost Spearpoint and ominous silence.

State Visits

Sagacity could not stand the unknown, "Only problems come from the unknown. We must know all there is to know about this outpost." He formed an expedition to travel to and study Outpost Spearpoint.

The expedition would split into two groups at Port Graikoi.

Oceanus would lead the ground unit to follow the shore, into the mountains, and on to Spearpoint. His group would contain himself, Sagacity, Piercer, Tethys, Themis, three Oceanids with deep water talents, and two stonemasons with rock climbing talents.

The second unit would continue by ship to the base of the mountain directly below Outpost Spearpoint. This unit would be led by Starmaster and included Kiya, Metis, Littlerock, Mnemosyne, three Oceanids, and an expert stonemason.

"Know your enemy?" Themis asked as they boarded their ship.

"Exactly," Sagacity answered.

PRINCIPALS: Kiya, Vanam, Pumi, Valki | ELDER TITANIDES: Themis, Mnemosyne, Phoebe, Tethys, Theia, Rhea | ELDER TITANES: Rivermaster/Oceanus, Sagacity/Coeus, Starmaster/Crius, Watchman/Hyperion, Piercer/Iapetus, Cronus

Port Graikoi

But on the way to Spearpoint, there was the matter of Affairs of State. Port Graikoi was the unofficial capital of the immediate area plus a large interior area. Chief Graikoi had leveraged his position as chief of Port Graikoi to incorporate vast swathes of the inland to come under his control. He had started referring to himself as 'King Graikoi,' in the fashion of the great peoples of Port Olympus with their 'Queen.' Pretentious, perhaps, but he was sure that he would eventually build a civilization worthy of the title. The King had attended several Winter Solstice Festivals and had been entertained at Port Olympus. He was a somewhat worldly man. But this was overwhelming. Entertaining Queen Kiya would be too much for his kingdom to properly accomplish. But there was also Oceanus, several Titans, and Metis herself. He frantically called his advisors together to create a plan to entertain these visiting dignitaries.

Port Graikoi

The Titan ship sailed into Port Graikoi.

Colorful flags flew throughout the port. They were greeted with drums, horns, dancers, and a chorus. The Titanides were delighted with the pageantry. Starmaster led the Titans onto the dock to meet the waiting receiving line of local leaders. The Titans were led down to the receiving line by a juggler keeping many fruits plus one sword expertly in the air. The Oceanids were infatuated. As everyone greeted everyone, the smell of fragrant incense drifted through the air. The greetings were completed, and everyone walked toward the main port building for a banquet.

They passed motionless figures of nudes in various athletic positions apparently carved from marmaros. Piercer was beside himself. *These are life-sized replicas of people carved directly from marmaros. I can train stonemasons to carve one in the likeness of Kiya and every elder titan. We could line the paths to Tartarus with them. And animals; why not animals, too? This is an entirely new building form I had never even thought of. The potential! Oh, the potential!*

Themis caught movement in the corner of her eye. She turned to look at the motionless figures. Each had turned slightly to follow the direction of the crowd. She shouted, "Those things are alive!"

ELDER OCEANIDS: Metis, Tyche, Clymene, Eurybia, Amphitrite
ELDER OLYMPIANS: Hestia, Demeter, Hera, Hades, Poseidon, Zeus
OTHER: Philyra, Dionysus, Heracles, Outis, Enceladus, Littlerock, Porphyrion

King Graikoi, pleased that someone had noticed, said, "Yes, we call them statues. It is an art our young people do to entertain us. They cover themselves with white powder and can remain motionless for hours. They look like stone, don't they?"

King Graikoi presented Prince Cadmus and his consort Harmonia to Queen Kiya. Cadmus was an enlightened chief from the far north who had pledged allegiance to King Graikoi to gain the benefits of the civilized resources the king had through his close relations with Port Olympus. Graikoi bestowed the title 'Prince' upon Cadmus to bind his allegiance and to increase the power of the king.

The Affairs of State came to completion. The Titans were impressed.

King Graikoi's guests were genuinely pleased and entertained. Toward the end, Metis drew him aside, put her arms around his shoulders, looked at him with big eyes, kissed him briefly on his lips, and said, "I am extremely proud of you. They are shocked by what you are building in your country. You are doing sooo well." She then turned and joined the Titans.

King Graikoi stood silent. *I will someday become a true king.*

All rose and profusely thanked their host for a delightful time. Kiya extended an invitation for King Graikoi to be her guest the season before the upcoming Winter Solstice festival. She was interested in the progress his kingdom was making. Perhaps they could exchange ideas on how to best serve their people.

I will someday become a true king.

Port Kaptara

Oceanus and his group did not reboard their ship but instead traveled by land toward Outpost Spearpoint.

Starmaster set sail to the base of the cliff by way of Port Kaptara. The land unit would take many more days to reach the outpost than would the ship. There would be ample time to make a State call to Chief Aeolus. A surprise State call. *Let's see how they handle a surprise visit from the queen of the Titans.*

PRINCIPALS: Kiya, Vanam, Pumi, Valki | ELDER TITANIDES: Themis, Mnemosyne, Phoebe, Tethys, Theia, Rhea | ELDER TITANES: Rivermaster/Oceanus, Sagacity/Coeus, Starmaster/Crius, Watchman/Hyperion, Piercer/Iapetus, Cronus

Book 2. The Beginning of Civilization: Mythologies Told True

Chief Aeolus was a practical leader. He was developing a sea-going nation and was delighted that Queen Kiya, herself, would drop by to see how they were progressing.

Aeolus asked, "And Daughter of the Sea, Metis, how are you!?"

All had a delightful time.

Outpost Spearpoint

A rope ladder had been lowered from the peak by the time Starmaster's ship arrived. Metis lowered a floating platform onto the water near the rope. The stonemason began drilling holes in the cliff face in which to place bolts with which to secure the floating platform. The platform was secured; they had a base of operations secured to the land. They tied their ship to the platform and tugged on the rope ladder to indicate they were prepared for the next operation. A stonemason started descending the ladder and creating safe places where a climber could rest. The ship's stonemason began doing the same but starting at the bottom of the cliff. They met halfway up. A route had been created from Oursea to Outpost Spearpoint.

Kiya was the first to climb the ladder and arrive at the upper level. That evening everyone gathered to watch the sun set over Oursea.

Sunrise

The complete documentation of the great wall of stone separating the two seas began in earnest: the land bridge itself and the two seas the bridge separated. Everyone began their assigned tasks.

Kiya stood alone looking over Oursea. She called Littlerock to join her. A breeze flowed through her hair. They stood together looking out over Oursea in silence. Then, Kiya half-turned toward him and said, "Littlerock, dear friend. I have a question of the utmost sensitivity. A question I command you never to address with anyone; even Piercer. Is this understood?"

"Yes, my Queen."

"What need be done to, in the blink of an eye, remove this wall?"

ELDER OCEANIDS: Metis, Tyche, Clymene, Eurybia, Amphitrite
ELDER OLYMPIANS: Hestia, Demeter, Hera, Hades, Poseidon, Zeus
OTHER: Philyra, Dionysus, Heracles, Outis, Enceladus, Littlerock, Porphyrion

16. The First Marriage
In the 59th year from the birth of Vanam
The Seduction of Rhea

Cronus woke from his tortured dream. He had done it, again. *No, no, no. I can't keep doing this!*

He sat up in his bed; then forcibly threw himself back down. *I can't keep doing this.*

He stared at his darkened ceiling and remembered his dream. He remembered her dress sliding from her body. And then he did it.

He got out of bed, cleaned himself, sat in his chair, and fantasized. *She will be in her party dress laughing with some random gigante. I will be dressed in my best uniform. I will be handsome. Manly. I will walk over, take her by the hand, and walk off with her. She will turn, smile, and wave goodbye to the gigante. I will lead her to a secluded fountain. I will turn to her and stare into her eyes. She will tilt her head and smile at me. I will unbutton the buttons on her dress. She will stare into my eyes as I do so. Her dress will slide down her perfect body onto the ground. She will stand before me totally unclothed.*

"Damn, damn, damn!" he said out loud. *Then what will you do, little boy? Do you think a woman like her is going to let a child like you touch her? She would be repulsed if she even thought I could think of these things. I am nothing! She is everything!*

He returned to his bed and lay down. But he knew he would not yet sleep. *She will be in her party dress laughing with some random gigante ...*

< >

The next morning, Cronus found his brother, Sagacity, in the port control center. "Brother, do you have time to talk with me?"

"Always, Cronus. Of what shall we talk?"

"Not here, Brother. In private, maybe we can walk or something."

"Let's go into the gardens. There is always a park bench by an out-of-the-way fountain. There we can solve all the world's problems, Little Brother."

They left, found a park bench, and sat down. "And so ..." Sagacity said.

PRINCIPALS: Kiya, Vanam, Pumi, Valki | ELDER TITANIDES: Themis, Mnemosyne, Phoebe, Tethys, Theia, Rhea | ELDER TITANES: Rivermaster/Oceanus, Sagacity/Coeus, Starmaster/Crius, Watchman/Hyperion, Piercer/Iapetus, Cronus

"Sex," Cronus replied. "I am tormented by it. I can't make it go away."

"You think about it all day? Before you go to bed? Nighttime ejaculations? That sort of thing?"

"YES!" Cronus replied. "How did you know?"

"Just a guess, Cronus. And I have just the solution for it. Let us walk down to the beach. There will be many Oceanids swimming. Most of them will be naked. Think about it, Cronus. At least one of them will be friendly. If one recognizes you as an Elder Titan, they will all be friendly. What say, Brother? Let us walk to the beach."

"No. I can't. I don't want to. I mean, how can I couple with a stranger? Someone I don't even know? That isn't right. You should know her. Know what she thinks, how she feels, what makes her laugh. How can you couple with somebody you don't even have feelings for? I don't understand it."

"Hmmm," Sagacity said. "This isn't usually a problem. This particular problem may take a moment or two to resolve. I, myself, in moments of weakness, and far from home, have been known to return the smile of an unfamiliar farmer woman, maybe an unknown Oceanid now and then. Nothing your Aunt Phoebe need know about. She wouldn't be that pleased to know these things, but, anyway, back to your problem. Hmmm."

He considered the issue. "Aha! Would there be a particular maiden who has stolen your heart? A particularly ravishing, interesting woman of great desirability? Hmmm?"

Cronus hesitated, "Yes. There is."

"Of course! Is it anyone I might know?"

Cronus hesitated, "You won't tell anyone? Promise."

"This is a private discussion of sex, Cronus. Such things are never discussed with anyone else. It is an issue of honor."

"Our sister, Rhea."

"Oh, my! She is a fireball. Yes, Rhea would turn the head of any red-blooded male. You set your standards high, my boy. She is attracted to Gigantes, you know. Bad boys. They don't treat their women with the

ELDER OCEANIDS: Metis, Tyche, Clymene, Eurybia, Amphitrite
ELDER OLYMPIANS: Hestia, Demeter, Hera, Hades, Poseidon, Zeus
OTHER: Philyra, Dionysus, Heracles, Outis, Enceladus, Littlerock, Porphyrion

same respect as Titans do. More respect than hunters, of course. But hunters are rather quick with their intimate relationships. Rhea, you say. She is not really your sister, you know. She was adopted by Mother way back in the day from tribes with too many girl children. Mother was always a soft touch for unwanted little girls. All our sisters are adopted, which makes no difference to Mother. We are all her children, whether she gave us birth or not. But what you have working for you is Rhea is not your biological sister. That, plus you are an Elder Titan. Never, ever, underestimate what a privilege and responsibility that carries with it. Plus, it is a magnet to the opposite sex. And, goodness knows, Sister Rhea is certainly of the opposite sex."

"What should I do, Brother Sagacity?"

"What should you do? Hmmm, I grew up with her, you know. I don't see Rhea in those terms. She was a brat. But, still, I recognize her charms. You did not grow up with her, either. She is what? Ten or fifteen years older than you? That will either work to your advantage or your disadvantage. Some women like the age thing; some don't. If you are to succeed in your quest assume it is to your advantage."

"My quest. What quest?"

"Why, to seduce Rhea, obviously. You have a great challenge here, Cronus. You are what? Thirteen? Fourteen? Inexperienced. A virgin. She thinks of you as her little brother. She is almost twice your age and very experienced and has never given you a sexual thought. Yes, indeed. You have an impossible challenge here. But you are a Titane. If there is one thing a Titane loves, it is an impossible challenge. You may well go down in humiliation, but success or not, what a time you will have! I propose a plan."

The Party Dress

It was a Full-moon family gathering. Full-moon gatherings were always formal. It gave the Titanides an excuse to dress up in their party clothes. New technology had yielded various string and wind instruments that created pleasing noises; 'music,' it was called. The players were extremely serious about advancing and perfecting their newfound art form. They played their instruments together and made quite harmonious music. Four

PRINCIPALS: Kiya, Vanam, Pumi, Valki | ELDER TITANIDES: Themis, Mnemosyne, Phoebe, Tethys, Theia, Rhea | ELDER TITANES: Rivermaster/Oceanus, Sagacity/Coeus, Starmaster/Crius, Watchman/Hyperion, Piercer/Iapetus, Cronus

older Oceanids supplied voices to coincide with the instruments. Together, they provided a most pleasing listening experience.

The moon was full. Dinner had finished. Everyone stood around talking, drinking Sweet or Bitters, and listening to the band of musicians.

She was in her party dress laughing with some random Gigante.

Cronus walked over to her in his best uniform. She turned to him and said, "My, how handsome you look tonight, Cronus."

He took her hand and asked, "Will you walk with me, Sister?"

She accepted the gentle pull of her hand, then turned, smiled, and waved goodbye to the Gigante. She asked, "To where do we walk, Cronus?"

He replied, "There is a place at Overlook Point I would like to show you."

"Overlook Point? That's quite a distance. I had better freshen my drink."

"That will be taken care of. Let's just walk under this beautiful full moon."

"All right, Cronus. We will walk under this beautiful full moon." His older sister absent-mindedly disengaged her hand. "What shall we talk about?"

"Me. I am a Titane. An elder Titane. I must grow into a person of great confidence and worth. Someone like you, Rhea. Confident, interesting. As handsome as you are beautiful."

"Well, you are certainly on your way, Cronus. The Oceanids and other young women often ask about you. 'How can we meet Cronus?' they ask."

"I am not at all interested in shallow, giddy women. I don't know how any man would couple with a woman whom he does not admire and have feelings for. Wait! We are approaching a way station. An Oceanid is serving drinks."

They walked over and Cronus said to the attentive Oceanid, "My friend would like a sweet drink but with a touch of ginger. I will have a Bitter, not stirred."

The Oceanid smiled, said, "Yes, Master Titan," and delivered the drinks.

"Rhea took her drink, took a sip, raised her eyebrows toward Cronus, and said, "Very nice. How did you know she would be here?"

ELDER OCEANIDS: Metis, Tyche, Clymene, Eurybia, Amphitrite
ELDER OLYMPIANS: Hestia, Demeter, Hera, Hades, Poseidon, Zeus
OTHER: Philyra, Dionysus, Heracles, Outis, Enceladus, Littlerock, Porphyrion

"I am a Titane. I must know these things. I am still young, perhaps. But I grow older with each moment. Shall we continue our talk? I believe we were discussing your great beauty."

"No. We were discussing your desirability among your young women admirers," Rhea laughed.

"Hah!" Cronus exclaimed. "And how old must one be to become attractive to a woman of substance and true desirability? These are the issues that concern me and impede my maturing into a true elder Titane. A Titane even more sexually desirable than the manly, but surely, mentally limited Gigantes."

Rhea giggled and sipped on her drink as they continued their walk. She considered his problem. "Many older women would be delighted if you approached them, Cronus. Women usually couple with men their own age or older but there is no shame in taking a younger man. You will find one who interests you."

"Look, another way station. Let us see what she has to offer."

They walked to it. The attending Oceanid asked, "Flowers for your friend?" The way station was covered with bouquets of beautiful flowers.

"No bouquets for my friend." He replied. "We are on a most interesting walk. A bouquet would be a burden for her to carry. But those hanging purple flowers. They are lovely and fragrant. Can you weave several into her hair?"

"Of course, Master Titane. That will make them even lovelier. It is a shame that she cannot see herself."

"I can see her," Cronus replied. He took her hand and said, "Walk closer so that I can smell the fragrance of your hair."

She hesitated. Then ... suddenly everything fell into place; the walk, the drinks, the flowers, the handholding, the attentiveness, each carefully chosen word. It all led to ...

She stopped abruptly, turned to him, and said, "You aren't my real brother. I mean not by biological brother."

PRINCIPALS: Kiya, Vanam, Pumi, Valki | ELDER TITANIDES: Themis, Mnemosyne, Phoebe, Tethys, Theia, Rhea | ELDER TITANES: Rivermaster/Oceanus, Sagacity/Coeus, Starmaster/Crius, Watchman/Hyperion, Piercer/Iapetus, Cronus

"No. Mother is my biological mother and your adopted mother. To her, we are all 'her children,' but no, Rhea. We are not related by blood. Isn't the moon glorious tonight? The most glorious I have ever seen."

Cronus moved to resume their walk. Rhea stood her ground.

"What is this view that you wish to share with me? What awaits me?"

He answered, "The best musicians are not at Tartarus tonight. They wait at Overlook Point near the statue of Mother. I have engaged them and some talented Oceanids. I have requested the Oceanids sing you some of their private songs. Songs they love. Songs of entering the sea. Of walking ever deeper into the sea. Of the sea wrapping itself around their bodies, pulling them deeper and deeper. Surrounding them. Loving them."

She hesitated. "Are you trying to seduce me, Cronus?"

"Not yet Rhea. I am not yet mature enough. But I hope to be by the time we reach Overlook Point."

Rhea laughed, removed her hand from his, and stared at him without expression for a long while. "They are fragrant, aren't they? Have you ever been with a woman, Cronus?"

"No." Unblinking, he returned her stare.

She was silent for a while, then said, "Cronus, I don't want to couple with a virgin at Overlook Point. It would ruin the ambiance." She continued her unblinking stare, tilted her head, and smiled up at him.

I will unbutton the buttons on her dress. She will stare into my eyes as I do so. Her dress will slide down her body onto the ground. She will stand before me unclothed ...

The Ceremony

Theirs was the first marriage. Ever.

Cronus had said, "Marriage is to be the coming thing." He thought it would strengthen the bond between the man and the woman. Promising to give up sexual liaisons with all others was considered avant-garde by both sexes. Could that even be done? Not that people were promiscuous, or anything, but the fact remained, people were promiscuous. Nonetheless, Cronus was sure that he would never wish to couple with

ELDER OCEANIDS: Metis, Tyche, Clymene, Eurybia, Amphitrite
ELDER OLYMPIANS: Hestia, Demeter, Hera, Hades, Poseidon, Zeus
OTHER: Philyra, Dionysus, Heracles, Outis, Enceladus, Littlerock, Porphyrion

any woman other than his beloved Rhea. Rhea, on the other hand, negotiated that her occasional liaison with a random, mentally inferior, muscled Gigante would not count as long as it was only one time. Per Gigante. Cronus laughingly agreed. "Now that we have that out of the way, let's get married."

The ceremony was held at Overlook Point. The pomp was unimaginable. Port Olympus could have handled the mass of people, but Cronus was insistent that he marry Rhea as they stood upon Overlook Point with everyone in the world standing on the sloping hill below them; watching their marriage take place.

Rhea's body was already showing signs of her daughter, Hestia, growing inside her. Beside Rhea, Kiya stood in a black form-fitting dress. Pumi had traveled from Tallstone to stand beside their son, Cronus. Oceanus would conduct a formal ceremony with formal words, where vows were exchanged, where Oceanus pronounced them husband and wife, where Cronus kissed Rhea, and where they turned to face their adoring public.

Where there was pandemonium.

A New Path

The formal party was held at the base of the hill below Overlook Point. Everyone came. Sagacity found Cronus and embraced him, "Impossible challenges, boy? Don't you love them?! By the way, your thoughts on extending our culture beyond our boundaries are most interesting. Get with me and Starmaster. And Metis, of course. Let's discuss it! You have got a great future as an Elder Titan. Young blood! We need young blood. Young leadership! New directions! New paths! Change! As soon as this is over, call a meeting. Let's get your projects moving."

The child, Hestia, would be born in six months.

Change would come.

Friends and Lovers

Kiya and Pumi left the merrymakers to their merrymaking. They retired to Kiya's quarters for an evening of catching up on old times.

PRINCIPALS: Kiya, Vanam, Pumi, Valki | ELDER TITANIDES: Themis, Mnemosyne, Phoebe, Tethys, Theia, Rhea | ELDER TITANES: Rivermaster/Oceanus, Sagacity/Coeus, Starmaster/Crius, Watchman/Hyperion, Piercer/Iapetus, Cronus

"Valki would have enjoyed this. My son, in a committed marriage. A first. She likes firsts. Although, she doesn't approve of the concept of marriage. 'If you are committed, you need no words to make it so,' she said." He stopped, gazed at Kiya, and quietly said, "You look no older than when we were children, Kiya."

"I try to keep myself fit. I eat and drink the right things. You are kind," she said and then laughed. "I also mix the Red Nectar that I make for me and my children. Few know of this but you and the elder Titanides. We continue to grow old, but only half as fast as one would expect. Now you know all my secrets." She giggled.

He laughed, "I see. There is much in life yet to learn." He held out his hand. She placed hers into his. He gently squeezed it. "My heart went out to you when you were banished. You have done well for yourself and your family, Kiya. Tartarus is the most glorious city in the world. When we negotiated our trade agreement, did you know where it would lead?"

"Oh, yes. Every detail."

"Did you suspect we might mate that night?"

She released her hand, stood up, removed her clothes, and stood naked before him, letting old eyes admire a young body, "Men! You are all so dense. Every move was rehearsed, Pumi. Every word. She sat on his lap and leaned back into his arms. She breathed deeply. "So much has happened. Life has been so good to us. It can't go on forever, but I shall enjoy every breath of life while I can." She laid her head against his shoulder and closed her eyes. "I have been remiss, I suppose. I have not been with any man since you. That was a long time ago. I had forgotten the warmth a man can bring."

He held her close.

< >

She lay exhausted on top of his body, purring softly. Pumi was pensive, staring at the ceiling. Kiya raised her head and looked at him. "What? Did I not please you?" she demanded.

He laughed. "Where did you learn these things, Kiya of the Clan of the Serpent? Who taught you?" He embraced her. She embraced back.

ELDER OCEANIDS: Metis, Tyche, Clymene, Eurybia, Amphitrite
ELDER OLYMPIANS: Hestia, Demeter, Hera, Hades, Poseidon, Zeus
OTHER: Philyra, Dionysus, Heracles, Outis, Enceladus, Littlerock, Porphyrion

She murmured, "Will you tell Valki of this? Will she be angry with me?"

"Valki told me that I owed you a great debt because you raised my son without my help. That I was to provide whatever poor compensation I could, as often as I could, to discharge this debt; that she did care to know how it was discharged; only that I had performed my duty well."

Kiya giggled. "As often as you can? Well, then. I am required to command you to perform your duty. And I do not want 'poor,' am I understood?"

Pumi understood.

< >

She awoke in the early morning, lying in his arms. He was again staring at the ceiling. "Where are you, now?" she asked.

He glanced at her and quietly said, "When we buried Breathson, Valki and I mated at his grave. It was not love. It was fury. She screamed at me; she screamed at the heavens. She was tormented. She spent her fury on me. She collapsed from exhaustion. I lay there without feeling on the border of nonexistence. As I approached unconscious sleep, our dead son spoke to me. He said, 'I have shed the body which was my prison. I am not only alive but at last, I live.' Does Breathson still live? If so, where is this place? The Scholars think about it. They suggest many things. But no one knows how this might be."

He laughed. "Perhaps a Tartarus research department can find this place."

She sat on top of him. "I don't know about that, Pumi. But let me see what *my* research department can find."

Consummation

The Titan world was perfect.

Kiya and her children prospered. They were expanding the civilized world—adding untold riches to all they encountered. There was peace, harmony, growth, expansion, and knowledge. It was a golden age, a brotherhood of man.

There was no indication, no hint, that sadness would come.

Infinite sadness.

PRINCIPALS: Kiya, Vanam, Pumi, Valki | ELDER TITANIDES: Themis, Mnemosyne, Phoebe, Tethys, Theia, Rhea | ELDER TITANES: Rivermaster/Oceanus, Sagacity/Coeus, Starmaster/Crius, Watchman/Hyperion, Piercer/Iapetus, Cronus

PART III. OLYMPIANS
17. Cronos
In the 69th year from the birth of Vanam

Chief-of-Chiefs

Cronus, Port Olympus 'Chief-of-Chiefs for All Projects,' sat at his desk overlooking the harbor at evening dusk and considered the long-term needs of the Titans. He had grown tall and lean.

He had suggested, and the family had agreed, that the day-to-day operation of the port would be handled with extreme efficiency by Themis. She enjoyed tracking complex, unending tasks. She was perfect to be given the title 'Olympus Portmaster.'

Assigning Starmaster as 'Olympus Trade Representative' to all trading partners was also met with universal family approval. Cronus's insistence that Starmaster's name be changed to something more professional and sophisticated was not met with universal approval. "What need does anyone have of a professional or sophisticated name?" as voiced by Kiya, was the consensus of the Elder Titans.

Nonetheless, Cronus prevailed. Starmaster became known as 'Crius,' a more professional and sophisticated name; presumably bringing greater status and gravitas to the office of 'Olympus Trade Representative;' and, therefore, greater power.

Cronus had assigned Sagacity to 'Director of Research for Olympian Interests.' Their interests lay in developing Piercer's work in colored rock; especially as it applied to metalworking applications; shipbuilding, rapid ground transportation, and weapons technologies. Piercer was, of course, 'Chief Research Scholar for Metal Research.' The aging Littlerock was his 'Assistant Director.' Creating stone items for trade purposes was assigned to 'Stone Art and Craft Manufacturing' managed by an entry-level executive.

Kiya's honorific, 'Queen' was formalized to indicate 'Head of State.' The duties and responsibilities of this office were spelled out in Sagacity's charter, 'Monarch: Duties and Powers of the Head of State.'

ELDER OCEANIDS: Metis, Tyche, Clymene, Eurybia, Amphitrite
ELDER OLYMPIANS: Hestia, Demeter, Hera, Hades, Poseidon, Zeus
OTHER: Philyra, Dionysus, Heracles, Outis, Enceladus, Littlerock, Porphyrion

Porphyrion gratefully accepted the offer to become 'General of the Army,' which included responsibility for training a defense corps and liaison to the 'Director of Research' for the development of weapons technology.

Phoebe was quite comfortable with developing a positive relationship with all known tribes as 'Secretary of Foreign Affairs.' Mnemosyne was her deputy. The position required considerable travel.

Oceanus declined, as did his mate, Tethys, the request to become 'Chief of Expeditionary Forces and Frontier Laison.'

Metis laughed at the very concept of 'business organization.' She declined all offers of increased responsibility.

All chiefs had at least one assistant chief. The intent was that a chief could leave, transfer, or retire at any time and there would be at least one competent candidate to replace them.

The Oceanids presented a special problem. Oceanids were not manageable. They were efficient, intelligent, quick-learning, and fulfilled their promises; otherwise, they were not manageable. Work a day, off a day, was their preferred work schedule. Sagacity proposed the concept of 'part-time' workers. Everyone compromised with 'three days on, three days off.' As it turned out, an Oceanid did not accept work unless they were interested in what they were doing. They had a quick learning curve and tremendous potential. But ... they were not manageable.

There was a caveat in the 'part-time' approach. Oceanids were natural-born childcare providers. A working mother had only to send their child to the beach and every Oceanid there considered it her joy and duty to teach and nurture the child. And Oceanids were natural-born teachers. Send the child to the beach with instructions of 'learn how to read' or 'learn how to write' or anything else, the child need only ask the first Oceanid they met and soon the child would be surrounded by qualified teachers on whatever subject was requested.

But it was their inclination to swim nude that most bothered Cronus. That just wasn't right. The Oceanids accepted the dress code of a high-neck blouse and knee-length skirt while at work but on the beach, it remained clothing optional. Cronus presented the problem to Theia, 'Chief of Textiles and Fashion Design.' Her solution was elegant. She opened a

PRINCIPALS: Kiya, Vanam, Pumi, Valki | ELDER TITANIDES: Themis, Mnemosyne, Phoebe, Tethys, Theia, Rhea | ELDER TITANES: Rivermaster/Oceanus, Sagacity/Coeus, Starmaster/Crius, Watchman/Hyperion, Piercer/Iapetus, Cronus

boutique near the beach and stocked it with little strips of colorful fabrics. One little bottom piece could be worn to cover the genitals and a matching piece could be selected to support the breasts. They were sassy and fun to wear, and it was like wearing nothing at all. An instant hit. They provided at least the trace of modesty that Cronus sought.

Yes, Cronus had organized the affairs of the Titans quite nicely. Their influence had increased a hundredfold, as had their riches. Cronus was not displeased. Yet, he remained, as always, uneasy. *These papyrus scrolls Mnemosyne developed are extremely useful. I wonder if we can develop a more efficient method to record and store information. Maps. I need more maps. We operate throughout the region, and we don't even have maps. But maps take up so much space.*

There was a knock on his door. He realized it was late and his assistant had probably left for the day. He turned in his chair to face the door, and said, "Come in."

The door opened. Kiya entered.

"Mother!" he said as he rose to greet her. "How delightful. I don't often see you at the port."

She extended her arms accepting his embrace. "And I did not see you at our Quarter-moon family dinner. All my children and grandchildren were there except you. We had a wonderful time. Metis and her sisters came and serenaded us. I missed you, Son."

"I'm sorry, Mother. This cursed work never ends. If I don't get it done, it will never get done. You know how it is."

"So many errors in one sentence, Son. It will all get done. Just not as quickly and to the standards of Cronus. You demand too much of yourself. Rhea and your children never see you. Hestia and Demeter need a father. You know they are not respectful children. Your influence would be a great benefit for both them and for Rhea."

Cronus laughed a cold laugh. "Rhea has her Gigantes. I'm sure she gets along well without me. As for my children, did they disrupt the family dinner, yet again?"

ELDER OCEANIDS: Metis, Tyche, Clymene, Eurybia, Amphitrite
ELDER OLYMPIANS: Hestia, Demeter, Hera, Hades, Poseidon, Zeus
OTHER: Philyra, Dionysus, Heracles, Outis, Enceladus, Littlerock, Porphyrion

Kiya laughed. "I will not complain about my grandchildren the only time I get to visit my son. Visit me at Tartarus if their behavior concerns you. We can discuss it then. Now, show me this empire you are so busy creating."

Laughing, he said, "Do you prefer to see organization charts or strategic planning documents? No? Well then, Mother, let's go to the roof and look out over your empire. It's just as magnificent as when you settled here a thousand years ago."

"Don't date me, Son. It wasn't that long ago."

"To the roof, Mother!"

He pulled a cord. A bell rang alerting Gigantes to prepare to operate the elevator. They entered. He pulled another cord indicating he wished to go to the roof. The elevator began to rise. "One of Sagacity's water people is working on replacing the Gigante-powered elevator with waterpower, but it is a complex issue, I'm afraid."

They arrived at the top level, stepped out onto the roof, and looked out over Oursea.

"I brought you up here many times when you were a child, Cronus. You loved it. Nothing was finished back then. I thought we were building a mighty structure that no one would ever see but my children. It is a different world we live in, now."

He put his arm around her shoulder. "All because of you, Mother. Mnemosyne tells me the story of you once being the Elder Woman in a tribe of hunter-gathers. Well, that world has ended. The hunter-gathers just don't know it yet. You ended it. Father Pumi ended it. Mother Valki ended it. Father's world is so enlightened; so learned. But it pales beside our world. We are turning wandering tribes into civilizations. Immigrants from their lands are raising Olympus, Tartarus, and all of our peoples toward greater enlightenment, greater knowledge, education, and riches. It benefits us and the world. I am so proud to be part of this. To have the opportunity to take all people to greater heights. The path you put the Titans on will be mimicked and copied by all that we meet. You told me once that people blindly follow the path they are on. Well, it is my duty to ensure they all are on the path of the Titans."

PRINCIPALS: Kiya, Vanam, Pumi, Valki | ELDER TITANIDES: Themis, Mnemosyne, Phoebe, Tethys, Theia, Rhea | ELDER TITANES: Rivermaster/Oceanus, Sagacity/Coeus, Starmaster/Crius, Watchman/Hyperion, Piercer/Iapetus, Cronus

"And the pressure to do so, Son? As the only given son of Pumi of Tallstone and Kiya of Tartarus?"

He paused. "Well, there is *that*, Mother! There is that."

She stood on her tiptoes and kissed him on his forehead. "Surprise me with a visit, Son. After you visit your wife and children."

He pulled the cord for the elevator. *We need a name for the whole island. We are overrun with scrolls. There are scrolls all over the place. All over the island. We need a better way.*

Family Man

It was time for a Quarter-moon family dinner. Cronus arrived at Tartarus to attend. He went first to Rhea's quarters and entered without knocking.

She lay naked upon their bed.

A random Gigante was putting on his tunic.

Matter-of-factly Rhea said to the Gigante, "All right, Sweet, that was nice, but you need to go now. My husband is here."

She rolled up onto one elbow and motioned Cronus to sit on the edge of her bed. Cronus waited until the Gigante had gone, walked over, and sat down.

She said, "You ignore me for an entire month. I finally invite a Gigante over and then *you* show up. It isn't fair, it's not fair at all! You know, they have contests to see who gets me next. I'm considered the highlight of their little sexual lives; not that I put that much into it. I only really get into it when I'm with you. And here you are. On my bed."

She grabbed his arm, pulled him onto the bed, and then straddled his chest. "He has warmed me up, Husband. Now, finish me off!"

Cronus said, "Rhea, all things considered, I think ..."

She cut him off. "You think too much, Cronus." She began unbuttoning his shirt. "I want it! I want it right now! Not after you think about it!"

Afterward, she insisted that he dress in a lightweight tunic instead of his formal attire. They walked hand-in-hand to the beach. Two light-haired children saw them approaching and ran toward them screaming, "Daddy,

ELDER OCEANIDS: Metis, Tyche, Clymene, Eurybia, Amphitrite
ELDER OLYMPIANS: Hestia, Demeter, Hera, Hades, Poseidon, Zeus
OTHER: Philyra, Dionysus, Heracles, Outis, Enceladus, Littlerock, Porphyrion

Daddy, Daddy." Three younger children toddled behind trying to keep up with their sisters.

He sat down on the beach making a lap for the two girls to climb into.

"What did you bring us, Daddy?" Hestia demanded.

"Yes, what did you bring us, Daddy?" Demeter parroted.

"Something too delicious to be shared with anyone. These are for you. Don't share it with anyone." He reached into his tunic and pulled out two wrapped soft food bars. "These are from the kitchens of Olympus. They are made from figs, honey, ground nuts, and secret ingredients. The latest in delectable sweets made only for the sweetest of people."

The girls unwrapped the bars and bit into them.

Hestia rolled her eyes skyward and said, "Delicious! Are there more?"

Cronus said, "Maybe after dinner. We will see." He looked up to see an Oceanid escorting his three toddlers to him.

The Oceanid wore the desired colorful bottom and halter. But on her, the outfit looked more provocative than demure. "Hey, Chief. Welcome to the beach. I'm Philyra. You probably don't remember me, but I work for you occasionally."

Cronus replied, "Of course, I remember you, Philyra. Are you ready to quit this beach life and come to work full-time as my executive assistant?"

She laughed. "No, not yet Chief. Besides, who but me, could have answered Hestia's call to learn about flow charts and organizational charts? We don't get that particular request from too many of our children. And, by the way, she is a dedicated student. She is going to make you proud, one day."

The five chatted on for a good while as the younger children milled around enjoying the treat their father had given them. Then Philyra excused herself, stood up to go, but then turned back and said, "Chief, be careful with Crius's Kemet project. The numbers they are offering don't add up."

"When can you work?" he asked.

"Whenever you need me. I've had my water days."

PRINCIPALS: Kiya, Vanam, Pumi, Valki | ELDER TITANIDES: Themis, Mnemosyne, Phoebe, Tethys, Theia, Rhea | ELDER TITANES: Rivermaster/Oceanus, Sagacity/Coeus, Starmaster/Crius, Watchman/Hyperion, Piercer/Iapetus, Cronus

"I'll tell my scheduler to be in touch with you."

She said, "Wonderful," turned, and walked away but snapped the back of her colorful bottom piece at him for effect.

"My, my," Rhea said. "All that and brains, too. It's good to be Cronus."

"Philyra is smart, Daddy, but she won't obey me like she's supposed to! You should have her killed!" Hestia complained.

Cronus laughed. "That's a little harsh, Daughter. Come on everybody. Let's go see Grandmother."

The Library of Olympus
In the 72nd year from the birth of Vanam

Mnemosyne had offered the solution at a Full-moon family dinner that Cronus had attended and raised his questions. She said, "Let's build a pretty building big enough to store my story scrolls and store all your maps along with Tethys' notes on their explorations. Design it so that anyone can enter and, if they can read, can read these things for themselves."

The family sat in silence as this suggestion was considered.

Sagacity immediately picked up on the new concept. He burst forth with, "And large enough so that the number of scrolls can double every year, and we can assign scribes to keep them in order and read them to illiterate people, and they can teach the illiterate to read, and others can bring their scrolls to add to our collection. A 'library.' We can call it a library. The 'Library of Olympus' could be one of the wonders of the world. Even scholars from Tallstone will go there to study. And our scribes can record their knowledge. It will be built with the finest marmaros with columns in front like giant tree trunks. It will contain the collected knowledge of all people. All can come and learn there. Yes, the 'Library of Olympus.' Where shall we build it? How large will it be?"

Mnemosyne was selected to be the 'Chief of the Library of Olympus.' Cronus, of course, would be chief in charge of construction.

And now, after three intense years of hard work and long hours, the great Library stood before them; ready to be opened to all that sought knowledge. Everyone of consequence in the known world was there; a mass of humanity standing before the building. Waiting.

ELDER OCEANIDS: Metis, Tyche, Clymene, Eurybia, Amphitrite
ELDER OLYMPIANS: Hestia, Demeter, Hera, Hades, Poseidon, Zeus
OTHER: Philyra, Dionysus, Heracles, Outis, Enceladus, Littlerock, Porphyrion

Mnemosyne strode up the marmaros steps to the first landing and turned to face the masses. Inscribed on the great portico above her were the symbols for "All Knowledge for All People." Between the high columns supporting the portico, she raised her arms. The crowd grew silent. She began, "Citizens of the world, the Titans present you a gift." She paused for effect, turned to her right with hand raised, and continued, "We give you all knowledge known to humanity."

To the sound of unending applause, Cronus and Kiya walked up the marmaros steps to join her.

Rhea stood to one side with her children at the base of the steps. She silently seethed within. Her three daughters, Hestia, Demeter, and Hera, jumped up and down, screaming, "Daddy, daddy, daddy." Her young sons, Hades and Poseidon, looked around with excitement.

The festivities lasted for almost two quarter-moons. All visiting dignitaries were properly recognized and entertained. All were left with feelings of exuberance and joy that they had been part of this great experience. Sagacity had met with Pumi and the Masters of Tallstone to discuss ways in which the library could support and document their continued quests to completely understand the world around them. Understandings were reached and protocols were established. There would be a continued dialog between Tallstone and the Library of Olympus.

< >

The Titans were exhausted.

Rather than meeting for a family dinner, the Elder Titanides retired to Kiya's quarters to relax and just be women. They changed from formal attire to casual, comfortable tunics.

Kiya listened to her daughter's chatter and exchange stories and anecdotes about themselves and how they had survived all the madness of designing and building the library while simultaneously running and growing the Port's power and trade. There was laughter and giggles.

"I don't know how you survived this, Rhea," Mnemosyne offered. "This project took me more hours than I have in a day and your husband worked harder than I did and continued his responsibilities as 'Chief of

Port Olympus Operations.' His was a superhuman effort. But it's finished now. I bet he will have a lot more time for you and your children."

"Yes, I suppose so," Rhea said.

Kiya said, "You have been quiet, Rhea. Is everything all right?"

Rhea responded, "Yes. Everything is as sweet as honey and figs," and again was silent.

Kiya rose, clapped her hands, and said, "Children, I have had a most delightful time. Now, each of you go to your own bed and sleep for two full days. I love all of you so much. Now go!"

Still laughing and giggling, each Titanide rose, embraced her mother, and left for their own quarters.

When Rhea, the youngest and last to leave, embraced Kiya, Kiya said, "Sit and stay with me awhile, Rhea. Together, we can solve all things."

Rhea burst into tears, sobbing violently, squeezing her mother in a desperate embrace. "Mother. I have failed. I cannot do this anymore. I have tried. I have tried so hard. I just can't do it anymore. I'm sorry. I'm so sorry. Forgive me, Mother. Forgive me."

The two sat down together, the embrace continued as did the crying.

"You are forgiven, child. For whatever it is you need forgiving for."

Rhea cried on; a lifetime of uncried tears.

At last, Rhea composed herself, leaned back in her chair, looked at her mother, and announced, "I am going to leave Cronus and move to Port Kaptara with the children. I'm going to tell him our marriage is ended."

The Divorce

Late at night, after all staff had gone, Rhea walked unannounced into the office of 'The Chief-of-Chiefs.'

"Cronus, we need to talk!"

"Rhea, what a delightful surprise. To what do I owe this pleasure?"

"We haven't been alone in over three months, Cronus. You have finished your library project. It's time for us to talk."

ELDER OCEANIDS: Metis, Tyche, Clymene, Eurybia, Amphitrite
ELDER OLYMPIANS: Hestia, Demeter, Hera, Hades, Poseidon, Zeus
OTHER: Philyra, Dionysus, Heracles, Outis, Enceladus, Littlerock, Porphyrion

"Well, of course. Have a seat and let's talk."

"Not here. On the roof overlooking Oursea."

"All the better, Rhea. We will have an even more magnificent view. I'll call for the elevator."

They rode to the rooftop, exited the elevator, and walked toward the two cushioned sofas angled side-by-side and positioned to overlook Oursea.

Cronus was surprised to see the flowing dark hair of a woman sitting on the far sofa with her arm resting on the back of the sofa. "Well, well. Who do we have here?"

The woman turned her head to look at him and said, "Hello, Chief. Don't get mad. I agreed to help Rhea with this. I hope it doesn't put a strain on our relationship."

"Philyra! What ...?" He stopped to stare at her sitting on the sofa with legs crossed, completely unclothed. "What ...?"

Rhea pushed him onto the adjacent couch and said, "She is helping us out, Cronus. We are getting a divorce."

"What? What are you talking about? What is Philyra doing here? What's going on?"

"We aren't going to be married any longer, Cronus. I can't take it anymore. We are getting a divorce. Tonight! I have kept my pledge to you through our entire, long marriage but I have run out of one-time use Gigantes and I'm tired of this. Three months! You have not been to me in three months! It's over, Sweet. But I'm not going to be the one to end it. You are!"

She looked over to Philyra and said, "Philyra, come and do this thing!"

Philyra rose and walked to stand before Cronus. He stared at her in wide-eyed disbelief and complete confusion, not understanding.

Rhea slid next to him, put one arm around his shoulder, and began unbuttoning his shirt. Philyra went to her knees and began removing his pants. Rhea said, "I know that you are one uptight Titane, Cronus. But you have my permission to enjoy this. It's my parting gift to you."

PRINCIPALS: Kiya, Vanam, Pumi, Valki | ELDER TITANIDES: Themis, Mnemosyne, Phoebe, Tethys, Theia, Rhea | ELDER TITANES: Rivermaster/Oceanus, Sagacity/Coeus, Starmaster/Crius, Watchman/Hyperion, Piercer/Iapetus, Cronus

She looked at Philyra and asked, "How do you want him, Sweet? On the sofa or the floor?"

Philyra simply took his legs and pulled him onto the floor.

Rhea asked, "He doesn't appear to be up for this, Philyra. Probably too confused and agitated. What are we going to do?"

Philyra knelt over him and began getting Cronus up for the task at hand. Cronus stared at Rhea in wide-eyed horror.

"I understand that Oceanids are excellent at this sort of thing. Maybe I can pick up some pointers." She paused, inspected his readiness, and said, "All right, Philyra, it looks like you can at least get started now."

Philyra swung her legs over his body and 'got started.'

Rhea knelt close to Cronus's face, stared back into his unblinking eyes, and said, softly, "It will be over soon, sweet, and, oh, if you don't want the divorce, then don't ejaculate. It's only official when you ejaculate."

She paused, and continued, "And since we are having this talk, I am taking the children to be raised at Port Kaptara. I hope to change the path they are on to one more to my liking; one more consistent with our upbringing. Our children are self-centered, spoiled, ungrateful, arrogant, obnoxious little brats. They have started referring to themselves as 'Olympians'."

Rhea looked at Philyra and asked, "How is he doing? It looks like you're giving more than you're getting."

With a husky voice, Philyra replied, "Well enough."

"Take your time."

Rhea then continued talking to Cronus, "I overheard Hestia telling Demeter how they would throw the lazy Titans out once they got to work with their daddy at Port Olympus. Hestia had memorized the organization chart. Can you believe that? She knew whose job she would take over first. That would be hilarious except she was deadly serious."

Rhea looked at Philyra, and asked, "Is he close? My talking isn't helping him pay you proper attention, but my watching is getting *me* excited."

Cronus clenched his eyes shut, groaned, and went limp.

ELDER OCEANIDS: Metis, Tyche, Clymene, Eurybia, Amphitrite
ELDER OLYMPIANS: Hestia, Demeter, Hera, Hades, Poseidon, Zeus
OTHER: Philyra, Dionysus, Heracles, Outis, Enceladus, Littlerock, Porphyrion

"Am I divorced?" Rhea asked Philyra.

"Yes," Philyra replied in a huskier voice.

"Give him a moment to recover then I want my turn."

Rhea stood and began removing her clothes. She said to Cronus, "You have one last duty and then I will leave you alone. You are going to give me one more child. A boy. His name will be Zeus. He will be raised far away from you at Port Kaptara. Don't worry. You will get your children back; one at a time. When they reach adulthood, I will send them back to you. I'm anxious to see how they will turn out."

She looked at Philyra and asked, "Can you get him up again? I don't want to touch that thing except where I have to."

Philyra once again went to work on his body. As Philyra worked on him, Cronus stared blankly at Rhea.

Rhea said to him, "We loved once. I felt it through my entire being. The exhilaration of being wanted. Then you took it from me and gave it to your job. Where did the affection go? The warmth? I craved it so. In each Gigante I took as my imaginary lover. I crave it still."

Finally, Philyra stood facing the now unclothed Rhea. "He appears to be capable, Rhea."

"Thank you, Philyra." She lowered herself onto his unwilling but capable body.

Rhea reached over, took Philyra's hand, squeezed it, and quietly asked, "Will you join me?"

Philyra considered the invitation but disengaged her hand as she said, "N-no. That wouldn't be appropriate."

With unshed tears seeping from clench-closed eyes, Rhea began her ritual as she said to no one there, "There should be warmth. There should be affection."

Philyra stared at the sad, cold, emotionless union between the once-husband and once-wife. Then ... Cronus watched as Philyra straddled his body and sank down to face Rhea. He watched Rhea's arms go around Philyra's shoulders; her nails digging into Philyra's flesh.

PRINCIPALS: Kiya, Vanam, Pumi, Valki | ELDER TITANIDES: Themis, Mnemosyne, Phoebe, Tethys, Theia, Rhea | ELDER TITANES: Rivermaster/Oceanus, Sagacity/Coeus, Starmaster/Crius, Watchman/Hyperion, Piercer/Iapetus, Cronus

He tried, to no avail, to ignore the moans coming from the two women. He turned his head away from that which played out upon his body to gaze, instead, over his beautiful harbor at Port Olympus. *There is so much yet to do. I must redouble my efforts to build the power and influence of Port Olympus. The library was a tremendous success, but we did not even record Mother's knowledge. Her knowledge is not in the library. She knows more than any person in the world about the healing power of plants. How did I overlook that? Why am I so inadequate!*

He groaned as he delivered Zeus into Rhea.

Fireworks
In the 75th year from the birth of Vanam

The night became the days became the seasons became the years.

Kiya was delighted that Rhea would, at long last, attend a family dinner. It had been three long, eventful years since she had seen her daughter and her granddaughter, Hestia. Immediately upon arrival at Port Olympus, Hestia had marched, with purpose, directly to her father's office. Rhea had not seen Hestia since. Rhea took the time for a long visit with her mother and sisters. It was not mentioned, but all took silent notice that Rhea laughed and giggled with them. She seemed to be as happy as she was before her marriage to Cronus.

"I am not hopeful about my children," Rhea told the Titanides." They still talk of nothing but when they can return and go to work for their father. Even the two boys, who barely remember their father have ingrained it into themselves that they are the children of Cronus, Port Olympus Chief-of-Chiefs, and that they are entitled to whatever they want, and all must obey them, or they will tell their father. Metis has grown tired of listening to it. She didn't want to keep them while I delivered Hestia to her father. She is not as child-friendly as most Oceanids. Be aware of what my children might scheme when they get together with their father."

Themis laughed. "I'm sure they will turn out fine. They will be good Titans."

"Olympians," Rhea corrected. "They will be good Olympians."

The Titanides laughed.

Kiya didn't.

ELDER OCEANIDS: Metis, Tyche, Clymene, Eurybia, Amphitrite
ELDER OLYMPIANS: Hestia, Demeter, Hera, Hades, Poseidon, Zeus
OTHER: Philyra, Dionysus, Heracles, Outis, Enceladus, Littlerock, Porphyrion

Hestia's Entrance

The family gathered in formal attire for the Full-moon family dinner. Kiya noticed that neither Cronus nor Hestia had yet arrived.

"I am here, Mother," Rhea responded. "I haven't seen my ex-husband in three years. I suspect he doesn't want to see me plus Hestia may consider herself a little too superior to mingle with commoners."

"I'm anxious to see this granddaughter of mine. She sounds all grown up."

The chatter continued. Dinner was served. The conversation was delightful. Sweetbreads were served and eaten. The band had begun playing, the Oceanids singing. Enceladus announced, "Queen Kiya, Cronus has asked me to announce that he and Olympian Hestia, now of Port Olympus, have arrived."

Except for Kiya, all rose and waited to again see Rhea's oldest child; gone for three years and now all grown up.

The two entered the patio. Hestia, nose in the air, announced, "I am so sorry that I was unable to accept your dinner invitation, but I had a scheduling conflict. I and Father, the 'Chief-of-Chiefs,' had already scheduled dinner together at the Port Olympus Elder Dining Room to discuss matters of great importance. It will soon be announced that I am to be his new executive assistant. I hope to make an immediate contribution and improve upon efficiencies of operation."

Tethys leaned and whispered into Sagacity's ear, "How old is she? Twelve? Thirteen? You were in your twenties before you could talk like that."

He replied, "And there are four more right behind her."

Hestia then graciously received her many admirers. It was quite a while before she thought to present herself to her Grandmother Kiya.

Rhea walked over to Cronus and said, "She is still quite the brat."

With nose in the air, Cronus replied, "She will make an excellent Executive Assistant. With her help, I hope to move our family business to great heights." He turned and walked off, leaving Rhea standing alone.

She giggled.

PRINCIPALS: Kiya, Vanam, Pumi, Valki | ELDER TITANIDES: Themis, Mnemosyne, Phoebe, Tethys, Theia, Rhea | ELDER TITANES: Rivermaster/Oceanus, Sagacity/Coeus, Starmaster/Crius, Watchman/Hyperion, Piercer/Iapetus, Cronus

The Fireworks Begin

The night continued, then Piercer walked to the fire pit, rang a bell, and announced, "We will have a magnificent show on the beach. For several years, Littlerock has been working on his special projects. I miss having him at my side, but he said that he is old, tired of hard work, and wanted to have some fun experimenting with his own useless projects. Well, he made an interesting discovery that I insisted he share with all of us tonight. But it is dangerous to be around. That's why the show will be at the beach. Now everyone, get a fresh Sweet or Bitter, and let's go to the beach!"

The women kicked off their shoes and everyone set off to Oursea.

Piercer and Kiya led the party to meet Littlerock and his apprentice stonemasons, now called 'Powder Applications Development Technicians,' who waited on the beach; their demonstration ready to begin. They had carried a large sitting rock in a prime location, especially for their queen.

"Welcome Great Queen Kiya and Master Iapetus," Littlerock gushed as he rushed over to take Kiya's extended hands.

Kiya looked at Piercer and asked, "'Iapetus?'"

"Corporate orders," he replied. "It's more sophisticated and powerful than 'Piercer.' I humor them."

Littlerock gushed, "Here. Sit over here, Great Queen. This sitting rock is especially for you."

"How nice! My, that's the largest sitting rock I have ever seen."

"Especially for you, my Queen. Are you ready? We made this discovery quite by accident, but we believe that it will amuse the masses. It will make quite an impression at your next meeting with the Heads of State. I am afraid that Porphyrion has taken notice and is inquiring about military applications. I misdirect him as best I can."

Kiya nodded, "Yes, I am ready."

Piercer, now Iapetus, shouted, "Let the show begin."

ELDER OCEANIDS: Metis, Tyche, Clymene, Eurybia, Amphitrite
ELDER OLYMPIANS: Hestia, Demeter, Hera, Hades, Poseidon, Zeus
OTHER: Philyra, Dionysus, Heracles, Outis, Enceladus, Littlerock, Porphyrion

All was silence. Then a pop. A streak of light sped toward the heavens. Then an explosion. Colored lights shot from a spot in the sky. Red. Blue. Yellow. Green. Followed by more pops, more streaks, more explosions of lights streaming across the sky. The sky filled with streaks of colored light. The Titans watched with dumbstruck awe and amazement. Finally, each burst was met with collective "Ooohs" and "aaahs."

Hestia turned to her father and demanded, "Why wasn't I informed of this?" She paused. "You *did* know, didn't you?"

The show ended. The excitement went on. So many questions. The 'Powder Applications Development' technicians were not accustomed to being the center of attention; to having the high-born hang onto their every word, to having other people interested in the things they were doing. The beach party continued. Kiya quietly listened to the chatter and conversations. She looked at Littlerock with a raised eyebrow.

Iapetus finally announced, "All right everyone. Let's take our guests back to the patio for music, drinks, and visiting. Let's go!"

Littlerock motioned for Kiya and two of his apprentices to remain. As the party disappeared toward Tartarus, the two assistants ran down the beach and raised a large flat piece of timber that had been lying unnoticed on the beach. "This way, my Queen," Littlerock said, taking her by the hand. We must stand behind this shield in case something goes wrong. Two of my technicians lost their lives working on this project."

"Lost their lives?" Kiya gasped, "How horrible!"

"Knowledge has a price. We seek to unlock the secrets of the earth itself, and the earth is a jealous guardian. Progress has been slow. We may never get there, but this will demonstrate where we are."

They walked behind the shield. Littlerock signaled to his technicians. They ran to their project. Kiya heard a muffled boom. They stepped from behind the shield and walked to the sitting rock. It had been shattered into many pieces. Kiya stared at the remains with amazement. Littlerock said simply, "It's all a matter of placing the powder in the correct location. Properly placed, the explosion can shatter the rock ... in the blink of an eye."

PRINCIPALS: Kiya, Vanam, Pumi, Valki | ELDER TITANIDES: Themis, Mnemosyne, Phoebe, Tethys, Theia, Rhea | ELDER TITANES: Rivermaster/Oceanus, Sagacity/Coeus, Starmaster/Crius, Watchman/Hyperion, Piercer/Iapetus, Cronus

Littlerock sent his special assistants ahead to the party. "They are my two most trusted associates, but still ..."

Kiya was deep in thought. "Does this have anything to do with the Port Spearpoint 'Deep Well' project?"

"Please, Queen Kiya, don't even use that term anywhere near me or my assistants. My best protection is no one ever thinks of my work and Oceanus's project on the same day. I wondered about deep wells at Spearpoint Port long ago while meeting with Sagacity. He took the concept and developed a plan. He has long since forgotten that it is not his original concept. My name has never been linked with it." He paused, "You will know better than I. How does the Deep Well project go?"

Kiya answered, "It will take several years to recover the tremendous costs, but Sagacity tells me that it is already past its break-even operational costs. The trade going through 'Deep Well' will double each year for the foreseeable future. The second well was completed earlier this year and it far more than doubled the Ports' capacity to lower goods from the upper sea to Oursea. Cronus gave the approval to start two new wells Sagacity had requested. And now, I find out that the entire Deep Well concept was initiated by you and the little question I once posed. A question that had no answer and would never be used even if it did. My little question has resulted in the loss of two lives, a show of many colors, and a massive investment in two holes in the ground. I must be careful what I ask you for, Littlerock."

"I advise Oceanus on the exact placement of the 'Deep Wells.' Their exact location is critical for my personal project. But the resulting shafts have created an unbroken flow of shipping from Port Olympus to Port Spearpoint's lower docks, transferred up through the Deep Well elevators to the Port Spearpoint upper docks, and then on to as many new ports as Oceanus can establish on the western sea. Your 'little question' is resulting in untold new riches for your people and is seeding civilization in the entire western lands. Those people are not as developed and civilized as even the hunter-gatherer tribes to our east. What they think they are receiving are goods and merchandise and pretty things. What they are actually receiving is enlightenment and civilization. All that plus exciting fireworks to trade to the outlands for their celebrations. I have made a

ELDER OCEANIDS: Metis, Tyche, Clymene, Eurybia, Amphitrite
ELDER OLYMPIANS: Hestia, Demeter, Hera, Hades, Poseidon, Zeus
OTHER: Philyra, Dionysus, Heracles, Outis, Enceladus, Littlerock, Porphyrion

shipment for you to gift Pumi for their next Winter Solstice Festival plus an apprentice to handle them. The fireworks are dangerous even in the simplest of configurations. And know this; asking the question, finding the answer, and using the answer are three different issues. As for my two martyrs, much was learned. Their death was not in vain."

They arrived back at the patio. The party proceeded loudly. They were met at the edge of the patio by Hestia, arms crossed, feet apart, demanding of Littlerock, "Why was my father not told of this project?"

Kiya smiled sweetly and answered for Littlerock, "Because I commanded him not to tell Cronus. Now, leave us, Hestia."

Livid, Hestia turned and stormed off to find her father.

Kiya called after her, "Oh, Hestia!"

Hestia turned, enraged, to face her grandmother. "You simply must learn Rule Number One: 'Know yourself.' Otherwise, you will continue to be an abject failure."

The child, in a fury only a thirteen-year-old woman can know, turned and fumed off.

"Be careful what enemies you make, my Queen," Littlerock said.

Kiya somberly replied, "I always am, my friend. And this one doesn't even have testicles. I don't think."

PRINCIPALS: Kiya, Vanam, Pumi, Valki | ELDER TITANIDES: Themis, Mnemosyne, Phoebe, Tethys, Theia, Rhea | ELDER TITANES: Rivermaster/Oceanus, Sagacity/Coeus, Starmaster/Crius, Watchman/Hyperion, Piercer/Iapetus, Cronus

18. Hestia, Zeus, and Athena
In the 84th year from the birth of Vanam
The Seduction of Semele

The years passed without too much drama.

On this day, Metis, as usual, swam naked. Today she swam off the coast of Kaptara with her new friend, Semele, the oldest daughter of Prince Cadmus. Cadmus had come to the Port to trade. The morning was warm, the ocean cool.

Semele was more modest than Metis and the other Oceanids. But in their company and the spirit of the occasion, and with no males present, especially her father, Semele, too, removed her tunic to swim naked in the ocean.

Semele's mother, Harmonia, had died leaving her father to raise and instruct their daughter. He was strict and not a good resource for knowledge required by a woman. She had suffered through puberty on her own. Males were justifiably afraid to request to mate with her. She was painfully aware of her innocence and ready to shed it. She watched the confident, outgoing, beautiful, unashamedly naked, Metis. She was enthralled.

The group retired to lie on the beach and rest. Semele sat beside Metis who was stretched out to sunbathe. Semele took a deep breath and asked, "Great Metis, can you instruct me in the art of mating?"

Metis was seldom startled but the question was unexpected. Metis leaned up on elbows and asked, "You have not yet mated? Have you been instructed in this matter."

Semele shook her head, "No."

Metis paused, considered the situation, and said, "It's simple enough. All you really need to know is to get on your hands and knees, raise your tunic above your waist, and present your rear to him. The rest will follow easily enough. See your elder woman if you don't want a baby."

Metis paused, again. "Of course," she said, as she once again propped up on her elbow, "Many people make mating complicated. I'm asked once a day to do it. I usually respectfully decline. If pressed, the male does not fare well. I can demonstrate various 'No!' techniques if you like. Were

ELDER OCEANIDS: Metis, Tyche, Clymene, Eurybia, Amphitrite
ELDER OLYMPIANS: Hestia, Demeter, Hera, Hades, Poseidon, Zeus
OTHER: Philyra, Dionysus, Heracles, Outis, Enceladus, Littlerock, Porphyrion

your chief to ask, I might. But otherwise, I generally prefer the touch of the sea to the touch of a male. But look at my sunbathing sisters. They seldom turn down an invitation from a respectful male. 'If it brings someone pleasure, let's do it!' is their attitude. I keep to the three basic positions, myself. But Clymene can show you how to mate upside down in a tree if that type of thing interests you. You can get through most of your life just knowing the big three; on hands and knees to get it over with; on your back, knees to your ears to drag it out in an intimate relationship; and, put him on his back and mount him if you want to maximize *your* pleasure. So, there you have it, Princess Semele. Do you want my sisters to find a suitable first-time mate for you?"

Semele put her hands to her lips and laughed. "I hardly think so, Great Metis. I would want to do that with someone special. But I am not as afraid as I was before your instruction."

Metis laughed. "I could go on and on if you have time and interest. After we became women, my sisters and I returned to visit our original home in Urfa and met with Great Mother Valki. She spent an entire evening with the four of us telling us about men, mating, different positions, different techniques, that sort of thing. I think she was inspired because she had an infatuated, appreciative audience. She knew a lot. We, of course, share all such knowledge with our sisters. How long are you here for?"

"I am here at least all day tomorrow. We leave for our camp after my father finishes trading with the Olympians."

"Stay with me and my sisters until you leave. You could stand a little loosening up. Who knows, an unattached male may wander through. My sisters have a way of attracting them."

Semele said, "Father would not like that, I'm afraid."

"Come on, let's go talk to him."

Semele hurriedly put on her tunic as Metis stood waiting. "You *will* put on your tunic? Won't you?" Semele asked.

"Nah. Come on. Let's go ask him if you can swim naked."

PRINCIPALS: Kiya, Vanam, Pumi, Valki | ELDER TITANIDES: Themis, Mnemosyne, Phoebe, Tethys, Theia, Rhea | ELDER TITANES: Rivermaster/Oceanus, Sagacity/Coeus, Starmaster/Crius, Watchman/Hyperion, Piercer/Iapetus, Cronus

Boy Transformed

The Oceanids and Semele returned to the beach the next morning. The chief had been greatly disoriented by the appearance of the Oceanids, but a male is no match for a determined Oceanid. So it was that Semele not only received permission to stay at the beach with her new sisters, but she received tacit approval to swim nude as long as no men were present.

Metis saw the incoming Olympian trading ship. It would be filled with valuable merchandise of great interest to the chiefs and their traders. They would be lost in negotiation for days. Several of her sisters put on their tunics and wandered up to the docks to see what might be happening.

Later, a naked Oceanid walked by on her way to the sea. She had a naked boy by her side.

Semele saw him, gasped, and tried to hide her own nakedness.

"Don't get excited, Semele," Metis said. "That's just Zeus. Consider him to be one of the girls. He's just a boy. Metis raised up on her elbows to get a better look. "Although he *is* filling out quite nicely. Much taller than he was, with a lot more muscles. He is an Olympian. Olympians are a big deal. He would most certainly 'be someone special.' Come on over. I'll introduce you. You can practice being naked around a male. Go play with him while he's still harmless."

Metis and Semele walked toward the Oceanid and Zeus. "Hey, Zeus," Metis called out. "Come meet Semele. She is an important person; a princess and everything. An Olympian should know all the princesses."

Zeus looked at Semele, a big smile on his face.

He then glanced at Metis but not into her eyes. Metis was the most developed female on the beach. Zeus stood staring at her body; his eyes widened; his lips parted.

Metis thought, *Well, well, that's interesting!*

She shoved Semele toward the entranced Zeus. "Jump on his back, Semele. Make him carry you into the surf. You can wrestle and play with each other."

Zeus reluctantly departed and ran into the sea with Semele on his back. "Stay with him, Semele!" Metis shouted.

ELDER OCEANIDS: Metis, Tyche, Clymene, Eurybia, Amphitrite
ELDER OLYMPIANS: Hestia, Demeter, Hera, Hades, Poseidon, Zeus
OTHER: Philyra, Dionysus, Heracles, Outis, Enceladus, Littlerock, Porphyrion

Metis retired to lie down on the beach to monitor her beloved Oursea and all the creatures in it.

Toward evening, sea creatures began returning to the beach. The evening was cool after a warm day. Zeus was pulling Semele's hand to make her keep up with him. He found Metis sitting on the beach watching them return. He brought Semele with him to stand before Metis. Metis glanced at his penis.

Zeus began to speak to Metis, but his voice cracked as his penis began enlarging. "What's happening? What are you doing to me?" Zeus demanded as he looked down in confusion at his first erection. Metis rose, smiled at him, reached over, stroked his penis several times, and said, "He's all yours, Semele. You know what to do."

Semele, not at all sure what to do, fell to her hands and knees and presented her rear to Zeus. Zeus was confused and overwhelmed with new, unknown sensations.

Metis muttered, "Do I have to do everything?" She then walked back to the two novices, pulled Zeus to stand behind Semele's waiting body, pushed him to his knees, lubricated their genitals with her saliva, and guided Zeus into Semele. *My, that's a big one!*

The two novices began their initiation.

After he was sated, Zeus grunted, stood, and began to walk away.

Metis was infuriated. "Hey, Dung-head! Where are you going? This woman just shared her body with you. That's the biggest compliment she can give you, and your response is 'Uhhh.' Is that all you got, Dung-head? Get back here! Show her the appreciation she deserves! Be a man!"

Zeus stopped and turned to face Metis in bewilderment.

She commanded, "Stand up, Semele! Zeus, get over here! Wrap your arms around your conquest. Whisper in her ear that she was the greatest experience of your life. Tell her how beautiful she is and that she is the most fascinating creature you have ever met. Tell her that you are unworthy to share her body. After you tell her all of that, make up some syrupy stuff. You don't have to mean it. She doesn't have to believe it. Just say it. It's a sign of respect, Dung-head! Show her respect and gratitude! Don't be a jerk!"

PRINCIPALS: Kiya, Vanam, Pumi, Valki | ELDER TITANIDES: Themis, Mnemosyne, Phoebe, Tethys, Theia, Rhea | ELDER TITANES: Rivermaster/Oceanus, Sagacity/Coeus, Starmaster/Crius, Watchman/Hyperion, Piercer/Iapetus, Cronus

Zeus wrapped his arms around Semele and held her close. He whispered things into her ear. His breath was hot in her ear.

Soon, Semele raised her arms and put them around Zeus' shoulders. Soon after, her fingernails dug into his shoulders. Soon after, she threw her head back and closed her eyes. Her breath became rapid. Soon after, she reached between the two of them, found Zeus rising, and holding on to him, stepped back, staring at him with intensity. She maintained her grip, slowly lay down upon her back, and brought her knees to her ears.

Zeus, on his own, initiated proper protocol.

Metis smiled. *Good job, you two!*

Zeus, finally spent, had learned his lesson well. He embraced Semele and whispered soft things into her ear. She believed every word. As did Zeus. For the moment, anyway.

They lay there a long, long time but eventually, Zeus called to the Oceanids. "Come, my sisters. Embrace and hold the love of my life, Semele. Let her see nothing that does not delight her. Let her hear nothing that does not thrill her. Hold her close while I do something which I know Semele wishes me to do. For her. For the both of us. For the three of us."

Metis thought, *Oh-oh ...*

Zeus stood and walked to where Metis sat watching. He held out both hands to her. Pulling her to her feet, Zeus said, "You, other than Semele, are the most beautiful and desirable woman that I have ever seen. You are the moon, the stars, you are the sea itself. Infinite, inviting. You are ..."

He continued on and on.

Metis glanced at Semele. *Dung! Semele has bought into this stuff. You poor, innocent woman. I have created a monster here!*

But Metis dutifully tilted her head with feigned fascination and stared deeply into his eyes. Her eyes widened; her lips parted. *The boy-man is doing all right, though. Saying good words. Plus, his penis is impressive. Semele is or will be soon enough, an important person around here. Zeus is an Olympian who has just now become a man, and, my goodness, he can take direction nicely! And, well, this is a teaching exercise, and it is my duty to be a good teacher.*

ELDER OCEANIDS: Metis, Tyche, Clymene, Eurybia, Amphitrite
ELDER OLYMPIANS: Hestia, Demeter, Hera, Hades, Poseidon, Zeus
OTHER: Philyra, Dionysus, Heracles, Outis, Enceladus, Littlerock, Porphyrion

With a husky voice, she whispered "No woman can resist your honeyed words, Zeus. Take me!"

And then, with normal voice, said, "Now, Sweet, lay down on your back."

Meeting of the Powerful

"Thank you for receiving me, Grandmother," Hestia said.

"It has been too long, Hestia. I hear of your triumphs and victories. You were a headstrong child and now you are a leader to be reckoned with."

"Yes, Grandmother. I am to be feared. But now I come to you as your granddaughter and with a trivial problem. It is so strange. I easily command and handle the power struggles between the strong egos of the world and now I am undone. By a nothing."

Kiya did not speak. She waited in silence.

"Know yourself was Rule Number One, you said. I thought you a horrid old hag, although, I must admit, you still appear younger and prettier than I. Still, at the time, I thought you horrid. But your words would not leave me. 'Know yourself.' What does that even mean? And if there is a Rule Number One then there must be a Rule Number Two. And 'abject failure' are not words I easily accept. But I put it all aside and I have done well. My father thinks I am wonderful, and really, I do a tremendous job. But always in my mind, 'abject failure.' And what is Rule Number Two? Life is strange, isn't it? The answers had always been there for the asking. The Library of Olympus. The chronicles of Mnemosyne, the history of our people, where we started, how we got here, Rule Number One, Rule Number Two. All there for the asking. The story of your beginning is abysmal, Grandmother. A member of a homeless tribe moving from camp to camp every month. You were an elder woman and that was a big deal. An elder woman! You were even the mate, not even a wife, of the tribal chief. The sadness of it overwhelms me. There is only one generation between that life and my life. That is terrifying. 'I chose a different path'—those are the words attributed to you. I have thought about that a lot. Who does that? Even I am on the path laid out before me. To step off the path that I am on and choose another, by my own violation, is unimaginable! Rule Number One—'know yourself.' Rule

---

PRINCIPALS: Kiya, Vanam, Pumi, Valki | ELDER TITANIDES: Themis, Mnemosyne, Phoebe, Tethys, Theia, Rhea | ELDER TITANES: Rivermaster/Oceanus, Sagacity/Coeus, Starmaster/Crius, Watchman/Hyperion, Piercer/Iapetus, Cronus

Number Two—'know your enemy.' So here I am Great Queen Kiya. I, at last, know myself and am at last ready to present myself to you. I am Hestia—your granddaughter."

"Welcome home, Granddaughter." Kiya rose and held out her arms to Hestia. Hestia came to her and tightly returned the embrace. Kiya held her and then pushed her granddaughter back to better see her. "And so, Granddaughter, what problem shall we solve today?"

"My little imbecilic brother; Zeus. Rhea presented Zeus to my father two seasons ago."

"Yes. I know. My beloved Rhea has at last returned to her home. She completed her exile and raised her children as best she could. Zeus was the last and he is now returned to his father, but Zeus has yet to present himself to me."

Kiya hesitated. "Imbecilic, you say?"

"Dumb. He is simply dumb. He thinks of nothing beyond himself. He comprehends nothing unless it brings him instant gratification. I assigned him to be 'Chief of Communications.' The easiest management position I have. He is responsible for ensuring all messages, scrolls, and materials reach the person to whom they are sent. He excels at it. He rejoices in it. 'Here comes our ray of sunshine,' they say when he walks into a room. He postures, he performs, he makes them laugh, and he revels in the adulation he is receiving. Hera is infatuated with him. He knows everyone in our organization by name and they know him. 'They love me!' he tells me. 'They really love me. And I love them.' It is disgusting. It is sickening. They are afraid of me BUT THEY LOVE THE IMBELCILLE!"

She tightly closed her eyes and lowered her forehead onto her clenched fist.

"I see," Kiya replied softly. "But do you?"

Hestia slowly raised her head to stare at Kiya. She stared for a long minute. Hestia laughed a bitter laugh. "So, I didn't know myself, at all. I had to come to my grandmother for her to reveal myself to me."

"I am only listening to you, child."

ELDER OCEANIDS: Metis, Tyche, Clymene, Eurybia, Amphitrite
ELDER OLYMPIANS: Hestia, Demeter, Hera, Hades, Poseidon, Zeus
OTHER: Philyra, Dionysus, Heracles, Outis, Enceladus, Littlerock, Porphyrion

"I am jealous. I am a jealous bitch. I am jealous of my little imbecilic brother. Of all that he has that I don't. I am weak!"

Kiya laughed. "Rephrase that."

Hestia paused, thought, and said, "I am a strong leader who has many strengths and a newfound weakness. It is not reasonable to be both universally loved and universally feared. Rule number two? I thought it was me against the world. For now, it is only Zeus, who neither understands himself nor can he comprehend that he has an enemy. The final pieces are now in place. I can finalize the re-organization. Thank you, Grandmother. I knew this would be a fruitful meeting."

Hestia stood to go.

"Don't leave, Hestia. Your aunts are coming over for daily gossip. You should join us. Gossip is so much more informative than daily briefings. Plus, if you leave, your ears might start burning. Your mother will probably be here. Perhaps you should practice facing her. 'Know your enemy,' Dear."

Hestia hesitated, smiled, and sat back down.

The Introduction of Zeus

The Full-moon family dinner was selected by Hestia as the appropriate vehicle to formally introduce Zeus to his family of Titans. Zeus had been raised in Port Kaptara and was unfamiliar with any of his relatives other than those who worked at Port Olympus.

The time came, Enceladus announced the arrival of Chief-of-Chiefs Cronus of Port Olympus and his ex-wife, Titanide Rhea, now of Tartarus. The two amicably walked down the receiving line together. He then announced Chief Executive Assistant to the Chief-of-Chiefs, Olympian Hestia with her brother, Olympian Poseidon. Then, Olympian Demeter with her brother, Olympian Hades. All were professionally amicable. And then, the guest of honor, "Titans, I present the Chief of Communications for Port Olympus, Olympian Zeus escorting his sister, Olympian Hera of Port Olympus."

The two strode in like the masters of the known world. Their smiles were electric. Zeus took every hand and shook it unmercifully. Hera was all smiles and gushing "How good to see you, again. We are so thrilled to be here." Their entrance was triumphant.

Rhea stood beside Cronus near the end of the receiving line. She leaned over and whispered, "You have such darling children, don't you?"

He caught no hint of sarcasm. He replied, "Yes, they are magnificent, aren't they? Every one of them."

Rhea giggled.

Enceladus announced, "Dinner is served."

Everyone went to their assigned seats. Hestia sat at the end of the table facing Kiya. Hera and Zeus sat on each side of Hestia. At first, Hestia was thrilled to be in the seat of honor. As the meal went on, a question crossed her mind, *Why isn't Zeus sitting here?*

Dinner finished, the band began playing, and Oceanids sang. A new entertainment had been imported from the south of Port Kemet; it was called 'dancing.' The elder Titans were not sure that dancing was appropriate but the second-generation Titans and everyone else, especially the Oceanids, thought this new concept to be wonderful. The original dances were modified to fit local tastes. 'Dancing' was still evolving into many forms, influenced greatly by whatever type of music the band was playing and who was dancing.

After a while, Hestia rang the bell to attract everyone's attention. All became quiet as Hestia stood and announced, "Chief-of-Chief Cronus has asked me to make an important announcement." Hestia did not look in Kiya's direction. "Zeus is the last child of Cronus and has, at last, joined our organization. I am pleased to announce that the Olympians have met and resolved to combine all the place names on our island to be under one encompassing name. These places include Tartarus, Port Olympus, Lookout Point, Camp Gigante, and all other parts of our island nation. A new name is long overdue. The name chosen for our nation is 'Kypros' in recognition of all the beautiful Kopar metal ore our island gives us. As part of this new model, a king for Kypros was also chosen. The King of Kypros will be Chief-of-Chiefs Cronus, son of Pumi of Tallstone. You may continue your festivities now."

ELDER OCEANIDS: Metis, Tyche, Clymene, Eurybia, Amphitrite
ELDER OLYMPIANS: Hestia, Demeter, Hera, Hades, Poseidon, Zeus
OTHER: Philyra, Dionysus, Heracles, Outis, Enceladus, Littlerock, Porphyrion

Hestia sat down.

Kiya did no more than hold up a hand for silence and gazed down the table at Hestia. The six Olympians were cheering wildly. No one else issued a sound. The Olympians were confused and quieted down. Zeus could not understand why everyone else was not wildly excited along with him. It didn't make sense.

Kiya simply stared at Hestia.

Cronus began to explain what a wonderful decision this was until Enceladus stepped over and put his hand on Cronus's shoulder and squeezed. A Gigante squeeze. Cronus became silent.

Kiya continued to stare at Hestia without expression.

Hestia broke under Kiya's cool gaze. "I hope this change meets with your approval, Kiya. You may retain any title you like, other than 'Queen' of course. It wouldn't be appropriate to have both a King and a Queen."

Kiya finally spoke, "Your proposal has merit, Hestia. I look forward to reviewing the details of your proposal. Perhaps I will approve the proposal; perhaps not. My decision will be based on the details. Especially the details of our relations with our trading partners. Will they be guaranteed access to all our knowledge and technology? Will they be nurtured to grow their civilization to the level of ours? Can we trade freely? Allow immigration without undue regulations? I, of course, as I assumed you knew, must approve any changes to our constitution as noted in our legally binding Charter. We will follow this protocol to the letter. Cronus will not disobey his queen. You aren't foolish enough to break our legally binding constitution, because if you did, Porphyrion would obey my directive to throw you from the roof of Port Olympus which most certainly be my directive. A leader must maintain discipline. Don't you agree?"

Kiya then stood, held out her arms, and said, "Now, Zeus, you are a wonderful, delightful young man. Come let your grandmother embrace you and let me share the glorious aura of the love that surrounds you."

As she stepped forward to embrace the excited, on-rushing Zeus, she smiled a sad little smile at Hestia.

PRINCIPALS: Kiya, Vanam, Pumi, Valki | ELDER TITANIDES: Themis, Mnemosyne, Phoebe, Tethys, Theia, Rhea | ELDER TITANES: Rivermaster/Oceanus, Sagacity/Coeus, Starmaster/Crius, Watchman/Hyperion, Piercer/Iapetus, Cronus

Book 2. The Beginning of Civilization: Mythologies Told True

Hestia sat silently fuming.

After chatting with Kiya, Zeus returned to the party and found Cronus. "Father," he said, "please introduce me again to Aunt Themis and Aunt Mnemosyne. They appear to be particularly interesting women."

Hera came up beside them. "Yes, father, introduce us to them. They are old enough to be our grandmothers, aren't they?"

"They don't look that old," Zeus offered as they walked over to chat with his aunts. *I wonder if old women like to couple with young men.*

The Seduction of Mnemosyne

The command to name the land 'Kypros' and appoint Cronus as King was rewritten to be in the form of a proposal as required by their Charter. Sagacity was called to direct the making of the necessary modifications. Hestia fumed that her father had not even noticed that he and she had been skewered and humiliated by Kiya. Office politics were all above his head. Asking Sagacity to manage the change would hopefully indicate to Kiya that Hestia admitted that she had been outwitted. A week passed. Zeus was tasked with delivering the document to Kiya for her review. A double message. Zeus was, after all, the 'Chief of Communications' plus Kiya had purposely used her first meeting with Zeus to send an unmistakable message to Hestia: "Don't mess with me, little girl."

Hestia thought, *And I'm the one who told you that Zeus is my nemesis. I can remain furious, or I can learn from a bad mistake. You defeated me without lifting a finger. I acknowledge that you defeated me, Kiya. But I shall come again! Smarter!*

Zeus arrived and presented the document to Kiya. Kiya flattered Zeus so much that it would have embarrassed anyone else. Zeus, however, considered his grandmother to be special. *She loves me sooo much! I can tell.*

Kiya said, "Join us for our evening meal, Zeus."

"That would be wonderful, Grandmother. But tell me, where do Aunt Themis and Aunt Mnemosyne dwell?"

"Their rooms in the Titanides quarters. Tell Enceladus you wish to speak with them. I'm sure they would be delighted to meet you on the patio."

ELDER OCEANIDS: Metis, Tyche, Clymene, Eurybia, Amphitrite
ELDER OLYMPIANS: Hestia, Demeter, Hera, Hades, Poseidon, Zeus
OTHER: Philyra, Dionysus, Heracles, Outis, Enceladus, Littlerock, Porphyrion

Zeus left but wandered the property. He came upon a farmer girl tending flowers. "Hello, my name is Zeus, and I am an Olympian." He continued, sweeping the girl into an enchanted world, plus he learned the floor plan of the Titanide's quarters; and which rooms were whose.

Mnemosyne sat at her recording desk inventing more symbols, markings, and signs to help her remember the stories she had been told about that which had befallen her people. She wore her simple white tunic. She answered a knock on her door.

Zeus stood there, naked, with a huge erection. He said, "Aunt Mnemosyne, it is I, your nephew, Zeus. I must talk to you."

She instinctively gasped, put her hand to her mouth, stepped back, and with wide eyes, stared at his erection.

He made a step toward her and said, "My dear aunt, I am in dire need of attention from a caring and affectionate woman. I know you can help me discharge this great burden I bear."

"Zeus!" she demanded. "What are you doing? You are completely unclothed. You should not be here like this!"

She looked into the corridor, saw no one, took his outstretched hands, and pulled him into her compartment.

"Dearest Aunt. I hurt. You can see that I cannot live much longer in this condition. Without your love, I will surely die. Help me! Please, help me."

"Zeus, you are not much more than a child. Young males have a way of relieving themselves from this condition. You know of it, surely."

"I made an oath to myself upon reaching manhood that I would never, under any circumstances, relieve my own condition. It is unmanly. Weak. Disgusting. No, Sweet Mnemosyne, I must always have help from a desirable woman to relieve this unbearable burden. Come with me to your bed, fair Mnemosyne. Relieve my pain."

"No, I am old enough to be your grandmother. You can mate with any young woman of your choosing. No, Zeus, it is not right that we couple."

He cupped her face in his hands and gently pushed her backward toward her bed. "Don't you understand, Mnemosyne, it is you whom I want; you

PRINCIPALS: Kiya, Vanam, Pumi, Valki | ELDER TITANIDES: Themis, Mnemosyne, Phoebe, Tethys, Theia, Rhea | ELDER TITANES: Rivermaster/Oceanus, Sagacity/Coeus, Starmaster/Crius, Watchman/Hyperion, Piercer/Iapetus, Cronus

whom I must have. A young girl is of no desire to me. It is you whom I must have. Now. Please."

He backed her into her bed. She fell back on it. He fell on top of her.

"No, Zeus, this is not right!"

"It *is* right, my dearest Mnemosyne. We shall make it right." He slipped his hands under her tunic and pulled it up over her body.

"NO!" Mnemosyne screamed as she tried to push him away. "We will not do this thing!"

Zeus put his hands under her calves and raised her knees above her head. He slipped himself into her body while whispering over and over, "Please, Mnemosyne. Do this with me, please."

After a while, she quit pushing.

Finally, he released himself into her. He rested a few moments and then stood above her. He grasped her feet, brought them to his lips, and kissed the soles of her feet. He gently massaged her feet while staring at her naked body. She lay silent, eyes closed. He positioned the souls of her feet together and laid her legs upon the bed, knees spread far apart, exposing the fullness of her body. "I want you to bear me a daughter. A daughter as beautiful as you. A daughter that will learn all that you know, that will inherit your greatness of knowledge, of wisdom. Thank you for this day, Mnemosyne. I will cherish our time together, forever."

He left her there.

< >

The Titans gathered for their evening meal.

Mnemosyne sat uncharacteristically silent; not offering one of her endless stories of family history. The meal began; Zeus entered and sat down. He was uncharacteristically animated and talkative. As sweets were being served for the final portion of the meal, Zeus stood up, raised his cup, and proclaimed, "I have an announcement that I would like to share."

Everyone accepted that Zeus must always be the center of attention. This evening would be no different.

ELDER OCEANIDS: Metis, Tyche, Clymene, Eurybia, Amphitrite
ELDER OLYMPIANS: Hestia, Demeter, Hera, Hades, Poseidon, Zeus
OTHER: Philyra, Dionysus, Heracles, Outis, Enceladus, Littlerock, Porphyrion

"Well, tell us then of your latest grand adventure, Zeus. We await your announcement with anticipation," Kiya said.

"I copulated with Aunt Mnemosyne this afternoon."

Themis choked on her sweet bread. The males sat up straighter. Mnemosyne's eyes widened—riveted on her plate. For a long moment there was complete silence.

Then Kiya said, "Zeus, you are still young. I must tell you that such matters are not announced in a public setting. They are intimacies not to be shared with the public. Bragging of one's conquests is not manly."

Zeus objected, "But Greatmother, I am not bragging. I am filled with joy that one as desirable and as worthy as Mnemosyne would take pity on a suitor as young and inexperienced as myself. And, too, I wish to publicly apologize to her if I was too forward and did not take the proper time to discuss the range of options she might consider. I am afraid that I may have been too brash and too demanding in the urgency of the moment. I did not properly answer all her reservations concerning our mating."

He addressed Mnemosyne, "Mnemosyne, I beg your forgiveness for my inexperience and urgency. I thank you for the beautiful and wondrous experience of our time together this afternoon. Do not think badly of me. I could not bear it. Do you think badly of me, Mnemosyne?"

Mnemosyne cast a sideways glance at her mother. Kiya glanced back, without expression. Mnemosyne then stood and replied, "You are an aggressive, arrogant, self-centered child who thinks only of himself. You will never force yourself upon me again. Am I understood?"

"Yes, Mnemosyne. I understand. I will obtain your express permission for our next mating. Thank you for your understanding. I am thrilled. Did you ask your mother for the potion that will ensure the baby you bear will be a girl?" He stared innocently and expectantly at her.

Mnemosyne rolled her eyes and sat down without responding.

Zeus looked at Kiya and said, "We wish a female child as beautiful and wise as her mother. She will learn the stories Mnemosyne knows and all stories yet to be told. We will name her 'Calliope.' She will be the first of many daughters we shall create together in mutual love and admiration."

PRINCIPALS: Kiya, Vanam, Pumi, Valki | ELDER TITANIDES: Themis, Mnemosyne, Phoebe, Tethys, Theia, Rhea | ELDER TITANES: Rivermaster/Oceanus, Sagacity/Coeus, Starmaster/Crius, Watchman/Hyperion, Piercer/Iapetus, Cronus

Pleased with himself and the attention he was commanding and oblivious to any consternation he might be causing, Zeus sat down to eagerly finish his sweetbread.

To the others at the table, Kiya said simply, "Well, there we have it. What did you do today, Themis?"

"I copulated with Zeus this morning, Mother. Obviously, I wasn't too memorable!"

Kiya's eyes widened.

Zeus rose in horror. "Not remember you! Sweet Themis, no man has ever been in a greater heaven ..." And on and on.

And so, it would come to pass nine months from this day, Mnemosyne would bear a daughter, Calliope, as would Themis bear a daughter, Clotho.

Athena

Cronus, King of Kypros, sat in his office on the floor immediately below the rooftop of Port Olympus. Hestia, Chief-of-Chiefs of Port Olympus Operations, sat in her office on the floor below him. Both were deep in thought as they wrestled with the many problems of running their gigantic enterprise. At first, neither noticed the modest craft sailing toward the port. Not until the docks began filling with Oceanids and workers and the docks became packed, did they notice that there was pandemonium below. Then they saw the craft flying the flag of Oceanid Metis. Hestia frowned. Metis was impossible to control. Hestia continued working. A message would be arriving soon enough if her entry were significant. She is probably just visiting the Elder Titanides.

"Chief of Communications" was intended to be a temporary job for entry into management, but Zeus would not hear of losing his job. It was perfect, everywhere he went there was love. Love of Zeus.

Hera, "Chief of Census Records," had an office, as did each of the Olympians, on the same floor as Hestia. Hestia had the only view of the harbor. Hera's desk faced toward the east, toward Tartarus. She was thrilled to see her younger brother, Zeus, enter the floor and come to his desk which was adjacent to hers. She stared at him wide-eyed, enthralled to hear of his morning delivering messages. Zeus was surprised when the

ELDER OCEANIDS: Metis, Tyche, Clymene, Eurybia, Amphitrite
ELDER OLYMPIANS: Hestia, Demeter, Hera, Hades, Poseidon, Zeus
OTHER: Philyra, Dionysus, Heracles, Outis, Enceladus, Littlerock, Porphyrion

Portmaster had sent him a message that a visiting dignitary had requested a special audience with him. Zeus was thrilled. *A visiting dignitary. Who could it be? Maybe someone bringing me gifts from afar. What could it be?*

Both Zeus and Hera were giddy with excitement. He had returned to his desk to receive this visiting dignitary.

Hestia, detecting too much activity coming from the far side of her floor, walked over and quickly deduced what was happening. Metis, who had just arrived, had helped Rhea raise Zeus. *She probably just wants to drop in and see how her efforts turned out. Don't be disappointed, Metis. He turned out just like you thought he would.*

She had no desire to see the Oceanid. Hestia returned to her desk.

Only two people entered the offices, Metis and a screaming baby. Metis headed straight to Zeus. All activity on the floor stopped as the Olympians gathered around Zeus's desk. Hestia returned when she heard the baby.

"Sorry about the screaming, Zeus. She's hungry," Metis said as she raised her blouse and began nursing her child. "Hey, can I have a chair to sit in, please? Being a mother is hard work. I have brought my daughter to see her daddy. Here she is, Zeus. What do you want to name her?"

The office became silent. Only the sound of a nursing baby could be heard. Zeus stared at Metis in complete confusion. None of her words registered in his brain. It was Hera who spoke first. "You claim this child is Zeus's? That's impossible. Zeus would never have a child with a commoner. His children will all be high-born. Not a common child."

Metis replied, "Well ... Hera, isn't it? It's been a while since I spanked your bare bottom. Not only is it possible, but here she is, waiting to be named and wanting to see her daddy. What do you think, Zeus? Do you like her?"

"She *is* pretty. Does she love me?" Zeus asked.

"She loves you more than the sky and the clouds and the sea. No daughter has ever loved a daddy more. Here. She's finished. Do you want to burp her?" She held out the baby to him. "So, what do you want to name her?"

Hera was frantic. "Zeus. Don't take that baby. It is a commoner."

PRINCIPALS: Kiya, Vanam, Pumi, Valki | ELDER TITANIDES: Themis, Mnemosyne, Phoebe, Tethys, Theia, Rhea | ELDER TITANES: Rivermaster/Oceanus, Sagacity/Coeus, Starmaster/Crius, Watchman/Hyperion, Piercer/Iapetus, Cronus

Zeus took the child and placed her on his shoulder. She spit up all over his shirt. "She loves me," Zeus exclaimed. "SHE LOVES ME!"

"Yes, she really loves you, Zeus," Metis said. "Now, she needs a name and a place to live. I will raise her in Tartarus but NOT in this place. Shall I go make plans with Grandmother for a place to live?"

Hera was adamant, "This child is a commoner. We will not raise a commoner!"

"She loves me!" Zeus exclaimed.

"I'm not sure you have many options, Hera," Metis said. "It's either you or me as her mother and you don't look like the mothering type."

"I most certainly am the mothering type," Hera said. "I am an Olympian. We excel at everything we do! And if I choose to raise a child, I most certainly will excel at it."

Hestia did not like where this was going, or where it had been for that matter. This problem must be resolved immediately. She commanded, "Zeus, give the child a name. Metis, go immediately to Kiya and make arrangements to raise it."

Hera was enraged. "THIS CHILD WILL NOT BE RAISED AS A COMMONER! I FORBID IT!"

"She loves me more than anyone else in the world!" Zeus said as his daughter fell asleep on his shoulder.

"GO AWAY, METIS. YOU WERE NEVER HERE. YOU ARE NOT THIS CHILD'S MOTHER. I AM HER MOTHER—AN OLYMPIAN. ZEUS'S DAUGHTER SHALL BE A PURE-BLOODED OLYMPIAN. SHE WILL NOT BE A COMMONER."

"I don't think so. I just wanted my daughter to see her father. I have no intention of giving her away."

"GO AWAY!!!" red-faced Hera screamed as she pointed toward the door.

Metis looked around the room at the Olympians gathered there, at the strange little children she had helped raise. Grown into what? All stared coldly at her, unblinking. All joined in the anger generated by their sister,

ELDER OCEANIDS: Metis, Tyche, Clymene, Eurybia, Amphitrite
ELDER OLYMPIANS: Hestia, Demeter, Hera, Hades, Poseidon, Zeus
OTHER: Philyra, Dionysus, Heracles, Outis, Enceladus, Littlerock, Porphyrion

Hera. A strange, unhinged, bloodless, collection of people unified against her. Metis trembled. *My child will be one of them!*

"SECURITY!!!"

Metis rose to leave but turned back to Zeus and asked, "Zeus, what is the name of my baby?"

"She is like a pointed spear lovingly driven deep into my heart. I will name her 'Athena.'"

Metis walked over and kissed her sleeping child on its head, said, "Goodbye, Athena. I hope you can make it in this place," and left before security arrived.

Hera happily took the child and called back to Zeus, "Come on, Zeus. Let's go show our new baby to Father."

Hestia was not pleased. *Oceanids simply cannot be controlled!*

PRINCIPALS: Kiya, Vanam, Pumi, Valki | ELDER TITANIDES: Themis, Mnemosyne, Phoebe, Tethys, Theia, Rhea | ELDER TITANES: Rivermaster/Oceanus, Sagacity/Coeus, Starmaster/Crius, Watchman/Hyperion, Piercer/Iapetus, Cronus

19. Decline

Kiya basked in the warmth of her family gathered around for the informal dinner. Her beloved Metis had returned from her long visit to Port Kaptara. Metis had helped Rhea in the upbringing of Rhea's children and had become a special friend and mentor to Prince Aeolus, leader of the Kaptarian civilization. The culture of his people grew rapidly under his leadership. Metis had matured into a beautiful woman who maintained her childlike awe of the world around her and her undying love of the sea. She remained unmanageable.

Stories were told. Songs were sung. Metis sang an 'earthy' song she had learned on her travels. Kiya blushed, but everyone, including Kiya, smiled and clapped their hands.

All were surprised that Metis had born a child and were eager to hear of her experiences. Her meeting with Zeus drew gasps from all but Kiya, who listened with stone-faced intensity.

Theia: "What will you do?"
Themis: "Shall I go and forcibly recover your baby?"
Mnemosyne: "Zeus and Hera cannot possibly raise Athena properly."
Phoebe: "This will not do."

It was Rhea who terminated the clucking. "You did correctly, Metis. We both know there is no hope for your daughter. She was born one of them. All you can do is love her and provide whatever guidance she may one day seek. You will be left with an unfillable emptiness, but you did as you should. Sing us another song, Metis. One of emptiness."

Metis replied, "I suppose I could jump up and run from the table in tears. But there is a song of an Oceanid forever torn from the sea."

Titanides cried. Kiya sat in stone-faced silence; Sagacity, lost in thought.

< >

In Port Olympus, the Olympians and their valued employees celebrated the arrival of Athena; the first second-generation Olympian. She would surely grow and embrace the values of the Olympians.

The Masters of the World.

ELDER OCEANIDS: Metis, Tyche, Clymene, Eurybia, Amphitrite
ELDER OLYMPIANS: Hestia, Demeter, Hera, Hades, Poseidon, Zeus
OTHER: Philyra, Dionysus, Heracles, Outis, Enceladus, Littlerock, Porphyrion

Notes on the Organization

Most elder Titans held top-level positions at Port Olympus. The second-generation Titans all held at least mid-level positions, if not higher.

The older three Potamoi brothers—Achelous, Alpheus, and Inachus—had fulfilled the demands of their parents, Oceanus and Tethys. They had risen to mid-level positions and learned all a Titan should master. They were then released to their parents in the far west where they were emissaries and ambassadors for the great civilization of Kypros. And, like their parents, scouts.

Leto and Asteria, the daughters of Phoebe and Sagacity—who was now referred to as 'Coeus' in Port Olympus circles—both rotated through high-level 'people-oriented' positions.

Astraeus, Pallas, and Perses, the three sons of mild-mannered Crius who was once named Starmaster, and Eurybia, became top executive assistants to Porphyrion in his 'Department of War and Defense.' A department that had never been called upon to act, but which continually spun off new technology and efficiencies.

Theia and Hyperion were especially proud of their three shining children. Eos was the first to work every morning and prepared the Port for the start of the day. Selene closed the port building each day ensuring all was safe and organized. Helios worked at the port the shortest time he could and then returned to his first love, the Port Spearpoint research department.

And lastly, the four sons of Iapetus and Clymene made it to middle management, but by the hardest. They had rather be in the field, visiting the common folk. The oldest, Atlas, was powerful and patient but much on the fool-hardy side. His brother, Prometheus, was extremely clever but always scheming. Epimetheus, bless his heart, was a bit guileless and not on the bright side. And Meoetius was a bit sullen and arrogant.

Olympians, Elder Titans, and second-generation Titans worked well together as a team. Their Mission Statement was to increase knowledge and wealth and share it with all peoples, to raise the standard of living and the enlightenment of all people throughout the world, and to promote

PRINCIPALS: Kiya, Vanam, Pumi, Valki | ELDER TITANIDES: Themis, Mnemosyne, Phoebe, Tethys, Theia, Rhea | ELDER TITANES: Rivermaster/Oceanus, Sagacity/Coeus, Starmaster/Crius, Watchman/Hyperion, Piercer/Iapetus, Cronus

immigration between all societies and to welcome the poor, the afflicted, and the hopeless into the welcoming arms of Kypros.

Granted, the Olympians were sometimes more concerned with the 'increase wealth' portion of the statement, but they understood that distribution beyond their borders was an investment in the future, which would someday return dividends. If they did not actively support the whole of the mission statement; they certainly did not interfere with it. Besides, it was in the official 'Charter of King and Queen of Kypros.' Their hands were tied even if they didn't want to share.

Port Olympus grew. Kypros continued to raise its standard of living. The world prospered.

It was a golden age.

Littlerock
In the 90th year from the birth of Vanam

The procession began at the fire pit.

Iapetus led them. He was followed, four abreast, by Kiya's grandchildren, then came Kiya and the elder Titans, and then the masses who respected and loved the old stone cutter. He was everyone's grandfather. He was the greatest metallurgist who had ever lived.

Iapetus marched with the urn containing the ashes held in front of him.

The grandchildren were led by Calliope.

Each grandchild wore a necklace of colored stones which was made for them by Littlerock as a birthing gift. Each year, on the anniversary of their birth, he gave them another beautiful, polished stone to add to their necklace. Each child had removed their favorite stone from their necklace and carried it clenched in their fist. Oceanids lined both sides of the path which led to the center of the Elysian Field. They softly sang their song of sadness.

Iapetus arrived at the destination. He sat the urn on the ground, sank to his knees, and put his forehead upon the urn. The procession circled Iapetus and the urn until the masses formed a huge circle around them. Iapetus lifted his head from the urn. The Oceanids ceased their song.

Iapetus said, in a loud and clear voice, "This is Littlerock. He was my friend."

ELDER OCEANIDS: Metis, Tyche, Clymene, Eurybia, Amphitrite
ELDER OLYMPIANS: Hestia, Demeter, Hera, Hades, Poseidon, Zeus
OTHER: Philyra, Dionysus, Heracles, Outis, Enceladus, Littlerock, Porphyrion

He emptied the urn onto the ground.

Calliope led the grandchildren to the ashes. She said to the ashes, "Master Littlerock, you were our friend." With that, she and the other children tossed their polished colored rocks into the ashes.

The Oceanids began their song of sadness.

The dinner that evening began somberly, but as stories, anecdotes, and jokes were told, laughter began, and the event became a joyful occasion. The music and singing became happier and more upbeat.

But at the children's table, the conversation remained somber.

Mnemosyne was monitoring the young Titanides as they talked. She glanced at Themis, who had also been observing. The sisters rose together and went to their daughters at the children's table. "May we join you for a little while?" Themis asked.

"Yes, Aunt Themis," Calliope replied. The children were silent. They were uncomfortable having adults at their table.

Mnemosyne asked, "You are all so serious. May I inquire as to what you have been discussing?"

The young Titanides looked at each other.

Their responses, at first tentative, became a torrent:
"Where is Master Little Rock?"
"Does he stay dead?"
"Where do you go when you die?"
"When I die, will I be gone forever?"
"If he is in my dreams, is that really him?"
"Can I see him again?"
"Can he come back to see us?"
"I liked him; I don't want him to be dead."
"Does he know we gave him a colored rock?"
"Will he come to see us if we go to Elysian Fields to visit him?"

Themis said, "Such interesting questions you have. This is more the talk of Scholars. Perhaps our children will grow into Scholars and learn about these things."

PRINCIPALS: Kiya, Vanam, Pumi, Valki | ELDER TITANIDES: Themis, Mnemosyne, Phoebe, Tethys, Theia, Rhea | ELDER TITANES: Rivermaster/Oceanus, Sagacity/Coeus, Starmaster/Crius, Watchman/Hyperion, Piercer/Iapetus, Cronus

Mnemosyne added, "These are not things we have considered. Such questions have not been raised before. But they are interesting and deserve to be answered. But where do we begin?"

Calliope asked, "Will Grandmother know?"

Everyone looked at Kiya, sitting at the head of the table. Kiya was aware of the concern at her Granddaughters' table and saw as they all looked at her. Kiya smiled and gave a little wave to them.

"Let's go ask," Themis said.

She listened quietly as her granddaughters expressed their concerns.

"I cannot answer these questions," Kiya said, "But I can guide you. Perhaps one of you will find the answers."

She paused and then continued, "I once had a friend named Pumi. He, too, is dead now." She stopped for a moment; sadness crossed her face. Then she looked up and around and said, in loud voice, "Pumi, can you hear me? Can you hear the questions of my grandchildren? If you can, give us the answers. Help us understand."

Everyone looked around for the voice of Pumi. No voice was heard.

Kiya shook her head in disappointment. "If Pumi could tell us, he would. He cannot do this thing. Why? I do not know. You must seek the answers to these things. When we last visited, Pumi told me that there are Tallstone Scholars who seek these answers. They call themselves Shamans. You can begin your search with them." She leaned toward her granddaughters and lowered her voice to a whisper. They leaned toward her. "He also told me this. That one time in the deep of night when he lay exhausted by his son's grave, his dead son spoke to him."

The eyes of the granddaughters widened. "What did he say?" Calliope asked in wonderment.

"His son said this, 'I have shed the body, which was my prison, and now, not only am I alive, at last, I live.'"

"Did he say where he lives?" Calliope asked.

Kiya replied, "Those are the only words Pumi shared with me."

ELDER OCEANIDS: Metis, Tyche, Clymene, Eurybia, Amphitrite
ELDER OLYMPIANS: Hestia, Demeter, Hera, Hades, Poseidon, Zeus
OTHER: Philyra, Dionysus, Heracles, Outis, Enceladus, Littlerock, Porphyrion

"I will find out where he lives," Clotho, Themis's oldest child, said. "I will find out if he lives in Elysian Fields or Overlook Point or in the colored stones we gave to him. Maybe he is in the wind or the sea or the clouds. Maybe he still lives in each of us because we love him or in Iapetus or Tallstone or trees. Maybe he lives in yesterday and can't speak to us anymore because we are living in today. Maybe Pumi can't speak to us because we haven't tried hard enough to speak to him. I shall go to Tallstone and learn from the Shaman. Will you take me, Mother?"

Themis said, "Of course, I will take you. I will take all my children plus any cousins who would like to go with us."

Eyes brightened. Little hands clapped. There was some jumping up and down.

"What have you started?" Mnemosyne asked her sister.

Themis replied, "Who knows? Perhaps a new path."

Zeus and Athena
In the 92nd year from the birth of Vanam

The days became the years.

They were absolutely the best; Chief of Communications Zeus and his delightful eight-year-old Executive Assistant daughter, the pure-blooded Olympian, Athena. Everywhere they went, they brought gaiety and delightfulness to those who loved to be in their presence. To those few who did not adore them, such as most Titans, less gaiety and more attitude. Zeus was far more loved than his remote, non-assessable father, King Cronus. And certainly, far more loved than his universally despised sister, Chief-of-Chiefs Hestia.

Everything ran smoothly. Secretary of Foreign Affairs Phoebe and her Executive Assistant Mnemosyne were surprised Hera had been assigned to be their Executive Assistant even though no such request had been made. Especially since Mnemosyne already had that title. Hera was to be privy to all meetings, decisions, and transactions involving that office.

"That's odd," Mnemosyne offered when first notified of the assignment.

The same notification announced that Hades would accept the assignment of 'Chief Executive Assistant' to the 'Chief Research Scholar

Book 2. *The Beginning of Civilization: Mythologies Told True*

for Metal Research,' Iapetus. Which was strange since Hades knew nothing of metals, research, or scholarship. Each Elder and second-generation Titan seemed to have an Olympian or one of their ardent admirers assigned to them to give them 'additional support and resources.'

Hestia imported three cadres of Hecatoncheires from a tribe far south of Port Kemet to be guards at the port. Each cadre consisted of fifty warriors who moved together as one unit. They were said to be unstoppable in warfare. Why Port Olympus needed warriors was not addressed. Each cadre had a name. The individuals didn't have names. They were simply part of their cadre. The names of the cadres were Cottos, Briareos, and Gyges. They were dedicated to King Cronos of Kypros and Port Olympus Chief-of-Chiefs Hestia.

Sagacity, now Coeus, noted one evening at a family gathering that the company emphasis seemed to be drifting from long-term investments to short-term profits. "Something's going on."

Hera's absolute devotion to Zeus was consummated when their father, King Cronus, approved the marriage of two beloved Olympian children. A marriage of blood-related brother and sister was unheard of, but they were both Olympians. How could there otherwise be pure-blood Olympian children? Other than Athena, of course.

From the everyday lunchtime consummations, two wonderful, delightful children had been born: Hephaestus—destined to join Hades at the Metal Working Operations, and Ares—destined to become a student of violent, physical war. Good Olympians both. Great futures with the company.

Zeus and Athena continued their encounters of love and admiration.

Pity Party

The Elder Titan women gathered on the patio for gossip time.

Phoebe said, "Did you hear that I have a new Executive Assistant, Mother? Hera of all people; Zeus's sister or wife or boss or mother or whatever she is. She's bad news. I don't know how this is supposed to work, since that's Mnemosyne's function."

ELDER OCEANIDS: Metis, Tyche, Clymene, Eurybia, Amphitrite
ELDER OLYMPIANS: Hestia, Demeter, Hera, Hades, Poseidon, Zeus
OTHER: Philyra, Dionysus, Heracles, Outis, Enceladus, Littlerock, Porphyrion

Mnemosyne replied, "Oh, Phoebe. Don't be dull. We both know Hestia is setting us up to get rid of us. That little self-centered Hades is now chief assistant to Iapetus. Save us all. We are on the road to destruction!"

"Road to destruction, Dear?" Kiya asked.

Phoebe answered, "Figuratively speaking, Mother. Hestia loves profits too much to allow things to go too far downhill. But we all know that she won't be at peace until all Titans are gone from her organization. Bitch!"

Kiya corrected her, "Strong leader!"

Obediently, Phoebe replied, "Of course, Mother. The bitch is a strong leader."

Mnemosyne said, "Come on, everybody. She wants us out. She wants her own people in. I'll admit that running an organization this size is difficult. It was easier when we were a small, tight-knit organization where most of us were related, and everybody knew everybody else. This is different. I've got five different cultures in my little section. The new man from Kemet doesn't even speak our language. I am sending him to Library School just to learn how to carry on a conversation. Bitch, strong leader, whatever, Hestia is doing a tremendous job in an exceedingly difficult position."

"Bitch!" Phoebe said. "Hestia runs the port while Cronus sits in his office looking out over the bay, planning things, and being King. Zeus stays busy by having everyone love him and getting his relatives pregnant. Life is so predictable, these days."

Mnemosyne replied, "Themis and I have no room to talk. Our children by Zeus are wonderful and delightful. We're fortunate that Zeus only comes sniffing around once a year to impregnate us again. We raise our children with good values. If they ever met their father, they would leave the righteous path and follow the path of self-centered, greedy Olympians. I make sure my little Muses are in the care of Oceanids whenever their father comes near Tartarus."

Themis added, "And my three Moirai don't even recognize his name as their father. It never comes up."

Kiya asked, "And the twins, Phoebe? I seldom see Leto. I never see her twins. They don't even pretend to visit their great-grandmother."

PRINCIPALS: Kiya, Vanam, Pumi, Valki | ELDER TITANIDES: Themis, Mnemosyne, Phoebe, Tethys, Theia, Rhea | ELDER TITANES: Rivermaster/Oceanus, Sagacity/Coeus, Starmaster/Crius, Watchman/Hyperion, Piercer/Iapetus, Cronus

Phoebe replied, "I am afraid that both Apollo and Artemis are infatuated with their Olympian cousins ... sisters, aunts, whatever they are. They are full of themselves at that age. Leto has hope that they will return to her teachings, but Zeus is far more dynamic than my sweet little Leto. Leto was impregnated by her uncle which is disgusting even if she is my child. And Asteria, I still weep for her. Whether Zeus drove her to suicide, or not, I suppose I will never know. But, still, I have more reason to despise Zeus than anyone here. But I remember my teachings: 'love everyone even if you despise them,' or something like that."

Theia offered, "Other than Metis, the only Oceanid I know that he has impregnated is Dione. I'm told her daughter Aphrodite is quite beautiful but wishes a great deal to be an Olympian. And his son, Hermes, by that Pleiades woman, Maia, is firmly on the path of his father. Maia was so young. And Zeus tricked that Alcmene girl. She was a happily married woman, to a prince, I hear. Zeus tricked her into thinking he was her husband and then impregnated her. Disgusting! But, her son Heracles, is said to be quite the man."

Phoebe groaned, "Well, that's Zeus. Age, relation, marital status, or species just doesn't matter when it comes to coupling."

Theia said again, "It's disgusting."

Rhea giggled. "That's my son you all are talking about and you're making me feel bad. You are all successful Titanides with your careers and your children. And look at me! Mother of six pure-bred, certified Olympian children, and no career. I have been back, what, nine years? And I don't contribute anything; to the port, to Tartarus, to Overlook Point. Nothing. I keep asking myself what am I doing here? Why do I exist?"

"I seem to remember, Rhea," Kiya said, "that the groundskeepers come to you for your guidance. Doesn't Outis show up occasionally to ask for advice on whatever new creatures he has tamed? Horses, I think he calls his latest. And the harvesting, packaging, and distribution of our honey farms go through your capable hands as do Theia's fashion design concepts and Iapetus's collection of jewelry. And you help Iapetus in his decision for new statues to create for the grounds and you counsel the young Oceanids in matters of womanhood. Honestly, Rhea, I have often wondered how you do all that you do."

ELDER OCEANIDS: Metis, Tyche, Clymene, Eurybia, Amphitrite
ELDER OLYMPIANS: Hestia, Demeter, Hera, Hades, Poseidon, Zeus
OTHER: Philyra, Dionysus, Heracles, Outis, Enceladus, Littlerock, Porphyrion

Rhea stood, walked over to Kiya, put her head in Kiya's lap, and softly cried. "I'm sorry, Mother. I'm so sorry."

Her sisters stood, hurried over, and put their arms around Rhea,

Themis asked, "What's the matter, Sweet? Still concerned for your children?"

Rhea choked on her soft sobs.

Theia said, "Sweet Sister. You were a good mother. You are still a good mother. The path your children take is their own decision; not yours; not their fathers.' You set them on the path of righteousness. Cronus is a good man, just not a good husband or father. He chose the path to grow Port Olympus to the exclusion of all else. He was the only son of Pumi and Kiya. He was driven to excel. His children idolized him, wanted to be him, and thought that they were entitled to everything just because they wanted it. Entitled because Cronus was their father. Entitled because they were born entitled. It is not up to you to save them. It is up to each of them. They can change at any time. All of us know this; I just remind you. It is up to your children. You are a good mother."

Rhea quietened and raised her head, looked blankly into space, and said, "They are little monsters. They think of nothing but themselves. Poseidon once kicked a dog because it was in his way. How can anyone kick a dog? They took things away from other children because they wanted it. I have heard 'Chief-of-Chief Cronus of Port Olympus is my father' so many times I choke on it. I am the mother of monsters. And these monsters are growing up to infiltrate and take over the Titan legacy of Port Olympus, the hope of the world. Sisters, cry with me! Raise your lamentations to the heavens! I am the mother of monsters, of Olympians!"

"Rhea," Kiya laughed, "I believe their father is *my* child."

PRINCIPALS: Kiya, Vanam, Pumi, Valki | ELDER TITANIDES: Themis, Mnemosyne, Phoebe, Tethys, Theia, Rhea | ELDER TITANES: Rivermaster/Oceanus, Sagacity/Coeus, Starmaster/Crius, Watchman/Hyperion, Piercer/Iapetus, Cronus

Book 2. The Beginning of Civilization: Mythologies Told True

20. Titanomachy
In the 96th year from the birth of Vanam

"From the Office of the Port Olympus Chief-of-Chiefs:

Olympian Hestia announced today the upcoming retirement of all Titans. Their retirement is effective immediately. The management of Port Olympus thanks the retirees for their years of dedicated service. A retirement party will be held at a date yet to be determined. Contact Port Olympus Chief of Communications Olympian Athena with any concerns or questions. Your co-operation in this matter is required.

s/Hestia, CoC P/O."

Titan Retirement

The band at the formal family gathering played rather loudly; the Oceanid singers bounced with the flow. Rhea, always ahead of the mainstream, demonstrated the latest dance moves which involved dancing with a partner, or without, or several.

A full month had passed since the Titans had returned home. All except for Oceanus and his family, who remained on the western frontier much to the delight of Sagacity.

"Hestia forgot one detail," Sagacity laughed. "She excels with day-to-day management, but her long-term planning isn't that good. To forget the entire western frontier is criminal. She forgot about Port Spearpoint and all points west. That would be hilarious if it weren't so sad!"

"You're just a bitter, old, fired employee, Sagacity. Or Coeus or whatever your name is. Get over it. Come dance with me," Mnemosyne said as she left him to go dance.

Kiya sat at the head of the table, laughing and clapping her hands to the music.

Coeus shouted back at her as she danced off, "You Titanides are not taking this seriously. Think of poor Iapetus. No more colored rocks!"

"So where did Zeus go?" Coeus asked Crius and Hyperion, who were standing with him.

ELDER OCEANIDS: Metis, Tyche, Clymene, Eurybia, Amphitrite
ELDER OLYMPIANS: Hestia, Demeter, Hera, Hades, Poseidon, Zeus
OTHER: Philyra, Dionysus, Heracles, Outis, Enceladus, Littlerock, Porphyrion

"I don't know," Crius answered. "He disappeared. Probably not a good sign. But we're not involved anymore."

"Well, actually," Hyperion said, "there is another factor at play. The Port doesn't produce anything. We Titans produce almost everything that's exported. Hestia is going to be livid when she discovers we can export goods without her port. It hasn't occurred to her that we are a separate operation. Cronus may be King of us all but that doesn't make Hestia chief of us all. She has fouled this takeover up, big time. She was so intent on taking over that she didn't think it through. I worry about those Hecatoncheires she imported. I never understood why she needs them. She has as many Gigantes at her disposal as she needs."

Crius interjected, "Most Gigante are loyal to Kiya, not Hestia. Maybe Mother should make a courtesy call on Chief Alcyoneous."

"What you are inferring is unthinkable, Crius," Coeus responded.

Crius responded, "Titans control the western frontier and control all manufacturing in Kypros. We are on the best of terms with Urfa, who pretty much controls the eastern frontier. What does Hestia have? A port. A port dependent on Titan goods. How long will it take her to figure that out? What will she do about it? Killing off the Titans would be a good start." He looked at Coeus and said, "Have Mother contact the Gigantes."

Rhea and Mnemosyne danced by and waved to their brothers. This was a song where it was appropriate for women to dance with women.

The music wound down. Enceladus announced that dinner would be served. Everyone found their places. Kiya rang her bell. "Enceladus, would you announce our special guest of honor for this evening?"

Enceladus walked to the entrance point. "Titans, our special guest for dinner this evening is Chief Alcyoneous of the Gigantes, a long-time friend, and ally of the Titans. Kiya has commanded me to assure everyone that figs will most certainly be served."

The Titans stood and applauded the old chief as he made his way to his seat of honor facing Kiya.

Crius, Hyperion, and Coeus looked at one another without expression.

PRINCIPALS: Kiya, Vanam, Pumi, Valki | ELDER TITANIDES: Themis, Mnemosyne, Phoebe, Tethys, Theia, Rhea | ELDER TITANES: Rivermaster/Oceanus, Sagacity/Coeus, Starmaster/Crius, Watchman/Hyperion, Piercer/Iapetus, Cronus

Cronus and Zeus
In the 97th year from the birth of Vanam

Executive Assistant Philyra led Zeus into his father's office. "I love this office, Father," he said as he walked around looking at each view. "I have to share my floor with the other Olympians. Hestia has the best view, and she won't give it to me. It's not fair."

"Well, Son. If you keep working hard perhaps you might obtain this office someday. You never know."

"Hestia took my good job away from me. She made me her assistant. All she does all day is tell me what to do. I don't like that."

"Hestia is the best of the best, Son. She knows what she's doing. She is probably grooming you for a much bigger role in the company. You would like that, wouldn't you?"

"I liked my old job. I saw everybody all the time. They all love me. Hera loves me. Athena loves me. Demeter, Hades, and Poseidon love me. They all love to listen to me talk."

"Well, yes. I am sure they do, but to what do I owe this pleasure?"

"What?" Zeus asked.

"Why are you here, Zeus?"

"Oh, I wanted to see my new office. Hestia told me that she is training me to be the new king."

Cronus Condemned

It happened soon enough, Athena and the Hecatoncheire cadre, Cottos, escorted Cronus to his new home in Tartarus. Cottos set up camp at the 300-pace pathway encircling Tartarus. Athena demanded to see Kiya.

She told Kiya that all Titans are now ordered to stay within the 300-pace circle. A Hecatoncheire cadre would be positioned at each entry point into Tartarus and all entering would need permission. She should collect all arms and turn them in to the Hecatoncheire. The area would be searched to ensure this order was met. Zeus was now the King of Kypros. Cronos would be allowed to live as long as he remained in Tartarus and did not

ELDER OCEANIDS: Metis, Tyche, Clymene, Eurybia, Amphitrite
ELDER OLYMPIANS: Hestia, Demeter, Hera, Hades, Poseidon, Zeus
OTHER: Philyra, Dionysus, Heracles, Outis, Enceladus, Littlerock, Porphyrion

try to instill an uprising. Cottos would be watching. "Is there anything you do not understand?"

"Why, nothing at all, dear. You may go," Kiya said.

Athena stared at Kiya with a blank look for several moments. *This was not the response I expected. Hestia was wrong. These people are stupid and compliant!*

Athena turned and rejoined Cottos. After a brief discussion, the Chief of Communications set off to return to Port Olympus.

"Welcome home, Son," Kiya said to Cronus. "You have had a difficult day. Bitter, if I remember. Sit down and rest. We will talk."

To Enceladus, she said, "A bitter for Cronus, please. And a meeting with an Oceanid."

They sat.

Cronus talked. "It was most upsetting, Mother. I was sitting at my desk, lost in work. My door opened and Hestia walked in, followed by Zeus and that Cottos group. She said, 'The Olympians have voted and unanimously elected Zeus as the new King of Kypros. Zeus has ordered that you retire to Tartarus and live there as long as you don't make any trouble. I wanted you dead, but Zeus declared that you love him, so you can live. Cottos will escort you directly to Tartarus. Speak to no one as you leave. I will send your things later.'"

Cronus paused, "Mother, I laughed and said, 'Dear Hestia, our Charter has a specific line of succession established and any change must be approved by the King, that's me. I certainly will not approve this proposal.' Hestia told me, 'Zeus has reviewed these details and proclaimed them trivial. He will clear up any violations at a later date. Now, the King grows impatient.' She told me that I had best leave quickly."

Again, he paused. "I said to her 'My dear Hestia ....' but she snapped her fingers and those Cottos people literally picked me up off my feet and carried me from my office. My daughter hates me. How can this be?" He hesitated, again. "Is it true, Mother? Am I no longer King?"

"You never really were, Son. You were a tool Hestia used to get rid of me."

PRINCIPALS: Kiya, Vanam, Pumi, Valki | ELDER TITANIDES: Themis, Mnemosyne, Phoebe, Tethys, Theia, Rhea | ELDER TITANES: Rivermaster/Oceanus, Sagacity/Coeus, Starmaster/Crius, Watchman/Hyperion, Piercer/Iapetus, Cronus

An Oceanid appeared and ran to Kiya for instructions. "Dear, we need to find the nature of these Hecatoncheire men. Will you gather your most clever sisters and find out what manner of creatures they are? What do they like? What do they respond to? What do they fear? That sort of thing."

The Oceanid's eyes brightened. "A reconnaissance mission, Grandmother? Are we going to war? Shall I send for General Porphyrion?"

"A wise suggestion, dear. But I suspect he is already in their custody. But if he can, yes, ask him to come to me. And keep me up to date on your mission."

The Oceanid ran off to gather some sisters. Kiya turned to Cronus and said, "Your quarters are just as you left them. Go and rest. Our family dinner tonight will be grand."

Even Rhea came to dinner. "You poor, sweet man," she said to Cronus as she went to her ex-husband and embraced him. "Your own children. Zeus, I can forgive. He just wants to be loved. Hestia turned out really smart and really mean, didn't she? I knew, but you didn't. You never even knew."

For the first time, Cronus wept.

Iapetus, too, had been banished to Tartarus. His precious rocks, his metalworking facilities, and his research labs were now under the control of Hades. He, too, was distraught.

But Kiya laughed. "We are where we started! Banished! Titans! Let's enjoy our good life while we can. As long as Hestia honors our constitution and continues exporting goods and civilization to the frontiers, what difference does it make who does it? Let's hope she continues to fulfill her duty and our constitution."

"She appears to have already skipped over the succession portion, Mother," Coeus said. "She has violated the Constitution. You could have Porphyrion throw her off the roof."

"That is a battle that we would lose, at least for now," Kiya said.

"Do we have a backup plan?"

"Several," she answered.

The banished talked for hours.

ELDER OCEANIDS: Metis, Tyche, Clymene, Eurybia, Amphitrite
ELDER OLYMPIANS: Hestia, Demeter, Hera, Hades, Poseidon, Zeus
OTHER: Philyra, Dionysus, Heracles, Outis, Enceladus, Littlerock, Porphyrion

Several Oceanids walked up from the south. They escorted General Porphyrion. "We found him at Port Olympus, Grandmother. He was under house arrest or something. We slipped him onto a skiff, sailed to Elysian Fields beach, and walked him up here. My sisters have their reports ready."

"Gather round, children," Kiya said. "Let's refine our plans for our future."

PRINCIPALS: Kiya, Vanam, Pumi, Valki | ELDER TITANIDES: Themis, Mnemosyne, Phoebe, Tethys, Theia, Rhea | ELDER TITANES: Rivermaster/Oceanus, Sagacity/Coeus, Starmaster/Crius, Watchman/Hyperion, Piercer/Iapetus, Cronus

21. Dionysus
In the 100th year from the birth of Vanam
Dionysus Bearing Gifts

The Olympians gathered every night on the roof of Port Olympus. They celebrated their greatness and poured unconditional love into Zeus, their king. The King of Kypros. They were dressed in their finest, which they always wore. If the masses did not know their greatness by their face, they would surely know, and bow before them, by their dress. They were simply the greatest.

Their servant, a Gigante, answered the knock on their door which was barely heard over the merrymaking of the Olympians. He opened the door. There stood a young, tall, handsome youth with a runner's build.

"May I see your invitation?" the Gigante politely asked.

"Invitation? Sorry, I don't have one. I'm here to see my father—Zeus. Do you know him?"

"Your father? I'm sorry. I don't recognize you and you are not on my list. Register at Port Reception in the morning. They will be able to help you there." The Gigante politely began to close the door.

The door slammed back into the Gigante with tremendous force. The youth had kicked it back open and stood there smiling. "My name is Dionysus. Tell Dad that my mother was Semele, the first woman he ever had sex with. I may well be the first ejaculation he ever had. Mother wasn't certain about that part. But tell Dad I'm here, and I want to meet him."

The Gigante was wide-eyed with fury but unsure of how to proceed. Dionysus looked around the Gigante, saw the party in progress, and waved to an Olympian woman staring at him. "This is my kind of place," Dionysus said. "And I have gifts for Dad that can liven this party up."

The Gigante stepped to physically eject the intruder but an Olympian, a powerful, woman armored in leather, arrived and said, "I am Olympian Athena. What is the meaning of this intrusion?!"

Dionysus held out both arms to the woman, "Sister Athena! I can't believe it! I'm your half-brother—Dionysus. You and I were conceived on the

---

ELDER OCEANIDS: Metis, Tyche, Clymene, Eurybia, Amphitrite
ELDER OLYMPIANS: Hestia, Demeter, Hera, Hades, Poseidon, Zeus
OTHER: Philyra, Dionysus, Heracles, Outis, Enceladus, Littlerock, Porphyrion

same beach at virtually the same time. Mother has told me the story many times about herself, her mentor, Metis, and Dad on the beach. Dad had a great time that day. Come embrace your brother!"

Athena was aghast. "I WAS NOT CONCEIVED!" she shouted. "Remove this imposter, Gigante-whatever-your-name-is!"

The Gigante attempted to physically remove Dionysius, but Dionysus kneed him in the groin, slammed the edge of his hand across the back of the Gigante's neck, and gently lowered the unconscious Gigante onto the floor.

"Come on, Sister Athena. Don't be mean to your brother. Introduce me to Dad."

"I AM NOT YOUR SISTER!"

The commotion at the door attracted the attention of Hera who walked over and said, "This is a private party. You are not welcome here."

His voice dropped an octave. "I am getting tired of this nonsense. Take me to my father or I will take myself to my father!"

"GUARDS! GUARDS!"

Three Gigante appeared at the door with swords out.

"Pleeease!" Dionysus said.

With quick, acrobatic moves he disarmed all three guards, laying two of them on the floor and glaring at the third. "Take me to Zeus! NOW!" he commanded.

The three people left standing stared at one another in confusion as young Dionysus said, "Never mind. I'll find him," and walked into the party. Talking and merrymaking stopped as Dionysus confidently strode into the room. All eyes were on the intruder. "Zeus?! Is that you, Dad? I love you, Dad," he said to the Olympian who appeared most likely to be Zeus. Dionysus knew the correct things to say to all of his relatives and, especially, to his father.

"Who are you?" Zeus asked.

Zeus and Dionysus had a long discussion and a nice, civil visit.

PRINCIPALS: Kiya, Vanam, Pumi, Valki | ELDER TITANIDES: Themis, Mnemosyne, Phoebe, Tethys, Theia, Rhea | ELDER TITANES: Rivermaster/Oceanus, Sagacity/Coeus, Starmaster/Crius, Watchman/Hyperion, Piercer/Iapetus, Cronus

But in the end, Zeus could not welcome just anybody into the select realm of Olympians and he was sure that he had never coupled with anyone other than his beloved wife, Hera, and, no, there had never been anyone named Metis, and, yes, Athena never had a mother. She was born one evening when Zeus slammed the palm of his hand to his forehead because he had a sharp pain in his stomach, and Athena popped out of his mouth fully dressed in her suit of armor. It was the armor that had given him the sharp pain. And no, Dionysus would not be received in the future. And no, Dionysus could not be an Olympian because he was not born of noble blood, and a princess mother did not count. Dionysus should not return. Gifts were always nice, but Dionysus should take his gifts and give them to beggars on the street. "Goodbye."

Dionysus said, "I see. Goodbye, Dad." He rose. As he left, he held out his arms to Athena and said, "Come give your brother a big goodbye hug."

Athena turned and stormed off.

As he left, Dionysus apologized to the four Gigantes.

Dionysus, Still Bearing Gifts

Kiya and the Titanides sat at their patio table. Enceladus came to them and said, "A visitor requests an audience with you, Queen Kiya."

"Of course, show him in. Ask what he would like for morning meal."

Enceladus returned shortly with the visitor. "Titans, this is Dionysus, a visitor from 'all over,' I believe he said."

The Titanides stood to greet their visitor, and Kiya extended her hands in greeting. "Welcome to our home, Dionysus. We look forward to visiting with you. Sit. Enceladus will bring you food and drink."

"You are kind, Kiya. I am told that you and your children ruled this land until the Olympians came and claimed it as their own."

Kiya said, "A concise summation. Short on details, perhaps, but a reasonable conclusion."

Dionysus asked, "May I tell you my story, Queen Kiya?"

ELDER OCEANIDS: Metis, Tyche, Clymene, Eurybia, Amphitrite
ELDER OLYMPIANS: Hestia, Demeter, Hera, Hades, Poseidon, Zeus
OTHER: Philyra, Dionysus, Heracles, Outis, Enceladus, Littlerock, Porphyrion

"Yes, please do. My daughter, Mnemosyne ..." she said as she motioned toward Mnemosyne, "... and her children are intrigued by good stories. Enceladus, invite the little Muses to join us. And I am now called Kiya; the name I prefer."

Dionysus bantered until his morning meal was finished and the Muses had gathered around. He began, "This is my story ..."

Hearing his story, Kiya was delighted. "We look forward to receiving your gracious gift. Present it to all my children tonight. We are having a family dinner and almost everyone will be there. How exciting!"

Titan Family Dinner

That evening, the family gathered for dinner.

Oceanus, Tethys, and most their children were, as usual, at Port Spearpoint or beyond. But attending from Port Spearpoint were Meoetius's daughters, Aidos and Pyrrha. The almost-red-headed-prim-and-proper Aidos, and her very-red-headed-wild-and-improper younger sister Pyrrha. Pyrrha had recently married her cousin, Deucalion, who worked for his father, Prometheus, at Port Spearpoint. Aidos had recently married Ziusudra, an intense young man of mysterious origin who had resided mostly in Tartarus. The sisters had gotten their red hair from their mother, Pandora, who had married Prometheus's sullen brother, Meoetius. In their childhood, the sisters were, as day and night, inseparable. Each captivated by her incomprehensible sister.

Also coming were Kiya's guests, Dionysus and his two followers who transported his merchandise and taught anyone interested in how to grow, harvest, and create that which they were about to experience.

Dinner was served and eaten. It was time for the gift to be presented. Dionysus signaled his people to begin. "Titans, I present to you the gift of the grape. I call it wine."

The assistants provided a drinking cup to each guest.

Dionysus continued, "It is either a blessing or a curse. It can carry you to the heights of ecstasy or the depths of despair or just give you a pleasant evening. It is a test of your nature, a test of your character. Treat it with respect. It will not do the same for you." Their cups were filled. "Your

PRINCIPALS: Kiya, Vanam, Pumi, Valki | ELDER TITANIDES: Themis, Mnemosyne, Phoebe, Tethys, Theia, Rhea | ELDER TITANES: Rivermaster/Oceanus, Sagacity/Coeus, Starmaster/Crius, Watchman/Hyperion, Piercer/Iapetus, Cronus

sweet drinks and bitter drinks have a new, formidable competitor: wine. I will not direct you on how to act or behave but I have led many to the cliffs of destruction and watched them merrily dance over."

"Shall I ask the band to play, Mother?" Rhea asked.

"A band of instruments?!" Dionysus exclaimed. "Most certainly. The perfect background for my gift!"

He raised his cup of wine into the air and proclaimed, "May you all have a long and merry life." The Titans mimicked his gesture. Dionysus swished the liquid in its vessel, stared at it a moment, sniffed the aroma, took an exploratory sip, swirled it in his mouth, and swallowed.

The Titans mimicked his actions and sipped their wine.

Random comments floated across the table:
"Interesting."
"It feels nice in my mouth."
"A bit sweet, I think."
"The aroma was pleasing."
"Much better than the bitter I usually have."
"This drink has substance to it."
"It has a fruity taste."
"Mine tastes like some of my rocks smell. I like it."
"Mushrooms? Leather? What's in this stuff?"

Dionysus said, "I have a sophisticated group. Titans may do all right with wine. But be warned, go slowly until you know what you are dealing with."

He glanced at Kiya, who had set her cup down without tasting it. "Kiya?" he said, raising his glass toward her and lifting his eyebrows.

"It sounds delightful. But, blessing or curse? Ecstasy or despair? Test of character? Let me see these things. Then I shall taste your wine."

Dionysus smiled a strange smile. "Yes, Kiya. Let us see these things together." He set his cup on the table and watched the Titans finish their first cup of wine. He motioned to the band to play louder.

The Titanes were fascinated with the texture, taste, and complexity of the drink. They were counseled by Dionysus's assistants who instructed them

ELDER OCEANIDS: Metis, Tyche, Clymene, Eurybia, Amphitrite
ELDER OLYMPIANS: Hestia, Demeter, Hera, Hades, Poseidon, Zeus
OTHER: Philyra, Dionysus, Heracles, Outis, Enceladus, Littlerock, Porphyrion

on a new vocabulary and what to look for in their drink. They were informed that theirs was a "new growth" and not complex at all. Dionysus did not want to waste "the good stuff" on neophytes. Dionysus would be informed of their interest. He would likely replace Kiya's drink with an older growth; perhaps their second drink could also be improved upon.

The Titanides were not at all concerned with the complexities of the taste but more interested in the gentle warmth it brought and the relaxation it caused. A counselor lectured them on lowered inhibitions and drinking too much. Too much might allow them to behave in what they would normally view as suggestive, lewd, and indecent behavior. It would certainly make them more festive, or fall asleep, whichever was their proclivity. But proceed with extreme caution until you master the effects of wine and know when to cease drinking, or at least slow down.

Rhea finished her third serving of wine. Finally, the beat of the music entered Rhea's body and forced her to stand. To dance. Rhea was the acknowledged 'Master of Dance.' And now, three glasses of wine had loosened her up. Her legs, arms, hands, hips, and head could all move in different directions simultaneously. She stood in front of the band, her head thrown back, her eyes closed, dancing a dance with herself.

Not to be upstaged, Pyrrha gulped down her third serving, joined Rhea on the dance floor, studied her moves, and decided she could do better.

The two women danced, each challenging the other.

The Titanides looked on with admiration.

Dionysus glanced at them, stood, walked to Kiya, and said, "Queen Kiya, I suppose you would like to see the extremes of what wine can do?"

Kiya nodded, "Yes."

Dionysus said, "Well, Kiya, what you will see is not even close to what wine can do to your senses. But don't worry, I don't take advantage of a woman because she has tasted my wine. At least not the first time."

He walked to stand in front of the two women. They opened their eyes and saw him standing there, smiling at them. They half-smiled back and began dancing for him. With him. Teasing him. Daring him. They thought they were impressing him with their moves. They did not suspect that it

PRINCIPALS: Kiya, Vanam, Pumi, Valki | ELDER TITANIDES: Themis, Mnemosyne, Phoebe, Tethys, Theia, Rhea | ELDER TITANES: Rivermaster/Oceanus, Sagacity/Coeus, Starmaster/Crius, Watchman/Hyperion, Piercer/Iapetus, Cronus

was they who were the amateurs; sweet young things just learning how to be suggestive, just learning how to tease, just learning how to dance.

Dionysus began parroting their moves. Rhea smiled. *A man who can at least pretend to dance.*

Pyrrha uncharacteristically stepped back to let Rhea take over.

Rhea added bounce to her step. Dionysus added bounce. She moved her body more wildly. He parroted her moves. She was delighted. She turned it on. Dionysus matched her every step, her every move.

He motioned to the band. Faster! Louder! Then Dionysus turned it on. Rhea was impressed and happy. She kept up. Dionysus moved closer to her, his body almost touching hers. They parried. Turned. Dionysus danced and pressed his chest into her back. They moved as one. She felt his body on hers. Moving together. She turned to face him; their bodies still glued together.

Any inhibitions Rhea had were now gone. She danced. Her hair waved in every direction. Her face was devoid of all worldly concerns. She would couple with any man who asked. Embrace any woman who offered. There was nothing she wouldn't do. Couldn't do. Shouldn't do.

Pyrrha could no longer stand it. She joined in. Her long red hair flowed over them like snakes dancing with a river. Making then one organism; one soul moving through time and space.

The Titanides watched the spectacle with wide-eyed wonder. Kiya with tight-eyed reservation.

Dionysus mercifully danced the two women to exhaustion. Returning to their chairs, they collapsed and sat gasping for breath. Titanides surrounded them.

Themis: "Are you all right, Rhea?"
Phoebe: "You were wild out there, Sister."
Mnemosyne: "I'm not at all sure some of that was appropriate."
Theia: "Do you want to lie down?"

Aidos took her sister's hand and said, "You did very well, Sister Pyrrha. I watched you with great interest. Your enthusiasm was inspiring."

ELDER OCEANIDS: Metis, Tyche, Clymene, Eurybia, Amphitrite
ELDER OLYMPIANS: Hestia, Demeter, Hera, Hades, Poseidon, Zeus
OTHER: Philyra, Dionysus, Heracles, Outis, Enceladus, Littlerock, Porphyrion

Deucalion turned to his wife, and drily asked, "Pye, do you want me to become someone who can do that?"

Pyrrha, pleased, gasped, "Husband, I married you because you are a boulder in a world of pebbles. Let me have my little excitements but change nothing of who you are. That was only a dessert, not a feast."

Dionysus returned to his chair and said to somber-faced Kiya, "With more wine, I can have them all that way. A room of men and women without inhibitions and filled with the warmth of wine will test their nature. It is a blessing or a curse."

Kiya loudly announced, "It's time to retire for the night, everyone. Say good night and go to bed, your *own* bed. We will talk tomorrow."

To Dionysus, she said, "The evening was both enjoyable and informative. In the name of the Titans, thank you for your gift of wine. I believe Coeus was learning its secrets from one of your assistants. We will all compare notes in the morning. Good night, Dionysus."

"Before I leave, Kiya, know that you have an exceedingly delightful and well-bred family, but Rhea and the red-headed one may not feel well in the morning. Also, my associates are at your disposal to teach you how to grow the plants I give you. They will teach you how to harvest and distill the wine. Wine has incredible trade value. My associates will be selling it in the market tomorrow. Your land looks perfect for the proper growing of grapes. And here, take this bottle to your quarters. It's a good bottle. You can assess the effect in the privacy of your room. I promise you won't end up running naked through Tartarus screaming, 'Take me! Take me!' Thank you for a pleasant evening."

He turned and left.

Kiya smiled, watched him go, and retired to her quarters with the flask of wine and a drinking cup. *I've been naked before!*

Dionysus and Zeus

Several days after the Titan party, Athena scoured the port for Dionysus. She found him on the dock cafe patio sipping wine with an extremely muscular man. "Dionysus, you are to come with me!" she demanded.

PRINCIPALS: Kiya, Vanam, Pumi, Valki | ELDER TITANIDES: Themis, Mnemosyne, Phoebe, Tethys, Theia, Rhea | ELDER TITANES: Rivermaster/Oceanus, Sagacity/Coeus, Starmaster/Crius, Watchman/Hyperion, Piercer/Iapetus, Cronus

"Little Sister," he said. "I could play word games with you, but you are so tiring to play with. May I bring my friend with me?"

"No! I mean, I don't know. I was only told to bring you."

He replied, "Well if I can bring my friend then I will come and do everything you command. If I can't, then I won't. Fair enough?"

Their first meeting had not gone at all to her liking and Father Zeus was having second thoughts about this cretin. She considered her options. "Very well. He may come but don't allow him to speak unless spoken to."

Dionysus agreed.

The three rode the elevator to Zeus's floor. Zeus met them at the door. "My dear son, how good to see you again. Why did you not inform me of this wine of yours? Hera, here, has been drinking it constantly since Demeter discovered it in the market. Demeter purchased a flask which she brought back and shared. Hera was at the market early the next morning buying more. Much more. It took Hestia a while, but she discovered that you are the supplier of this most excellent drink. I will take all that you have. I have been discussing your situation with my beloved Hera, to whom I am constantly faithful. I have decided to accept your gift, which must have been this wine! And I will recognize you as an Olympian, too. Are you excited? Do you love me?"

"Oh, joy! Dear Father! I am so excited, and I love you so much! Yes, take all that I have! All that I have remaining is in the market. I will have it sent to you immediately so that my brothers and sisters can enjoy it this very night! You can throw a real party! I will dispatch a messenger this day to bring you copious amounts directly from my vineyard north of Port Graikoi. I am so excited, Dad. And I love you so much!"

Hera giggled. "I have a son I had forgotten I bore. Zeus reminded me what a fabulous time we had making you. I'm so glad you came home and that you brought us this exquisite wine! And who is this handsome young friend of yours? He has so many muscles!"

"This is my friend, Heracles. He and I are from the same region. We have a lot in common, including the same father."

ELDER OCEANIDS: Metis, Tyche, Clymene, Eurybia, Amphitrite
ELDER OLYMPIANS: Hestia, Demeter, Hera, Hades, Poseidon, Zeus
OTHER: Philyra, Dionysus, Heracles, Outis, Enceladus, Littlerock, Porphyrion

Hera smiled blankly as she considered the implications of what she had just heard.

"Don't worry your pretty little head over it, Mother. Let's you and I get another glass of wine while Heracles and Dad get to know each other." Dionysus led Hera off by her elbow.

Dionysus failed to mention that he had already given the bulk of his wine, and all his plants, to his newly found relatives, the Titans.

Zeus and Heracles talked. They had a good conversation and agreed on many things.

An Olympian Party

Each Olympian attended what would be the first of many grand and glorious parties on the Port Olympus rooftop. The attendees included everyone in the world of any importance; Olympians, and Olympian want-to-be's.

King Zeus was the King of all Kypros and, with it, the titular head of the port and the Olympians. Hera was his second-in-command and his beloved wife, sister, and sometimes mother. Zeus was always loudly faithful to his wife. She was a jealous wife, seeing infidelities where there were none.

Hestia was the official Chief-of-Chief of Port Operations, a position Zeus let her maintain because Hestia loved him so much; although it was not exceedingly clear who let who hold what position. Demeter and Poseidon were key executives in running port operations. Hades missed many Olympian parties because he was always away in the north someplace, which was fine, since they didn't like Hades that much, anyway.

The second generation of Olympians was coming up nicely. They had the family values of "mine, mine, mine" plus the added advantage of never feeling guilt when demanding things just because they could.

The second generation included Zeus's children by Hera plus an assortment of his high-born children whom Hera did not exactly remember bearing until Zeus reminded her what fun they had conceiving the child. Zeus had grown so weary of explaining away the mothers of these children. He was delighted when he hit upon the ploy; "Of course, this is your child, Hera. Don't you remember? We had such a wonderful time making it." Hera did not want to appear to be dense. She would

PRINCIPALS: Kiya, Vanam, Pumi, Valki | ELDER TITANIDES: Themis, Mnemosyne, Phoebe, Tethys, Theia, Rhea | ELDER TITANES: Rivermaster/Oceanus, Sagacity/Coeus, Starmaster/Crius, Watchman/Hyperion, Piercer/Iapetus, Cronus

suddenly remember, "Of course, that's my child. I had such a delightful time making it."

Zeus could already see that Hera's discovery of wine was going to make his life much easier.

The two Titan grandchildren, Apollo and Artemis, seemed conflicted at times but were embracing the Olympian worldview.

Aphrodite was in her element; being allowed to be an Olympian, having every pretty thing she wanted, allowed to do anything she wanted to do. And all Zeus required of her, other than the usual boy-girl stuff, was to sometimes call Hera, "Mother." Yes, Aphrodite had found her calling. She was an Olympian.

Hermes, one of Zeus's sons by a distant relative, was allowed entry into the Olympian club because Hermes was an outstanding asset to Port Olympus as the Chief of Communications and the greatest Messenger in the corps; jobs Zeus once held and remembered with extreme fondness. Hera quickly remembered bearing Hermes. It had been a difficult labor.

Athena was virgin born. No female had been involved. She having popped out of Zeus' mouth and all.

Ares and Hephaestus were the children Hera best-remembered bearing.

Heracles wanted to join this elite club, but Zeus considered him to be low-born and Zeus did not remember the boy's mother, anyway.

Zeus certainly remembered Dionysus's mother, Princess Semele, and, if truth be told, he most certainly remembered Athena's non-existent mother, the Oceanid Metis. *Where is Metis, anyway?*

After the feast was eaten, Heracles entered the roof with a cask of wine on each shoulder. "There is more where this came from, but this is more than enough for every Olympian to drink their fill."

Dionysus stood, said a few words about wine and drinking, and then a few words about how much he loved Zeus and his beloved mother, Hera. "Mother Hera, let's find out how much wine you can drink this evening!"

ELDER OCEANIDS: Metis, Tyche, Clymene, Eurybia, Amphitrite
ELDER OLYMPIANS: Hestia, Demeter, Hera, Hades, Poseidon, Zeus
OTHER: Philyra, Dionysus, Heracles, Outis, Enceladus, Littlerock, Porphyrion

Associates served wine to all. Dionysus found an out-of-the-way chair, sat down, took a cup of wine, leaned back, and, with great anticipation, watched the party of parties begin.

The Founding of Evil

The next evening, Dionysus sat uncharacteristically silent at the Titan dinner.

"Dionysus, you are so quiet," Kiya said, raising her wine in his direction.

Coeus asked, "You say that the taste and aroma take on the characteristics of the ground it is grown in? That's interesting. That must be why your associates instructed us to make the plantings in different parts of our island. We will be able to compare subtle differences in each growth."

Dionysus raised his wine toward Coeus. "Astute observation, Coeus. And with no prior knowledge or training in these arts. My new Titan family is far more enlightened than any family I ever hoped to find."

Kiya said, "Share your thoughts with us, Dionysus. Perhaps we can help."

He stared at his wine as he twirled it in his cup. He stood. After a while, he said, "I fear that I have unleashed evil upon your land."

The Titans remained silent, waiting for him to continue. He said, "I may be young but I'm not a child. I know the power of the gift I have given you. I have played my aulos and led loud parades of naked men and women through their village streets. I have encouraged them to abandon all inhibitions and frolic and play in whatever combinations they might devise. Their couplings are of no concern to me. I have liberated their minds, taken them to higher planes, and allowed them to glimpse themselves as they really are. What they do with the gift I gave them is their test of themselves."

He stopped, sat down, looked at Kiya, and repeated, "I fear, Mother Kiya, I have unleashed evil in your land." His eyes went vacant. He was silent.

"I see," Kiya said. "Well, we have trained for evil, are prepared for evil, and shall destroy evil when it comes. Now, sweet Dionysus, how shall we know this evil?"

"You know it, already, Mother. But not the depths, not its capabilities, not its desires. Whatever you thought, whatever you feared, whatever you planned for is upon you. The Olympians have drunk the wine and discovered their true selves. They revealed it to themselves and will reveal it to you and the world soon enough. I have unleashed evil upon you."

"Don't be melodramatic, Son. Tell us what happened so that we can refine our plans and move forward. Now, what happened?"

Dionysus laughed and held his cup for more wine. "You people are incredible! Theia, cover your ears!"

He began. "Their party began innocently enough. Aphrodite was naked on the table before their second cup was finished. She and Poseidon provided the first round of the evening's entertainment. Another cup or two and the evening livened up a bit. Rhea, in her wildest, most drunken erotic fantasies, could not begin to imagine the various ways a woman can entertain men—at the same time. As it turns out, Aphrodite is an imaginative woman. By then, other couples were getting into it. Good clean fun so far. But they did not stop drinking the wine. Zeus demanded everyone drink more wine, and then, more wine. Ares demanded a live goat be brought to him. When the goat eventually arrived, Ares copulated with it as Athena cut its throat and Hera drank its blood. They all laughed. They thought these acts to be hilarious. Zeus demanded 'More wine!' Ares shouted, 'That was fun with the goat! Let's do it with an Oceanid!' Everyone cheered. I looked around in terror. Heracles was of no use; he was trying to be one of them. I attracted my servers and told one to go quickly and warn the Oceanids and whatever other innocents might be on the streets. I told the other server to distract their errand Gigante in any manner possible. Perhaps this would be forgotten if no one returned. 'More wine for everyone,' I shouted, thinking they might drink themselves into oblivion. I won't repeat the words they vomited that night, but they are what you fear, what you have prepared for. They now recognize their true selves. Hestia commanded that they prepare a plan to begin acquiring everything in the world as their private possessions."

Dionysus was silent for a moment. "And Kiya, I had come to Kypros wanting to be one of them."

Kiya replied, "We are fortunate, Dear Dionysus. You are a Titan." She turned to Enceladus and said, "Find an Oceanid. Tell her that Kiya needs her granddaughter, Metis."

ELDER OCEANIDS: Metis, Tyche, Clymene, Eurybia, Amphitrite
ELDER OLYMPIANS: Hestia, Demeter, Hera, Hades, Poseidon, Zeus
OTHER: Philyra, Dionysus, Heracles, Outis, Enceladus, Littlerock, Porphyrion

"When will the war begin, Mother?" Coeus asked.

She replied, "It began long ago, Coeus. Now comes the blood."

22. Gigantomachy

"They have not denied the Constitution, Kiya. Until they do, I will not challenge them," Alcyoneous said.

"A wise course," Kiya replied. "Are you prepared once they do?"

"We will be victorious. The Gigantes who remain loyal are training to their peak fighting capability. I force them to train under the guise of punishment for not demonstrating their undying fealty to our King. Gigantes who favor the Olympians will be on a trade mission to Overlook Point when I strike. Hestia keeps one Hecatoncheire guarding the port and two stationed away from the port. Innocent workers will die trying to stop us from reaching the Olympians. We will spare whoever we can. Receiving the severed heads of Hestia and Zeus will neutralize the two remaining Hecatoncheire when they arrive. They will no longer have a commander. Victory will be yours, Queen Kiya. It shall be so!"

"You are a dear and powerful friend to the Titans, Alcyoneous. I will try to be worthy of your friendship. I trust the future you see shall come to pass. If you fail, I will have a difficult choice to make. Difficult because the decision has not yet been made. I see clearly where the path of the Olympians leads. They shall not go there. You will stop them, or I will stop them, or the good earth, herself, will stop them. If not now, then in ten thousand years. But they will be stopped."

Coeus volunteered, "The Winter Solstice Festival approaches. Princes, chiefs, and kings from the frontiers will be entertained at Port Olympus and then transported to the festival as honored guests of Zeus. If I were Hestia, I would choose this time to present new terms of trade."

Kiya said, "Dionysus brings me the day-to-day words of the Olympians. They consider him to be one of them. But his heart is in the right place although his morals may be a bit flexible. By whose word will you accept that the Constitution has been violated, Alcyoneous?"

Alcyoneous replied, "Do not give me that command unless our Constitution is clearly violated. I place my honor in your hands. By your word shall I bring war."

ELDER OCEANIDS: Metis, Tyche, Clymene, Eurybia, Amphitrite
ELDER OLYMPIANS: Hestia, Demeter, Hera, Hades, Poseidon, Zeus
OTHER: Philyra, Dionysus, Heracles, Outis, Enceladus, Littlerock, Porphyrion

She raised her cup toward Alcyoneous, "I place your honor above mine. The command will not be given if hope remains. Let us drink to peace."

He raised his cup, "To Peace!"

New Trade Terms—and Onerous

Leaders from the frontiers gathered at Port Olympus on the Quartermoon before the Winter Solstice Festival began. Trade discussions were held; new terms were announced; new agreements were demanded.

So, they gathered, negotiated, and were appalled by the terms now demanded. They could continue their trade with and through Port Olympus but a tribute of 50% of the value of all transactions would be paid directly to the Olympians. Technology and research would need to be purchased rather than accessed for free. Unskilled or low-status immigrants would no longer be allowed into Kypros. All new immigrants must have useful skills. Hestia was tired of supporting the rest of the world. Surely everyone saw the need for Kypros to allow the provinces to stand on their own feet and pay their own way. If the port made an extra profit from the transactions, that was simply payback for their past investments. Hestia felt that she must renegotiate all the bad trade agreements made by Kiya, who was a bad negotiator. And a bad Queen.

Surely everyone knew these things.

Tartarus Trade Terms

Hermes demanded an audience with Kiya. He described the tribute which Hestia required of Tartarus.

"I would expect Hestia to tell me of these things."

"Hestia is too busy carrying out the business of the port. Besides these terms are simple to understand and require no negotiation. Is that understood?"

"Not quite, Messenger Hermes. You demand more than we produce."

"Then work harder. Your people appear to be lazy. Working harder will benefit both you and the Olympians. Surely you understand this."

"Will Hestia grant me an audience so that these terms can be negotiated?"

PRINCIPALS: Kiya, Vanam, Pumi, Valki | ELDER TITANIDES: Themis, Mnemosyne, Phoebe, Tethys, Theia, Rhea | ELDER TITANES: Rivermaster/Oceanus, Sagacity/Coeus, Starmaster/Crius, Watchman/Hyperion, Piercer/Iapetus, Cronus

"I have already told you that Hestia is far too busy to meet with you."

"And if we are not able, or won't, pay your tribute, what then?"

"Then Gigantes will come and take what is ours. Hestia has admired the statues of the Titans lining your pathways. These would make adequate payment for your first delinquent payment. Hestia would enjoy decorating these statues with festive adornments and markings."

"You did not mention when the first tribute is due."

"It is due and payable upon receipt of this message. She will allow you until the end of the month to send payment."

"The terms are NOT accepted. I demand Hestia meet with me to negotiate acceptable terms."

"I have told you that Hestia will not meet with you. Hestia will not negotiate. These are the terms that you will acknowledge and accept."

Kiya simply sat and stared at Hermes. She signaled for a Bitter. It was brought to her.

She sipped as she continued her silent, unyielding stare.

The Last Family Campfire

The next morning, Kiya sent a message to Alcyoneous. "Dearest Friend, the Titans will gather in Tartarus to celebrate this New Year. Join us for a few days of feasting. There will be fireworks."

The new year came.

The family gathered for a formal dinner.

The Titanides wore their finest party ensembles. Metis and her four sisters were there, as was Dionysus plus the guest of honor, the Great Gigantes Chief Alcyoneous. The feast food was wonderful. The laughter was unending. After dinner, everyone rose to obtain more wine, to talk, to laugh, to listen to the band, and, perhaps to dance.

Immediately after they rose, Kiya asked her elder children to join her around the ceremonial fire pit. They gathered around. Kiya took the hand of the Titanide standing on either side of her. The remaining Titans saw this, and they, too, joined hands. Kiya said, "This shall most likely be our

ELDER OCEANIDS: Metis, Tyche, Clymene, Eurybia, Amphitrite
ELDER OLYMPIANS: Hestia, Demeter, Hera, Hades, Poseidon, Zeus
OTHER: Philyra, Dionysus, Heracles, Outis, Enceladus, Littlerock, Porphyrion

last family gathering, children. I have had a wonderful time. Metis, Tyche, Clymene, Eurybia, Amphitrite—sing us a song. A song of joy.

After the singing, Outis found Rhea. "Great Elder Titanide Rhea, allow me to express my appreciation for the attention and warmth you extended to me in our youth. You made me feel like a worthy and respected member of our people."

Rhea embraced him and replied, "Oh, my sweet honey, Outis. You were one of my favorites. You would hover over me like a bee seducing a flower. Your mighty sting brought me joy. If Cronus hadn't swept off my feet, we might have little Outis's running around. I liked that thing you did with the honey. If we survive, we will get together, again. Promise?"

"If we survive, I promise," he said as he smiled sadly and left her.

Gigantomachy

The Titans and their honored guests sat at their morning meal when Hermes arrived with the platoon of Gigantes. He loudly announced, "Kiya of Tartarus. Your tribute was not received on time. Olympians now claim their rightful tribute consisting of the statues lining the incoming pathway. My Gigantes will now collect them. Do not resist. Anyone who resists will be killed."

"By what right, under our Constitution, do you do this?!" Kiya demanded.

"Zeus demands it! That is the only right I need!" Hermes barked.

The Gigantes began collecting the statues for transport back to Port Olympus.

Kiya gazed at Alcyoneous. "I have given both Enceladus and Porphyrion permission to return to the Gigantes if you will have them. They wish to be with you in your great quest."

"My honor and the might of the Gigante are all the greater with their return. I rejoice for my good fortune."

Kiya softly said, "Let there be war."

23. Fall of the Titans

The Titans began refining their final battle plan and the last, terrible plan to be implemented if they lost the war.

The time came for the Gigante attack on Port Olympus.

The Titans and their friends gathered on the patio around the ceremonial fire pit. The fire of bonding burned brightly. They told stories and sang songs. They embraced and shared laughter.

Outis had provided a tamed horse for Dionysus to ride to bring the news. They awaited the arrival of Dionysus, on horseback, to bring word of defeat or of victory!

If defeat, then if one Hecatoncheire came for them, every Titan down to the last child would fight them to the death. If two Hecatoncheire came, there was no hope for victory; the resulting slaughter of the untrained younger Titans would be meaningless.

Instead, the Final Plan would be initiated. Only the Elder Titans would stand and fight the two Hecatoncheires. Kiya and all Elder Titans were trained and practiced hand-to-hand in-fighting daily. They had lived long, and their deaths would allow time for family and friends to retreat to the waiting sailing vessels. From there, the survivors would sail to the frontiers and make their way into the highlands. Metis would watch until the outcome was without question. She would deliver the result of this day to her father at Port Spearpoint, along with Kiya's dreadful last command.

In joy and laughter, they waited. There would be time enough for tears another day.

In the distance, the galloping horse was seen. Everyone gathered at their designated positions.

Dionysus arrived, immediately dismounted, and shouted, "We are defeated! The Gigantes destroyed the Cottos Hecatoncheires. Alcyoneous, Enceladus, and Porphyrion fought their way to the Olympians. But Heracles and Athena killed them. I followed Hestia down as she hurried to summon her two remaining Hecatoncheires. She shouted back at me, 'Go tell your Titan friends what is to come!' She now marches toward Tartarus with the two remaining Hecatoncheires."

ELDER OCEANIDS: Metis, Tyche, Clymene, Eurybia, Amphitrite
ELDER OLYMPIANS: Hestia, Demeter, Hera, Hades, Poseidon, Zeus
OTHER: Philyra, Dionysus, Heracles, Outis, Enceladus, Littlerock, Porphyrion

They exchanged a few more words, then Kiya turned toward the throng gathered before her, raised her fist into the air, and loudly proclaimed, "Death comes for us! Long live the Titans!"

They understood what they were now to do. They responded, "Long Live the Titans!" turned, and, upon their new path, hurried toward the beach to the waiting Oceanids.

All left the patio except Kiya and her children.

Coeus was on point; he would be the first to die. Behind and to his left, stood Iapetus. Behind and to his right stood Hyperion. Completing the diamond formation would be Crius. The Titanides would die in single file, oldest to youngest. Behind the Titanides, stood the youngest Elder Titan, Cronus.

Kiya was last. She wore a simple necklace made of five thin, colored, pierced stones.

Hecatoncheires Briareus and Gyges came for them. Kiya watched her children prepare. *You will have your way at last, CHIEF Vanam. I and my children will die. But know this. We do not despair.*

Coeus killed Gyges 1 and 2 before his head was removed by Gyges 3. Iapetus and Hyperion killed Gyges 3, 4, and 5. Crius killed number 6. Themis killed 7 and 8 before being struck down by 9. Mnemosyne killed 10 and 11; Phoebe killed 12; Theia 13; and little, athletic Rhea killed 14, 15, and 16. Cronus, son of Pumi, killed 17 and 18.

Kiya watched her children with pride. *Porphyrion trained us well.*

She closed her eyes, lowered her head, and prepared herself. *I am well trained, quick, agile, and have two perfect daggers. I am calm, tranquil, and prepared. They are large, clumsy, slow, and move with predictability. They are not trained for infighting. They are filled with the rage of war.*

Her eyes snapped open. She saw the swords starting positions and knew the path they would take. She was motionless until 19 and 20 committed. She glided from where the swords thought she would be, swerved behind 19 and 20, and smoothly glided daggers into their hearts from behind. She reversed her course from where the next swords were already headed, delivering a dagger into the chests of 21 and 22. She shifted course to glide by the side of 23, delivering a dagger into his side. She then delivered a

PRINCIPALS: Kiya, Vanam, Pumi, Valki | ELDER TITANIDES: Themis, Mnemosyne, Phoebe, Tethys, Theia, Rhea | ELDER TITANES: Rivermaster/Oceanus, Sagacity/Coeus, Starmaster/Crius, Watchman/Hyperion, Piercer/Iapetus, Cronus

dagger into the heart of 25 before swiveling to kill 24. Gyges 26 was swinging erratically; it took an extra tenth of a second to predict where his sword be. Her brain signaled her muscles where not to be. Her muscles were already moving her body when her dagger caught on the rib of 25, slowing her for a twentieth of a second. Gyges 26 sword separated her head from her body. Gyges 27 ran his sword through the headless body.

The remaining Gyges surveyed the field and immediately began removing the heads of those still attached to their bodies. Completing their assigned tasks, they gathered along the path for inspection.

Seeing the excitement ended, Hestia inspected her troops, congratulating them on a job well done but silently wondering if she had gotten what she had paid for. *Eleven old people killed 25 of the finest fighting force in the world?!*

She sipped from a large cup of wine as she came to the remains of Coeus. *Pompous loudmouth.*

She kicked his head out of her way, sipped her wine, and continued down the line, sipping and kicking. She came upon Themis's head. *Bitch!*

Finally, she came upon Rhea. *You never let me have what I wanted, Mother. I always hated you. I guess you knew that.*

She sipped, she kicked. She came to Cronus and became melancholy. *Father! I am so proud of you. I always thought of you as a dried-up, useless, old man. But look at you. Single-handedly killing two of my finest fighters. Hooray for you.*

She sipped. She kicked.

Hestia looked down the path to the fire pit and became giddy. *Grandmother. We meet again! I am so delighted to see you!*

She walked to stand over Kiya and stared at her body for a long time. Suddenly, involuntarily, she threw her wine onto the severed head. *Why did I do that, Grandmother? Now you have the wine, and I don't. Life isn't fair.*

Hestia chuckled as she picked the head up by the hair and pitched it into the flames of the fire pit. She then returned to the remaining Gyges.

She said, "Clean this mess up in the morning. They will be here waiting for you. Now, follow me to Port Olympus. The Olympians will be having

ELDER OCEANIDS: Metis, Tyche, Clymene, Eurybia, Amphitrite
ELDER OLYMPIANS: Hestia, Demeter, Hera, Hades, Poseidon, Zeus
OTHER: Philyra, Dionysus, Heracles, Outis, Enceladus, Littlerock, Porphyrion

a major party. They will be so excited to hear about the downfall of the Titans and the glorious triumph of the Olympians."

She began their march back to Port Olympus. Her wine cup was empty. *I wish I had the wine I shared with you, Grandmother. You never were very nice to me!*

24. Triumph of the Olympians

Metis arrived at Port Spearpoint late in the night.

She found and then embraced her mother and then her father. They sat together. "It's over. Grandmother lost. I saw her and each of your sisters and brothers die under the sword. My cousins retreated by boat. All made it to the shores surrounding Oursea."

She paused, "My Oceanid sisters saw the ending. After all was quiet, some went into the Elysian Fields and built a great pyre. Others gathered the remains of Kiya and her children and took them to the pyre. The Oceanids lit the pyre and sang our song of sadness. The higher the flames grew, the louder they sang."

Again, she paused, "If Grandmother died, Father, I am to give you her last command: 'Remove the wall.'"

With a quieter voice, she said, "My sisters will tell all they meet that Queen Kiya commands them to gather their belongings and retreat to higher ground, that a great flood is coming."

Oceanus sat in silence. Eventually, he said, "Mother is dead? My brothers and my sisters are dead? Remove the wall?"

He was silent again then muttered to no one, "That was just a concept. It was never to actually happen. We have stockpiled the powders and mixtures to do it. There is a plan to do it, but I never thought ..."

He stood, left his wife and daughter, and walked to stare out over Oursea. *It probably wouldn't work, anyway. Littlerock said that it might not work. But to even attempt it would destroy Port Spearpoint, whether the wall came down or not. And if it did somehow work, then Kypros would be destroyed and every port on Oursea would be under stades of water. Tens of thousands of our people would die. And to what end? So that mother can kill the Olympians? Maybe the Olympians do deserve to die. And mother believes that by killing them, we would be ridding the world of a horrible plague. Even so, why would not their plague appear again? Civilization flows through Port Olympus. Destroy it? The Olympians killed my mother. They killed my family. They are evil. But ... remove the wall?*

ELDER OCEANIDS: Metis, Tyche, Clymene, Eurybia, Amphitrite
ELDER OLYMPIANS: Hestia, Demeter, Hera, Hades, Poseidon, Zeus
OTHER: Philyra, Dionysus, Heracles, Outis, Enceladus, Littlerock, Porphyrion

There was little for Tethys and Metis to do but wait. Metis pleased her mother by begging her to tell the story of the rock and bear claw necklace she always wore, "Tell it just one more time, Mother."

Tethys would tell that story and then the one about becoming her mother, "I have never seen bigger eyes than the four little Oceanids had when they stood before their new father awaiting his reaction to the news that he now had four brand new daughters. Older daughters but precious daughters, nonetheless. Mother was furious, but she finally accepted what was to be and loved you all the more."

Tethys talked of the new worlds she and Oceanus had discovered. Of the tribes, of the wonders, of how much larger the world than anyone had imagined when Oceanus, then named Rivermaster, and Coeus, then named Sagacity, had left the Clan of the Serpent. "That was a lifetime, ago," Tethys said. "We were children. Wild, savage little children."

Metis laughed. "We still are. We never really fit in with genteel society. We just pretended." Metis paused and then said, "Uhhh, I don't think I ever officially told you, but I had a baby."

"I have a grandchild you didn't tell me about?!" Tethys asked.

"Uhhh, yes. You do. I'm not particularly proud of it. I mean I love my daughter and all, but she wasn't my best performance. I kind of messed up. Zeus is her father. He took her away from me. He named her Athena, and she's one of them, an Olympian. So, if everything goes like Grandmother wants it to, if Father does this thing and is successful, we are going to kill my daughter."

Metis choked on the last words.

Tethys embraced her daughter. "Each of us does what must be done. Despair only if your path is not straight and true. Let what must be, be. Now, tell me about Athena. The good and the bad!"

"Well, I don't know exactly where to start but I was lying on the beach one day with my friend, Semele ..."

PRINCIPALS: Kiya, Vanam, Pumi, Valki | ELDER TITANIDES: Themis, Mnemosyne, Phoebe, Tethys, Theia, Rhea | ELDER TITANES: Rivermaster/Oceanus, Sagacity/Coeus, Starmaster/Crius, Watchman/Hyperion, Piercer/Iapetus, Cronus

Sunrise

Tethys and Metis heard the approaching footsteps of Oceanus. They rose to meet the haggard man with bloodshot eyes.

His only words were, "I will not do this thing."

Then he walked away.

Olympians Victorious

Hestia stared at the moon rising over beautiful, peaceful Port Olympus Harbor. She knew, two floors above, Zeus would be bringing the Olympians into full party mode. Aphrodite would be gyrating on the table by now, her clothes strewn on the heads of her adoring admirers.

Hestia savored the triumph. *I have rid the world of the insufferable Kiya and her sanctimonious, self-righteous children. Their day with their low-class, disrespectful, attitudes is over. Olympians now own the world! All people will pay us tribute, honor and obey us. They will acknowledge our magnificence and glory.*

Olympian Hestia closed her eyes and threw back her head in ecstasy. *We will rule for ten thousand years!*

###

ELDER OCEANIDS: Metis, Tyche, Clymene, Eurybia, Amphitrite
ELDER OLYMPIANS: Hestia, Demeter, Hera, Hades, Poseidon, Zeus
OTHER: Philyra, Dionysus, Heracles, Outis, Enceladus, Littlerock, Porphyrion

###

The Beginning of Civilization: Mythologies Told True
continues in
Book 3. *Dionysus and Hestia: Rise and Fall of the Olympians, Second Edition*
which tells the story of Dionysus and his friends
as they attempt to save civilization from
the self-serving, insatiable Olympians.

PRINCIPALS: Kiya, Vanam, Pumi, Valki | ELDER TITANIDES: Themis, Mnemosyne, Phoebe, Tethys, Theia, Rhea | ELDER TITANES: Rivermaster/Oceanus, Sagacity/Coeus, Starmaster/Crius, Watchman/Hyperion, Piercer/Iapetus, Cronus

IV. APPENDIX
Author's Notes

TITAN etymology is given by the Greek writer, Hesiod, who gave a double etymology for "Titan." He derived it from titaino, "to strain" and tisis, "vengeance." He wrote that Ouranos gave them the name Titans "in reproach; for they strained and did a fearful deed, and that vengeance for it would come afterward."

ATLANTIS lies in the exact location of my fictional Tartarus as described by Robert Sarmast in his book *Discovery of Atlantis, the Startling Case for the Island of Cyprus* by Origen Press. Sarmast maintains that in 10,000 B.C.E. the plains of Cypress were not submerged by the Mediterranean and this now-submerged landmass matches Plato's description of Atlantis in all respects.

GOBEKLI TEPE is an archeological site in eastern Turkey and is the world's oldest megalithic site. It was built by hunter-gatherers 12,000 years ago and predates agriculture, animal domestication, and settlements. It has no known reason to exist. Wheat domestication is thought to have occurred within 60 miles of Gobekli Tepe. It provides the basis for my fictional Tallstone.

SANLIURFA, a modern city in Turkey, is the basis for my fictional Urfa which is my first permanent settlement of hunter-gatherers and where Valki domesticated wheat. Sanliurfa lies twelve miles from Gobekli Tepe.

STRAIT OF MESSINA is the submerged narrow strait between eastern Sicily and Calabria, Italy. At its most narrow point, it is less than two miles wide. The maximum depth is 820 feet. My fictional Port Spearpoint lies directly over it.

ELDER OCEANIDS: Metis, Tyche, Clymene, Eurybia, Amphitrite
ELDER OLYMPIANS: Hestia, Demeter, Hera, Hades, Poseidon, Zeus
OTHER: Philyra, Dionysus, Heracles, Outis, Enceladus, Littlerock, Porphyrion

Greek Mythology Primer

The Earth gave birth to the Sky, the Mountains, and the Sea. These four gave birth to everyone else.

Anthropomorphically, Gaia gave birth to Ouranos, Ourea, and Pontus. Then it got complicated.

By Ouranos, Gaia gave birth to the twelve Elder Titans, the three Cyclops, and the three Hecatoncheires.

By Pontus, Gaia gave birth to Nereus, Thaumas, Phorcys, Ceto, and Eurybia. These gave birth to myriad sea gods, goddesses, and nymphs.

By his splattered blood, Ouranos gave virgin birth to the Giants, the Erinyes, the Meliads, and maybe Aphrodite.

By Oceanus, Tethys gave birth to the many Oceanids, Ocean and River Goddesses, and many Potamoi—River Gods.

By Coeus, Phoebe gave birth to Leto and Asteria.

By Crius, Eurybia gave birth to Astraeus, Pallas, and Perses.

By Hyperion, Theia gave birth to Helios, Selene, and Eos—the Sun, the Moon, and the Dawn.

By Iapetus, Oceanid Clymene gave birth to Atlas, Prometheus, Epimetheus, and Menoetius—the Fathers of Mankind.

By Cronus, Rhea gave birth to the six Elder Olympians—Hestia, Demeter, Hera, Hades, Poseidon, and Zeus.

By Zeus:
Oceanid Metis possibly gave birth to Olympian Athena;
Olympian sister Hera gave birth to Olympians Ares and Hephaestus and mortal Hebe;
Titanide Leto gave birth to twin Olympians Apollo and Artemis;
Pleiades Maia gave birth to Olympian Hermes;
Theban mortal Princess Semele gave birth to Olympian Dionysus;
Titanide Aunt Mnemosyne gave birth to the "Muses;"
Titanide Aunt Themis gave birth to the "Horae" and "The Fates;"

PRINCIPALS: Kiya, Vanam, Pumi, Valki | ELDER TITANIDES: Themis, Mnemosyne, Phoebe, Tethys, Theia, Rhea | ELDER TITANES: Rivermaster/Oceanus, Sagacity/Coeus, Starmaster/Crius, Watchman/Hyperion, Piercer/Iapetus, Cronus

Book 2. The Beginning of Civilization: Mythologies Told True

the rape of Olympian sister Demeter gave birth to Persephone; the mortal Alcmene gave birth to Heracles.

The twelve **Elder Titans** were Oceanus, Coeus, Crius, Hyperion, Iapetus, Cronus, Themis, Mnemosyne, Phoebe, Tethys, Theia, and Rhea.

The six **Elder Olympians** were the six children of Cronus and Rhea including Hestia, Demeter, Hera, Hades, Poseidon, and Zeus.

The six younger **Olympians** were six of the many children fathered by Zeus including Apollo, Ares, Artemis, Athena, Demeter, Aphrodite, Dionysus, Hermes, and Hephaestus. The last six names vary within different traditions.

ELDER OCEANIDS: Metis, Tyche, Clymene, Eurybia, Amphitrite
ELDER OLYMPIANS: Hestia, Demeter, Hera, Hades, Poseidon, Zeus
OTHER: Philyra, Dionysus, Heracles, Outis, Enceladus, Littlerock, Porphyrion

Glossary of Names and Places

Biy = "born in the year" is referenced from the birth of Vanam.
Diy = "Died in the year' referenced to the birth of Vanam.
cf = "contracted from" is the source name etymology.
IGR = "In Greek Mythology"

Aeolus was the first elected chief of Port Kaptara. See Kaptara.

Achaeous was the appointed general of Port Kaptara.

Achelous was the first son of Oceanus and Tethys. Tethys gave birth to him in a river and called him a Potamoi.
IGM Achelous was a son of Oceanus and Tethys, a river god, father to the Sirens and nymphs.

Aidos was the daughter of Meoetius and Pandora, wife of Ziusudra, and the older sister of Pyrrha.

Alcyoneous was the great Chief of the Gigantes. He led the battle of the Gigantes against the Olympians attempting to regain control of Port Olympus for Queen Kiya.
IGM Alcyoneous was one of the Giants, the traditional opponent of Heracles during the Gigantomachy.

Alpheus was the second son of Oceanus and Tethys. She gave birth to him in a river and called him a Potamoi.
IGM Son of Oceanus and Tethys. A river god.

Amphitrite was the biological daughter of Oceanus and Tethys and an Elder Oceanid.
IGM Wife of Poseidon and Queen of the Sea.

Aphrodite was a party girl who would do anything and everyone to be an Olympian. She was everyone's favorite partner. Biy 47.
IGM Aphrodite was the daughter of Zeus and Oceanid Dione (in one tradition). She was consort to all the male Olympians and many others. Goddess of love, beauty, and sexuality.

Apollo was the son of Zeus and Titanide Leto and twin to Artemis. He was born a Titan but gravitated toward the Olympian lifestyle. Biy 47.
IGM Apollo was the son of Zeus and Titanide Leto and the God of many things.

Ares was the son of Zeus and Zeus's sister Hera. He was a brutal, sadistic Olympian.
IGM Ares was the son of Zeus and Hera. He fathered many children. One of his consorts was Aphrodite. He was the God of War.

Artemis was the daughter of Zeus and Titanide Leto. She was twin to Apollo, born a Titan but gravitated toward the Olympian lifestyle. Biy 87.
IGM Artemis was the daughter of Zeus and Titanide Leto. She was the Goddess of the Hunt and had no consorts or children.

Athena was the daughter of Zeus and Oceanid Metis; possibly from Zeus's third ejaculation. She was a loud and dominating Olympian who dressed in armor and maintained that hers was a virgin birth directly from her father's mouth. Biy 84.
IGM Athena was the firstborn and favorite child of Zeus. She sprang fully grown from his head in full armor. She had no consorts or children. She was the patron of Athens and other cities. Goddess of wisdom and battle strategy.

Atlas was the son of Elder Titane Iapetus and Oceanid Clymene. Biy 47.
IGM Atlas was one of the four fathers of mankind.

Calpeia was a local woman who befriended Tethys and Oceanus at what is now the Strait of Gibraltar.
In archeology, the name is given to the remains of a woman who lived in 7500 B.C.E. and whose DNA is identical to a modern-day woman.

Clan of the Lion was the first tribe to be designated "Clan" and was a founding tribe of the Winter Solstice Festival. Notable members include Chief Nanatan, Master Skywatcher Vaniyal, Skywatchers Littlestar and Voutch, and Elder Woman Vivekamulla. Notable members acquired include the foundling Valki.

Clan of the Serpent was the second tribe to be designated "Clan" and was a founding member of the Winter Solstice Festival. Notable members include Chief Talaimai, Hunter/Chief Vanam, Moonwatchers Karan and Nilla, Elder Women Panti and Palai, Hunters Valuvana, Maiyana, Master Stonecutters Pumi and Kattar, and Gatherer Amma. Notable members acquired from other tribes include Kiya, Valki, and Skywatcher Voutch. The tribe was originally Chief Talaimai's and then Chief Vanam's.

Clymene was the adopted daughter of Rivermaster and Tethys and the third of the Elder Oceanids. She married Elder Titan Piercer and gave birth to four sons. Biy 33.
IGM Iapetus and Clymene gave birth to Atlas, Prometheus, Epimetheus, and Meoetius—the Fathers of Mankind.

ELDER OCEANIDS: Metis, Tyche, Clymene, Eurybia, Amphitrite
ELDER OLYMPIANS: Hestia, Demeter, Hera, Hades, Poseidon, Zeus
OTHER: Philyra, Dionysus, Heracles, Outis, Enceladus, Littlerock, Porphyrion

Coeus. See Sagacity.
IGM Coeus and Phoebe gave birth to Leto and Asteria.

The **Common Language** was the language spoken by most Neolithic tribes within the Levant and the more northern lands. Even the most inarticulate tribes recognized the universal "thou, ye, we, not, what, this, that, old, black, mother, man, worm, hand, bark, fire, ashes, to flow, to hear, to pull, to spit." The Common Language evolved as the tribes traded young women as mates to men in other tribes. The women of their new tribe would learn the words, motions, and philosophies of the new member's tribe and their expanded vocabularies would be passed on to their children. Different levels of sophistication evolved as the tribes moved from a nomadic lifestyle, without possessions, to a sedimentary lifestyle, with possessions. By the Neolithic period, people were at least, if not more, as intelligent and forward-looking as we are.

Crius. See Starmaster.
IGM: Elder Titane Crius and Oceanid Eurybia gave birth to Astraeus, Pallas, and Perses.

Cronos was the sixth son of Kiya and her only son by Pumi. Because of his parentage, he was driven to be successful in all things. He became the Chief-of-Chief of Port Olympus and eventually became King of the Titans. He married Elder Titanide Rhea in the first true marriage. The two gave birth to six children who would become the Elder Olympians. By his executive assistant, Philyra, Cronos fathered Chiron, who was physically deformed.
IGM Elder Titan Cronus and sister Elder Titanide Rhea gave birth to all Elder Olympians. Cronus also fathered the first Centaur by Oceanid Philyra.

Cyclops.
IGM The Cyclops were three giant, one-eyed creatures named Brontes, Steropes, and Arges.

Deep Lab was the remote research facility established by Littlerock with the original intent of researching Queen Kiya's question "How would one remove the granite wall which Spearpoint Port sits upon?" It evolved into a research center for advanced technology.

Deep Well was one of six elevator shafts drilled through the cliff upon which Port Spearpoint sat and used to transport goods between Oursea and Middlesea.

PRINCIPALS: Kiya, Vanam, Pumi, Valki | ELDER TITANIDES: Themis, Mnemosyne, Phoebe, Tethys, Theia, Rhea | ELDER TITANES: Rivermaster/Oceanus, Sagacity/Coeus, Starmaster/Crius, Watchman/Hyperion, Piercer/Iapetus, Cronus

Demeter was the second child of Cronus and Rhea. She was an Olympian. Biy 62.
IGM Demeter was raped by Zeus and bore Persephone. The birth order of the Elder Olympians is convoluted. Demeter was the Goddess of the Harvest, Fertility, and Law.

Deucalion was the son of Prometheus and Hesione and husband of Aidos.

Dionysus was a son of Zeus by Princess Semele; possibly from Zeus's first ejaculation. Dionysus was the inventor and bringer of wine. Initially spurned by his father, he adopted the Titans as his real family. In his youth, he was a party animal and drinking friend with his half-brother, Heracles. He became an Olympian but rejected Olympian ideals. Biy 84.
IGM Dionysus was an Olympian in some traditions but not an Olympian in other traditions. His mythology is great, complex, and important. He was the God of Wine among other things.

Einkorn was a wild grain domesticated into wheat by Valki.

Elder Olympians were the six children of Cronus and Rhea. They were Hestia, Demeter, Hera, Hades, Poseidon, and Zeus.
IGM, the same.

Elder Titans were the six sons and six adopted daughters of Kiya. The Titanes were Oceanus a.k.a Rivermaster a.k.a Firstson, Coeus a.k.a Sagacity a.k.a Secondson, Crius a.k.a Starmaster a.k.a Thirdson, Hyperion a.k.a Watchman a.k.a Fourthson, a.k.a Piercer a.k.a Fifthson, and Cronus. The Titanides were Themis, Mnemosyne, Phoebe, Tethys, Theia, and Rhea. The Titanes were all children by Vanam except for Cronus who was fathered by Pumi. The Titanides were all adopted.
IGM the Elder Titans were all children of Gaia by Ouranos.

Enceladus was a Gigante who was the aid to Kiya. He immigrated from Urfa after being brought there as a child to presumably die.
IGM Enceladus was one of the Giants and the traditional opponent of Athena during Gigantomachy.

Elysium Fields was the southern area between Tartarus and Oursea.
IGM Elysium Fields was one of the areas of the underworld and it was reserved for heroes.

Eurybia was an adopted daughter of Rivermaster and Tethys and the fourth of the first four Elder Oceanids. She married Elder Titane Starmaster.
IGM Elder Titan Crius and Oceanid Eurybia gave birth to Astraeus, Pallas, and Perses.

ELDER OCEANIDS: Metis, Tyche, Clymene, Eurybia, Amphitrite
ELDER OLYMPIANS: Hestia, Demeter, Hera, Hades, Poseidon, Zeus
OTHER: Philyra, Dionysus, Heracles, Outis, Enceladus, Littlerock, Porphyrion

Giants. See Gigantes.
IGM Giants were a race of extremely strong, aggressive normal-sized people. They were the bane of the Olympians.

The **Gigantomachy** was the great battle whereby the Olympians defeated the Gigantes and gained complete control of the lands of Tartarus.
IGM the Gigantomachy was the great war whereby the Olympians defeated the Giants.

Gigantes were a tribe of exceptionally strong but otherwise normal sized. people who befriended the Titans.
IGM see Giants.

Hades was the third child born to Elder Titane Cronus and Elder Titanide Rhea. Biy 65.
IGM. He abducted and married his niece, Persephone. He eventually became the God of the Underworld.

Hephaestus was the son of Zeus and his sister Hera and was an elder Olympian. He worked in the Port Olympus Metals Department and became a master in metalworking.
IGM Hephaestus was a son of Zeus and Hera, God of fire and metalworking. Aphrodite and Aglaea were his consorts. He had several children.

Hera was the third child of Cronus and Rhea and an Elder Olympian. She married her brother Zeus and was insanely jealous of her husband's many affairs. She was not as bright as her siblings. She loved her wine. Biy 63.
IGM Hera was the wife of her brother Zeus, Goddess of Marriage and Birth, and was insanely jealous and vindictive of his many liaisons. She gave birth to Olympians Ares and Hephaestus and non-Olympians Hebe and Eileithyia.

Hecatoncheires was a cadre of 50 fighting men trained to fight together as a fierce single unit. The men did not have individual names, only the name of their cadre. The three cadres initially retained by Hestia were Briareus, Cottus, and Gyges.
IGM the Hecatoncheires were three giant extremely strong creatures with 50 heads and 100 hands. Their names were Briareus, Cottus, and Gyges.

Heracles was a half-brother of Dionysus through Zeus. His exceptional strength was instrumental in defeating the Gigantes at the Battle of Port Olympus. He was eventually accepted as an Olympian. Biy 85.
IGM, a son of Zeus who, in some tradition, became an Olympian.

PRINCIPALS: Kiya, Vanam, Pumi, Valki | ELDER TITANIDES: Themis, Mnemosyne, Phoebe, Tethys, Theia, Rhea | ELDER TITANES: Rivermaster/Oceanus, Sagacity/Coeus, Starmaster/Crius, Watchman/Hyperion, Piercer/Iapetus, Cronus

Book 2. The Beginning of Civilization: Mythologies Told True

Hermes was a son of Zeus by a distant relative. He became an Olympian and was a chief messenger at Port Olympus.
IGM Hermes was the son of Zeus by Pleiades Maia. He had several consorts and several children. He is considered the herald of the gods.

Hestia was the firstborn child of Titane Cronus and Titanide Rhea. She became the dominant member of her family and Chief-of-Chiefs of Port Olympus. She made and unmade kings, initiated the ouster of the Titans, and was victorious in the war with the Gigantes. Biy 60.
IGM Hestia had no consorts or children, remained a perpetual virgin, and was Goddess of Hearth, Home, the State, and Virginity. The birth order of the Elder Olympians is convoluted.

Horae.
IGM the Horae were the three Goddesses of the Seasons named Thallo, Auxo, and Carpo.

Hyperion. See Watchman.
IGM Elder Titane Hyperion and his sister Elder Titanide Theia gave birth to the Shining Children. These were Helios the Sun, Selene the Moon, and Eos the Dawn.

Hyperion. See Watchman.
IGM Elder Titane Hyperion and his sister Elder Titanide Theia gave birth to the Shining Children. These were Helios the Sun, Selene the Moon, and Eos the Dawn.

Iapetus. See Piercer.
IGM Elder Titane Iapetus and Oceanid Clymene gave birth to Atlas, Prometheus, Epimetheus, and Meoetius. They are considered the Fathers of Mankind.

Inachus was the third son of Elder Titane Oceanus and Elder Titanide Tethys. Tethys gave birth to him in a river.

Kaptara. See Port Kaptara.

Kemet, the man, was the leader of a tribe encountered by Starmaster and Metis during their circumference of Oursea. See Port Kemet.

Kemet, the lands, was the lands of Chief Kemet which eventually became the land of Egypt.

Kiya was the high-born, intellectual daughter of Chief Irakka and Elder Woman Naman of the Tribe of Irakka. In year 18, she was charged to Vanam of the Tribe of Chief Talaimai. In year 43, she and her children were banished. She founded Tartarus, directed the building of Port Olympus, and became Queen of the Titans. Biy 4, Diy 99.
IGM Gaia was the Earth. See Greek Mythology.

ELDER OCEANIDS: Metis, Tyche, Clymene, Eurybia, Amphitrite
ELDER OLYMPIANS: Hestia, Demeter, Hera, Hades, Poseidon, Zeus
OTHER: Philyra, Dionysus, Heracles, Outis, Enceladus, Littlerock, Porphyrion

Kiya's adopted daughters were
1. Themis,
2. Mnemosyne,
3. Phoebe,
4. Tethys,
5. Theia,
6. Rhea.

Kiya's sons were
1. Firstson by Vanam a.k.a Rivermaster a.k.a Oceanus,
2. Secondson by Vanam a.k.a Sagacity a.k.a Coeus,
3. Thirdson by Vanam a.k.a Crius,
4. Fourthson by Vanam a.k.a Hyperion,
5. Fifthson by Vanam a.k.a Piercer a.k.a Iapetus,
6. Cronus by Pumi.

Lands of Tartarus was the island of extant Cypress including Tartarus, Port Olympus, Elysian Fields, Phlegethon Mines, Overlook Point, et al.

Last Camp was a euphemism for "left to die." The elderly or disabled tribal member was given food, water, a spear, tribal best wishes, and left behind at their *Last Camp*.

Littlerock was Clan of the Serpent Stone Cutter for Chief Vanam's tribe and a one-time apprentice to Pumi. Late in life, he became an apprentice to Piercer in geology and, with Piercer, founded Metallurgy.

Littlestar was an apprentice to Vaniyal, Clan of the Lion Skywatcher. He developed the concept of using shadows cast by Tallstone to better understand the motion of the constellations. He eventually became Master-of-Masters at Tallstone.

Marmaros was a white rock found in massive quantities at the cliffs of Tartarus near Overlook Point. i.e., marble.

Metis was the dominant of the four daughters adopted by Tethys and Rivermaster and was the first of the Elder Oceanids. She was influential in founding new civilizations. She was the mother of Athena by Zeus.
IGM Metis gave birth to Athena by Zeus but there are several different traditions.

Middlesea was the body of water between Port Spearpoint and the Atlantic Ocean and separated from the lower Oursea by the sheer wall upon which Port Spearpoint is located.

Mnemosyne was the second adopted daughter of Kiya. She was an Elder Titanide and third in power among the Titans. She was a consort to Zeus and mothered several of his children.
IGM by Zeus, Mnemosyne gave birth to the Muses. Their names were Calliope, Clio, Melpomene, and possibly six others.

Firstson. see Rivermaster.

Oceanus. See Rivermaster.
IGM Elder Titane Oceanus and his sister Elder Titanide Tethys gave birth to the Oceanids and the Potamoi. They were water goddesses and river gods.

Oceanids were a sorority of unrelated, free-spirited women who learned to love and live off the sea independently of any traditional lifestyle. Their founders were Metis, Tyche, Clymene, and Eurybia; all of whom were adopted by Titans Rivermaster and Tethys. Their influence and attitudes spread to other young girls without families who collectively called themselves Oceanids. They self-taught one another all arts including reading, writing, and sexuality. They were nurturing, helpful, and intelligent.
IGM Oceanids were the 3000 water nymphs who were the daughters of Oceanus and Tethys.

Kopar was copper.

Kypros was the name given to the lands of Tartarus by the Olympians because the island contained large quantities of Kypros (Copper).

Olympians were the six Elder Olympians plus six more fathered by Zeus with various women. The second-generation Olympians were Apollo, Ares, Artemis, Athena, Demeter, Aphrodite, Dionysus, Hermes, and Hephaestus. The names of the last six vary within different traditions.

Oursea was the sea discovered by Rivermaster and Sagacity on their scouting expedition. It surrounds the island containing Tartarus. It is the western portion of the Mediterranean from the Strait of Messina to the shores of Syria. The western bank was delineated, at the time, by the sheer cliffs rising from the Strait of Messina.

ELDER OCEANIDS: Metis, Tyche, Clymene, Eurybia, Amphitrite
ELDER OLYMPIANS: Hestia, Demeter, Hera, Hades, Poseidon, Zeus
OTHER: Philyra, Dionysus, Heracles, Outis, Enceladus, Littlerock, Porphyrion

Overlook Point was the entry point into the land of the Titans. It was located at the end of the narrow neck of land connecting the mainland with the almost island.

Pace. One Pace is approximately 60 inches.

Palai was an original inhabitant, and the first Elder Woman, of Urfa. When younger, she was the Clan of the Serpent Elder Woman.

Panti was Kiya's successor as Clan of the Serpent Elder Woman. She was originally in line for the position rather than Kiya.

Periphas was a Prince, then King, of the Graikoi frontier.

Paravi was a senior Urfa Elder Woman. When younger, she was the Clan of the Aurochs Elder Woman.

Persephone was the daughter of Demeter by Zeus. She was abducted by Hades and became his wife. She eventually ruled Tartarus as "Queen of the Colored Fields."
IGM a.k.a Kore. She was the wife of Hades with whom she ruled the Underworld. She was an important figure, along with her mother, in the Eleusinian mysteries which predate Greek Mythology. She had several children including, in some traditions, Dionysus.

Phlegethon was the copper mine near Overlook Point that housed Piercer's mines and workshops.
IGM Phlegethon was "Fire Flaming," one of the six rivers of the Underworld running parallel to the river Styx.

Philyra was an Oceanid who became Executive Assistant to Port Olympus Chief-of-Chiefs Hestia and then Hestia's replacement. Biy 52.
IGM Philyra gave birth to the first Centaur which was fathered by Cronus. She may have later become the wife of Dionysus.

Phoebe was an adopted daughter of Kiya and an Elder Titanide. She married Elder Titan Sagacity.
IGM Phoebe and Coeus gave birth to Leto and Asteria.

Piercer was the fifth son of Kiya by Vanam and an Elder Titane. He was fascinated with colored stones and became the first geologist and metallurgist. He married Elder Oceanid Clymene. The two parented Atlas, Prometheus, Epimetheus, and Meoetius. He was later named Iapetus by the direction of Port Olympus management.
IGM See Iapetus.

PRINCIPALS: Kiya, Vanam, Pumi, Valki | ELDER TITANIDES: Themis, Mnemosyne, Phoebe, Tethys, Theia, Rhea | ELDER TITANES: Rivermaster/Oceanus, Sagacity/Coeus, Starmaster/Crius, Watchman/Hyperion, Piercer/Iapetus, Cronus

Porphyrion was a Gigante extremely skilled in warfare who trained Kiya and her children in the intricacies of hand-to-hand attacks which was not widely known at the time.
IGM Porphyrion was one of the Giants who fought in the Gigantomachy.

Port Graikoi was the third seaport founded by the Titans. It was the second founded by Oceanus and Tethys. Graikoi evolved into Greece.

Port Kaptara was the second seaport founded by the Titans and the first founded by Oceanus and Tethys. Kaptara evolved into Crete.

Port Kemet was the fifth seaport founded by the Titans and was founded by Starmaster and Metis. Originally, it was an obelisk marking a rendezvous for the Titans and Chief Kemet. The port evolved into Egypt.

Port Olympus was the first port built by the Titans. It contained the great step pyramid Port Olympus office/resident building.

Port Olympus Building was the great step pyramid Port Olympus office/resident building. The roof was a viewing deck.

Port Spearpoint was the third seaport founded by the Titans. It was the third founded by Oceanus and Tethys. Initially, it was only a spear marking a spot. It then became an Outpost, then the major seaport connecting Oursea to all land west of the great granite seawall.

Poseidon was the fifth child, second male, born to Elder Titane Cronus and Elder Titanide Rhea. He eventually usurped Hestia as the dominant Olympian. He was an adversary of Elder Titan Oceanus.
IGM Poseidon was the God of Sea, Storms, Earthquakes, and Horses.

Potamoi were male children of Tethys and Oceanus. They were each born in a different major river.
IGM the Potamoi were gods of rivers and streams.

Prometheus was the son of Elder Titane Iapetus and Oceanid Clymene.
IGM Prometheus was one of the fathers of mankind. Known for his intelligence and for being a champion of humankind. Author of the arts and sciences.

Protector was the title given to a male who agreed to accept a female from another tribe to be under his protection.

Pumi was the Clan of the Serpent Stonecutter and the premier stonecutter in the known lands. He founded the Tallstone Camp and

---

ELDER OCEANIDS: Metis, Tyche, Clymene, Eurybia, Amphitrite
ELDER OLYMPIANS: Hestia, Demeter, Hera, Hades, Poseidon, Zeus
OTHER: Philyra, Dionysus, Heracles, Outis, Enceladus, Littlerock, Porphyrion

Urfa Camp. He was mate to Valki, and he adopted sons Breathson and Putt. Biy 10, Diy 97. He was the biological father to Replaceson. cf "Earth."

Pyrrha was the daughter of Meoetius and Pandora, wife of Deucalion, and younger sister of Aidos.

Red Nectar was a drink developed by Kiya which reduced the aging process by 50%. The recipe was shared with her daughters upon their reaching maturity. The Titanides were tasked with surreptitiously providing the drink to only their family members and sharing the recipe only with their own "worthy" daughters upon their maturity.

Rhea was the last daughter adopted by Kiya, the youngest of the Elder Titans, and "the wild child" of the family. She married Elder Titane Cronus and was the mother to the six Elder Titans.
IGM Rhea, by Cronus, gave birth to Hestia, Demeter, Hera, Hades, Poseidon, and Zeus. The tradition concerning the order of their birth is convoluted.

Rivermaster was the first-born son of Kiya and Vanam. He was an elder Titane and married Elder Titanide Tethys. They adopted four girls who became the Elder Oceanids, and she gave birth to several sons and daughters. Rivermaster and Tethys explored the lands surrounding Oursea and the great Middlesea which the two discovered. Originally named Firstson, Tethys eventually renamed him Oceanus.
IGM. See Oceanus.

Riverport was a river-crossing dock established by Rivermaster and Sagacity on the banks of a wide river five days westward run from Urfa, it was the primary entry point into the eastern lands from Tartarus and was the scene of Kiya and Vanam's final challenge.

Sagacity was the second son of Kiya by Vanam. He was an Elder Titane who married Elder Titanide Phoebe who gave birth to Leto and Asteria. Sagacity was an intellectual fascinated with words, the power of words, and the power of planning. Originally named Secondson, he was renamed Coeus by the direction of the Port Olympus management.
IGM See Coeus.

Season was the basic unit of measuring time as measured from one full moon to the next. Tribes tended to camp at one site for one season and then migrate to another camp for the next hunting season.

PRINCIPALS: Kiya, Vanam, Pumi, Valki | ELDER TITANIDES: Themis, Mnemosyne, Phoebe, Tethys, Theia, Rhea | ELDER TITANES: Rivermaster/Oceanus, Sagacity/Coeus, Starmaster/Crius, Watchman/Hyperion, Piercer/Iapetus, Cronus

Secondson. See Sagacity.

Seilenos was an older aide, mentor, and wagon driver to Dionysus.
IGM Seilenos was the oldest of the Satyrs. He was a father, teacher, and companion to Dionysus.

Selene was the daughter of Elder Titane Hyperion and Elder Titanide Theia and became an influential resident of Urfa.
IGM Selene was one of the three children of Hyperion and Theia called "The Shining Ones." Selene drove her moon chariot across the heavens and was Goddess of the Moon."

Spearpoint. See Port Spearpoint.

Stade. One stade is 607.2 feet. Ten stades are 1.15 miles.

Starmaster was the third son of Kiya by Vanam. He was an Elder Titane jack-of-all-trades but interested in astronomy. He married Elder Oceanid Eurybia who parented Astraeus, Pallas, and Perses. He was renamed Crius by demand of Port Olympus management.
IGM See Crius.

Tall stone was the stone obelisk four times the height of a man placed in the center of the hill marking the location of Tallstone Camp. The site could be easily seen from a distance.

Tallstone Camp, or Tallstone, was a hilly site Pumi marked as a potential campsite favorable to his tribe's gatherers because of the nearby abundant plant life. Pumi manipulated his elders into accepting the site as a recurring camp. Pumi relocated his utilitarian Rock Table, containing engravings of hunters and antelopes, from his favorite source of stones – Rockplace Camp. He then erected a tall stone obelisk on the hill so the site could be easily seen from a distance. Circumstances caused him to surround the tall stone with Guardian stones and personalize Sitting Stones for each chief that attended the eventual Winter Solstice Festival. The tall stone cast shadows which helped the Skywatchers understand the motion of the sun and constellations.

Tartarus was the camp where the Titans settled. It was the center of Titan life. It contained the ceremonial fire pit, an entertaining patio, and Titan residences. "Land of the Titans" is my invented etymology.
IGM while Tartarus is not considered to be directly a part of the underworld, it is described as being as far beneath the underworld as the earth is beneath the sky It was reserved for the worst people which, according to Ouranos, included the Titans. Zeus cast the Titans along with his father Cronus into Tartarus after defeating them.

ELDER OCEANIDS: Metis, Tyche, Clymene, Eurybia, Amphitrite
ELDER OLYMPIANS: Hestia, Demeter, Hera, Hades, Poseidon, Zeus
OTHER: Philyra, Dionysus, Heracles, Outis, Enceladus, Littlerock, Porphyrion

Tethys was an adopted daughter of Kiya. She was an Elder Titanide who married Elder Titane Rivermaster. The two adopted Metis, Tyche, Clymene, and Eurybia who became the first Oceanids. She gave birth to the Potamoi brothers who she named Achelous, Alpheus, and Inachus. She was an explorer and was fascinated with the power of water.
IGM Tethys, by Oceanus, gave birth to the Oceanids and the Potamoi who were water goddesses and river gods.

Theia was an adopted daughter of Kiya. She was Elder Titanide who married Elder Titane Watchman. They had three children, including Selene. Theia was the first and premier seamstress of her time.
IGM Theia, by Hyperion, gave birth to the Shining Children. They were Helios the Sun, Selene the Moon, and Eos the Dawn.

Themis was the first daughter adopted by Kiya. She was the oldest Titanide and second in power among the Titans after her mother. She was a consort to Zeus and bore him several children.
IGM by Zeus, Themis gave birth to the "Horae" who were the Goddess' of the Seasons. Their names were Thallo, Auxo, and Carpo. She also gave birth to "The Fates" Their names were Clotho, "The Spinner," Lachesis, "The Allotter," and Atropos, "Death."

Titans were Kiya, the Elder Titans, the children of the Elder Titans, plus those accepted into the Titan family.

Titanes were male Titans.

Titanides were female Titans.

The **Titanomachy** was Hestia's successful project to remove all Titans from positions of power in Port Olympus.
IGM the Titanomachy was the war between the Titans and the Olympians.

Tyche was an adopted daughter of Rivermaster and Tethys. She was the second of the first four Elder Oceanids. She assisted her parents in founding new civilizations Biy 32.
IGM there are several traditions as to Tyche's parents. None suggest a consort or offspring.

Urfa was the first city. It evolved from a hunting camp founded by Pumi but developed by Valki as a Last Camp for the elderly and other cast-offs. Valki domesticated einkorn in her fields at Urfa. Building trades and animal domestication also evolved at Urfa.

Valki was a foundling by Vivekamulla, Clan of the Lion Elder Woman. She became the mate of Pumi. She grew Urfa from a camp for the

PRINCIPALS: Kiya, Vanam, Pumi, Valki | ELDER TITANIDES: Themis, Mnemosyne, Phoebe, Tethys, Theia, Rhea | ELDER TITANES: Rivermaster/Oceanus, Sagacity/Coeus, Starmaster/Crius, Watchman/Hyperion, Piercer/Iapetus, Cronus

elderly and tribal misfits into the major city of its time. She domesticated Einkorn into modern wheat. She developed the Winter Solstice Festival into a major yearly event. She adopted sons Breathson and Putt and was the biological mother to Replaceson. Biy 13, Diy 65. cf "Valkkai" or "Life."

Vanam was the ambitious successor to the great Clan of the Serpent Chief Talaimai. He became the mate of Kiya, fathered five sons, and adopted six daughters whom he eventually banished from his tribe. Biy 0. Diy 44. cf "Uyar-Vanam" or "High Sky."
IGM See Ouranos, "The Sky."

Watchman was the fourth son of Kiya by Vanam. Elder Titane Watchman married Elder Titanide Theia. The two were parents of Helios, Selene, and Eos. He was renamed Hyperion by the direction of Port Olympus management.
IGM See Hyperion.

Winter Solstice Festival was a festival held at Tallstone Camp each Winter's Solstice. The first Festival was the first planned Encounter between two tribes, the Clan of the Lion and the Clan of the Serpent. The festival grew each year as more tribes came to the planned encounter. It solidified the position of Tallstone and Urfa as the cultural and scientific center of the world and was the catalyst for the beginning of civilization.

Zeus was the sixth child, the third male, born to Cronus and Rhea. The Olympian was flamboyant, gushing, overpowering, and a womanizer. He required ongoing and universal love from everyone. He eventually became God of the Sky. Biy 72.
IGM Zeus was the King of the Gods. His wife Hera gave birth to Olympians Ares and Hephaestus and non-Olympians Hebe and Eileithyia. Zeus mated with most females and fathered many children including Olympians Athena and Dionysus plus Greek Hero Heracles. The birth order of the Elder Olympians is convoluted. Zeus was the God of Sky, Lightning, and Justice.

Ziusudra was the husband of Aidos.

ELDER OCEANIDS: Metis, Tyche, Clymene, Eurybia, Amphitrite
ELDER OLYMPIANS: Hestia, Demeter, Hera, Hades, Poseidon, Zeus
OTHER: Philyra, Dionysus, Heracles, Outis, Enceladus, Littlerock, Porphyrion

Changes to the Second Edition

1. Simplified the childhood names of Kiya's sons to "Firstson," "Secondson," through "Fifthson."

2. Introduced Deucalion, Ziusudra, Aidos, and Pyrrha at the Titan party for Dionysus in order to lay a foundation for subsequent "Great Flood" and Sumerian mythological references.

3. Gave Rhea and Philyra motivation for their scene with Cronus.

4. Changed the name "Olympia" to "Kypros" based on the large amounts of copper found there.

5. Gave Tyche motivation for distaste of sexual activity.

6. Improved page design and cover.

PRINCIPALS: Kiya, Vanam, Pumi, Valki | ELDER TITANIDES: Themis, Mnemosyne, Phoebe, Tethys, Theia, Rhea | ELDER TITANES: Rivermaster/Oceanus, Sagacity/Coeus, Starmaster/Crius, Watchman/Hyperion, Piercer/Iapetus, Cronus

Book 2. The Beginning of Civilization: Mythologies Told True

ELDER OCEANIDS: Metis, Tyche, Clymene, Eurybia, Amphitrite
ELDER OLYMPIANS: Hestia, Demeter, Hera, Hades, Poseidon, Zeus
OTHER: Philyra, Dionysus, Heracles, Outis, Enceladus, Littlerock, Porphyrion

Printed in the USA
CPSIA information can be obtained
at www.ICGtesting.com
LVHW040803130924
790906LV00013B/48/J